INTIMATE ENCOUNTER

INTIMATE ENCOUNTER

DEREN ICKE

*Createspace, Amazon,
Ingramsparks.
United States*

Copyright 2017 by Deren Icke.

ISBN:

Hardcover   978-0-9945740-9-1

Softcover   978-0-9945740-7-7

eBook   978-0-9945740-6-0

Print information available on the last page.

To order additional copies of this book, contact:

www.derenicke.com

Amazon.com

Kindle

Createspace

IngramSparks

PressBooks.com

DEREN ICKE

Intimate Encounter

DEREN ICKE

Dedicated to all trafficking victims from or in Cambodia, Thailand, Nepal, India, Africa, The United States, England, Haiti, and South America...and the wicked ones who exploit them from around the world. Ignorance is not bliss.

Back of every wasted life is a bad philosophy, an erroneous conception of life's worth and purpose. The man who believes that he was born to get all he can, will spend his life trying to get it, and whatever he gets will be but a cage of spotted mice. The man who believes he was created to enjoy fleshly pleasures will devote himself to pleasure seeking, and if by a combination of favourable circumstances he manages to get a lot of fun out of life, his pleasures will all turn to ashes in his mouth at the last. He will find out too late that God made him too noble to be satisfied with those tawdry pleasures he had devoted his life to here under the sun.

– A.W. Tozer

1

CHAPTER 1

Jeff sat for hours on his worn-out sofa thinking a million thoughts at once. His mind just would not turn off. The wedding was already in progress but he felt too tired to go. The car key was on the stool beside him and he made a second personal commitment to grab it and leave in exactly thirty minutes. The television was on but he was only partially interested. There was nothing but bad news on television. The kidnapped Chibok girls were yet to be found and the low cost of crude was crippling the oil based economy. He would have turned it off if he had the energy to get the remote control. Instead he sat there and took the negativity in like a sponge.

His wife, Nneka, was in her room. They had not spoken much to each other in months. There was the occasional question which required a monotonous yes or no answer. Sometimes she tried to initiate a conversation but he was too self-engrossed to be of any use. There were times when he wished they had never got married.

She was a good woman no doubt but it seemed he had fallen into that place his good friend, or rather associate, Mike, had said he would. Mike had assured him that Nneka, unfortunately, belonged to an era when all that was necessary in a woman was fidelity, good housekeeping skills, and good manners. Humanity had outgrown that era. Women had to be much more than domesticated wives and great mothers. Mike believed a player such as he was would never be satisfied with a woman like that. He would always yearn for that wildness that characterised their school days. He had found his views strange at the time. Now he wondered if he was right. He had after all cheated on her several times and, hard as he tried, he always fell into the same temptation.

He was thankful when Mike's car pulled up in front of the house. It was just the motivation he needed to get up. There was this energy around him that was infectious. He was sure his testosterone level was sky high. As soon as he saw him his mood instantly improved. He grabbed his keys and, without a word to his wife, left the house without locking the front door. There was a time when he would never have gone anywhere without letting her know. During their pre-marriage class, it had been emphasised that this was a key necessity if trust was to be maintained. He tried his best to adhere to all he had learnt during those months preceding their wedding. Reality eventually clashed with good intentions and it became increasingly convenient to just leave the house without saying where he was going.

Nneka did not like Mike. Mike never felt comfortable around her. She understood he was an old friend but had advised him from the beginning of their marriage that it was time to move on from men such as him from his immoral past. She referred to him as the door to the past he had long cut ties with. Like a prophetess, she had predicted he would be the one to lure him back to his old ways when the opportunity came. How right she had been.

Mike was already lighting a cigarette when he came out. He was leaning against his car and smiled when he saw him.

"You look sharp man," he said smiling broadly, smoke spilling out of his nostrils. "I thought you were no longer coming. They are done with the boring church part. I thought I would come by before proceeding to the reception."

"You don't look bad yourself," he said trying to smile back. "How was the ceremony?"

"It was alright," Mike replied. "You know the usual stuff that women like to hear but never like to accept. All that talk about submission and the man being the head of the home crap. I mean it's not crap but might as well be. If they let us be the head, there will be no problem. They just must ask unnecessary questions and meddle in our manly affairs. Get in. We go in my car. You not going to embarrass us in that locomotive you have there."

Jeff got into the passenger seat of his new BMW SUV. The leather still smelt fresh. It was a different experience from when he was in his. Mike never revealed anything about his source of income. They worked in the same place though they had very different roles. He had an idea how much he earned. The car was way out of his league.

"I need to get me one of these someday," he said looking around the car like a child in a cockpit."

"Don't wait till you are sixty to start enjoying life," Mike said. "What will be the point then?"

He said nothing. Mike pressed the start button and the engine roared into life. He briefly had an image of himself driving a similar car with Nneka beside him. He quickly shook the image off. He knew such things never interested her. Little was of interest to her which was part of the problem.

"She home?" Mike asked as he eased the car out of the narrow driveway.

"Who?"

"Who else?"

He nodded.

They drove on in silence for a while. He felt guilty for not having her with him. It did not feel right to be attending a wedding without his wife. The thought of her being all alone in the house made him feel guilty. He wished she had never miscarried. She was not the type to blame anyone for her misfortune but he sometimes wondered if the stress of the discovery had not caused it.

"Don't drink too much," Mike said after a while.

"What are you now, a pastor?"

Mike laughed.

"I wouldn't mind being a pastor," he said. "They are rich, drive fancy cars and have all these beautiful women at their beck and call. Not a bad life at all. They don't even have to be holy no more."

"You do have a crooked way of seeing things," Jeff said. "You know that, don't you?"

Mike shrugged.

"I'm just a realist," he said. "I say it as I see it. They make millions, those pastors, and don't pay tax."

"Not all of them," Jeff said.

"Just don't get wasted," he said. "I want to take you to this place. You've not been looking your usual bubbly self for a while now. Breaks my heart to see you like this. I told you she was not your type."

"She's a good woman," he said defensively.

"No doubt," he said nodding. "But are you?"

The question rattled him a bit.

"You started going to church just because of her," Mike went on. "That's just pathetic. Deep down you are still the same you and it is time to unleash that beast."

He jabbed a finger at his arm as he said this.

"That is just so wrong, what you just said," Jeff said.

"It's the truth and you needed to hear it. I tried to make it obvious to you before you committed but you were just too eager to hook up with the 'most decent' girl on campus. How's her decency helping you out now?"

"Did you drink or something?"

Mike laughed sarcastically.

"A little bit. What does that matter? The truth is no less true even when spoken by a drunk lunatic."

Jeff nodded to himself as if making a personal resolve to break off from him for good. There was another brief period of silence.

"So," Jeff asked. "What is this place you plan to take me to?"

Mike smiled mischievously.

"Just relax. It's a secret. You will thank me later."

He spent the next few minutes answering and making calls. Some were from his numerous mistresses scattered around the country. Jeff realised just why his wife never liked him. He had no conscience, unlike himself. At least he struggled with his infidelities which were essentially opportunistic and not frequent. Mike on the other hand lived infidelity. A faithful marriage was never his plan and he claimed to have made his ex-wife understand this before they tied the knot which sounded unbelievable. But then, Ronke was a poor girl from a very poor family who, unlike Nneka, made a big deal out of the material things in life. She liked to move in the circles of the rich and popular when they were still on campus. Rumour had it then that she even dated a couple of lecturers. Self-imposed desperation could drive many into the unusual, including marriage to a known player.

The venue was already bustling with activity when they arrived. The music was so loud he wished he had ear plugs. Exquisitely dressed men and women danced to the tune of the music with reckless abandon. The band was a popular one and did not disappoint. Their drummers were known throughout the country to be the best. They could make even a shy nun dance without any reservation. Mike excused himself and hurried back outside, phone to his ear. Jeff found a spot close to the window to sit. A waiter approached him with a tray full of half-filled wine glasses. He took one, downed it, set the glass down and reached for another. This time he held it in his hand and sipped slowly.

The MC took over the stage when he was satisfied he had given everyone a chance to gyrate. He congratulated the big mamas for rocking their assets and announced the arrival of some more important personalities including Mike who was nowhere to be seen. The bride and groom were engrossed with each other, kissing, tugging and laughing like they had never seen each other before the day. Cameramen walked around snapping away at anyone who caught their attention. When Mike finally returned, there was a lipstick stain on his lips. He pointed it out and he hurriedly and furiously wiped it off.

"I told you to be gentle on the booze," he said almost accusingly.

"Relax man," Jeff said. "It's only my second. Those two look like they are madly in love."

Mike did not answer. He had one of his three cell phones in his hand and was sending a text. He eventually smiled to himself and hurried outside again. The MC invited the couple to the dance floor for a dance. The crowd cheered as they rose and the band began playing their latest hit music. Apparently the newly wedded couple were no strangers to dancing. They were good at it and danced like their very lives depended on it. As he watched them he could not help relieving the sense of happiness and exhilaration he had felt during his own wedding. He had been certain his would last forever. It was funny how one silly mistake could rob one of his dreams and happiness.

Nneka was a good woman. He could never deny that. He could never blame her for acting the way she was acting. Most women would have left him a long time ago. But she stayed. She still loved him. He knew. All she needed was an apology, an assurance that he would commit to the vows they had made before a similar crowd and God. She was not bothered about the embarrassment as much as his reassurance.

"Sir?"

Without a word, he returned his empty glass of wine and picked up another one. The waiter nodded slightly and left. Mike was again out of sight. His head was beginning to feel light, a sign that he had probably had enough to drink. At this point he did not mind getting drunk. Hopefully he would have sobered up by the time they were ready to leave. The sane world made no sense to him. Perhaps if he got drunk; saw things from the point of view of a drunkard, there might be some answers, some sense to life.

He gulped down the whole of it and belched. He nodded to himself as the drunken world began to take shape. It was a queer world of blurred images and no problems. He smiled.

"Yeah!" he yelled.

Several heads turned in his direction. He did not mind. The music eventually ended abruptly and the crowd applauded as the couple, hand in hand, returned to their seats. Her bridesmaids hurriedly picked up the money they had been showered with while they danced. There was a lot of it. The guests were apparently rich and generous. Being an investigative journalist and a columnist in the media company he worked for, the contrast between extreme poverty and riches never ceased to baffle him. It was a mystery that wealthy men and women could afford to shower money on a couple whocould evidently take care of themselves yet turn a blind eye on the plight of countless poor orphans and widows the world over.

His mind switched back to Nneka. She was a very beautiful woman. In the university, she had been one of the few decent women around. Other equally beautiful women had signed away their decencies by agreeing to some movie or fashion contract where they were essentially expected to parade their nakedness to the whole world. She was offered similar immoral contracts but refused them all. He, on the other hand, had been a playboy. His affairs were no secret. Twice he had won the campus award for the most charming couple of the year with two different girls. To him, keeping girls was like keeping empires. He felt like Alexander the Great whenever he conquered a new girl's heart. He knew the trick. A car, some cash, and a good accommodation was all that was needed to conquer in a society where these things were overvalued. He had it all. After a while even he began to tire of it all. It was a senseless habit he could not stop.

Everything changed the day he set eyes on Nneka. There was something unique about her that most others lacked. She was a good Christian woman with no interest whatsoever in any of the materialistic stuff most others would easily sell their souls for. Her life was the truth that had eluded him. She embodied the morality he thought was humanly impossible. It was a moment of self-awareness. Most girls fell for the money and fun he offered and not himself. He knew not even one of them would stay a day longer if his money vanished. He was the fool, not them. They were like bees that sucked the nectar out of any blossomed flower. They would simply move on to the next man with money to burn. Who could blame them? The culture was based on money.

"Sir?"

Jeff took the glass of wine, hesitated for a moment then gulped down its content. The waiter waited for him to pick up another glass but moved on when he showed no further interest. He was already far gone in his mental journey.

Nneka showed him how deficient he was. For the first time in his life he realised he was living in a fool's paradise. He had seen a girl who would not be enticed with the very things other girls would jump at and realized he had nothing in himself to offer. His ego had been based on materialism. When confronted with a materialistic female all he had to do was meet her needs. What could he offer a woman like Nneka? He had played the game for so long the way most others did which was essentially based on an unwritten give and take principle. When faced with a situation where no money was required and no sex was offered in return, he felt deficient. Her personality made him feel like a worm. He was rotten to the chore, rotten, dirty and stinking.

When he made his feelings known to his brothers in sin, they laughed at him and asked him to give it up. He was not the first sinner to admire Nneka. Sinful men were attracted to noble women. Ironically, sinful men always corrupt noble women. She knew what she wanted and would never settle for any one until she found him. She was not one of those who lived like pigs while waiting for some prince charming before committing. She would only commit to the one. They even dared compare his intentions to those of a bat wanting to bond with a dove. This infuriated him.

For many nights, he would lay awake thinking of her and hating his rotten life. He hated all his girlfriends for being she bats; immoral creatures of darkness who were readily bought over with crumbs. He began to detest them for being so cheap. He stopped smoking weed and cut down his drinking drastically. He even stopped frequenting night clubs and other shady places of the night.

The lady behind the wedding cake began to educate the guests on the idea behind its design. They listened as if they would be asked to answer questions based on her talk.

"Purple represents royalty..."

He shook his head. It was the same old talk. His had been white, white for peace. There was no peace! He wished she would shut her mouth and let the guests eat their cake, white or purple. It was just a cake and the colours meant nothing. He signalled a passing waiter and grabbed a can of beer. He quickly lost interest in the cake talk.

It was at the peak of his psychological torture over Nneka that a thought crossed his mind. Why not turn himself into a dove? He could start attending church and live a holy life. The idea was so invigorating that the next day he bought himself a bible, the big type he had seen some television preachers use. It weighed a ton but at least she would never miss it. His friends expectedly laughed when he told them of his intention to start going to church. They laughed even harder when he told them it was her church he would be attending. Why go to any other?

Nneka was not the sole reason he wanted to turn his life around. He had always wanted a good family. His family was functional only because his promiscuous father could at least pay the bills. He rarely came home before eleven in the night and sometimes never even bothered coming home at all. There were times when he would be gone for weeks. When he was a kid, his mother would make excuses for his absence; busy schedules, out of state assignments, etc. When he got older, he knew. He also knew his mother knew all along. Good old father loved his women. He was shocked. He talked morality but lived like a Babylonian. He wondered why she stayed if she knew all along. She explained that she stayed because of her children. She knew exactly what step mums did to their step children and did not want any of her kids going through that. He did not want to be that kind of a father and husband. Good wishes did not build homes. He needed to change.

After the surprising revelation, he began to hate his father. He thought he was a selfish man who did not give a damn how his wife felt. His mother noticed the change in his attitude towards him and decided to have a chat with him one day. She told him his father, her husband, was in bondage, in chains. He was a man so blinded by his ways that he could not understand the full extent of his actions on others. He needed to be pitied, not hated. She it was who taught him how hate poisons the hater while leaving the hated untouched. Hate was as evil as the reason for the hate.

He softened a bit afterwards even though he felt she was the one who was blind. When he became a teenager and began seeing women in a different light he became closer to his father. Who could stay away from all the pretty women mother earth had been blessed with? Only a eunuch could. They were irresistible. He turned to the master womaniser for advice. It was his own father who taught him the principle of give and take. He believed all relationships were based on an exchange, whatever that exchange was.

One thing led to another and Nneka finally noticed him. He had joined her activity group in church, the Prayer Warriors. It was their duty to pray for the world and all its evils. That same year his father died. His mother wept for weeks. She believed he had died a sinner and believed he was languishing in hell.

"What did you gain?" she had asked repeatedly during his wake. "Why could you not just change your ways?"

On his part, he was more concerned about his monthly allowance. His father's expensive habits had translated into a lot of loans and unpaid debts. They had been living a false life financed by loans. His allowances were to be no more and that was just the easy part. Fortunately, it was his last year in school. All he had to do was persevere to the end and hope for a good job.

Nneka heard of his plight. She offered all she could and even gave him money from time to time. Initially his ego could not take her sympathy but eventually he learnt to relax and be helped. The ways of the world were not her ways. Everything she did was out of sincere love and she expected nothing in return. No one knew of this for she believed when you do good only God had to know. Sometimes he wondered where all the other gold diggers came from. They all read the same bible she did and some even claimed to be Christians. He often wondered what would have happened if he was still living his old life when his father passed. His superficial girlfriends would have simply left him high and dry.

One day he decided he was going to make his intentions known to her. He had only a few months left to graduate at the time. Once out of school he would not be seeing her as often. She was pleased. Surprisingly, she was not surprised.

The student pastors and many of the Christian students' community were not amused. They regarded him as a sinner, a wolf in sheep clothing who had snuck into their midst with one sinister goal in mind. She told him of all the objections raised. He was a sinner pretending to have repented. He would return to his old ways once they tied the knot. This only made him more determined to prove them wrong. He knew some of them wanted her for themselves. Her virtues were lost on no one. Even in church good girls were still hard to find.

When they eventually got married against all the odds, he vowed to himself that he would never make her regret saying "I do" to him. The wedding was full of her so-called brethren who only came because it would have been bad not to have come. He could feel their judgmental eyes drilling hell hot holes at the back of his head. Getting married to her was all worth the hate. He left genuinely believing he would never disappoint her. Then came his great fall from his moral high castle.

An announcement was made. The guests may start bringing forward their gifts. He had completely forgotten that part about weddings. Nneka always took care of the gifts. He signalled to one of the waiters. When she came, he asked her for an envelope. Few moments later she returned with a brown one. He put some money into it and was about sealing it when he changed his mind. They were already rich. He would rather give it to some beggar in the street. He got a piece of paper instead from his pocket and scribbled on it:

Good intentions and love are never enough for a healthy marriage. Read your bible together, stay away from bad friends and don't let in-laws and friends interfere.

He put the paper into the envelope, sealed it and made his way to the front of the hall where the gifts were piling up. By the time he got there it looked as if Santa had crashed there. He was sure there were families who would do better with the gifts. Unfortunately for them, they did not belong in the social circles of those who could afford them. He dropped his envelope and walked back to his seat. Suddenly a sense of overwhelming heaviness came over him. He had just had a flashback of his wedding day. He hated the thought of divorce. He still loved Nneka. Even if he did get a divorce his next marriage would have a ninety-five percent chance of failing if the statistics were right. He understood the implication of this.

"Sir?"

This time he glared at him angrily. He checked himself on time. Why be angry with him? He was only trying to do his job and put food on his family's table. With a smile, he took the glass of wine and emptied its content on the floor.

"Sorry," he said with a polite smile. "I don't want to get drunk."

With that he stood and left the hall. The waiter stood transfixed in shock. He did not move until the drunken man was out of sight.

2

CHAPTER 2

As an undergraduate, Jeff used to belong to a club called The Hell Raisers. Their motto was simple: Raise Hell. Every bona fide member was dedicated to that motto. They even pledged allegiance to Lucifer whom they referred to as 'the god of all fun'. It seemed like a joke back then but looking back now he wondered if there was really anything funny about what they did. The damage they caused was far from funny. Mike had been a member too. He always had a thing for the bizarre. He was the one who introduced him to the club. Then they only had fifteen members and unknown to him were looking for rich kids to recruit.

He liked the idea of like-minded people coming together to have fun without any fear of judgment. They organised the craziest parties on campus and soon their numbers swelled. Every fun-loving student wanted to be a member once their presence was well known. Soon they started to screen would be members. There were just too many interested in being Hell Raisers. They even started charging recruitment fees and annual fees. This did not deter them.

One day, Mike suggested they float a magazine that would raise hell. He had money to spend and liked the idea of poking his nose into other people's garbage. They called it Our Monthly Garbage. It was an instant hit. People loved garbage and with everyone having a phone with a camera, there was a lot of it being produced to satisfy the appetite of the public. Many bought the magazine just to make sure their own garbage was not made public. A lot of lives were ruined. They paid money for stories that those involved during times of drunken foolishness would rather keep secret. Video or photo evidence meant more money. Many became depressed because of what was published about them. He had been too narcissistic at the time to even take notice. Blackmail became the unintended consequence. Mike was the one who came up with the idea to ask people for money to avoid a particularly damaging story being published. They would leak headlines of intended publications with promises of photographic proof in the main issue, hoping those involved would pay up to keep it quiet. Children of the rich were usually their target.

The magazine's end came after the suicide of a first-year female student. She had been invited to a party by a jealous friend. Something was slipped into her drink and one thing led to another. When a young man came to their make shift office with pictures to sell they did not question him. When the monthly edition hit the shelves, details of what really happened began to emerge. He instantly knew there would be trouble. After her suicide the police were called in. They were lucky to escape any criminal prosecution and could prove they had nothing to do with her ordeal. Part of the deal they made with the police was that they would never publish another issue. That was the end of it. Sometimes Mike would talk about restarting it. He, on his part, never stopped thinking about the poor girl.

Mike was always a strangely lucky fellow. If anything came up he was always the first to know. After their graduation, he got a job in a media company as an accountant while he worked as a freelance journalist. At the time, he was trying his best to stay away from him. He was quickly realizing how much of a bad influence he was having over him. He was just too morally corrupt and sometimes he feared he was not completely normal in the head. Nothing was off limits. He began to find his jokes to be too vulgar and his social interests extremely outrageous. To think they were the very things he used to find interest in made him disgusted with himself.

After his marriage to Nneka, Mike soon got the message that he was an unwanted guest in his home and loathed her for it. He believed she had separated him from his best friend. It was for this reason that he kept rejecting his offer to come and work in the same media company he worked for. They needed journalists on a permanent or contractual basis. The window of opportunity was closing. Many would die for the job but he had convinced his boss to reserve a spot for him. He eventually had to make the tough decision to accept his offer. The money was good and the stability it brought convenient. The internet meant freelance journalism was not as lucrative as it used to be and it was getting worse.

Initially he did not tell Nneka about this. When she found out her response was as expected. She had a bad feeling about it all. His heart skipped a beat when she said it. The good-looking secretary he had been assigned was already plaguing his free time. He knew it was only a matter of time. Mike urged him on. He knew it was partly because of his grudge with Nneka. Despite this knowledge, he still succumbed to her incessant seductions. How she found out was still a mystery to him. He still believed it was Mike who found a way to make sure she knew.

For weeks after the infamous affair he refused to speak to Mike and kept his distance from the secretary. Some of Nneka's Christian friends heard about the scandalous affair and even came home to offer their support. Their judgmental stares said it all. He was the devil their sister had come to be stuck with. If they could help it, they would put an end to it all and get a more deserving brother for her. He swallowed his pride and tried to maintain a straight face through it all.

She kept to herself for days on end afterwards. Sometimes he would hear her crying out to God. She would ask why he had given her the go ahead to marry him knowing this would happen. It was during this period that they grew apart. He feared they would never be able to have the sort of carefree relationship they used to have. How would she ever trust him again? He knew they could not carry on like that forever. Divorce might be the only way out after all. She was already humiliated. Hopefully, time would heal her heart. Thankfully, they had no children to complicate things. He was sure there were men out there who would still jump at the opportunity of marrying her even as a divorcee. Mike may have been right after all. He was not meant for women like her.

The further he grew from his wife the closer he became to Mike. They were not back to their old ways but occasionally they had lunch together in some coffee shop. When he invited him to the wedding, he accepted. It was a wedding after all, not some crazy party in some night club.

Outside, he found Mike in his car with a woman he had never seen before. He shook his head before knocking on the window. She bolted without any introductions.

"Is the wedding reception over yet?" he asked looking confused.

"It's over for me," he said.

Mike looked at him for a while.

"You are drunk," he said laughing. "I told you not to get drunk."

"I'm not drunk," Jeff said. "Let's get out of here."

Mike checked himself out in the mirror and combed his hair with a comb he always left in his car. Jeff shook his head as he watched him with a puzzled look on his face.

"Take me straight home," he said.

Mike laughed.

"No way man," he said. "You don't need to go home just yet. Look at you. You are dying inside. Nneka is..."

"Leave my wife out if it," he cut in angrily.

Mike shrugged. He inserted the key into the ignition and adjusted his seat. Jeff sat on the passenger's seat and drifted into sleep almost immediately. Mike looked at him for a while, shook his head and drove off. He knew his friend's conscience was eating him up and blamed his wife for this. They used to be able to just have fun without the burden of conscience. Fun could not be fun if you get troubled by it afterwards. He still had hopes that his good old friend could be rehabilitated back to the way he used to be; unhinged and wild. His wife was putting him into the same cage she was in herself. He hated religion and religious people. They made life as boring as hell and judged anyone who did not share their same boring beliefs in consequences.

"Sit tight man," he said to himself with genuine conviction. "They are not going to cage that free spirit anymore."

He put on the radio and listened to the news as he drove. The economy was not looking good but what did he care? He waited till the exchange rate was announced before turning it off. The rest of the trip was spent in silence. Occasionally he looked at his friend to make sure he was fine. Jeff was snoring away quietly.

After almost an hour he arrived his destination. It was a house in the middle of apparently nowhere. For miles around there was nothing to represent civilisation. Various exotic cars were parked around the house in no order. He hesitated as he contemplated waking Jeff up but decided to leave him behind. He alighted and lit a cigarette as he approached the entrance. The two huge men mounting the entrance did not bother looking at the card he produced from his pocket. They knew who he was. Instead they took turns shaking his hand and smacking him playfully on the back. Mike always thought shaking their hands was like shaking the hands of gorillas. He often wondered what they ate besides the inevitable steroids he was sure they injected regularly. After some dirty small talk, he went inside but not before explaining that he had a friend inside his car who would be coming in later. They asked if his friend had an invite. He said no but that he would sort out a temporary card once inside.

The scene inside the hall was a sharp contrast to what was outside. The hall had been designed by someone who knew a thing or two about architecture and arts. The ceiling was high and glittering chandeliers hung from them. Everything had a touch of class to it, including the expensive life sized paintings on the walls of popular musicians and other personalities apparently known only to certain people. Mike himself could recognize Hugh Hefner, founder of the infamous playboy magazine. He always meant to ask Caro who the others were but assumed they were involved in similar trades as Hugh. The soft jazz music that filled the air had the desired calming effect on his nerves.

Caro managed the place. She was a woman in her late forties. She looked like she had been a stunner in her youthful days. She still had a pretty face even though she was quite fat. She preferred to describe herself as being plump. Most referred to her as Madam Caro, or simply as Madam. He preferred to call her Caro. He had already seen her as she moved from one table to the other making sure her clients were happy. He had also spotted at least two faces he recognized from television. One of them was a senator. It could easily have been another serene restaurant scene except for the fact that most of the female partners were underage and lived there.

He smoked as he waited. There was no designated smoking area and the hall was thick with smoke. From the scents in the air he could perceive that some of the people there were smoking weed and other stuff. No one bothered any other and that was why he loved the place. Not a soul would tell anyone come morning that they saw a senator the previous night. Even a Hollywood celebrity would feel relaxed without fear of the paparazzi.

His mind wondered to his personal issues. He wondered if Jeff was still asleep and if not, how he was reacting to his strange environment. He blamed him for a lot of the bad fortune that had come his way, one of which was his now terminated marriage. He had felt broken hearted with the way his old-time friend had treated him just because of some so called angel he wanted to marry. It had seemed like a joke at first but suddenly Jeff was talking about a wife, a home, kids, and eternal life. These were strange topics to them. They were used to talking about booze, cash and women. He began to make him feel like some childish, irresponsible fool.

After Jeff got married to Nneka he decided to give marriage a shot. He had hoped that would make him welcome in their home. Nneka was not dissuaded. She treated him like a leper and managed to convince his friend to do the same. It hurt like hell. Unlike them, he had two children with his wife. The fool kept forgetting to take her contraceptive pills. Sometimes he believed she did it on purpose believing that kids would force him to settle. He never one day had the intention of quitting his playboy lifestyle and never gave her the impression that he would. Perhaps she thought after the wedding something would click in his primate brain and turn him from a roving gorilla to a monk. Women!

He adored his children and would do everything in his power to make sure they were in no way disadvantaged. He provided enough money for whatever they needed. That to him was enough. Ronke had quickly got used to the idea that she was married to a playboy. Unlike Nneka, she was no saint herself and found solace in his money. She used to complain during the first few years after their marriage. Afterwards she stopped complaining. Why would she? Her family members treated him like a god. He was, after all, the cash cow that made most of their dreams come true. The only reason he divorced her was because one of his most persistent mistresses insisted he did so.

Madam Caro eventually arrived at his table. Her heavily made up face reminded him of an older and less attractive version of Kim Kardashian. He wondered if anyone had ever found the courage to tell her that she should sue her makeup artist. She probably would not have taken any offence. She was just that carefree.

"Don't tell me you just came here to look at people having fun," she said planting a kiss on his cheek before sitting. She was breathing heavily and he thought he could hear a slight wheeze. Her voice was always hoarse and he had advised her to see a doctor about it. Who would not develop COPD after spending night after night in a smoke-filled hall. Plus, she was a smoker herself.

"I'm just taking time to unwind. This place has not slowed down one bit," he said. "I thought we are in a recession."

Madam Caro's laughter sounded like a misfiring truck. She laughed and coughed and wheezed at the same time. She made laughing seem like a happy but painful experience. The problem with her was that she loved to laugh despite her ailing lungs.

"Don't make me laugh," she said when she finally caught her breath. "Recession ko, recession ni. The irony of it all is that the worse the economy performs, the more people come."

Mike seemed puzzled. "How's that?"

She shrugged her huge shoulders. "I'm not a socio-economic analyst. I just say what I see. You know I don't have time to ask questions.

Business is booming and that is all that matters. Shebi you want talk abi you want…"

He leaned forward.

"I brought a friend today," he said. "This is his first time here. Can I get a card for him?"

"How did he come in without a card?" she asked suddenly looking furious. "I should fire those lazy guards."

"He is still outside," he said. "Relax. He is sleeping in my car, probably a bit drunk too. I want him to get some special treatment. The type of treatment that will keep him coming back."

Madam Caro pulled his ear jokingly.

"Naughty boy," she said. "What if he is some kind of spy? No bring wahala come give me for here. This is not how we do things. You of all people suppose know."

"I've known him since way back," he said. "He is clean."

She looked at the door that led to her office as if contemplating the torture of having to walk all the way there. She took out her cell phone and made a call. Moments later one of the ugliest men he had ever seen, if not the ugliest, came hurrying to their table. She gave him a key and instructed him to go to her office, unlock her drawer and get one of the cards in it.

"Don't open any other drawer," she warned. "Just open the top one, get the card, lock it, and bring it back."

The man nodded and hurried away. Mike observed him until he disappeared behind the door.

"That guy is ugly," Mike said. He was frowning. "What was his name again?"

"Robert. What of you?" She asked. "Who convinced you of your good looks?"

"I handsome no be small," he said smiling. "Ladies dig me like eye pencil."

"Who told you women like handsome men? Besides, if women dig you like that then why are you here?" she mocked.

"Freedom," he said. "This place is all about the freedom it represents. I can come here and forget the rigid and judgmental world exists for a few hours. It is one of a kind."

Madam did not reply. She fumed as she wondered what was taking Robert so long. Just as she decided to go and see for herself he emerged from the door and hurried back to her.

"I gave you a simple instruction," she scolded in a tone of voice that showed how ruthless she could be. "What were you doing in there?"

Robert scratched his head.

"The lock was hard to open," he said.

She gave him a stern look before dismissing him with a wave of her hand. She gave him the card.

"Don't ever do this again," she said. "It's just because it is you that I am turning a blind eye. You should have at least tried to explain to me over the phone before bringing him here."

"Thanks a lot," he said. "You are the best."

They agreed to meet in the VIP section. She wanted to personally chat with his friend before formally welcoming him as one of theirs. It was a smaller section where illegal gambling went on. He had seen men gamble away millions of dollars in minutes in there. Gambling was not his thing. He never won. He finished his cigarette before going outside again. Jeff was awake but sleepy when he got to the car. He thought he would be furious.

"Where are we?" he asked weakly. "What is that building over there?"

Mike smiled in the darkness.

"This is heaven on earth," he said. "Come on man. Let's go get that fun you've been missing for too long."

"Just take me home," he said. "I need to sleep. Seriously. I have work tomorrow."

Mike laughed.

"You've got to be kidding me," he said. "Come on out. You can sleep here if you want. They've got very nice rooms."

"Is it a hotel?"

Mike took him by the hand and led him out of the car with the air of a doctor about to administer treatment to a psychiatric patient. Jeff followed like a lamb. He let go of his hand when they got close to the entrance. Jeff kept looking around like a lost man.

"There's not a building in view besides this one," he said.

"This place is out of town," Mike said. "Few people know it even exists. I've been wanting to bring you here for a long time. Can't be selfish with all the fun. You should have been here long time ago if not for that wife of yours. Give these women a chance and they'll turn us all into caged animals."

"Who's he?" one of the huge guards asked when they got to the entrance.

"A friend," Jeff answered producing the golden card Madam had given him earlier. This time he took it, had a good look and passed it to his colleague.

"Let him through, Zudock," he said.

Zudock stepped aside to let them pass. All the while he never stopped looking at Jeff who, on his part, looked uneasy.

"Stop staring at him like that," his colleague said when they were out of hearing distance. "You got the man looking uncomfortable."

"I don't like the guy, Barry" Zudock said. "Looks like a cop to me."

"He's not the first cop to come here," Barry said. "If he has a card, he has a card. Relax."

Once inside Jeff could not stop staring. He could recognise no less than five popular faces within the first few seconds of stepping into the hall. Mike had to tell him repeatedly to stop acting like a kid in a zoo. They made their way to the VIP section where Madam was already waiting. The section was separated from the main hall by a huge oak door that had the sign PRIVATE engraved on it in golden letters. It was never locked but everyone knew never to go through it unless by invitation. It was designed to be discrete rather than grand and had only a dim light to light up the room. Huge leather sofas with high backrests faced the walls. Jeff strained his eyes. He could barely make out her features in the poorly lit room. Mike knew that insane sums of money was being won and lost behind some of the chairs.

"Is this the man?" she asked.

"This is the man," Mike replied sitting and urging Jeff to sit too. "This is Jeff. He was my best man during my wedding."

"Why do men even get married?" she asked rhetorically.

"Culture," Mike replied. "It is expected. If you don't they will think you are gay or in some cult. Marriage is not too bad in itself. Monogamy is the problem. My friend here has been grappling with this issue for years now. He is a good man with a conscience. He used to be like me. Just want something to take the stress out of his life a little bit. This is Madam Caro. She runs this place better than most African presidents run their countries. Madam is a real businesswoman who understands our needs. She works around the clock with one aim in mind: the happiness of all men. She is one of those feminists who does not hate men. She believes men and women can have exactly what they want and still be happy with each other. Isn't that brilliant? She works really hard. Give her the Israeli-Palestinian conflict and she would solve it in twelve months. She thinks more night clubs in the area would solve the problem."

Madam proceeded to light a cigarette. She took her time.

"I've worked hard during my youth," she said after inhaling and exhaling thick smoke several times. "Now I have to rest while others follow the path I left behind. I consider myself a facilitator these days.

We are ahead of the times. The age of reason would soon come and the rest of society would catch up with my views. What is it that you do?"

Mike tapped his leg with his shoe.

"I'm an accountant," he lied.

"We work in the same place," Mike said.

"Two accountants in one company?" she asked. "Must be a rich company."

"They do alright," Jeff said.

Robert came to take their orders.

"Later," Mike said. "My friend here is still trying to recover from a day of binge drinking."

He left. Madam Caro soon dozed off, the lit cigarette still in her hand. The two men exchanged looks as she began snoring softly. Mike coughed loudly, causing her to wake up.

"You chaps are still here," she said. "I thought Robert had sorted you out. Where is he?"

"I can go fetch him," Mike offered eagerly.

"Don't worry," she said. "I'll use my phone. But you know where the girls are, don't you? Just go upstairs."

Mike suddenly became restless and in a hurry to leave. He stood and thanked her.

"Try fix up something for my pal here," he said before leaving.

"Hey?!" Jeff called after him. He did not turn back. He was like a dog on his way to fetch a ball.

Madam made a call from her phone. He was beginning to figure out what the place was about and why Mike had brought him there.

"Come on," Madam said as she stood. "Don't be shy here. Everybody is here for the same thing. There is no cause for alarm. Let mummy find you the perfect girl. Did he tell you I am a match maker as well? Except I don't match people up so they can get married and spoil the fun. What you need is different depending on your mood and status in life. We are not the same each new day. Why should we stick to the same woman every day? That is precisely the problem."

He wanted to tell her that he was not interested, that he was not aware his friend was bringing him to such a place. He realised he was fiddling with his wedding ring and stopped abruptly. She was too sleepy to notice anything. He followed as she walked into the main hall. It was even busier than when they had arrived. For some reason, he focused on a pot-bellied man sitting at a table with two other women. There was something wrong with the picture that he could not entirely put a finger on. Suddenly it occurred to him who the man was. He also realised the people he was with were not women but girls. He was sure the older of the two could not have been more than fourteen years old. They acted like mature women. The older one kissed him on the lips while the other had her hand on his thigh. It seemed a bit too much to bear and he shook his head as if to shake off the image. He did not have children but could not help thinking how the two were some others' daughters and wondered how they had ended up there. Where were their parents?

"There's enough fun to go around," Madam who had misunderstood his stare said. "Come."

Suddenly the instinct that was natural to every journalist began to urge him on. Out of curiosity more than anything else he followed her as she struggled up a flight of stairs. She led the way to another door. It led to a long corridor. A heavily built man who looked like a crossbreed between a gorilla and The Rock sat at the end of it. He wondered if she got all her guards on steroids.

He was reading a magazine and did not even as much as look up. He counted five doors on either side of the corridor. He could here laughter coming from one of them. What sounded like a scuffle between two people could be heard from within another room. The other rooms were quiet. Suddenly one of the doors burst open and an angry looking man walked out fuming. He was rubbing his knuckles as if he had just been in a fist fight.

"What is the problem, Musa?" Madam Caro asked looking angry and embarrassed.

"It's the girl again," he said touching his cheek tenderly. "That bitch scratch my face. She's possessed man. I tell you say we need to get rid of her. She be truck load of trouble."

He could see scratch marks on his face. His clothes were torn too. Whoever had done such damage to a man that huge must have a lot of fight in her, he thought.

"As big as you are, you cannot control a little girl," she said. "What do I pay you for?"

"Madam na beat I dey beat am since," he said defensively. "That girl possess demons no be small. She fight like someone wey get legion demon inside. E be like say she dey craze self. She claim say she no fit work. She say she get fever."

She scoffed at him then cast a quick embarrassed look at Jeff. She placed her hands on her waist and looked at the door as if in deep thought.

"Was she really having a fever?" she asked.

He was blowing at the hand. It was slightly blood stained.

"Her body hot small sha," he said. "But other girls dey fit work with that kind small fever."

"You be doctor?" she asked accusingly. "If she tell you say she sick you for tell me. You know how much I buy that girl? You just big like Michelin with no brain. If say you kill am you for see trouble. Go wait for me for main hall. Pray say Robert no catch you tonight."

Musa left, cursing beneath his breath. She turned to him. She was looking stressed and irritated.

"This is not looking like a good night for you," she said. "Hope you are not one of those men with bad luck. We should go back to the hall. I have others to attend to you know. If that big fool had told me what the situation is I would not have wasted my time coming here."

"May I see her?" he asked.

"Who?" she asked with a sneer on her face. "The sick one?"

"If you don't mind," he said.

"You are the customer," she said. "You are the one who should mind. I'll advise you to get someone else. Besides being sick she seems to be having one of her anger fits today. If I did not know better, I would have thought she was one rich folk's child before coming here. So rude. If you don't want your face looking like it went through a paper shredder just forget about her. I will deal with her myself later."

"Let me just see her," he insisted. "Perhaps she needs to be handled differently. Violence sometimes brings out the worst in people."

She looked at him, hesitated, then shrugged. "You must be one of those masochistic men I've heard about who enjoy pain. Anyway, hope your friend explained how this place works in terms of settlement. Don't want any complaints from anybody. If you have any problem, call Jack sitting over there pretending he can read and he'll fix you something better."

He nodded. Jack did not raise his head from the magazine he was reading. Apparently, he was there for some other kind of trouble. He noted her reference to the girls as 'something'. This worried him. His journalistic instincts were kicking in and he wanted to know just what was going on.

"Jack does not say much but he has his own way of dealing with problems," she said. "He can sit there all day looking at magazines like some statue but I assure you he will spring to action like Flash when necessary. Jack say hello to our guest. This is his first time here."

Jack looked up. His eyes were cold as ice. A corner of his mouth lifted in a smile, revealing some gold teeth that gleamed in the light.

"Let us hope we will not be needing him," Jeff said and headed for the room Musa had exited earlier.

"Have a nice time," Madam Caro said. "I'll be in the hall if you need me."

Jack was already engrossed in his magazine. He hesitated in front of the door which was ajar, listened for any sounds from within, heard nothing then knocked. No one answered. He knocked again.

"Just go in," Jack said irritatingly. "It's not your bloody wife's bedroom."

Jeff looked at him, shocked by the unwarranted rudeness and hostility.

"Now don't stand there looking at me like you gay," he said. "I generally do not like people waiting around on my corridor. It is distracting."

He ignored him and pushed the door gently. The room was simply furnished. A queen size bed was in the middle, leaving little space for much else. They had managed to squeeze in a dressing table and it had all sorts of make-up kits on it. No one was in sight and not a single sound could be heard.

He strolled slowly further into the room. The cushioned rug underneath made his movement silent. There was another door on the other end of the wall which he believed led to the bathroom. He stood in front of it wondering if he should proceed or not. So far, he could tell no one treated her with any dignity but he felt like he was invading her personal space. A sound behind the main door caused him to turn.

She was sitting on the floor, her knees drawn up to her chest and her face buried in them. Much of it was hidden in a mass of hair that looked very much ruffled. He did not know what he had expected but the pathetic figure in front of him did not match the damage he had seen on Musa.

He advanced slowly towards her, stopped, then squatted in front of her. He was aware of Jack's presence. As gently as he could he closed the door and locked it. Not knowing what to say or do he just remained there observing the pitiful figure. She did not move. He wondered if she was even aware of his presence.

"How is the fever now?" he asked as gently as he could.

She did not reply.

His head was by now clearing up from the alcohol. He tried to recall anything of help from the psychology lessons he had attended during his training as a journalist on how to deal with traumatised kids in war situations. He tried again.

"I'm here for your good," he said realising to his surprise that his voice was a bit shaky. He cursed himself for drinking too much at the wedding and wondered if his breath smelled of alcohol.

The head rose slowly. A defiant smile was on her face and there was this look in her eyes that reminded him of a torture victim he had once examined during the Liberian civil war. The head fell back to its former position before they made any reasonable eye contact. Other than the strange look, he was taken aback by her extreme beauty. She was pretty, very pretty. He had always had an eye for pretty girls and he could see that even though her hair was dishevelled and her face a mess. Her eyes were moist and red, the long lashes matted together by tears and make-up. Her lips were pressed together tightly in a stubborn gesture. On one side of her face he had seen the unmistakable hand print of a slap. The finger marks were red and stood in sharp contrast to her light skin. She was young, too young. His guess was that she was thirteen or fourteen.

"You should get something warm to cover yourself with," he said. "It is quite cold. You will make your fever worse."

He might have been talking to a statue.

"Why don't you go see a doctor?" he asked. "I'm sure my doctor will take good care of you."

She lifted her head once more, this time with a look of incredibility on her face. Through narrowed lids she studied him.

"You are new here?" she finally asked. Her voice was hoarse, like that of someone who had been crying or had a cold.

"Yes," he replied. "A friend brought me here. I thought we were going to a restaurant or something."

"She looked away and stared at the window but said nothing. It was completely dark outside. He could see she was thinking. The look of defiance was beginning to ebb and a sad look was creeping in. He observed the gradual change, not sure if it was a good sign. She let out a long sigh and rose slowly to her feet. She was much taller than he had imagined. He stood too.

"Feeling better now?" he asked.

She shot him a look that would have made a python recoil. Without a word, she walked to the door, opened it and stepped into what he confirmed to be a bathroom. She began to close the door slowly, hesitated, swung it open and then slammed it shut. The noise was deafening.

"Oh boy," he said to himself wearily and sat on the bed. He could hear running water from the bathroom. He began to recall his school days when Mike had been his pal. He laughed softly as he recalled how he could hardly stay a minute without thinking of women. His life at the time had been dominated by what some described as the lusts of the flesh. He had lost the appetite and was not sure if it was growing up or the reformation. Mike was still like that and they were almost the same age. Perhaps it was the guilt of sins past. Back then he would have been thinking of the best strategy to get her into bed despite the situation. He might even have raped her. Men! He could not blame any woman who hates men. He would be the first to admit that he had been a selfish man back then who lived only to gratify his selfish desires. Women were not innocent either. Every mother had a chance to raise her son well.

As he listened to the running water he thought of her. It was obvious she did not have much free will. Her presence there was a puzzle he found difficult to solve. How did she come to be in such a place in the first place? Had a friend lured her in and she did not find it as adventurous as she had imagined? Perhaps she had come on her own, wanted to quit after a change of heart only to realise she was trapped; they would not let her go. Perhaps. One thing was certain and that was the fact that she had little chance of leaving. The machinery he had seen around her was not one she could overcome without substantial help from some powerful figure. He reckoned it must be overwhelming being in such a place and feeling trapped for life.

The door to the bathroom eventually opened and she walked in rubbing her hair with a towel. She had only a large towel wrapped around her. She paused when she saw him as if surprised he was still there.

"Are you still here?" she asked. There was irritation in her tone

"You wanted me to go?" he asked.

"You know what brought you here," she said. "You are definitely not getting it here. You better turn your fun search light elsewhere. I am prepared to die tonight."

She sat on the chair in front of the mirror, her back to him. As she combed her hair he could see her face in the mirror. He winced and looked away. She was such a beauty. He could still not imagine how she had come to be in her present situation. An unintended sigh escaped his lips. She heard it, paused, then continued combing her hair. He was unaware of the fact that she was observing him from the mirror. He buried his face in his hands. She continued watching him, now with some curiosity while she systematically ran the comb through her moist hair. She gathered it behind her neck and held it together with an elastic band that was on the table. He straightened up and looked at her, or rather her image in the mirror.

"How old are you?" he asked.

She made a face.

"I can't see of what use that would be to you," she said rudely.

"I'll like to know you better…"

"Goodness!" she exclaimed. "What is this? Another round of mental torture?"

He laughed inwardly, sadly. It was the fact that he had used the same line during his campus days and had sometimes got a similar response. It was funny how he was getting a similar reaction in completely different scenarios. He had no selfish motives now and genuinely wanted to know her better.

"I sincerely wish we met under different situations," he said.

"You really do not have to waste your words here," she said standing. She changed into a black, tight fitting gown while she spoke. "We are all slaves here. You don't have to woo us. It's not as if I have any opinion or choice here."

He sighed again.

"Getting bored already?" she asked laughing sarcastically. "I'm sure the poor woman you left at home would be even more bored. It's a pity because this very night, not even a hot iron to my face will make me change my mind. I can be stubborn. See."

She raised the gown, turned her back to him and bent her knee to show him her sole. He could see dark lines on the sole of her foot. He looked from the foot to her face quizzically.

"Hot iron rods," she said as if she was talking about a new tattoo. "I can be stubborn when I want to be. Why the soles of my feet? Because they don't want my skin burnt where men like you will be turned off. It would spoil their business. Ha!"

"I'm so sorry," he said.

"Good. Well, I'm sorry too. For you, that is. Why don't you just leave?"

"I don't want you to get into any trouble," he said.

"You are my trouble tonight," she said. "Why can't you just leave me alone? Leave me alone everyone!"

Someone knocked on the door. Despite her stance, a look of horror came to her face.

"Any problem in there?" a harsh voice asked.

Jeff walked to the door and opened it. Jack stood there with his magazine in one hand. He looked even more menacing now he was much closer. It was a face that would have frightened the devil himself, he thought. It did not do him any good trying to look tough all the time.

"Is she being difficult?" he asked looking as if he was eager to come in and put her in her place.

Jeff looked back at her. She stood with a look of fear on her face and seemed to plead with her eyes.

"Everything's fine," he said and banged the door shut. He waited and listened. Jack stood on the other side for some time then walked back to his station. He turned to face her. She looked scared and most of her defiant disposition was gone.

"Listen to me," he said, his tone low but firm. "I never came here for any of this. Like I said, this is my first time here. I never heard of this place before tonight. A colleague of mine brought me here and until Madam Caro brought me in here I had no idea it was more than a restaurant. I am married. I respect my marriage vows. I have a kid sister and, one day, I hope to have a daughter. This is not my kind of life. Do you understand?"

She nodded repeatedly. He moved closer and placed his hands on her shoulders. She was trembling. This made him angry. No human should be made to feel that frightened by another. It was just wrong. Pages from his counselling book flashed through his mind. He had to build some trust; establish a relationship.

"I have noticed some strange things here," he went on. "This place stinks to say the least and some rich and powerful men know it exists. If my guess is right, then I believe you can't leave because those bullies won't let you?"

She nodded. He touched the red marks on her cheek. Her eyes were beginning to get moist.

"Musa did this?"

She nodded.

He led her to the bed and they both sat. He could not find the right words to say for a while. Eventually he pulled himself together.

"I am a journalist," he said. "My job is to make the public aware of the evils of our society so that necessary actions can be taken. Your fundamental human rights have been violated to say the least and in the evilest of ways. Now, I want you to pull yourself together. You must tell me everything about yourself and this place. Listen!"

Even before he finished talking she was already shaking her head in fear. He knew he had to be more persuasive. She had seen all sorts of men, women too. None or few had given her any reason to put her faith in humanity. They had all come to take. None gave. Why should he be any different?

"This is no time to be fearful," he said shaking her gently. "You've got..."

He realised he was acting out of anger. Per the books, it was a bad sign.

Emotions cloud judgment. He relaxed, apologised and placed a hand across her shoulders. Tears began to flow down her cheeks. He handed her a handkerchief he always carried in his pocket and waited. As she wiped the tears away he saw the scars on her wrist. He held the hand and felt the scars with his thumbs.

"You tried to commit suicide," he said just a bit louder than a whisper. He had been thinking aloud.

Suddenly her mouth tightened and the defiant look began to return. At this point he wanted the stubborn side. Sadness and self-pity would hardly achieve anything. He would redirect her anger.

"Listen," he said still holding the hand. "Life is a precious gift. It is so precious that we should all cherish it. People grow old and wish their days of youth would somehow come back. But no one reverses the progress of time. We can only recall the past in our minds. People kill, cheat, even steal so that they may survive. Now, when a young girl decides that there is no more reason to continue to live, something must be terribly wrong which cannot be her fault."

Her face began to soften. There was now a look of bewilderment. He knew he was striking the right cords. She needed to believe in life, people, and herself again.

"When we get to a point where we are willing to die, we have reached a stage where we can face the enemy squarely because we no longer have anything to lose. This is where many make the mistake; suicide is like taking the enemy's sword and using it on ourselves. No! We should die fighting. Those who fight with nothing to lose often win. Why? Because they fight with their whole might."

She considered his words in silence.

"Now, listen to me. God gave you life for a good reason. You have a right to live. No being, not even the devil, has the right to make you hate your existence. These people are demons. They are in bondage just like you but in a way that they are not even aware of. They are prisoners of the demons ruling them. To be a slave and not know it is the worst kind of slavery.

"You must begin to fight. I will fight with you. God will help us. I'm sure you don't want to continue living like this. Think of the other girls too."

She sighed. Suddenly someone knocked.

"You're not done yet?" Mike asked mockingly.

"Give me a few minutes," he said. "I'll join you guys downstairs."

He stood. She looked at him as if afraid he was going to leave and she would never see him again. He knew he had gained her trust. He lowered his tone.

"I'll be back tomorrow. I promise. You must tell me everything then. I'll try to make them leave you alone. I'll sell my car if I must but we are getting you out of this place. You understand? Just hang in there. Be patient. Can't believe I did not ask your name."

"Ehi," she said. "Don't worry. You are not the first to leave here not knowing my name. It means nobody."

They laughed at her attempt at humour.

"Jeff," he said. "I'll see you tomorrow."

She nodded rapidly. He walked to the door, took a deep breath and opened it. Joe stood there with Madam Caro. They had been listening.

"How did it go man?" Mike asked beaming happily and mischievously.

"Blissful," he replied. "Madam really knows the tricks. Must have coached her girls well."

"Any woman that needs coaching is no woman at all," she said looking flattered. "It is all instinct."

"Coming tomorrow?" Mike asked.

"You paying?"

"Come on man," Mike said laughing. "Who do you think paid for you tonight? You take care of yourself tomorrow."

"Then I guess I'll just stay home...."

"Hell no," Mike cut in hurriedly. "Alright. I'll pay tomorrow. Afterwards, it's all on you."

Jeff's suspicions were confirmed. The man just wanted his marriage destroyed. His guess was that he wanted to get back at his wife. He was truly a sick, wicked being.

"My legs ache," Madam Caro said. "You two can argue all you want. All we want is our money. We really don't care where it comes from. I'm sure Jack does not care which of you pays tomorrow. He just wants his pay check at the end of the month. Isn't it true Jack?"

Jack nodded without lifting his head.

"Join me in the hall when you are done arguing about money," she said walking away. "I can't remember the last time I heard anyone argue over money in this place."

They followed close behind.

"You need a foot massage?" Mike asked as they walked. "You do work too hard."

She cast him a naughty look.

"I have my boys to help me with that if I need one. Thanks anyway. At least you appreciate the hard work I do for society."

The hall was still very busy when they got there. Jeff could see even more recognisable faces. Caro led them to her usual table and they sat.

"Now where's that lousy waiter?" Mike asked. "I need my drink now."

Madam signalled to one of the waiters. He walked up to them.

"Gin and tonic," Mike said. "Jeff?"

"Lemon and lime bitters," he said.

"Hope the evening was not that bitter," Caro said.

She shared a hysterical laugh with Mike. Jeff waited patiently for them to get over their hysteria.

"On the contrary," he said when they were done making fun of him. "I did have one of the best nights of my life."

"With a sick girl?" she asked.

"No way!" Mike asked in shock. "Of all the girls in here you gave my main man here a sick girl on his first night? How do we know she does not have AIDS? Hope you used protection?"

"He chose her," she defended, her finger pointing at Jeff.

"I'm not a kid," he said. "I know about protection. Now if you two do not mind, I really don't like sharing private details with others."

"My man here has changed," Mike told her. He was in high spirits. "We used to share every detail about everything. I don't know what has got into his mind."

"We do test our girls from time to time by the way," she said. "We have a doctor who comes here every weekend or so."

"How come he has not seen her yet?" Jeff asked.

"He may be coming tomorrow," she said. "I think she just has a cold."

"I am more interested in the meaning of 'from time to time'," Mike said. "How often is that and what if they get HIV between that interval."

"Life is full of risks," she said. "Many men have got the disease from their wives and vice versa. We do not pose any more risk than what you get out there. As a matter of fact, our risk is lower."

"What's the doctor's name?" Jeff asked.

"Why on earth do you want to know?" Mike asked.

Madam Caro observed him critically, her eyes narrowed in suspicion. Jeff was unaware of this. The waiter arrived with the drinks. Mike drained his glass in an instant and asked for another.

"What's eating you up man?" Mike asked. "The sick girl? Want to try another one? I'll wait."

"You do remember I have a wife, don't you?" Jeff asked.

"Now you are feeling all guilty and blue?" Mike asked. "You'll get over that very soon. I promise you. Let her do the choosing next time. She knows exactly what every man needs at any point in time."

"The conscience will ease with time dear," Caro said. "Hope you've not caught her bug. Viruses can make you feel down. There's one they called Einstein Barr. Weird name. Can make you feel all depressed and fatigued. Not sure why God made these tiny things in the first place. Anyway, most men who come here are also married. Look around you. They would have been home and depressed. Think of this place as some sort of psychotherapy."

"He got this 'holier than thou' attitude after he got married," Mike said. "This man used to be my mentor in sin. I'm trying to get him out of the trap he got himself into. Used to be a very bubbly fellow."

Jeff grimaced as Mike began to sing: *I was lost but now I'm found...*

The waiter arrived with his second drink. This time he drank slowly.

"Tomorrow," Mike said. "We'll show him some good girls. No more sick girls for my pal."

"I'll rather see her again tomorrow," Jeff said.

Mike and Caro exchanged glances.

"You've fallen in love with her or what?" Caro asked. "I can tell you now that it is not love. Men have a thing for vulnerable women. That is why as a feminist I detest women exhibiting weakness. We are not the weaker sex. Strong is the new sexy."

"Who said anything about love?" Jeff asked coldly. "By the way, how much does this thing cost?"

"Eight hundred dollars a night," Mike answered. "We do get international guests here too. Australia and the UK are the most regular."

"What if I want her to myself for, let's say, two to three months?" Jeff asked.

"Are you nuts?" Mike asked. "Such an expense for a whore?"

"Who's not a whore these days?" Caro asked. "The whore you know is better than the saint you don't. If he can afford it, let him pay."

"You will not be coming here every day you know," Mike pointed out.

Jeff shrugged.

"I just don't like the idea of sharing," he said. "Besides, your question about AIDS got me worried."

"Could be love," Caro said. "Who knows? I won't let you marry her though. I have the right to refuse."

"How much?" Jeff asked. He was serious.

"Don't do it man," Mike pleaded. "You will go bankrupt. You can ask for her any time you come. Just call in advance and she will make her available."

"Seven thousand two hundred dollars," she said looking up from her cell phone. "I can give you some discount. Let's make it a flat rate of seven thousand. My boys will be pleased too. They are tired of her troubles. That ugly man called Robert keeps defending her. He is her self-appointed guardian angel. They won't have to worry about her until you come."

"I'll send you the cheque," Jeff said.

"You must be nuts," Mike said.

"No, he's not," Caro said. "Leave the man alone. We only take cash by the way. Just come with the money next time. I'll get you a permanent card so you can come and go whenever you want. Your friend here wants to ruin our business transaction. Give me your email address and I'll send you the location map. It is remote. Without a map, no one will be able to find it."

"Get me a sheet of paper," Jeff said.

She signalled to a waiter standing nearby and instructed him to get a sheet of paper and a pen. When he brought them, she handed them to Jeff who wrote down his details. She scribbled a contract and made him sign it.

"I'll ask the doctor to come around and get her checked," Caro who was obviously pleased with her business deal said. "We will check her for HIV, gonorrhoea, syphilis, and even Ebola. I can ask him to give her a broad range of antibiotics just in case. That's what I call special service."

Jeff sipped his lemon and lime bitters. Mike could not help wondering what had got into his pal. He shook his head.

"You should consider doing the same," she said to Mike. "There is always a risk of getting the disease during a window period."

"No, thank you, ma'am," he said emphatically. "If I wanted to settle down with one woman I would have stuck to my wife. I thought that was the whole point of having such a place. If I was Donald Trump I would pay for all the ladies here, except Obiageli of course."

"What's wrong with her?" Jeff asked.

"Getting too old for the place," she said. "She's twenty-five. If I don't get a good deal from one of those brothels in town we will have to fly her off to Dubai or Italy. I told her that the other day and she cried all night. Our girls know they are better off here. But then, business is business and we have to maintain our standard."

"What goes on in Italy?" Jeff asked.

"Trust me, you do not want to know," Mike said.

They both laughed knowingly and did a high five. Jeff shook his head. He could not believe the level of apathy, depravity, and callousness they were portraying. The two had absolutely no conscience and he loathed himself for ever being like that. Back in the day he would have reacted with the same sadistic joy they shared.

They talked about all the rotten stuff going on in the world and all the dirty games played by corrupt politicians and public figures. Jeff said little. When he got tired of it all he announced his intention to leave. By this time, Mike was drunk and unsteady on his feet. She begged him to take the key from him. It was obvious she wanted him alive long enough to bring in the cash.

She walked with them to Mike's car and got one of her guards to help put him on the back seat where he was securely strapped in. While this was going on she gave him directions on how to join the main road.

"See you tomorrow with my money," she said before he got into the driver's seat. "Not a word of this place to anyone."

"See you," he said and ignited the engine.

He drove slowly. The road was bumpy and he wanted to ensure Mike's car lived long. He could not help noticing the cold stare the guards gave him as he left. They stood there until he was out of sight.

He realised just how remote the place was as he drove. Huge trees lined the road and there was not a single light anywhere. As far as he could tell the place was in the middle of a very thick forest. That men would go to that extent to have fun was scary. That they would choose underage girls as the objects of their indulgence sickened him. Even as a player, he had his rules. He could never imagine himself exploiting a child. The world must have been worse than it was at a time when he thought he was the worst humanity could ever become. Perhaps the world had changed for the worse during his absence from the game.

When they got to more even ground Mike who had snapped out of his drunken slumber suddenly became all chatty. He wanted him to listen to every detail of his escapade. He let him talk. When it got too unsettling he had to ask him to keep the details to himself. He went on anyway.

He eventually managed to shut out his voice from his mind and instead focus on Ehi. The poor girl must have been through a lot. He could tell from the look in her eyes. That men like Mike found any excitement in what they did to people like her without any thought to her dignity as a human made his stomach churn. They had in some way managed to make people mere objects to be used and abused.

He remembered Nneka's advice about pornography. She believed it was the devil's biggest offensive against the humanity of mankind. Pornography was a weapon that created sick desires in people; desires they would never have known and did not need. Like drugs, it was the unnecessary high that led to an inevitable low aka depression unless the victim refuels with something more extreme than the last. It also made the objects of those weird desires dehumanised. Any porn addict would eventually become a pervert per her. He agreed.

He had interviewed a lot of sex offenders. Every one of them was addicted to extreme porn. It was the silent killer eating away at society's moral conscience. He personally stayed away from it. The only problem was that mainstream media was now pornographic in its content. Her advice was for him to stay away from anything pornographic in any shape or form, even seemingly innocent television programs. If there is sex in it then it should be avoided. She had no interest in anything from Hollywood and had no respect for any actor or actress who was ever involved in a sex scene.

When they got to the city he decided it would be safer to take Mike to his house and then go home in the car. Mike insisted he was sober enough to drive but he refused to let him. He let him out when they got to his place and then drove home.

Nneka was inbed when he arrived. He knew she was awake. He knew the way she breathed when she was asleep. He also knew what she would be thinking. How was he to tell her that none of what she was thinking was true, that he had been faithful to her even though he was coming home at such an unholy hour? What exactly would he say to convince her? He wished he could tell her about his encounter with Ehi. Even he knew the story would sound silly.

He removed his shoes and got into bed. For hours, he lay there staring into the darkness and wondering how on earth he was going to get Ehi out of there. Something told him his encounter with her was just the beginning of something bigger. He had an uneasy feeling in his gut. Common sense told him to just forget the whole encounter and never set his foot there again. There must be many like her all over the world. He could never rescue them all. He was no super hero. He wished he was. He knew he would never be able to abandon her there. He would have to find a way or die in the process. He also knew that any wrong move could spell disaster for her. They could decide to ship her away to Italy as punishment or worse. He had to tread carefully. With people as dangerous as that, even he could be at risk of harm.

3

CHAPTER 3

The next day at work he got a message that the manager wanted to see him. Being that he was late for work that morning he assumed it was for some sort of chastisement. He braced himself and went to his office. Gbenga was always in a bad mood. He always acted like he had some deadline to meet. The company was doing well and there was really no reason for him to be so uptight. He was always irritable and the only time they saw him relax a bit was after a few glasses of wine during the annual Christmas party.

"Sit down Jeff," he said without looking up from the paper he was reading.

"Good morning," Jeff said as he sat.

Gbenga grunted something back in response. He was scouring through clips from very old newspapers tagged to equally old looking files some unfortunate orderly had found from the archives probably after hours of searching.

"I know it's somewhere here," he said to himself as he searched. "Where on earth is that clip?"

Jeff shrugged and let him do his searching. Eventually he gave up and looked up.

"You were late this morning," he said.

"Traffic," Jeff said.

"I also go through traffic on my way to work," he said. "Anyway. The reason I called you is because I have a special assignment for you. Ever heard of The Ethiopian?"

Jeff nodded and frowned at the same time. The man everyone referred to as The Ethiopian was a strange character who lived by the lagoon. No one knew how long he had been staying there or for what purpose. Those who had seen him say he looks like he came from Ethiopia and had a foreign accent. All sorts of rumours had spread about him. Some even believed he had mystical powers and there were claims of certain supernatural powers. Jeff had no idea what to believe. The tabloids always had something spectacular to say about him when they ran out of stories and the public seem to have a healthy appetite for any news that involved him. It was not the type of story he expected a reputable company like theirs to be covering. Many flocked to see him. He was, in a sense, a guru to thousands. Then the other rumour started circulating. He preferred not to discuss it.

"Sure have," he said. "Don't tell me you want to dedicate some columns to that man?"

"That is exactly what we are going to do," he said.

"He is a nobody," Jeff protested. "At best, he is some weird figure who some superstitious folks believe to be a guru with special powers. We are not the type of company to be publishing such stuff."

"Yet each time a paper mentions him, its sales goes up," Gbenga said. "That is something. He is not just a nobody. He is like the wind. We don't see it but we can feel it everywhere. He is not a normal human being, I admit, but definitely not a nobody. People do not flock to see a nobody in the middle of nowhere."

"Why the sudden interest?" Jeff asked.

"I had a dream last night about him," he said.

"A dream?" Jeff asked. "You just had a dream last night about someone and this morning you decide we are going to do a story about him?"

"Why not?" he asked. "Maybe I have special powers myself."

"What was this dream about, if I may ask?" Jeff asked.

"Not now," Gbenga said. "I will tell you some other day. Would have made more sense to you if I had found the clip I was looking for. Now go get ready."

"Anything in particular you want me to focus on?"

Gbenga shook his head. "Not really. You are the investigative journalist. Gather as much as you can. We want enough to be able to write something on him for the next ten years if necessary."

"Sounds like this will not be a one-off coverage," Jeff said standing.

"We will find out," Gbenga said. "That will depend on how the public receive the first issue. Now don't look so dejected. We are not going to put out some sensational stuff like those tabloids. They are only interested in stuff that get the public talking. I am asking you to get material on a person who has some mystique about him. He is a myth. I want you to demystify him. Let us present the man behind the myth. Find out, for instance, what his childhood was like. Who are his parents? Where did he come from? Dig around. Travel to Ethiopia and dig there as well. While there find out if the ark of the covenant is really there. Just make sure you keep every invoice."

Jeff nodded. He knew never to argue with him.

"I will do my best. It is all impromptu but I will try."

"And wipe that frown off your face," Gbenga said. "Others would be happy to do this job. You don't have to come in here unless you have to. Do your thing from home. Just don't sleep from morning till night. At least you will not have to worry about traffic for a while. When you are done, I want some good stuff on my table. Verifiable stuff. I want evidence of anything you dig up."

A confused Jeff nodded, thanked him and left. Back in his office he sat down to think of the whole project. He decided it was not such a bad idea after all. He would have enough time to himself and would not bother about being late for work for at least a month. He always liked the investigative part of his job. It involved a lot of interviews and what he called covert operations. At times like this he employed the services of a private detective he had known for some years. Mason, as he called himself, was the best there was out there. He used to be a cop but retired to open his own private detective business. He soon became very popular, thanks to the part he played in finding out where the daughter of a lecturer who had been kidnapped was being kept and the coverage he had given the story in their magazine. His business took off after this event and he was eternally indebted to him. However busy he was, he would always make his job a priority as a result.

He made a call to the lady in charge of the storeroom and ordered the gadgets he felt he would need. He was assured the items would be ready for pick up in less than thirty minutes. He proceeded to put finishing touches to any pending task he had. Being at the office was not the best part of his job and he did not intend coming in unless he had to. Gbenga had basically given him a wonderful gift.

While he waited for his equipment, Mike came into his office beaming happily. His eyes were bloodshot. He had no intentions of telling him anything about his new assignment.

"Had some serious fun last night," Mike said settling into the chair opposite him as if ready for a long gist. "Boy that was something. What's your plan tonight?"

"Are you planning on returning there tonight?" he asked. "What's up with your eyes?"

"Not sure," Mike said. "Do they look that bad?"

"You look like something from hell," he said seriously. "Better go check it out. Could be Ebola. Just don't come too close."

"It doesn't hurt," Mike said. "It will clear up. I can take you there if you want."

"I can get there myself," Jeff said pretending to read something from a file on his table.

"The way can be tricky even with a map," Mike said. "You don't want to get lost in that jungle. Do you know how dangerous that place is? One wrong turn and you could find yourself driving straight into a kidnapper's den. They use that forest a lot and tend to be a bit paranoid."

"The road is pretty straightforward," he said. "Madam showed me how to get there."

"Why would she do that?" Mike asked suddenly becoming apprehensive. "Usually she does not trust first timers. That sort of business needs to be kept under a tight lid."

"Relax. You were drunk, remember?" Jeff said. "Someone had to get you out."

"So, you want to go on your own?" Mike asked. There was a hint of disappointment in his tone.

"Okay," Jeff said feeling sorry for him. "We go together but I go in my own car. I will follow you behind so I don't drive into some criminals' hideout and get shot."

"When?" he asked.

"You decide and let me know," he said. "Send me a text or something."

The phone rang and he picked it up. The items were ready. He thanked the lady and promised to be there in less than two minutes. Mike was already standing before the call ended.

"I'll send you a text," he said. "See you in the evening."

"See you," Jeff said.

As soon as Mike left he hurried to the storeroom where the items were neatly packed in little white boxes. He checked each item and then signed at the bottom of the list the lady had handed him. Most of the gadgets he picked were not for the assignment but for Ehi. He was already making plans to get her out of there. It was obvious to him that he would never have any reasonable peace of mind until she was out of the abusive environment. He thanked her, packed the boxes into a bigger one and carried them straight to a waiting company car. He asked the driver to wait then returned to his office to get some files and lock his door. He hoped he would not see it again for the next month or so.

Once back home he headed straight to the garage where he kept an old wooden box that contained all sorts of documents including his primary school certificate. The clips that he suspected Gbenga was looking for was in the box somewhere. He was supposed to have returned them but had not. He kept procrastinating until he forgot about it altogether. Feeling a bit guilty for not telling his boss of his crime he searched frantically through other similar looking files until he found it. It contained cut-outs from magazines and newspapers. Anything that referenced The Ethiopian was in there. It was a good starting point. He took the file, closed the box, returned it to its place and headed for the living area.

The house was quiet and he assumed Nneka was in her room or the laundry area. In the past, she would have come to ask him why he was back so early. Those good old days seemed like ages ago. He went through the clips. It was surprising how much of The Ethiopian he had forgotten. The archive was rich.

An hour later he felt he had done enough research for the task ahead. He spent another thirty minutes or so planning his approach. There was still no evidence he came from Ethiopia. He realised he could save himself a whole lot of money and travel time if he could secure an hour or two long interview with him. If he was honest, he might get all the answers he needed from the horse's mouth. The problem was that he was not sure if he would believe everything or anything that came from that mouth. Many saw him as a holy man with rare gifts. If half the claims were true, he may be in for the experience of his life. Then there were the unproven scandals. He would leave them for the end. When he had got all he needed, he would enquire about them. There was no point ruining an interview by bringing up such issues early.

It was really because of Ehi that he did not want to travel. He believed every day was crucial. If he left the country things might get stale and the trust he had managed to generate would be broken. He had to stay until at least something reasonable had been done.

Satisfied he was more than ready he put away the file and made himself a coffee. The coffee machine was a wedding gift from an uncle. It was quite handy and at the press of a button he was guaranteed great coffee. He sat on the sofa and sipped his coffee while thinking of Ehi. The thought of seeing her again actually gave him some excitement.

That frightened him. It was not just the excitement of seeing her again. He was worried he was feeling the same way he used to feel when one of his ex-girlfriends was about to visit.

He was by no means a monk. She was extremely pretty and had a great body. The last thing he wanted was to develop anything but a healthy desire to see her removed from her current predicament and rehabilitated back to normal life. Unhealthy and unholy thoughts were playing around the periphery of his mind and struggling to take hold. They swarmed his head like evening mosquitoes that kept coming back after he brushed them aside. They must not be allowed to take hold. If he succumbed to them he would become no better than all the monsters who had seen her as nothing but another piece of flesh to satisfy their deviant appetites. He would become his former self and that must not be allowed to happen.

He had other fears. If he succeeded in getting her out of there, where would he keep her? Nneka would never believe his story and even if she did they would come looking for her in his house once they figure out what had happened. He still had not worked out how she was going to be removed from there. Mason could have ideas. He always found ways of solving seemingly complex problems in record time. His brain worked like a computer. He knew Madam Caro was not someone to be taken for granted. He was not for once fooled by her seemingly jovial and carefree attitude. No one could maintain that much order with that number of dangerous entities without being ruthless. She would come at him and anyone associated with him with everything she had if she ever knew he was responsible for her escape.

Different plans were developed, tried and tested before being discarded. There was always an obvious flaw by the time he ran the plot through his mind. He knew it was time to rest when he started thinking of hiring thugs to charge the place with guns to rescue her. He had to stick to reality. There had to be a flaw in their seemingly airtight security. He only needed to find it. He realised Mike may be of help. The only problem was that he would become suspicious if he started asking too many questions. Mike, like many who exploited such helpless people around the world, was not just part of the problem but the problem. He could not expect him to be sympathetic to his cause unless he presented a lie.

He finished his now cold coffee, stood, stretched and yawned before proceeding to the bedroom to lie down. Suddenly it occurred to him that Ehi might be the key to the puzzle. Who better to know about any potential security flaw than the captive herself? If she had ever thought of escape, she might already have a plan. It was possible her already crafted plan only needed someone from the outside to take her through the dangerous jungle. He would have to ask her when he saw her later in the evening.

He called Mason while he was lying on the bed. He gave him as much detail as he would need without revealing anything that would jeopardize his plans. Ehi was left out of the conversation completely. Madam Caro was the focus. Mason wanted to know her full name. Thankfully he had heard about the place. It was decided he would call him back once he had anything of importance or if he needed more information. He was confident he would have something in less than a week.

He closed his eyes and tried to focus on the task ahead that his boss had entrusted to him. He did not envisage any difficulty. The Ethiopian was apparently a simple man. His only concern was that he may be surrounded by too many people, all wanting one thing or the other from the man.

In a superstitious society such as the one he found himself, it was inevitable that many would always blame their bad fortune on someone or some external forces. Mother-in-laws were the popular objects of such blame. Few were willing to own up to their mistakes and responsibilities. Generation Y, especially, wanted fun all day with no regard to consequence or responsibility. It was inevitable that they would always seek out those perceived to have enough power to wish away their bad fortune. He hoped he would find the time to have a one on one session with him.

It was almost two in the afternoon when he woke. He felt like closing his eyes and dozing for another hour or two. Who would know? Reluctantly, he got up and headed for the bathroom where he splashed some water on his face. He knew in an hour he would want another hour until the day was gone. He was at home but not on holiday. He dressed up, picked up his stuffed work bag and left the house.

It was a sunny day. The route he chose took him through the very heart of Lagos. Gbenga had been wrong when he said he would not have to worry about traffic. He had to endure one gruelling traffic jam after another. Street vendors who took advantage of the situation to market their wares bombarded him with various goods from China. He bought a car phone charger and vowed never to purchase anything else. He was forced to part with some money to pay some folk who rightly felt his windscreen needed cleaning.

At first, the whole thing irritated him. He regarded them as pests who should have gone to school or learnt a trade. It was only when he bothered to consider the eyes of one of the vendors that he softened his stance. There was nothing but despair and a certain hopelessness in them. He ended up buying some device that was supposed to charge his phone using solar energy. He was not sure he would ever need such a thing. He was just doing his part to alleviate the man's situation. What troubled him the most was that they were about the same age. For some reason the desperation he saw in his eyes stayed with him for a while. He realised he was one of the fortunate ones to have had an education and a job. He ended up spending a small fortune buying other items he would usually never have thought of buying. The economic situation was terrible. He planned to give away much of them as gifts when it was convenient. Someone's birthday would come up soon.

Thankfully, he eventually left the heart of the city and its mayhem behind and started concentrating on the task ahead. He had not prepared any set of questions as he usually did. He wanted it to feel like a normal conversation. He had never interviewed such a man before. He was used to interviewing politicians, lecturers, businessmen, and even criminals. This would be his first and his instinct told him it would be an entirely new experience. As he drove through great expanses of uninhabited land he wondered why many chose to pack themselves in the city when there was so much space elsewhere. Lagos was a city bursting at its seams. There was just too many people and not enough space.

He found the lagoon. He was surprised to see only a handful of people at the site. This was no modern-day guru with throngs of people around him. Perhaps those who thought he was a mad man were right. He parked his car under a tree and proceeded to the spot where he had been told the man would be found. A man of average height dressed in a pair of black denim and a matching plain white T-shirt approached. He thought white would have been more appropriate. Without asking his name he advised him to sit on a small bench that looked like it was made from a thousand-year old tree. It even had wrinkles.

He was advised to take off his shoes. He was on holy ground. He wanted to argue but decided against it. He took them off. The feeling of the grass beneath his feet was one he had not experienced in a long time. It felt relaxing. There were at least three other people sitting on similar benches and another four lying face down on the ground apparently in a trance. The silence was quite unusual. Even at home when he was alone there was always some background noise. The only background noise here was the sound of birds chirping away happily. It felt like he was in another world. The feel of the soft breeze against his face was divine. He really began to feel like he was indeed on holy ground.

The Ethiopian was in a make shift hut made of mud walls, bamboo sticks, and a thatch roof. He could not see him but he could hear his conversation with a young man. The others did not seem interested in their talk but he found himself straining to hear what was being said. The man sounded anxious, even agitated, while The Ethiopian sounded relaxed.

"I feel like my time is going," the man was saying. "I am almost thirty and I still don't have a job, no girlfriend, no home, and certainly no hope. I know you told me to believe but with nothing working for me I find it hard. I wish I was never born."

He found it hard to hear The Ethiopian's response. He was soft spoken and gentle. Suddenly the man began to weep. His sobs pierced the serene atmosphere like knives through butter. His sobs went on for almost five minutes. The sound of it made his heart beat fast for no explainable reason. There was something about a grown man's cry of hopelessness that was disconcerting to him. When he regained his composure, they talked for another fifteen minutes after which he was led out by the man he naturally assumed was his assistant. The young man sat on a bench and turned his gaze to the skies. He was surprised when he was asked to go in. No one seemed to protest. Leaving his shoes behind, he went in.

The Ethiopian had his eyes focused on the part of the lagoon that was visible through a deliberate gap in the wall. He did not say a word for almost a minute. He sat on a bench like the one he had just left and surveyed the place. He would describe it later in his article. The inside of the hut was made of bamboo sticks jammed into the ground. Its walls were made of nicely woven palm leaves on the inside and mud on the outside. The Ethiopian sat by one of two openings in the wall with one leg on the bench. He had on a white cloth that matched his white hair and beard. It reached all the way to his ankles. The ground was earth. There was nothing in the hut except the two benches. It reminded him of how far from simplicity he had strayed.

After a while The Ethiopian turned to look at him, stood and apologised for his brief period of absent mindedness. The two men shook hands. He was quite tall. He did not beam happily like some of the Indian gurus he had seen on television. He did look like a man without a worry in the world. He did not hesitate like most others did when he introduced himself as a journalist and stated the purpose of his visit.

He was invited to take a walk with him. They left the hut and strolled down the bank of the lagoon. Occasionally he would retrieve some sort of feed from his pocket and throw them into the water. This usually triggered a feeding frenzy from the fish beneath, temporarily disrupting the calmness of the water's surface.

"They are following us," he said.

"Who?" Jeff asked looking back and seeing no one.

"The fish," he said. "They will follow us all the way to that tree over there."

"What happens there?" Jeff asked.

"That is my favourite spot," he said. "When I am alone I like to sit there and feed the fish."

"Are you some sort of fisherman?" he asked.

The Ethiopian laughed. "I am who I am. You are who you are. We are. You are human, not a journalist. You are not what you do."

Jeff frowned as he struggled to make sense of his response. Eventually they got to the tree. They both sat on a rock close to the edge. It was then he saw the fish. They swam as if in formation. They moved in unison at each movement either of them made, breaking formation only when he threw some feed into the water and returning to their positions once the feeding was over. He watched with keen interest as the man fed them. When the last of the feed was thrown in the fish swam away. He was amazed. They acted like they had intelligence. He never thought of them as anything but a food source.

"How did they know that was the last?" he asked perplexed.

"They've got eyes," he said. "They saw me empty out my pocket and turn it inside out. I feed them every day."

Jeff nodded. He found it amazing that the fish behaved much like dogs.

"What is it that you do as a journalist?" he asked.

"I gather news and then make the public aware of what is going on," he replied. "We have a magazine where these stories are published."

He nodded thoughtfully. "And you are here to know more about me."

"In a sense, yes," Jeff said.

The man smiled, all the while staring into the distance. Jeff on his part observed him. He could not be more than seventy years old. He had a serene aura around him and was quite different from every other man he had met. His tall, lean frame was carried elegantly. Even when he sat his torso was held straight. He would not have been surprised if he was told he belonged to some royal family. The impression he was getting was that of royalty without the arrogance that comes with it. The colour of his skin reminded him of toffee. He did look Ethiopian with his fine features; narrow pointed nose and all.

"What questions would you ask a man you want to know?" he asked smiling. The crow's feet at the corners of his eyes deepened as he did so.

Jeff shrugged. "How old are you? Where are you from? Why are you here?"

He left out the "Are you sane or insane?" He figured it was not a question to be asked but an observation to be made. So far there was nothing to suggest insanity. He had been to a mental institution once and had come to realise that some of the so called insane could function quite well and have meaningful conversation contrary to popular belief.

"And people really are interested in all that?"

"Sure."

"Why? If they want to know me they can come and ask me themselves."

"It is a busy world," Jeff said. "We gather the stories so that they can just sit back, relax and read about them."

He stood and placed his arms behind his back, his gaze still focused on the horizon as if he was observing some event unfolding there. Jeff remained sitting. He was beginning to get worried. Soon it would be dusk. So far, he had nothing and the man did not seem to be worried about time.

"The best way to know a man is to encounter the man," he said calmly. "I have encountered you. I know you. If someone asks me if I know Jeff I would certainly say yes. Yes, I know Jeff. I have encountered you. I know you are a man on a mission. I know you are a man of passion. You are hardworking or you would not have got to where you are now in life. You have a dark past but you are a man who possesses what many today no longer have. You have compassion, sympathy, and generosity. When many are out there thinking of what they can acquire to add to themselves, you don't. That is where many have missed it. You have it right mostly. Yet, there still is that flaw that threatens to unravel everything."

Jeff was not sure if the man was being patronising. He was flattered by what he just heard, except for the last part.

"I will not tell you about myself," The Ethiopian said. "I will tell you what you need to know. You will, from my words, make up your mind about me but I assure you that your opinion of me will benefit no one. You are here for something much more important than I. The people out there do not have to know me if they have no business with me. I will implore you to listen carefully. Even when what I say does not make any sense, do not worry. One day they will.

"I believe you were meant to be here. Few things in life happen by chance. You are here because you needed to be here. When a man encounters an impossible problem, if he cries out for help, help will come. Men with noble intentions will sooner than later realise that there is a force for good that engages all those with noble intentions. The righteous need to be as bold as a lion. Forces come from persons. God is the force behind good and the evil one is behind evil and dark forces."

Jeff watched him as he spoke. The man spoke for what seemed like hours. He soon lost all concerns about time or his assignment. The words that came out of his mouth were not like anything he had ever heard. It was like the old man had opened a portal through which universal truths came pouring into his being. He spoke with ease, with the assurance of one who knew and understood that which was hidden from humanity. In the end, he felt like a newborn baby whose eyes had been opened to a world he thought he knew, yet did not know at all.

"Come again," the old man said at the end of the long sermon. By this time, the sun was long gone and a huge moon hung low in the sky. "You are the instrument God will use. There is much I must tell you. Tread carefully, but not with fear. Be cautious, but never fear."

It was only when he was in his car that he realised how much time he had spent there. He wondered if The Ethiopian slept there. Everyone was gone by the time they returned to the hut, including the assistant. He reasoned it would be better to head straight to Madam Caro's resort as he now termed it. Going back home and then coming back again would take hours.

He drove slowly. Cars whisked past him. His mind was still unravelling from his experience with The Ethiopian. Never in all his life had anyone spoken with such understanding of life. He still did not know where he was from. He still did not have anything to present to his boss. One thing he was certain of was that nothing would ever remain the same. He hoped he had recorded every word. There were times when he had been half asleep as the man had talked. The whole experience seemed like a trance. He had been drifting in and out of consciousness.

He turned off the highway and followed the now rugged road as best he could remember from the map she sent to his email and her descriptions the previous night. He was relieved when the light of the resort appeared in the distance. There were more cars that night than he could remember seeing the first time. Mike's car was easily recognisable.

He presented his card to the guards who showed little interest this time. They waved him in and resumed their interrupted conversation.

Mike apparently had been on the lookout for him. He approached him and led him to a table with a half-eaten plate of fried rice and a bottle of beer on it.

"Madam Caro was wondering if you would come," he said. "I told her there was no way in the world you would not come."

"Where is she?" he asked.

"Somewhere in the VIP section attending to some very important guests," he said. "Hungry?"

Jeff shook his head.

"Beer?"

"I'm fine," he said. "I was wondering why there were so many cars outside."

"Some top politicians are in the house," he said. "Those exotic cars were actually paid for by your tax money. There is no accountability anywhere. I bet your tax money is what they are burning here and Madam Caro has no qualms being on the receiving end of such corruption. Can't say I blame her. She spent a lot of money setting up this place. You reap when you sow."

Jeff shrugged. It was always about money and pleasure with Mike. He thought of Ehi. He tried to act calm but was dying to see her.

"The nation is encountering the biggest economic decline in its history yet the looters are unwilling to slow down," Mike said. "Make cuts everywhere else but not the rich politicians' wages. The people always suffer. The real problem on earth is the class war. Ever been to India?"

"What are you?" Jeff asked. "An anti-corruption activist?".

Mike shook his head as he drained the last of his beer.

"It's just annoying," he said. "Anyway, I'm not about to spoil my day. Grab a beer man."

"Maybe later," Jeff said.

"You still sticking to that girl?"

"Mind your own business," Jeff said.

Mike shrugged then ate the rest of his meal hurriedly while Jeff broodingly considered the night ahead. When he was done, Mike gave out a loud burp, winked naughtily at Jeff before hurrying off. Moments later Robert appeared looking as ugly as ever. He wanted to know if Jeff needed anything as he had observed he was yet to eat or drink. Jeff advised him to return later. As soon as he was gone he turned to observe the scene.

Madam Caro did know what men really wanted. The most beautiful and shapely of the opposite sex he had ever seen were in the room. He kept forgetting most of them were underage. He wondered if he was being rather foolish to be ignoring the beautiful variety that was before him. Why focus on Ehi? Why were the natural inclinations of man always towards that which would create disorder? Why couldn't he be inclined to be good the same way he tended so easily towards evil? Good was something he had to strive for. Evil on the other hand was something he had to fight against. The Ethiopian had talked about this strange inclination but it still plagued him nonetheless. Knowledge did not amount to victory. He needed inner strength.

One lady caught his attention above all else. She was tall and dark skinned with hair that was well braided and oiled. They reached to the middle of her back. She wore a tightfitting dress that revealed her perfect figure and sat with a gentle smile on her lips. For some reason their eyes had met several times. He wondered what she was doing there. She did not look like one of Caro's. She looked like someone born into a life of privilege.

The Ethiopian's words echoed at the back of his mind. This was surely a distraction. She had given him an obvious invitation and the possibilities that could be was hard to pass up. Thrice he had managed to tear his gaze away from her beauty. Thrice he had resumed his lustful stare. She was like a work of art that lingered in the mind long after you leave its presence. She was a feast to the eyes as Mike would say.

He soon got tired of fighting his instincts and stood. For some reason, he remembered a classmate called Shagamu. He often used to joke that the best way to end a temptation was to fall into it. "Take the bait and the torment would cease," he would say. As he walked across the room he felt like he was taking a walk of destiny. Something told him that if he walked up to her he would never be able to do anything for Ehi. He felt his heart pound as he made his way towards her. He knew he shouldn't but his old self had suddenly burst out from somewhere deep inside his being. She knew he was approaching even though she now had her side to him. He could see the smile playing at the corner of her mouth. It was the smile of victory.

4

CHAPTER 4

All evening she sat on her bed wondering what was going on. She could hear the men and some of the women talking in the backyard below her window. Musa was threatening one of the girls. He wanted his clothes washed and ironed or she would be made to face his wrath. Musa's voice always made her heart skip a beat. She was not the only one who feared him. He was the most vicious of all of them. Robert was ugly but at least had a heart. They all were capable of unspeakable brutality but she could tell Robert was only brutal when he had to. Madam Caro knew just how to manipulate men, and women.

Sometimes she wondered how it was that they could do whatever they wanted without fear of any consequence. They had ultimate power over them. The feeling of helplessness was quite overwhelming. How come not one of the men that came there could see what they were going through?

She thought of Jeff. She had never stopped thinking of him since he left. He was the only man who had ever taken any personal interest in her. He was the only man that saw her as a human being and not just another piece of flesh placed there to satisfy his every desire no matter how depraved. He was the only man that had come to see her without leaving her feeling battered and worthless. She smiled for some reason at the thought of him being the only person on the outside whose name she knew. Did he still remember hers? Was she still in his memory? Would he come back?

They had left her alone after his visit. No one came close to her and no one told her anything except the doctor that had checked on her the next day. The silent treatment was a relief as well as torture. She could at least rest for a while. The beatings had ceased at least. Was it something he told Madam Caro? Did he threaten her? Worse still, had he complained to her? Had they decided to sell her off to Italy or Spain? Could it be that the man she thought so highly of was only a two-faced back stabber who had treated her so kindly only to go back to Caro to say negative things about her? The thought was scary. If that degree of kindness and concern could be faked, then she did have much to fear from men. She could deal with the outright evil. At least she knew what she was dealing with. Deception was something new.

What if they were preparing to ship her to Dubai or Saudi? What if they had had enough and had decided to kill her? That would explain the silence. That would explain the new treatment. They had had enough and were going to sell her off as a slave! But where was he? Had he come to some harm? Had Jack overheard their conversation and reported to Madam? Had he been murdered that night? The thought of this brought tears to her eyes. She would feel responsible for his death for as long as she lived. The thought of not knowing what was going on was unbelievably tormenting.

She had never known any kindness. For once, someone out of the blue had touched her soul; shown her some love. Till now love was only a word she had read about in the pages of incomplete and worn out romantic novels. Robert was the only one among the men that read such novels. The ugly beast had a heart. She read of women being swept off their feet by the power of love knowing she would never experience such. As far as she knew all men were beasts. That was until she met him. Was it too early to start changing her mind? All her life she had known fear, the fear of torment, of pain. Now she was experiencing a new fear; the fear of betrayal, of abandonment. He said he would come. It was not fair. The women in those novels at least enjoyed times of bliss before the inevitable betrayal. She had gone straight from the height of love to the bottom of the cliff. Why must her life be so miserable and different?

Every sound outside the door caused her heart to skip a beat. The sounds evoked both fear and excitement. Fear that Musa would come, bundle her into some car that would take her to the port where she would be shipped away to a faraway country full of men as evil and selfish as the ones she had known all her life. Excitement that it would be him coming back as promised. She had wiped away tears from her face and reapplied her makeup countless times. If he never came back, then it would have been better he never came into her life at all. At least she had learnt to live with the evil she had known. How unfair for him to come into that life and offer false hope.

She was half asleep when she heard a knock on the door. Worn down with fear and dashed expectation she sat up, aware of her wildly beating heart. She had left the door unlocked. Slowly the knob began to turn.

"God," she prayed. "Let it be him."

The door opened. Jeff stood there. Unable to control herself she let out a cry of joy, leaped off the bed and flung herself at him. She held on tightly as if afraid if she let go he would leave and never come back. Jeff was taken by surprise at her action. He held her. They stood there for what seemed like hours. She trembled and shuddered as she held on.

"Are you still ill?" he asked concerned. "I asked them to take you to the doctor."

She shook her head. He could tell she was happy to see him. It made him feel unbelievably good. He struggled to hold back tears. He had often wondered what having a daughter would be like. There and then he knew the answer.

She led him to the bed and they both sat. She still held on to his hand. He let her hold on even when his shoulder began to ache.

"It's been very strange since you came," she said in hushed but excited tones. "No one has bothered me since. I don't understand what is going on. What did you tell them?"

He told her. For a while she did not speak. He thought she would be excited.

"That is a lot of money," she said looking worried. "Do you think you will be able to afford it?"

"I have learnt," he said. "It is not the means but the purpose, the intention. If the cause is noble, the means will come. The one who calls always provides."

She began to look sad.

"What's the problem?" he asked.

"I don't want you getting into any trouble," she said. "The money's too much."

"Let me worry about that," he said. "I should not have told you. How much is a life worth? You are worth every cent. Come on. Cheer up."

She laughed. He decided it was time to get down to business. He disengaged himself from her hold and got the bag he had dropped during the hug. He unzipped it and brought out his recorder.

"I want everything here," he said holding up the recorder. "This is the much you can do for me. I will ask you some questions. Answer to the best of your knowledge. If you feel like crying, cry, but please, do not stop talking till I tell you to, okay?"

She nodded.

"Good."

He set the tape down on the bed, pressed the red button, let it record for some time then looked at her.

"What is your name?"

"Ehi."

"Ehi who?"

She stared at him curiously.

"Your surname."

"I don't have one. My name's Ehi. That's it."

He was at a loss for words for some seconds. A documentary about the street kids of Rio came to his mind.

"Alright," he went on. "Ehi. Tell me everything. Tell me about your life before now. How did you get here? How has life been? I want you to say everything you remember: Your suicide attempt, the treatment you've been receiving, the men that come here, what they do to you, how Musa and the others have been treating you...everything till when I met you. Just talk as if you are telling me the story of your life. Let it flow."

She looked away and sighed. She began to recall and recount another life, a life she often believed was never even real. It was like a dream one had dreamt years ago, muddled and vague. It seemed to belong to someone else. She had been four years old.

While she spoke, Jeff listened. She was like one in a trance. He could see she had managed to remove herself from her memories, especially the hurtful ones. Dissociation was often a sign of extreme abuse. It was a coping mechanism employed by the mind to deal with distressful situations. This often led to multiple personalities. Occasionally he would ask a question and she would answer. This went on for hours. Eight hours later he decided she needed to rest. His heart felt like lead but he managed to keep the tears back. He knew he had to be professional and strong for her sake. In addition to the pain he felt guilt. He could easily have been one of those men. He had been one of those men.

"Life has been most unfair to you," he told her after a period of silent reflection. She did not reply. He gathered his devices and carefully placed them in his bag. When he was through he sat on the bed and gazed at the floor. The silence was heavy.

"You think this will work?" she asked. She sounded weak.

"It has to," he said. "That's my problem. Don't spend a minute thinking over it. Rest well. Eat well and laugh well. One thing I know is that you will be out of this place one day."

She nodded. It was an almost imperceptible nod.

"Breath no word of this to anyone, not even your most trusted friend," he said.

She nodded.

"Good," he said and stood. He looked around the room. He found it quite disheartening that she and many others had been confined to their small rooms for years now. It was enslavement. She had been a prisoner without even realising it. "I should be going downstairs now. I'm pretty sure Mike would be wondering why I am taking so long."

"That man is not your friend," she said. "Anyone who can bring you to such a place knowing you are married cannot be your friend."

He regarded her curiously then smiled. "You are indeed wise at your young age. You will make a good wife and mother someday. I do share equal guilt. I am an adult. I came along. If I cannot defend my values why should I expect another to care about them?"

"It's funny," she said. "Life is indeed mysterious."

"Why do you say that?" he asked.

"How else would I have met you if you had not come?" she asked. "I guess we can say he is the reason for our meeting."

He shrugged.

"Quite true," he said. "I did not know where he was taking me until we got here. See you soon."

"When are you coming again?" she asked.

"I can't say," he said.

"Tomorrow?" she asked standing and hugging him.

He sighed as he put his arms around her and looked down on her childishly eager face.

"I wish I could come tomorrow," he said. "I don't want to raise any suspicions. Besides, I need to start making serious plans to get you out of here. I have thought about it again and again. Give me time and I will figure it out."

"The best way is to escape from the doctor's clinic," she said. "I have thought about it before. I just could not bring myself to do it. There was no way I could have outrun any of the men. Even if I did, I never could figure out what I would do afterwards. The police come here too. Can't just run to them."

"Do you know his name?" he asked.

"They just call him Doc. The name on his desk says Dr. F. Salami. His clinic is somewhere in the city."

He kissed her on the forehead in excitement.

"That might be the opportunity we are looking for," he said. "I will get someone to look the name up. We should be able to find him in the registry."

"What do you plan to do if you find him?" she asked, a bit apprehensive.

"Leave that to me," he said. "I will not do anything that will put you at risk. He will only know your name if it becomes necessary. I have to go now."

"Do you really have to?" she asked.

"Unfortunately," he said.

They disengaged. He picked up his bag. She was sitting on the bed when he left, her eyes on the floor. Jack was as usual reading his magazine at the end of the corridor. He did not look up when he emerged. He wondered if he had been eavesdropping. Initially he had disliked him. He was unsure if he and the other men were not themselves as much victims as the girls they oversaw.

Madam Caro was in the hall with a sleepy Mike when he got there. For some reason, Mike was cranky.

"What took you so long?" he asked. "I need to sleep. Got work in less than five hours."

"Poor you," he replied. "I never asked you to wait for me."

"He only arrived a few minutes ago," Caro said. "How was your night?"

"Great," he replied. "And how are your diplomatic guests?"

"They've gone now," she said yawning. "The world is in the hands of the immoral. Scary to think of it. Bad men control this earth."

"That does not mean they lack good judgment," Mike said. "Come on man, let's go."

The two men stood. Caro remained sitting, claiming extreme fatigue. Mike said little as they walked to the parking lot. He wondered what was up with him. He said a grumpy good night before getting into his car and driving off. Before he got into his, he looked around. It had to be the clinic, he thought. There was no way she was going to be able to leave the place unnoticed. He took in as much detail as he could. Hard as he tried he could not see anything more than a huge building surrounded by a very unforgiving forest. Mason would have no doubt seen up to ten things hidden in plain sight. The man had that gift. It was about time he contacted him.

The tail lights of Mike's car could be seen ahead as he drove. The man drove like he had been angered by something. As he drove bits and pieces of Ehi's narration played back in his mind. He could not believe how someone that young could have already been subjected to that amount of pain.

Her story reminded him of Vivian. He had put her in the family way. When she had told him she was pregnant he had panicked and denied he could be responsible. There was no evidence she had ever cheated on him but back then his mentality was that all women were cheats. The thought of being a father scared him to death. Marriage was equally scary and he was not sure which he dreaded more. His father would have disowned him. He was the adulterer that expected his sons to be saints.

Vivian had cried for days. He talked and joked about her with his friends. She even begged him for some money to have an abortion. He had refused, his reasoning then being that he would be admitting ownership if he did that. When her pregnancy became obvious she left school. He never heard of her again and never bothered to check on her. He even wished she had died. For a while the thought of her showing up at his doorstep with a baby scared him. He even had a nightmare once in which she had showed up with a set of twins during class. His friends teased him with his fears when he told them.

He could not believe how insensitive he had been back then. Nneka was right. He had indeed been blind at the time and in darkness. Like many others still in darkness, all he had cared about was himself. Ehi's experience had him thinking. What if Vivian had gone to one of those so-called baby factories where underage girls were offered money by patronising women to stay till the end of their pregnancies after which they were paid pathetic sums of money to relinquish every right to their babies? What if his baby was alive somewhere and experiencing something like what Ehi was experiencing?

He began to have some chest pain as he considered the possibility. He found solace in the thought that a nice Christian American or Canadian couple had adopted the baby. He used to think the westerners were the civilised folks. He now knew better. All of mankind suffered from that mysterious evilness that plagued them from birth. It was only when his vision got blurry that he realised tears had welled up in his eyes. He wiped them off feeling a bit embarrassed. It was a cruel world. It was a cruel world not because there was no God or that God was evil but because men and women were in darkness, a darkness that felt like fun to only those generating the evil that was wrecking the lives of themselves and others.

5

CHAPTER 5

They were friends. They lived in Ajegunle, the worst ghetto in the whole of Africa. Not even the worst slums in Kenya, South Africa or Brazil could compete with its squalor and crime. They had grown up together amidst the filth, pain, laughter, and hope. In their teenage years, all they talked about was women and the day they would leave the slum behind, grand style. When they became adults, they spent their days talking about the day they would become big time crooks, politicians, businessmen, and millionaires in that order. Money was and would always remain the central theme. They had lived too long in poverty. Women came second.

When they became adults, they did not speak with the same zeal they used to as teens. It was the same words and the same dreams, just a bit more cautiously said. Years had gone by and some of those they had known as babies had hit the very jackpot they had often talked about. The new generation of crooks were more vicious and aggressive in their ambitions.

Many years back, they had been loud. They were loud in their dressing and loud in their speech. They had boasted with certainty of the days they would be the talk of the town like the reigning rich men before them who had left the ghetto for safer abodes. Having little but full of the arrogance that the assurance of future wealth would bring, they had lived recklessly and immorally. Not that they had been different from the others. When society defines self-worth in terms of material possession then that becomes the primary goal. Priests have no honour here. The rich, no matter the source of their wealth, are the gods of the land.

As the years went by without the realisation of the expected wealth in the expected timeframe, desperation began to set in. Like many others who had shunned education for various reasons, their desperation meant more daring crimes. The prison system was full of comrades caught. Prison was something they feared. They had all done their respective times. A year here, three years there...it was the norm and there was no shame in it. 'Just be careful next time,' their apathetic mothers would say.

The sort of term they feared was life in prison. Nothing could be worse except a lifetime of poverty. To them the two were essentially the same. In a world where the poor had limited options, a lifetime of poverty was akin to a life sentence. The only difference was that in prison you were at least fed some crappy meal and had a roof over your head.

One day Osun, the most daring of them, came into Ani's room where they normally met with a black plastic bag in his hand and looking very excited. They eyed the bag with suspicious expectation. Could it be money? Osun would not come to them with a bag full of money that none of them had earned. They were no fools. Their friendship did not stretch that far. He set the bag down on the floor and opened it. He reached inside and brought out a dirty brown paper bag that looked like it had been dug up from the ground. It still had dirt on it. He tore the paper off. They watched patiently. When it was eventually revealed, they all reacted differently. It was shiny, too shiny for the sort of package it had come in. They all stared in disbelief. They were used to crime, petty crimes committed preferably in the absence of the home owner. Guns meant confrontation and possibly murder. Murder meant life in prison or even the death sentence.

Osun glared at them. He looked like a man possessed. They wondered if he had been using a new drug.

"For how long shall we continue languishing in our poverty while money flies all around us?" he asked like his ancestors had organised the bloody French revolution. "No one is going to call you and give you their money. You've got to take it by force. The rich love their money. They pursue money with even more vigour than any poor person I know. The only thing they cherish more than money is their lives. Threaten that life and they will give you anything you want."

They stared at him in disbelief. They were sure in one of their get-rich-quick meetings they had condemned armed robbery in no uncertain terms. Could anyone blame him? His dreams, like theirs, were becoming impossible. In a way, he was right. They believed they were poor only because the rich folks had taken up all opportunities for themselves and their families, including those still unborn and swimming in their testicles.

They liked the money. They did not like the idea of violence. Yet, which crook ever got rich from pickpocketing or selling second hand items stolen from homes? Why should they stick to some silly moral code when they were already criminals? If you must eat a frog, at least eat a fat one.

"No big man has clean hands," Osun went on. "I have wondered why we have remained where we are. I used to think we may be cursed or something. There is no curse. We have talked big and acted small. You've got to stain your hands to get rich. Get the money then wash your hands clean. We will pay our tithes afterwards if we must. I will ask a pastor to conduct a deliverance sermon on me. The demons will go. The money will stay."

Someone laughed. It was Ani. He loved the idea. Why not? The one they called Smallie because of his size shrugged. He was neither frightened nor eager. Whatever they wanted to do would be fine with him. He now lived a life of resignation. Since his last girlfriend left he had been depressed even though he never admitted it. She had believed in love and always said love was not based on riches. They had met after a robbery in which he had stumbled upon some expensive gold watches and chains. He had sold them and had money to spend. As soon as the money was gone she left. He learnt his lesson then: there was no love without money. She was now married to a teacher who did not have much but at least got something at the end of each month. He was still in love with her. When he considered the future, all he saw was a lifetime of poverty, doom and gloom. His biggest fear was growing old and not having the strength to rob houses anymore. What would he do then?

Sunday gazed at the guns. He was called Sunday simply because he liked to rob people's homes on Sundays when they had gone to church. Osun never saw the wisdom in that since most people wore their gold chains and watches to church. He was comfortable robbing homes. At least he was guaranteed a decent meal now and then. After a while he shrugged. Better die trying. He saw a lot of possibilities with the gun. He too had had enough of poverty. He needed money. It was his fundamental human right.

Bull sat perfectly still. Built like a body builder, he often escorted neighbourhood folks when they go to get money owed them. Everyone knew his fee was ten percent of whatever was paid. No one failed to pay up after one look at him. Just the threat of going to him for help made people suddenly feel like paying up their debts. He liked to beat people up and once said he preferred an opportunity to beat someone up to his ten percent. His last victim was still undergoing psychiatric treatment.

The moment Osun walked in he knew what the bag contained. Guns were not new to him. His father had been a soldier who had died abroad during one of the country's numerous and useless peace keeping missions. It was said that his father used to invite him to a no-rules fist fight whenever he tried to challenge his authority. He was always badly beaten up until he became good at fighting. Despite this horrific treatment, they remained close until the day he was killed. The same country he served had not cared about his family after his death. Why should they now care about his son's means of survival? He felt entitled. It was about time.

Osun, satisfied with their response, brought out a rough sheet of paper from his pocket and squatted next to the gun. He had prepared well in advance. It was the sketch of a street with at least four exit roads with the expected time of escape written on each. His plan was simple. The bank was in a small town. His source had disclosed that at least twenty million in cash was deposited there at a particular day of each month. The neighbouring towns relied on this deposit for their salaries. They only had one security guard. On this day, they would have anything between two to four. These were not hardened cops inspired by dedication but pot-bellied men in their late forties and fifties who happened to know someone who connected them to the job. No one had ever robbed the bank because no one thought it was worth the effort. This was why they must act fast or else wait another month.

His plan was simple. The money would be deposited at night. They would go in the wee hours of the morning, take whatever security that was there by surprise, grab the money and go. They needed a car or two. One that no one would recognise. He was confident they would be able to steal one just in time for the operation. It seemed his main concern was not immediate success but that someone would expose their secret by spending the new money recklessly. His solution was that they would keep the money somewhere safe, lay low and endure poverty for another month or two before sharing the loot. That way no one would suspect they had anything to do with the heist. Most crooks were caught not during the operation but when they started spending the money. All the cops had to do was ask who in the ghetto had stumbled upon new money. The ghetto was rife with jealousy and people would always snitch.

They listened as he spoke with authority. He had suddenly assumed the role of boss and they obliged him. It was, after all, his plan and his gun. He was making a whole lot of sense too. Laying low and living the life of the living dead for another two months would be gruesome. It was one thing enduring a lifestyle because there was no choice. It was another thing enduring poverty when you had the money hidden somewhere.

"Why not wait till next month?" Ani asked. "This thing is so rushed. Don't get me wrong, I love the idea of having some money tomorrow. The problem is I also hate the idea that tomorrow I could be dead or in prison in a few days."

Sunday shook himself out of his day dream. His fears were legitimate.

"He's right in a way," he said in agreement. "Armed robbery is not supposed to be something you wake up one day and decided to do the next day. You must plan, think over it. You have to make family arrangements in case you get shot or even killed."

Osun looked like a politician about to lose an election. He glared at Ani.

"In life, sentimentalists never achieve anything," he said trying to control his rage. "I have done the planning. I did not just wake up today and decide I was going to rob a bank tomorrow. Tomorrow we go. If we succeed, we are rich. If we don't...."

He shrugged.

"Let's do it," Bull said. "Smallie?"

Smallie nodded. In the end, they all agreed. No one wanted to blame himself for the rest of his life for not being part of the operation that could have changed his fortune. Generations to come will hear and blame him for ignoring the chance that would have elevated them out of poverty. It was a gamble. Yet, everything in life, from politics to business was a gamble.

Sunday protested the last part of the plan that had to do with laying low while the money lay beneath the ground. What if they returned to find it had been eaten up by termites? The Rolex and flashy clothes could wait but he loved his good food, beer and women. The others lent their support. It was agreed that each would receive fifty thousand. The rest would be hidden in the bush. Osun already had a metal box ready as well as shovels and flash lights. No termite would be able to chew through this box.

They gave Smallie and Ani the task of finding two cars, nothing fancy but not the type that would break down during a pursuit. They must also check the fuel gauge before stealing them. They needed full tanks. The two shrugged. For their effort, they would receive a hundred thousand each as bonus. Osun had already announced that he would be getting forty percent for being the mastermind. They reluctantly agreed. No point arguing when the money was not yet real. The issue would be revisited. It would be twenty percent each.

The plan was fine-tuned and polished. They all liked the final look. The thought that they would finally be rich men in less than a few hours was exhilarating. Even Smallie's depression mysteriously vanished, supporting Ani's theory that depression had something to do with lack of money and not the serotonin that doctors say was the problem. Stealing a car was never his problem. He always ended up selling to the wrong person and had done some months in prison for being that stupid. This time he was not required to sell to anyone.

Once they were sure every aspect of the plan was a possibility they talked like they always had when they were teens; loud and with confidence. The money was spent before it even came. Sunday planned to buy a house and pay the dowry his girlfriend's family had been pestering him to pay for years now. Ani planned to move to a hotel and enjoy the good life for a week before deciding what to do next. Bull had always wanted a gymnasium. The money would provide the capital. Smallie wanted to return to school. They laughed at his ridiculous plan. There were already too many graduates on the street looking for jobs. What would be the point of that?

Osun was the only one who did not say much. When asked why he was so quiet his reply was that he was busy thinking about the next day's operation. They urged him to think hard because the last place they needed to be was in jail or, in case it was real, hell.

The next day after the operation they gathered at the agreed location. It was an uncompleted building on the outskirts of town. Smallie was not with them. He had been shot by one of the security guards as they were breaking through the door. The guard had been quickly overpowered and tied up with the rest who had guns but no bullets, thanks to the corrupt superiors who were supposed to make sure they were well armed. They all had masks on and none spoke a word. The gun did the talking.

They held a minute of silence in Smallie's honour and then quickly moved to the topic at hand. Osun gave everyone fifty thousand each as promised. Someone suggested they take Smallie's share to his siblings. Osun disagreed. How would they explain it? They had thrown his body into a bush as they fled the scene. They would go back to bury it later. His family would never know what happened to him. The story must be that he tried to migrate to Europe via sea and may have drowned.

The rest of the money was buried as planned. They took an oath never to reveal their secret to anyone and never to return to the spot until the agreed date. No member of the team was going to visit another member and they must go easy on the booze and women. They all agreed before dispersing.

Sunday's fifty thousand was gone in a week. He went to Osun's house to ask for more but was told by his brother he had gone to visit a friend in another state to be back around the agreed date. When he tried to call him, the number was not available. Fuming and impatient he waited for the day when his woes would end. They were all aware the police were investigating the brutal crime. Another gang of five had been arrested in connection with the crime and reports were that they were being tortured in one of the underground cells. Rumour had it that one had confessed. This was received as good news.

When the day and time eventually came, they began to arrive the scene in cautiously optimistic moods. Never in their lives had they been more punctual. Some had borrowed money from family and neighbours promising to pay back soon. Osun did not show up. When three hours after the agreed time he still had not shown up, Sunday suggested they dig up the box and start sharing the money. They would leave his share in the box and put it back in the ground. Ani wondered if the oath would be broken by such an act. Sunday was not listening. He grabbed the shovel and started digging like a lunatic in search of his sanity. He had his suspicions. They all watched. Ani joked that if he dropped dead from a heart attack there would be less of them and more money. Sunday did not find it funny. Instantly he issued instructions on what to do with the money if anything happened to him.

"Give it to my mother or face the wrath of my ghost," he said before resuming his frantic dig.

When the shovel hit the box, they cheered. It was lifted out of the hole. It was heavier than they remembered but Ani thought it may be because the adrenalin had been high at the time. With the shovel, Sunday broke the lock. Bull lifted the lid. The box contained nothing but bricks and a few notes. They removed the bricks hoping to find the money underneath. All they found was more bricks until they got to the bottom. The gun was there but no money. It was then reality hit them. Osun had played them all and given himself two months' head start to vanish. Bull grabbed the gun and went into a fit of rage that scared the rest despite the situation. Sunday sat on the ground and felt like weeping. Ani was stupefied and stared at the now empty box in shock.

They could not believe that their childhood friend would do such a thing. They had been so close to being rich. His share of the money would have been enough for whatever he wanted to do with it. Why be greedy? He could have at least left something substantial. The thought of continuing in the path of poverty was frustrating. They had at least begun to get used to it. The whole plot had lifted their hopes and given them a foretaste of the good life to come. With this assurance, they had gone borrowing. Some had even assured their loved ones that things were about to change for the better. They wondered how a human being could be so heartless.

Despite the evidence, they decided to wait till dusk just in case Osun showed up. They offered possible reasons why he was not there. It was possible he had moved the money for some valid reason and was running late. It was also possible he had forgotten the date. Sunday told them to give it up and to admit that they had been duped. He was the first to leave. No one stopped him.

A now calm Bull and Ani stayed on and chatted. Their conversation had a tinge of sadness to it as they recalled past hardships especially as kids. They had all grown up under tough situations. Osun had endured the worst. He of all should have understood the impact the money would have had not just on them but their families. He, like the corrupt African leaders he often complained about, had taken away the hopes and aspirations of many.

When the crickets began chirping Ani urged Bull to get up. It was too dark to stay there. They left, hardly saying anything as they walked back to their respective homes. The reality of their battered hopes was overwhelming. Ani went straight to bed without eating. Bull sat in front of the one room he shared with his mother, sister, and brother and stared at the moon, gun in hand and wondering what life was all about. He sat there till past midnight. By the time he was ready for bed he vowed that he would dedicate the rest of his life to finding Osun and making sure he paid for his crime. Smallie was dead because of him. That was unforgivable.

Sunday committed suicide five months later. They attended his funeral. As his immediate family wept and rolled in the dirt they wondered how everything could have been different if only Osun had not done what he did. Ani recalled he had made plans to send every member of his family to school or to learn some trade. He really wanted to break the cycle of poverty that had plagued them for generations.

During the meal at the funeral Ani and Bull sat and talked in hushed tones. They shared any information they had gathered on Osun. Ani believed he had gone to South Africa from where he planned to fly to the US. Bull believed he had gone to Dubai. They realised there was not much they could do to get him if he was out of the country. They simply did not have the means. They knew he would one day return. When that day came, they would be waiting. They would never forget. Word of what he did began to spread. No gang condoned betrayal. Everyone was on the lookout for him. He dared not return.

Their conversation soon shifted to themselves. They asked questions that portrayed guilt and regret. Perhaps they should have taken school more seriously. They had been five friends. Two were dead and another had eloped with their money. The nerds they used to laugh at earned their money month after month doing work they considered enslavement. They were the ones who got it right by sitting in classes and enduring what they had at the time called boring mental slavery.

"Remember when we used to call ourselves the Fantastic Five?" Ani asked.

Bull spat on the ground. "I regret the day that evil bastard came into my life," he said.

After the funeral, they hardly ever met. Bull started smoking weed like a lunatic. Ani on the other hand went to a high priest and spent thirteen hours uttering unthinkable curses on Osun: "May he never have peace. May he never die a good death. Let his better eye go blind...leave one eye so he can see me laugh at him."

The high priest looked on with a proud smile on his face as he spat out the words that showed the venom in his heart. Never had he seen any so viciously evil. That made him proud of his work. His spiritual father, Eke the serpent, would be proud too.

One man knew what was going on with the group of friends. His name was Inspector Dele. After the robbery, he had monitored every five-man gang in their bad book. The fact that this group was not generating any activity was a bit suspicious. They did not communicate with each other which was what he expected any smart group of thieves to do after a robbery. The five men they had in custody had endured a lot of torture before they finally confessed.

He only took their confession to his boss because the politicians wanted results and he wanted rewards. The public needed to know that the men and women paid to protect them were doing a good job. One of the guards had sworn he had shot one of the robbers. That part of his statement had been ignored since it did not match his report. His policy was that every thief needed to be in jail even if it was not for the particular crime he was convicted for. So, he let the men take the blame.

He continued to monitor every one of the remaining groups. The money had to be found. One of his undercover cops had been at Sunday's funeral. Ani and Bull did not look like they were rolling in money. They looked as broke as he had known them to be. These were men known to him for years. Crime was not serving them well. Why they did not quit and try something legit beat him. Osun went to live in Ikoyi. After a while he vanished from their radar. Before he did they had gathered enough intel to know he planned to travel to South Africa from where he would eventually migrate to either Australia or Canada. The inspector dedicated his men to watch every immigration agent and embassy in Ikoyi.

One day they got their big break. Osun was spotted leaving the South African embassy in Ikoyi with an apparently new girlfriend. His visa had been granted and he was very much elated. They were followed to a nearby restaurant where they celebrated and discussed the future. The girlfriend wanted to know how long she would have to wait for him. He promised he would be back in less than three years. He sounded happy and excited. She, on the other hand, was worried about the future of their relationship.

Inspector Dele decided to pay him a visit one evening. He went with one of his men. Osun was watching a soccer match when they entered his apartment uninvited. He was shocked and scared to death. Once they assured him they did not represent any form of vengeance he relaxed a little. Inspector Dele wasted no time in announcing the purpose of his visit. He was not there to arrest him. The politicians steal and waste enough money to make Osun look like a saint. Besides, the case had already been closed and the unfortunate culprits behind bars. He wanted his cut. He wanted half the money he knew Osun was hiding somewhere, half the money plus a small favour when he got to South Africa. Osun began to relax when he realised he was talking to just another crook in police uniform. The negotiation lasted only a few minutes. In the end, they agreed twenty percent was a fair share for someone who did not take any risk.

Mason was the cop who had escorted Inspector Dele to Osun's apartment. He sat in Jeff's sitting room one day and narrated the story. It was just one of his numerous stories. As an ex-cop, he always had one story or another to tell. He got some money for his time at the apartment. It turned out the inspector was a stingy man. When he protested, he advised him to be grateful for what he got. It was after all money he had earned for just a few minutes' work. This was one of the stories he described as 'for your ears only'. He was never to publish any of it. But then he knew the true story of the August twenty-first bank robbery in which millions was stolen. The wrong but not innocent people were still paying the price for the crime.

"Every crime has a solution," Mason said as he put his usual finishing touch to the story that took the better part of two hours to tell. "Those that seem unsolved are actually covered-up."

Jeff nodded in agreement. It was an interesting narration. He had come across Ani one day. The man was on his way to the bus rank. Unknown to him he had stood for minutes just watching him. He seemed withdrawn and had aged a lot. He had felt sorry for him. Unable to rob homes anymore, he was now an errand boy for some new gang. His fate would have been different had things played out differently. He knew the man had taken a solemn oath to kill Osun the day he ever laid eyes on him. He suspected the only thing that kept him alive was this hope of revenge.

He knew he would publish the story someday. Something told him it was not complete yet. One day Osun would come back to the country and then they would have their conclusion. As for the inspector, he was still a cop, only much higher up in rank.

6

CHAPTER 6

Madam Caro liked to believe she was doing humanity and her girls a huge favour. She often liked to hold a meeting occasionally to remind them that their lives would have been worthless without her timely intervention. Gratitude was a virtue they would do well to nurture. Usually she would make the girls wait for hours in the dining area while she applied her make up. Barry, the guard who was made to stand guard outside her door sometimes for unknown reasons, often commented that she was better off without her often heavy make-up.

On this day, she had a woman in her late twenties beside her. The woman was extremely pretty and looked like she was straight out of the cover of a fashion magazine. She had a good and expensive taste. Her diamond rings sparkled and her whitened teeth gleamed as she beamed a generous smile at the girls. They gasped and gushed when they saw her. She was that pretty. Madam Caro on the other hand had the look of a proud mother. She sat close to the lady and even had her arm linked in hers as if to emphasise ownership. When the girls finally became quiet she disengaged her arm and cleared her throat.

"Hi girls," she said. "I hope you are all happy?"

They nodded. Some said yes. Others said yeah nonchalantly. Happiness was not something they could relate to.

"We have a very important visitor in our midst today," she went on.

"She came to see me personally but I felt it would be very important that you see her. Meet Violet. You are looking at your future. Violet was once like you before I stepped in; unsure of herself, poor, unloved, unprotected, and abused. I made her what she is today and she has never forgotten that. I wanted you to see that being obedient and working hard has its rewards.

"There are some of you who think I am wicked. Some of you think we are taking advantage of you. I am not going to lie and tell you that life is rosy and smooth. That is why I never read those silly romantic novels. No one gives you anything in life unless they are your parents and they have it to give. I'm not going to say too much. Men are evil beings. They talk love but only want one thing from women, sex and submission. We are not their bitches and the only way you can have the voice to speak in this life as a woman is to make your own way out of oblivion. Easier said than done in today's patriarch world."

Violet was nodding her head in agreement as she spoke. Her smile waned somethings but quickly came back. When she was eventually given the permission to speak she basically repeated Madam Caro's words. Life was tough. They should be grateful for the sanctuary they had, a sanctuary provided by Madam Caro. Women out there did worse for nothing in the name of love. Love was nothing without both parties being free to choose each other. Most choose out of duress and financial pressure. In the end, she flashed her diamond ring, announcing that she was getting married to a wealthy businessman in less than a month. They were all invited. It was her choice as much as his. She was not marrying him for the money but because she wanted to. She was already rich in her own right. A lot of his rich friends would be coming. They were single and searching. Some of the girls might get lucky that day. When she asked for volunteers for her bridal train lots of hands went up.

She talked about Hollywood and Nollywood. Life was all about using what you have to get what you want. Again, she repeated her warning: men will always be selfish. It was up to women to protect their dreams and aspirations and make sure they do not end up being someone's maid in the name of love or marriage.

"Many women are working like donkeys while the men they are trying to please are busy showering their affection and money on some young mistress. It is sad but true. Love is nothing but a trap," she said like a guru in the love business. "You can fall in love with any man when the time is right. Men will worship at your feet when you have beauty and independence. When you have beauty and a heart that aches for love you will lose that beauty in a few years and he will move on to someone else. I know. I have been there. You do not have to learn from my experience.

"I personally came to Madam Caro for help and she took me in. I had no education, no family and no self-esteem. I was determined never to rely on anyone again. In the end, I did it. It was hard but I knew one day it would pay off. Work now, play later. All those movie stars and super-models, what do you think they are doing? You think they are doing anything different from what you are doing? Fashion walks are never really about fashion but hooking up with the rich and mighty. Why do you think celebrities are always dating models? It is just an escort business in disguise. The whole world revolves around these principles and only the dumb think otherwise."

"Work hard my children," Madam Caro said in conclusion. "If I am hard on you it is because I want you to understand that life out there is very harsh and you must get ready for it. Soft people will not make it out there. You will not be here forever. You will all come back to thank me one day like Violet here."

When they were finally dismissed they had looks of confusion and admiration on their faces. Some wanted to ask if it meant she had been keeping some money aside for them which would be used when the time for the eventual face off with the real world came. Even the seemingly jovial atmosphere did not give any the guts to ask such a question. They will find out in due time. Caro was known to be unpredictable. She could be charming one moment and a monster the next. A girl had been made to stand almost naked all through the night just because she asked to be taken to the zoo. The men were made to keep watch in turns just to make sure she carried out her punishment fully. Afterwards they learnt to think before talking.

The topic of the day was obviously Violet and whether they were being exploited or protected. She had injected fresh air into a place that was hitherto monotonous and boring. They all wanted to look like her and be like her some day; pretty, independent, outspoken, and rich. Most had never been to a wedding. They hoped Madam Caro would let them attend. If they were lucky they would meet some prince charming.

She spent another hour or two walking around the facility and chatting to a girl or guard now and then. When it was time to leave a lot of the girls escorted her to the parking lot. She was like a hero to them. They saw a lot of men. Not a lot of women came around there. They sniffed her perfume, felt her hair and silky smooth skin and even caressed her fabric. Her car matched her personality; elegant and colourful. When she was gone, they felt like they had been in a dream.

Suddenly it all began to make sense and they began to regard Madam Caro as a hero and not the villain they had thought she was. If Violet represented the future, that future was worth waiting for.

Ehi was not fooled by Violet's glitz and glamour. She had learnt from Jeff that not all men were evil and not all women represented her best interest. She could easily see the contradiction in her words. On the one hand, she wanted them to think of a future when they would be independent and free to choose whatever and whoever they wanted. On the other hand, she was inviting them to this glorious wedding where the same men they were supposed to wear body amour against would be analysing them like animals for sale.

She knew Caro would never let any girl leave unless someone paid for her. They were commodities to her. She had already decided she was not interested in the wedding. Suddenly a thought struck her. It might be in her best interest to hook up with some rich man. It was a way out. It would make the chances of escape even better. She could not wait to see Jeff to discuss it with him.

The thought of Jeff made her feel different. He was her sunshine and true hero. He had bought her, so to speak, but not for himself. The thought of him made her day feel light and merry. She was beginning to think she was in love with him. She was in love with married Jeff and had no idea what to do with her emotions. She even found herself getting jealous each time he mentioned his wife. He was a good man and deserved his good wife. She only wished he had been single when they met. Scary thoughts that made her question her sanity sometimes came to her mind, thoughts that she would never dare reveal to anyone, least of all Jeff. Her comfort lay in the fact that she would never be able to do such a thing. She was not that evil. She had read that love was a form of insanity that had driven men and women to do the unthinkable. This frightened her.

Madam Caro was so happy that day that she declared it a day of partying and rest. She would send out messages to her clients. They would not be happy but she did not have any contract with them. What would they do, sue her? She was certain their wives or girlfriends would be happy.

The guards were sent to town to buy food and drinks. The girls had never felt happier in all the years they were there. When she heard their excited screams and laughter she went into her room and shed a tear or two. To think they could have been out there in the cruel streets without her intervention was overwhelming. It was not only the streets that was evil, people's homes could be as cold and dark as the streets. She knew.

Her own cousin was sick and dying of AIDS yet had to do chores like she was a maid in the name of marriage. Horrific abuses took place behind closed doors of homes that seemed nice to the outsider.

She had a son who had cut all ties with her for various reasons. She often wished he had been female. There was a time she tried desperately for another child hoping it would be a girl. After three miscarriages and a near death experience during which she experienced the mystical outer darkness, she decided it was safer to just appreciate her one incommunicado son. She would do anything to hold him in her arms again. As far as she was concerned he was still her baby. She had named him Tony for no good reason at all. She had been tired and the labour had been worse than she had imagined it would be. When the fat midwife walked in with her pen and paper wanting to know the baby's name Tony just popped into her head.

Tony always wanted to know who his father was. All she could tell him was that he had walked out on them and may never come back. She did not want to tell him he was dead in case he showed up one day or he decided to search for him and succeeded. He used the absence of his father to excuse his stubbornness. At school, he was always getting into fights. It was only during a session with a psychologist that she realised she should have told him his father had died. Apparently, it was better to believe one's absentee father was dead. That way the feeling of rejection was avoided. It was too late to change the story at that point.

Tony began to 'experiment with his dark side' as he put it. This started after he became friends with a Luciferian who taught him that men ought to embrace their dark side rather than seek to overcome it. She was not religious and had issues with a God who tolerated men like Hitler but this new concept frightened even her. He hooked up with the darkest of people and listened to the darkest of music. The books he chose from their school library were always the scary ones with evil characters on the covers. Sometimes she felt the devil had personally given him to her.

That he would drop out of school to join a street gang was almost inevitable. At the age of thirteen he was already spending nights away from home. She had heard there was a street figure called Ivory who had this big house where all sorts of shady characters were always welcome. Tony had apparently struck up some sort of relationship with him and he had taken him under his wings. If she had had the guts she would have gone there to confront him. Ivory was not the sort of person you want to mess with.

Initially, Tony came home occasionally. One day he came with a girl he introduced to her as his girlfriend. He was only sixteen at the time and was talking marriage and stuff. She could not remember her name. She was covered in tattoos and was the first girl she had ever seen to have a tongue ring. She instantly disliked her and the feeling was mutual. That was the last time she saw her son again. Apparently, the girl must have had something to do with it.

She went to her window and parted the curtain a little bit. She could see the girls partying in the courtyard below. She retreated before anyone saw her. Violet's speech about love had brought back painful memories. She still believed in love even though she had lost all faith in men. In her quest for love she had been used and abused by them. It took her a while to realise that the best way not to be hurt by any man was not to put your heart and soul into the relationship.

She began to date men for the fun of it. It was less scary and more rewarding financially. She did not have to worry about if he was the one or who else he was seeing. She dated them in their dozens and never went for broke. Soon she began to learn their secrets. Men liked pleasure without responsibility. They only gave where they had something to gain. The further from their reach you are the more they would fight to get you even though you can never predict what they would do once they get you. She quickly realised it was never about love with men but ego. When a man sees a woman who had it all and needed nothing from them, they become insecure.

She played them like a game. Old, young, rich, poor, married, about to get married, single... she played them all. Without her heart on the line she actually began to enjoy the game. She had seen a lot of them fall from riches to rags because of her. She did not have time for remorse.

In her younger days, she was extremely pretty and knew it. She had a knockout body too. Only those who could meet her price tag could come close. Those who could not tried to. In the end, they got what they wanted but were left broken hearted and financially destroyed. Some even proposed marriage. She would go with them to see their parents and relatives even though she already knew how it was going to end up. They would parade her like some trophy to their parents and friends with pride. They wanted the world to see what they had conquered. While they trotted around like proud peacocks she would smile inwardly at the coming disappointment.

She sighed heavily. Violet had reminded her that, for all her callousness, she still had a hole in her heart that only love would fill. She still believed in love. She was a feminist but was no lesbian. Some women had tried to seduce her which had angered her. It seemed only the female of the species knew what love meant. Her own heart was still open to one man alone. Unfortunately, she had no idea where he was or if he was even alive. Violet had not found love. She had only found someone she could settle down with and start raising the kids she had always wanted. That was good enough for her. During their chat, she had wondered if she could still find what her heart had been yearning for even after years of giving up. Violet's response had been shocking and true.

"You will find the one," she had said. "The problem is that when you find him, he would be taken already. If you want to find true love, just get married. He always shows up late. It is the cruel nature of love to be found when it is already too late."

Violet believed that now she was tying the knot with her wealthy mate true love would come calling. She had no intentions of letting him go. She will not play by any rules and will pursue true love whenever he comes knocking. She was advised to tread carefully. Her new ATM machine was not like the others she could dump when she wanted to. This was a dangerous man with the means to make her as well as her loved ones disappear. It could be her head on the line, literally.

She had her own theory about love, one based on her experience. True love disappears and makes you wait forever. He would never come back but will leave you wondering if he will. True love will mess with your mind years after you think you have moved on with the next best thing. She believed she had met him. They had shared the most incredible moments of her life. It had been short-lived but memorable. He had promised to come back. That was over fifteen years back and she was still waiting. Her one true love had turned her into the beast that she had become and she blamed every broken heart she had left behind on him. He was responsible for all her misdeeds, not her. She could have been married. Tony would have had a different life. He might have even become a doctor or a lawyer.

She sighed heavily. It was a chain of thought the psychologist had advised her to break before it took hold of her mind and led to another episode of depression. This time she did not want to break the chain of thoughts. She wanted to feel the pain of being abandoned and broken hearted. She reached for the whiskey on her bedside table and poured herself some good measure. She still had his picture but was too lazy to take it out of the box. She was sure he had grown older and must look different. Sometimes she would take it out and gaze at it for hours. His handsome smile would come alive and she would hear the echoes of his rich laughter.

There was something about the way he had promised he would return that made her believe he would. She had seen pain in his eyes. He had not wanted to disclose the reason why he had to leave. She had begged him to stay. After all, he had enough money. They would settle down and have kids. His mind was made up. Africa was not his future. It was too volatile, too unstable. He would go and find stability and then come back to get her. Their children would never have to go through what he went through. He had given her a large amount of money for safe keeping. It would be his last resort in case things did not work out as planned. Too many had left the country hoping to return years later as kings only to be deported with no dime to their name. Would he have entrusted her with such an amount if he did not intend to return? That was one of the reasons she still believed in him. Everything pointed to the fact that he did plan to return to her. He did truly love her. Something must have happened to him.

She had cried when he left. They talked almost every day on the phone for the first few months after his departure. His plans were working out fine. His only fear was that he may be deported before he got his papers. His primary concern was the immigration department. Suddenly he had stopped calling and his number became unreachable. She would wake up at night and dial his number up to a hundred times. She even developed a certain anger for the metallic female voice that told her repeatedly that the number she was trying to call was unavailable. When she started wondering if the same electronic voice was dating him she knew she was losing her mind and needed to seek help.

One possibility she did not want to consider was the fact that he was dead. In a way, she would have been glad if this was the case. The psychologist was right. Death was better than rejection or abandonment. It was the finality of death that frightened her. Death meant she would never see him again ever. She could not accept this possibility. It was something to do with the death of her father at a very young age. He had been her source of strength, pride and security. He had been a very wealthy man who had inherited a lot of money from his own father, a renowned hunter of elephants. Ivory was what got him his wealth. Her father did not like hunting but with what he got he started cocoa farms in the southern part of the country where the rain was good. The cocoa plantations were often deep in the jungle and he often stayed there for weeks on end especially during the harvest season. He also owned rubber tree plantations.

She always looked forward to his return from such trips with joyful expectation. He always had a gift for her. One day she was told he was never coming back. He Had died in a car accident. The body was so badly mangled that she had not been allowed to see it. All she saw was his coffin. His death marked the end of her dreams of a good education. Greedy and evil relatives moved in and took everything. The farms were mismanaged and eventually abandoned after everything that could be sold for cash was sold for cash. If they could have found buyers for the farm houses they would have sold them too. Fortunately, no one wanted buildings in the middle of nowhere.

Years later, she decided to visit one of them. She was shocked to see the farm house where her father used to take her to on some weekends looking like someone had dropped a bomb on it. She vowed to rebuild it. She did. The cocoa business had become very competitive at the time. Her plan was to pick up from where her father left things. It was around this time that she dated a wealthy night club owner. He had been deported from the UK where he worked as a bouncer in a night club. He knew a lot about the dirty night life of the west and used his experience to establish various night clubs.

She got her idea from him. Using the money her absentee lover entrusted to her she renovated the dilapidated farm house and made it into a resort. One thing led to another and the rest was history. The money her true love left with her had grown in value ever since. She had more money than she would ever need and had the exact amount he had left in a bag in her bedroom. She wanted him back. Money was not her problem, love was. Violet would learn later that love was the one thing every woman yearned for especially after the age of forty. It was not her duty to tell her. She would find out herself.

7

CHAPTER 7

Mason, the private detective, drove through the jungle wondering what would happen that night. It was Friday. Jeff had chosen Friday because it would be busy and he would have a better chance of success. He had Jeff's card in his breast pocket. Without it there was no way he was going to be let into the resort. He was not nervous. Years as a cop and even more years as a private detective had eliminated every fear factor for such missions. He was rather thrilled.

He chewed roasted almonds as he drove. They were in a plastic bag on the passenger's seat. The true purpose of the bag was not to supply him with magnesium but to conceal a small pistol underneath that he hoped he would not have to use that night.

Earlier in the week he had met with Jeff in a restaurant and they had both agreed that the best way for him to succeed was for him to visit the resort as a guest. That way he would analyse their security measures from the inside and plot an escape or rescue plan with the intel gathered. He did not expect any trouble. As a matter of fact, he considered it a routine operation. All he needed to do was order drinks and maybe some food, use the toilet, lose his way deliberately now and then and try to befriend one of the men who worked there. He had learnt the art of conversation and could strike up a conversation with a chameleon if that would serve his purpose.

The nuts were tasty. He had bought them from one of the street vendors. Fortunately, he had bought four packs. His wife would be more than delighted. She was the compulsive healthy eater who exercised every day with the belief that she was prolonging her life. He knew she had other reasons for her fitness craze, reasons he tried not to worry about. He had his own exit strategy.

He believed life was not about numbers but about quality. Exercise to him was self-harm. He would, as usual, give her the full details of his night's mission. She did not trust him in the least. He did not trust her either. She was one of those feminists who went to countless meetings every week where they discussed how to dethrone men from society. Why she even got married was still a mystery to him. She and her like-minded feminists believe men sat on some invisible throne that he was yet to feel as a man. Maybe the ancestors should have allowed women to go to war back in the day. That way they would have appreciated the sacrifice they had made and understood that war was not funny.

He already knew what the area surrounding the building looked like. He had done surveillance of the environment earlier with a night vision camera. There was no way anyone was going to escape from there without some help either from the inside or outside. He stopped the car beside a tree with the front facing the entrance in case he had to make a fast exit. It had happened before. Next, he grabbed a handful of nuts before exiting the car with the gun tucked behind his trousers. The two guards did not even look at him twice as he waved Jeff's card and made his entry while pretending to light a cigar to conceal his face. He had noticed the cameras.

The interior was just as Jeff had described it. The girls were pretty. They were young too. He had been warned to be careful and not get carried away. They could be very seductive. He was feeling like a monk that night, the only thing in his mind being the mission. He quickly downed a bottle of beer before making his way to the toilet. After missing his way twice and memorising every hallway and every door or window, he returned to his seat.

When he saw Robert, he knew at once it was Robert. Jeff had not minced his words when he described how ugly the man was. He had been right. He had learnt though that oftentimes the ugliest people were the ones with the best of hearts. He also knew a lot of ugly crooks in prison. The extremely handsome or pretty ones were likely to be bipolar. Robert seemed to be the down to earth fellow who would not hurt a fly. The only problem was that he had hurt more than a fly. When Jeff described his features, he had a feeling he had seen such an ugly fellow before.

There could not be two of such faces. Nature was not that unkind. Such faces do not happen that frequently. Seeing him in real life confirmed his suspicion. Robert was a murderer on the run who happened to be on the wanted persons list. The fact that a lot of top police officers were in the room told him Madam Caro must be the sort of woman who pulled strings that went all the way to the top.

The place was very relaxing and he was already having a good time. The music was not too loud and the light just bright enough. A man came to join him. He announced proudly that he was the commissioner for agriculture in a nearby state. He reeked of alcohol as he talked and even offered to pay for his drinks. He let him. The woman known as Madam Caro could be seen crossing the floor now and then with a different guest each time. She looked vaguely familiar.

The commissioner talked about the progress his state was making in the agriculture sector. Rubber production had risen fifteen percent since he became the commissioner. He tried to appear to listen. He was paying for his drink after all. He was relieved when a third man who knew the commissioner joined them and before long they were chatting away. He drank his beer and watched Robert.

As soon as he had his chance he signalled to Robert. He came with a notepad and a pen expecting to take an order.

"Monkey Face!" he hailed. He would never have said it if he did not have a gun and a beer.

Robert looked like someone had punched him in the gut. It was a name that belonged to another place and another life he had escaped from. Back then he would have fought anyone who dared call him that. He recovered from his shock quickly. There were people who wanted him dead if only they knew where to find him. Fear gripped him but he managed to keep a straight face.

Mason asked him if they could go to a private area to talk. It was very important. Robert did not like him but agreed they could talk in the VIP section. He was as eager to get away from the crowd and had broken out in a cold sweat. He had to make it quick though. The place was busy. Mason excused himself from the two men and went with him. Robert walked fast.

Madam Caro was chatting with some men who looked like they were from India when they got there. They sat on the only available chair which was close to the entrance.

"Wetin you wan talk about?" Robert asked. "You be police?"

"Do I look like one?" he asked.

"You resemble police," he said. "We see police here all the time."

"I am a cop," he lied. "But not your average cop. I belong to a special unit dedicated to tracking down terrorists. Relax. I know you are not one."

"No shaking," Robert said. "I know you?"

He did look relaxed and the sweat was gone. The man had seen so many cops that he believed he would never be arrested.

"Let's just say I know a lot about you, Robert," Mason said.

"So?" he asked. "Wetin you want?" There was no hint of fear in his tone.

"Now," he said. "I would like you to do something for me. Before I let you know what it is though I must know that I can trust you."

Robert shrugged. "I no fit guarantee until I know wetin you want. For this life, the only person you fit trust na God. We trust pastors those days. Even pastor dey thief now and I no be pastor."

Mason smiled. "What is it you want in life, Robert? You want to be a fugitive all your life? You want to work for Madam Caro till when? Till you become so old you can't even spell your name? She will discard you when you are no longer useful. When are you going to get settled in life?"

"I no be fuji musician," he said getting angry. "And how I want to spend my time no be your damn business, abi you be Doctor Phil. Be like say we don talk finish. I need to return for work."

Mason decided it was time to change tactics. He had done his research. He cleared his throat.

"I know you send money to your mother and siblings from time to time," he said. "They know you are a wanted man. I can get them arrested for aiding a fugitive and obstruction of justice. That can get them at least ten years in jail each. I know your sister is almost through with her degree program. I think you are doing a good job. I am not the kind of person who dashes people's dreams unless I must. I know a certain group of very evil men who will be happy to know you work here. I can leave them an anonymous tip."

Robert hesitated. The two men looked at each other while Madam Caro and her guests chatted away unaware of their presence. One of them was saying something about building a similar resort in India and Dubai. Robert's face looked deadly. Mason remained calm. He could see the other man was struggling with rage. He had seen photographs of the man he had murdered with his bare hands. It had been a brutal fight but Robert had come out of it alive. He was only sixteen at the time and the man he had murdered was in his twenties and a known thug. He had run not necessarily from the law but from fear of vengeance. The man had belonged to a deadly local gang that was known to kill at will. His mother and siblings had fled the town too.

"You stay away from me and my people," he hissed while struggling to keep his tone low. "I no care if you be part of some special squad or SSS. No ever threaten my family again."

Mason raised his hands in apology.

"We are wasting time," he said. "What I ask is very small. I just have to make sure I can trust you. Do this one small favour for me and I vow to never trouble you again. You will never see me again and I can actually get your file erased."

"No worry about my file," he said.

"Then why are you hiding?"

"Who tell you say I dey hide?"

"Alright," Mason said. "I will leave my card with you. Give me a call when you want to talk nice. My number is on it. If you don't call me within a week some old friends of yours will be paying you a visit. I might even tell them where your family is staying just for the fun of it."

He placed his card on the table.

"I fit make sure you no leave this place alive," Robert said ignoring the card. "How you want run your big mouth if you don die?"

"Say that again and I will ensure you never walk again," Mason said. "Do I look stupid to you?"

Robert decided to back down a little bit. He had learnt that when a man is not afraid of threats there was usually more to him than meets the eye.

"Wetin exactly you want?" he asked.

"Finally, you are asking the right questions," Mason said. "It is a delicate issue. Not a big one, just delicate. I must know that whatever I discuss with you will be between you and me. Do I have your word?"

He nodded.

"Take my card before anyone sees it," Mason said.

"People give me card all the time," he said. "No big deal. Just talk."

At this point, Madam Caro and her guests finalised whatever it was they were discussing. They all got up and began to leave. As they walked past she saw Mason. Her eyes narrowed in suspicion. There was a hint of recognition in her eyes.

"What are you doing here, Robert?" she asked.

He took the card on the table and slid it into his pocket surreptitiously then stood.

"Who is this? Do I know you sir?" she asked. "I have never seen you here before. Have you seen him before?"

"No ma'am," Robert said.

She looked at her Indian guests apologetically.

"Sort this out let me walk my guests to their car," she said. "I don't want to see you here chatting with a client when I return. This is Friday and you know how busy it is."

He nodded. Mason stood. Madam Caro left with her guests. As she walked through the door she paused and looked back. She went on, hurrying a bit to catch up with her fast walking guests.

"You get gate pass?" Robert asked as she left.

"Of course, I do," Mason replied.

"Make I see."

"No, you may not. I will be leaving now. Call me."

With that he left.

Robert hurried to the main hall. He stood close to the entrance long enough to see Madam Caro was in no hurry to return then hurried to her room. The next day they would have to take money to her bank. He opened her drawer and tore off a page from her cheque book. He knew he had to start withdrawing larger amounts than he had been. There would be a higher chance of being caught but now was not the time to be discrete. It was time to move on yet again. He had always planned to leave when the time was right. His past was catching up.

Madam Caro paid them peanuts even though she made a lot of money every week. The last time he asked for a raise she called him the most ungrateful fool on earth. Her argument was that she gave them free accommodation, food, and protection from the cops. The men who worked for her had all been involved in one crime or the other. In a way, she was right. He earned above the minimum wage and did not have to pay rent. The only problem was that he needed more than that if he was ever going to meet his targets in life.

She trusted him enough to take her cash to the bank at the end of every week. She also considered him not smart enough to steal from her which worked to his advantage because he had been stealing from her. His plan had always been to disappear once he had what he considered to be enough money. The visit from the mystery man who knew his past told him the time had come to move on. He had always had recurring nightmares of being finally captured by the gang he had referred to and undergoing the most horrific torture. That nightmare was about to become real if he did not act fast. If he could find him then they may not be too far behind.

He left the room just in time. She did not know he had his own copy of the key which he had made a while ago in a hardware shop. If the others saw him in her room they would simply assume he was running some errand for her. He spent the rest of the busy night planning how best to vanish and when. At the back of his mind he kept wondering what the mystery man wanted with him. What could he possibly be able to offer such a person that was apparently very important?

As soon as her happy guests were gone a fuming Madam Caro pounced on the guards at the entrance.

"I saw a strange face in here," she said. "How did he get in?"

They vowed they checked every man's card before entry. Every man who was in there was supposed to be in there, they assured with confidence. She glared at them for a while before going inside to look for Robert and download her anger on him.

"Who was that man?" she asked. "Did you check to see if he had a card?"

"That one no be my job," he said. "My job na to serve any guest wey dey inside."

"What did he want?"

He shrugged. He already had his answer ready. "He say he no wan make people see him face since him be secondary school principal. He wan make I arrange room for am."

"Where is he now?" she asked. "Which principal can afford to come here? You should use your brain sometimes."

"Be like say he don go," he said. "You panic the man."

"How convenient," she said. "Tell Zudock to come and see me immediately. I want every tape from all surveillance cameras checked. Check with him and get me the man's face. Give it to the inspector whenever he comes. We can't have strangers coming here without my permission. What if he was here to plant a bomb or kidnap someone? Did you even think about that? Don't you read the news? Why am I even asking? You are just too dumb to know what is happening around you. These are dangerous times."

Robert looked down sheepishly. Over the years, he had learnt to play the role of the unintelligent fool. She fumed as she analysed his ugly face. It made her even more angry.

"How can a man be so dumb and ugly?" she asked. "How old are you? You are not a kid. How can you be so dumb? Without me you will just self-destruct. Let me hear you or any of you ask for a raise again, you ungrateful idiots!"

With that she stormed out of the kitchen. Robert bit his lower lip. He had endured her humiliation for years. She claimed to have helped him when he had nothing. He saw it differently. As far as he was concerned they both had helped each other. As for being dumb, she would find out soon enough just how dumb he really was. He put his hands in his pocket and leaned against a wall. One hand was in contact with the mystery man's card while the other was in contact with her cheque book. He could tell another chapter of his life was about to start. He was going to hit her hard before he left. She was going to pay for all the insults and humiliation he had endured at her hand.

He went outside for a smoke and to make a phone call. There were a lot of orders from the kitchen waiting to be delivered but he could not be bothered at that point. He called home. His elderly mother picked it up.

"How are you, my son?" she asked.

"I dey fine mama," he replied. Sometimes he wondered if she was the only one who really cared about him in the whole world. "How Emmanuel and Tessy?"

She sighed. He could tell something was wrong. Something was always wrong.

"Tessy is fine as always. She is focused on her studies and will soon be graduating. Just a few months to go," she said. "As for Emmanuel, he is just busy doing what he knows best. Two girls came here just this week claiming to be pregnant for him. He is not even worried about this HIV thing going around. I have asked you to stop sending him money."

"Na you refuse to open bank account," he said almost accusingly. "Tessy dey school most of the time. Na only Emma I fit send money to."

"I will open the account," she said.

He shook his head. That was not the first time she was saying that. He had called home to take his mind off things but it seemed there was always one trouble or the other anywhere he turned.

"Emmanuel dey home?" he asked.

"Yes. Let me go and call him," she said.

He waited, his forehead creased in thought. She sounded worn out. Emmanuel was the oldest. He sometimes wondered if he had some form of mental disorder. He was slow in everything except women. The reason he sent money to him was because of the trust they shared. The man was just proving incapable of surviving without the financial lifeline he offered. Occasionally he would come up with some "mega project" that would earn him millions in just a few months. He would plead for capital. Once the money was sent he would vanish for a few weeks only to resurface with nothing but apologies for another wasted opportunity. His patience was wearing thin.

He listened as she knocked on his bedroom door. He would have found it funny when she argued briefly with him about bringing strange women to the house had he been in a different mood. His defence was that he was not a kid. He shook his head.

"Hey bro!" Emmanuel saluted when he eventually came to the phone. "What's up? When we wan finally see you?"

"Soon," he said. "How life?"

"Tough but can't complain," he said. "I don learn to be positive. Just keep sending the love into my account and I'll be alright."

"Listen," he said. "I need to leave this work soon. I wan make you find another house for another state. No tell mama yet. Matter of fact no tell anyone."

"Wetin dey happen?" Emmanuel asked yawning.

"I no fit explain now," he said. "If you fit move go different city, move fast. Make sure no one know where you dey go. As soon as you settle down call me and give me the address."

"What of the money? Accommodation expensive these days you know."

Robert paused for a few seconds. He was too angry to speak. It was always about money. He had found people were more wasteful with money when they did not earn it themselves. When he finally relaxed enough not to go into an outburst he resumed talking.

"Take some money from the one wey you dey put aside for me," he said. "You really need to learn how to manage money."

"Things are hard," he said. "No be everybody dey find am easy."

"And who e easy for?" he asked.

"Just send some money," Emmanuel said. "Your money dey tied up for some business deal now. E go take a few months before I fit access the equity."

"You dey tell me say you use my money?" Robert asked. He was biting his lip in a desperate attempt to stay calm. He knew the money was gone.

"I no say use," he said. "I just invest am. Calm down bro. You go get am back."

He knew arguing with him was a useless exercise. He blamed himself for ever entrusting his money to him. He should have entrusted it to his sister. His problem then was that he believed women to be vulnerable. A smart guy could easily gain access to her heart and through her heart his money. He could see how absurd his thinking had been at the time. In the game of love, which, to him, was all about lust and advantage, men were the real suckers. This to him was the reason many African economies were in shambles. Their leaders were showering too many mistresses with public money.

"Put mama back for the line," he said angrily.

"Don't be mad bro," Emmanuel said. "Are you sending the money or what?"

"Just put mama back on the line," he snapped.

He realised he was shaking with rage as he waited. He felt like bashing his head against a concrete wall. The man was just irresponsible and lacked a conscience.

"My son."

"Mama," he said. "Emma still dey there?"

"He has gone back to his latest girlfriend," she said. "You need to talk to that one."

"How I go advise grown man mama?" he asked. "Which advise you wan give a grown man wey he no already know? Tell Tessy to send me her account number as soon as possible. Anyone come look for me?"

"There was this man who came some weeks ago," she said. "He said he was from the National Bureau of Statistics and wanted a list of all my children."

"You tell am where I dey?" he asked.

"Do I know where you are?"

"Listen mama," he said. "You must leave the house. Emmanuel don eat all my money. I think I don get enough of him. From now on he dey on his own. Tell Tessy to send me her account number. I go send her some money so she fit look for another place for you. I no get time to explain. Just do as I tell you. No tell Emmanuel about this. No let am know where you dey go. Once you relocate let me know where you dey. I go see you soon."

"Is there a problem?" she asked sounding alarmed.

"Nothing I no fit handle," he said. "Just do as I say. No worry about anything. I have to go now."

He ended the call. He decided to have another smoke before going in. Wasting time outside was his own way of getting paid for Caro's insults. He lit a cigarette and sat on the ground facing the building.

He could see her window from there. She was the prettiest girl he had ever laid his eyes on. There were times when he had made up his mind to finally make his feelings known to her. His face was always the barrier. It had been the source of trouble and insecurity since he was a child. His father had left believing his wife had had an affair after he was born. His basis was that he looked nothing like him. His good mother had endured the insult patiently. It was time she got her well-deserved break. He would spare no expenses to make sure she got it before she left the planet.

He had researched plastic surgeries online. The amount needed was astronomical. He was going to find it no matter what. Caro would pay for his plastic surgery as certainly as Mexico was going to pay for Trump's wall.

The spot he was sitting on was his favourite simply because from there he could see her window. Sometimes he would see her silhouette in the night. The day she had tried to kill herself he had had a fight with Musa. If not for the intervention of Madam Caro, he would have committed another murder that night. They knew he was always defensive of her. If she knew, she never showed it.

Occasionally she would come out of her shell and they would chat. The other girls thought she was a snob. He knew better. He was the closest to a friend she had in the place. She was close to two other girls. One had been shipped off to Italy or Spain. Madam Caro played her game close to her chest. Nothing would make him happier than to leave the place with her. Sometimes he would fantasise about a future with her as his wife and their kids running around a beautiful home with a garden full of flowers and butterflies. It was his escape from the real world that he had found to be so harsh and insensitive.

Growing up had been hard. Many blamed him for being the cause of his parent's divorce. For years, he had believed he was some sort of cursed creature. In school, many made fun of him because of his face. One day someone called him Monkey Face. A brutal fight had erupted in which he had lost. To add to the humiliation, the name stuck. Monkey Face was used by any who wanted to provoke him.

He had to drop out after too many fights. Unfortunately, some of his school mates lived in his neighbourhood. There was no respite from the constant bullying and taunting. His mother would weep when she saw a new bruise or wound. She knew he was getting into fights almost daily. The fact that she was helpless to do anything worsened her plight.

He soon became recluse. There was no future as far as he was concerned and he often prayed he would sleep and never wake up. Sometimes he would ask God why he was given such a face. Sometimes he would pray for a new face. This was when he was younger and still had a lot of childlike faith. The next day he would rush to the mirror to see if his prayers had been answered. The same ugly face would stare back at him like a scene from a nightmare. He had long stopped believing in God.

The day Ehi had attempted suicide he realised just how much like him she was. Up till then he had never given much thought to his role in the place. All he did was obey orders. He had personally beaten up a few of the girls who had tried to be rude to the boss or had committed one crime or the other. Ehi was different from the others and it was not just because of her exceptional beauty. She was just different. He was not sure why he was drawn to her. He sometimes thought it was because she was pretty and he was ugly. Someone had once joked that he had to marry a very pretty woman or his kids would have no hope in life. The thought of having kids who would go through what he had been through was worrying. Plastic surgery would not fix his DNA.

She lived in her own world. She did not speak much. All she did was mind her business and stay in her room except when she had to come down for one reason or the other. Musa and some of the others were in the habit of sleeping around with the girls when they felt like it. If they refused they would be beaten up. They knew not to come close to her. He would kill the person. They all knew he was there because of a murder he had committed and they feared him because of this.

He wondered if he would one day find the guts to finally tell her how he felt about her. It was the fear of her response more than his insecurities that held him back. He had known rejection most of his life and had learnt to deal with it. He was not sure he would be able to live with her rejection. Of what use would living be? All the money he stole or earned was for a better future free from his past and his face. She, he believed, would make everything meaningful and worthwhile.

He sat smoking and looking in the direction of her window. That night she did not leave her curtain open. He finished his cigarette and toyed with the idea of calling Mason. He decided he would do that the next day. There was no guarantee his family would be safe even if he did whatever it was he wanted. While he stalled for time, he would make sure they moved to someplace where no one would be able to find them.

He eventually went in to meet an angry kitchen staff. The head chef wanted to know where he had been. He told him he had been out to have a smoke. He knew there was nothing anyone could do to him. Even Madam Caro could only yell and run her big mouth. She was not going to tie him to some pole and have him flogged like she sometimes did to the girls. He picked up a plate of food and went to the hall. It was even busier than before. He wondered why all those men preferred to be with women they barely knew when they had people who loved them at home. All he wanted was the one person who would accept and love him for who he was. No amount of pleasure seeking or whatever it was that made men cheat would make him leave her for any other woman for even a minute.

Emmanuel's latest girlfriend was a woman in her late twenties called Belinda. She claimed to be on the run from an abusive ex. If he found her, he would kill her. She told stories of his brutality. Emmanuel would seethe with rage as he listened to horrific tales of abuse. She was reading a book when he returned from his brief communication with his brother. He made people believe Robert was abroad working in a factory. She expected Emmanuel to be rich since he had someone to send him some foreign currency occasionally. He tried to live up to her expectations which were often unrealistic. In the two months she had been staying in the house he had spent a fortune.

"Who be that?" she asked without looking up from the book.

"My brother," he replied. "We need to get that money back. He no happy at all."

"I tell you say e go take some months before we begin see some profit," she replied with a look of impatience. "You no explain am to him?"

"My brother no be businessman," he said. "He makes his money by hard work and stinginess. He no go understand."

"Too bad," she said. "Nothing wey I fit do."

"What if the business fail?" he asked.

She shrugged. "Every business get risk. I no explain all this from start?"

He looked at her for a while then shook his head. For someone running from an abusive situation she sure did have no sense of gratitude or modesty. Sometimes he wondered if she had been abused for those very reasons. Not that any man should have any reason to raise his hand against a woman. Despite his attraction to her his patience was wearing thin.

He lay on the bed, stretched and yawned.

"I'm hungry," he said.

"Your mama no cook?" she asked.

"My mama no be your maid," he said.

"But she be your mama," she said unapologetically. "You know say she no like me and I try to avoid her as much as I fit. If you been get your own house e for better. Make we go that new restaurant go eat."

He shook his head. He had tried being reasonable with her. She was not the reasoning type. All she cared about was what she wanted. Bad as he thought his former girlfriend was, Belinda made him realise she had a lot of good qualities he had not appreciated when they were together.

The problem was that he could not give her the boot until he recovered his money. He also did not want her carrying his baby. He still had not convinced her to get an abortion.

He rolled over on the bed and planted his face in the pillow.

"So?" she asked. "We dey go the place to eat or not? Now wey you don mention food, I don begin starve."

He ignored her. His mind was as busy as a beehive.

8

CHAPTER 8

Mason sat on a couch in Jeff's house where he was giving him an update that would have made a North Korean commander in chief proud when his cell phone rang. It was Robert. He signalled to Jeff to remain quiet then answered. Jeff listened, trying to make some sense of the one-sided conversation. Apart from the fact that he could tell something was not right he had to wait for Mason to explain what was going on. He focused his gaze on the detective's hat which was on the coffee table.

"Waoh!" Mason said after the call. He rattled his fingers on the side table, a sign that he was uneasy.

"What's wrong?" Jeff asked.

"Madam Caro knows what I look like," he said.

"How so?" Jeff asked.

"Apparently, she had seen me before somewhere in the distant past," he said. "Got suspicious and got her boys to go through the surveillance videos. She has asked that he send my picture to one of her police friends to get me identified. The images are not that good. Always had a part of my face covered with my hand. This is not good. Never know what facial identifying program these cops have."

"Do you think they know I gave you the card?" Jeff asked.

"No evidence of that yet," he said. "They may if they dig further. We need to speed things up. It is only a matter of time before she figures out my true mission. Trust me on this."

"What do we do now?" Jeff asked.

"Just give me time to think," Mason said. He had the cell phone pressed against his right temple, his eyes shut.

Jeff watched him, unsure of what to say.

"If Mike sees that picture he would be able to link me to you," he said after a while. "He is the only one who can make that connection. Do you think we should let him know what we are up to?"

"Can never trust that man," Jeff said.

"I thought he was your friend?" Mason asked.

"We were close at a time when I was stupid," Jeff said. "No telling what he will do with the information if we let him in on our plan. He may go running straight to Madam Caro with it. I still don't know the full extent of the connection between those two."

"What would be the rationale for that?" Mason asked looking a bit confused. "What exactly does he stand to gain if he stops one girl he barely knows from leaving that place?"

"I know Mike," Jeff said. "He is a psychopath. He is very unsteady. We cannot rely on him. You have to think up something else."

"The clock is ticking here Jeff," he said. "I have done what you asked me to do. Robert can be of help. From what I gather he is not a fan of that fat woman. I saw her and witnessed how she treats him first hand. I have not told him who our girl is but once you give the green light we can start the engine going. Have you rented a place for her yet?"

"Not yet," Jeff said. "I'm a bit low on cash."

"You are not planning on bringing her here, are you?" Mason asked. "Once she goes missing they will look here, thanks to your unusual interest. By the way, is your wife aware of this?"

"Not yet," a tired Jeff said. "How do you explain all this to your wife? We are not communicating that well now, if you know what I mean."

"If she finds out another way it will not look good," Mason said. "Unless..."

He raised his hand and left his statement hanging.

Jeff looked at him curiously.

"Unless what?" he asked.

"Never mind," Mason said. "I just want to do my part. As long as you are happy, I am happy."

"If you have anything to say to me, just say it," Jeff said. "You know I don't like unfinished statements."

"I've seen the way you talk about her," he said. "Now I understand your intentions are noble and all that. I'm just saying…if I did not know better I would have thought you were in love with her. People have a way of concealing personal agendas and cloaking them in nobility."

Jeff sighed. Mason was not someone known to mince his words. Ehi had been featuring in his day dreams of late, a fact as troubling as it was puzzling. He had often wondered if his true intentions were personal. There were dozens of girls there, millions in similar circumstances around the world. Why Ehi?

He did not plan to stop at just her. He wanted to bring the whole thing that Madam Caro and her people had going crashing to the ground. She believed she was doing them a great favour. He believed she was diminishing the potential of many. Being a prostitute was nothing about choice or empowerment but survival. Many could be lawyers and even engineers if given the chance. On the other hand, there were many lawyers and engineers who were jobless. It was confusing.

He still had not figured out who their parents were, if they were aware of their children's situation or not, and if not what exactly their stories were.

"Have you gone to the orphanage?" he asked.

"Tomorrow I'll do that," Mason said noting the diversion. He had known Nneka for some years. Unlike Mike, she welcomed him with open arms. She was the ideal wife; faithful, moral, wise, hardworking, supportive, and doting. She believed that the man was the head of the home and would never be a part of the silly feminist movement his wife was a champion of. Only an idiot would not appreciate a woman like that at a time when more and more women were biting what he called the evil fruit of independence aka anarchy.

He suspected she was somewhere in the house. When discussing the issue, Jeff spoke in low tones and he followed suit. Something was wrong but he had learnt not to interfere in other people's marital problems unless by invitation. If his suspicions were right, then Jeff was in a very vulnerable situation. He had gone to the resort after all, a place no married man should have ever gone.

"Do you think I should go there myself?" Jeff asked.

Mason was surprised. "Why? You don't trust me to do a good job?"

"Not that," Jeff said. "If they have your picture then they will follow your trail. The less you appear from now on the better for us and the safer for her. I am a journalist after all. You have done most of the work. You found the orphanage. I'll give you your due credit when I write the book. I will pay them a visit and pretend to be looking for a child to adopt. Who knows, I may end up coming home with one."

"Not funny," Mason said laughing.

"Might happen," Jeff said. "Who knows?"

Mason thought about it. It was not such a bad idea after all.

Jeff's phone rang. He went to answer it. Mason used the opportunity to go through his list of text messages, half listening to what Jeff was saying. When he was through with the call he returned to his seat.

"That was Mike," he said.

Mason sat up.

"Wanted to know if I gave my card to anyone," Jeff went on. "I told him no. They have excluded everyone that came that night. Those like myself who were not around are being checked out. I asked him if the card could not have been forged."

"And what was his response?"

"To forge them you must know the place exists in the first place," Jeff said. "I wonder why they are making such a big fuss about the whole thing? I mean, who goes to this length just because one man managed to sneak into their establishment?"

"People do crazy things when their livelihood is threatened," Mason said. "The good thing is that we have Robert. He is on our side."

"How do you know this?" Jeff asked. "How do you know he is not co-operating with Caro and just nudging you on until your full intentions are known?"

"Which is why I have not divulged anything crucial to him yet," he said. "I have thought of all this. You forget I do this for a living. Robert has a lot of reasons not to stab me in the back. His family is one."

"You think someone like that will care about his family that much?"

"Don't judge him by his looks," Mason said. "The man has a beating heart. For now, he is our best chance at succeeding. I just hope you understand who you are dealing with. This thing goes beyond that fat woman. One slipup and your life may be on the line here. I believe I have made the risk clear to you. These people will do anything to protect their machine. They are in it for various reasons and I assure you it goes all the way to politics and even finance. I mean top senators are involved. Tread carefully. It is not just an entertainment spot but an international lobbying machine that involves blackmail."

"I understand the risks," Jeff said. "I heard you the first time."

He picked up his hat.

"Going already?" Jeff asked.

"I have other cases besides this one," he said. "Not as if you are paying me much. Must make up the cash from elsewhere. Right now, I am investigating a hot kidnap case. The man is a lecturer. The family have been warned not to contact the police. They have contacted me. Guess how much they are demanding? Twenty million. If a lecturer has that kind of money, why would he remain a lecturer? These folks are so dumb it makes them dangerous. They don't care what your earning capacity is. They just yank you off the street and demand whatever it is they feel they can demand."

"Sounds scary," Jeff said frowning.

"It is scary," Mason agreed. "They blame poverty yet squander millions like they are some spoilt kids brought up in a castle. My wife and I are still waiting for the day you will honour our last invitation."

"Tell her I said soon," Jeff said.

"I'm not telling her anything," he said putting on his signature hat. "Whenever you are sure of the day just let me know. You going to the orphanage tomorrow?"

"Sure."

"Be careful."

"It's just an orphanage, Mason," Jeff said. "Relax. Have a good day."

"I'll be careful just going to the toilet if I were you," Mason said. "I'm telling you."

"Your job is making you excessively paranoid," Jeff said.

"Which is why I am alive," he replied. "Have a good day. Since you are going there tomorrow I'll focus on the doctor. Say hi to your wife when she returns."

"I will. I'll see the doctor if I can. The less you are involved the better."

He shrugged and left.

As soon as he was gone Jeff picked up the file he had left on the table and began to go through it. It had everything Mason had gathered so far on the case. The doctor's name and address were all there. Robert's cell phone number was there as well. Mason was a well organised man and everything had been typed and printed. He could have just scribbled them.

The orphanage in question was well known to him. A lot of prominent men, women and organisations often made donations to them. The place was run by a woman twice the size of Madam Caro. He had never met her personally but had seen her during the few occasions he had gone there to cover some widely-publicised donation usually made by a politician just before a major election. Orphanages were their favourites. No politician ever gave quietly. The whole world had to know how generous they were.

He decided the best time to go would be in the afternoon. That was when the children would be taking their nap. He planned to find information about Ehi. Should he fail, Mason may have to do his usual thing later and sneak inside to get the file. If Ehi had a file there he would find it. Conventional wisdom told him that if something fishy was going on there then asking for a particular file would only trigger a chain of events that would ruin everything they planned to achieve.

He went to the study and did a little research on the place. There was not much about it on the internet. They had a Facebook page. The only thing he found in it were pictures of politicians, past, present and future, smiling usually beside some bags of rice with some carefully selected children in the background.

He decided to do some search on the Ethiopian. He wondered if he should visit him again on his way from the orphanage. It had been a while since their last meeting. There was nothing except newspaper articles. Eventually he did some scouting for a good apartment to lease. He found some and wrote down the contact details of the respective agents. It was time he started preparing. She would have to stay somewhere if their plans worked. The thought of her being finally free was a bit overwhelming for him and he closed his eyes for a few seconds. If the doctor could be convinced then the rest would be easy, easier than he had ever hoped.

Along with the excitement of the possible end to her ordeal came the fact of real challenges. Only in the modern era would someone escape slavery only to be unable to cope with freedom. Being free was proving as difficult as being enslaved. Many ex-convicts found themselves back in prison again and again for the same reason. Mankind had to own up to the fact that the earth was running on artificial mode. The electricity was expensive. The free water was treated and then made expensive to consumers. If not for China, clothing would have remained expensive. Mobility was expensive. You had to buy a car then the fuel and every other expensive thing that went with it including periodic maintenance. This excluded the unseen cost of burnt fuel to the environment. Back in the day, all you needed was a cart and a donkey or horse. All they had to do to survive was eat grass.

Then there was education. She needed a good education. That was her real ticket out of her predicament or she may quickly relapse into the only thing she knew how to. It was no secret that hundreds of thousands of undergraduates the world over were engaging in some sort of money for sex lifestyle to fund their education. He found it pathetic. In Australia, they even had websites where students hooked up with rich people who were willing to pay their fees for pleasure. It was all modernised prostitution to him; different forms of the same problem.

A good education in a reputable institution meant good money. The more he punched the numbers the more he wondered if Madam Caro did not have the right to her claim of being a saviour rather than a villain. They quickly added up. It would take a middle-class family all their income to attend to the needs of just two students. For those on minimum wage, he had no idea how they did it. When it cameto the unemployed, there simply was no way they could cope. His little mental activity was opening his eyes to a reality he had always thought he knew but was realising he did not. There was desperation in the society and that desperation was breeding crime and lawlessness. It was easy to pride oneself with being law abiding when all was financially well. By his recent line of reasoning, the worst criminals were those who committed crimes despite being financially comfortable. The politicians were at the head of that group.

He called two of the real estate agents and scheduled a meeting. One was available that afternoon and would be happy to meet him in thirty minutes. He logged into his bank account and whistled when he saw his balance. He hoped he would be paid his salary on time. His savings were depreciating faster than the arctic ice and with it his peace of mind. It was a long time since he had lived from pay check to pay check. It was not a good way to live. The amount of money he would be spending over the next few months or even years was enough to give him a slight headache. He instinctively thought of seeing a doctor. It had been a while. Too many friends were having heart attacks. His guess was that none of them saw it coming.

The meeting was easier than he had imagined. The agent, a smartly dressed woman who preferred to be called Lauren, was already at the apartment when he arrived. He immediately liked the place. It was not in a noisy neighbourhood. She would need time to learn the ways of humanity before being ushered into the world of conflict and unpleasant people. Most of the other tenants were working class men and women who left in the morning only to return in the evening to prepare for a new day. They will not have time to be interested in the affairs of their neighbours. Few had kids. The place was as quiet as a graveyard.

"May I ask what you do for a living?" she asked when he wrote her a cheque.

"I'm a writer," he replied. He had come to realise that people were always wary of journalists. This often amused him. It was not as if he was going to write some damning article about the apartment or refuse to pay rent. Next to lawyers, they were the most loathed. The tax man at least did not have to meet people and could always claim the ambiguous title of Public Servant.

He had the keys to the apartment by the time he left and she remarked before they parted ways that that was her easiest deal till date. He intended to visit a furniture shop sometime during the week. Just the most basic items like a bed, a small refrigerator, sofas, and a reading table would do. He may spend time there himself from time to time until she eventually occupied it.

It was with a sense of accomplishment and foreseeable financial hardship that he drove back home. He drove as cautiously as his busy mind would allow. The other unruly drivers did not make the task any easier. He was in the middle of a major traffic jam when his cell phone rang. It was in his hip pocket. He blamed himself for not putting it somewhere more accessible before getting into the car. Mike always teased him about getting a new car. His had Bluetooth features with which he could answer his cell phone while driving at the press of a button.

The phone rang incessantly. He decided whoever was calling really needed to speak to him. With a look of irritation on his face and a wary eye on the road he kept a hand on the wheel, lifted his butt as much as the seatbelt would allow and reached into the hip pocket. After several attempts while the phone rang on he managed to retrieve it between two fingers. He was not one of those who believed answering a call while driving was dangerous. Texting while driving was something he never did. That was dangerous.

It was Mason. He answered.

"Listen pal," he said with a sense of urgency. "I am being followed. Write down these numbers."

"Who are they?" Jeff asked. Mason was not a man easily scared. He always carried a gun. For him to be talking like that showed he was in some very grave danger.

"Just get these numbers."

"I am driving," Jeff said.

"Stop in the middle of the road if you have to!" Mason yelled.

"Give me the number."

"LAA414A. Got it?"

"Got it. Where are you? I will call the cops."

"It is a police car," Mason said sarcastically. "The occupants do not look like cops at all. I can see at least four men inside. Go to my wife. Make sure she is safe. Tell her to leave the house with the kids."

"Stay on the line Mason," Jeff said.

"Just do as I say and let me handle this. Something tells me it has to do with either that fat Madam Caro or the lecturer. I told you she was dangerous. Didn't think they'll come for me. I believe they are looking for the perfect place to attack."

"You think they want to assassinate you?"

"I'm of more use to them alive. Head home. Call Becky and tell her to start packing before you arrive. If you need any help, contact my partner Toby. He will know what to do. He knows all about the cases I am working on except the Caro one. I'll try not to mention your name if I get tortured. Can't guarantee how long I'll last though. Never did well with pain. Remember not to go to the cops. Do not call this number again in case they get my phone. Here we go."

Mason ended the call. Jeff took a few seconds to clear his head. He called Mason's wife and delivered the message. She was all hysterical and kept yelling incomprehensible words. When he finally got her to calm down he asked her to pack a few things. He would be meeting her in a few minutes. The kids were in school so it was decided she would pack only vital stuff like documents, passports, and money before heading to their school to pick them up. She had her own gun too. Being married to a private detective always had its hazards. He would meet her in front of the school. From there they would head to his home. He knew he had to inform his wife under normal circumstances. The circumstances were far from normal. They were about to have guests in their home and even he could not say how long they were going to stay. She had to get ready even if it meant having only a few minutes' notice.

He drove with his mind torn in several directions. It was a struggle to think and stay focused on the road at the same time. If Caro had sent her people to get Mason, what did she know? What would she find out? What if he was wrong and they were completely unrelated? What if he, Mason, was the primary target? Many kidnappers made outrageous demands. The amount of money they demanded often led families to borrow huge sums of money. Mason was by no means a wealthy man. His guess was that the man could not be worth more than a hundred grand. He was just a hardworking man who invested in his family. Money had never been his motivation. He was popular but not rich. How would the criminals know this? Most equated popularity with wealth.

He kept hoping Mason would call to tell him he had just been overly paranoid. When he arrived the school and he had not called yet he had to assume the worst. Becky who had been waiting with her two sons under a tree when he arrived walked up to him firing off a barrage of questions.

"Let's get the kids settled then we can talk privately," he said.

"They are old enough to understand," she replied. "Just tell me what is going on."

He took a deep breath, asked the kids to wait in their mother's car and then waited for them to leave.

"I think your husband has been kidnapped," he said. "He called me. He said some people in a police car were following him."

She placed her arms akimbo.

"You think," she said. "Did you call the police?"

"No," Jeff said. "He specifically advised me not to call the cops. I told you the men were in a police car."

"Which they could have stolen," she said.

"Let's just get to my place," a frustrated Jeff said. "I am as shocked as you."

She made no attempt to leave.

"I am still wondering why he called you," she said. "Why didn't he call me? My guess is that whatever it is that is going on must be connected to you. Do you know who could have kidnapped him, if indeed he has been kidnapped?"

He shook his head. "No."

"My husband should better not come to any harm," she warned pointing a finger at him.

"Let's just stay positive," he said. "Follow me. I'll lead the way."

"I know where your house is," she said and walked back to her car.

Jeff drove slowly, making sure she was always in sight in the rear-view mirror. He knew the route could be tricky. When the traffic got easier he called Nneka and delivered the news as simply as he could. She took it calmly. She knew Becky. His house had only three bedrooms. They decided Becky should have a room to herself while the kids shared one. That meant they would have to go back to sleeping in the same room.

Nneka was waiting in front of the house when they arrived. The two women hugged casually. They were led inside. He announced he had some urgent business to attend to. Becky was still adamant and insisted on calling the police. He tried his best to persuade her otherwise. Mason had been involved in a lot of kidnap cases. If he did not want the police involved then that must be the best option. He left a fuming Becky and a busy Nneka behind. The kids did not seem too bothered and were already watching their favourite cartoon. They had agreed their mother would have to explain to them why they could not return home.

His destination was the doctor's home. He saw no point in delaying anything. His house was in the same compound as his clinic. He knew the clinic but had never met the man. As he drove he tried to calm himself down. The doctor was his only outside link to Caro and her establishment.

The place was busy when he arrived. He wondered if the patients would mind if they knew the man they literally entrusted their lives to was unqualified. He would not have been that busy if he was not good at what he did. He walked up to the reception and told her he wanted to see Doctor Salami. She gave him a form to fill which he did. Everything he wrote down was false including his name. She advised him to take a seat when he returned it.

The patients were of all age groups. For some reason the baby being held by the woman beside him began to yell uncontrollably, its eyes fixed on him like he was the problem. The place was so noisy he almost wished he had not come. He soon realised there were three other doctors in the place, one female and two males. One looked like he was fresh out of medical school. The other looked more like a thug than a doctor.

9

CHAPTER 9

Dr F. Salami was well respected in his community. He was a man most looked up to and his success had inspired a lot of neighbourhood kids who would have been content just working in a local post office to venture into the medical profession. Many wanted to be like Salami. He was happily married with two kids. His son was predictably in medical school. He was named Salami Jnr. His daughter was a pharmacy student. The official story was that Dr Salami's late parents had been peasant farmers. They had survived by growing cassava which they then processed into garri, one of the staple foods in the south of the country. This was then transported into town in bags to be sold to so called garri merchants. The merchants then took them to the major cities where they were sold for a huge profit. The further away from the farm it was sold the higher the profit, much like cocaine. Garri was hard work to the farmer but big business to the merchant.

Late Mr. Salami believed in raw hard work. He was an honest man who went to his farm before the sun rose and returned just before sunset. His approach to life was simple: work hard, do good to others, and invest in your children. It did not take him long to figure out that the world was evolving and that soon the successful would be those who had a good education. His own father had looked upon the western education and culture as a sort of corruption to the well-established Ibo culture

101

he had grown to know and respect. He could complete his primary education only because his teacher at the time was impressed with his level of intelligence and felt it would be a shame if he did not go further. Unfortunately, he was later transferred to another school where no one paid him any attention.

Salami senior's father had five wives and countless number of children. Those days, lots of children meant lots of hands in the farm. Needs then were simple. All you needed was a place to sleep, food, clothing, and a reliable water source. Nobody paid for anything. Nobody needed electricity or pipe borne water that they had to pay for. The bush was everyone's toilet. The old man could see that change was in the air. The new road that cut through their village was a constant reminder of the new world that was coming. The cars that drove past and the new council buildings that were erected told of a new order and new rulers. The kings they had known were now answerable to a system of government only few could understand.

During his trips to the town to sell garri he saw men who had embraced the western education and what they had achieved through it. It was not just the money. He had seen doctors and engineers at work. He knew his children had to be educated all the way to university level. Many of his mates mocked him. They nicknamed him Owl because he was only seen at night. He did not mind. The bags of garri was his assurance that his children would not be denied the education he had lost out on. Many of those who mocked him did not understand how the world was changing. He had given up trying to convince them.

As often as he could he would call his son into his hut and talk to him about why he should take his studies very seriously. He too had a nickname; The Book Slave. He was always reading. He understood the pressures he faced. He explained to him that they were living at an interface and when men lived at a time of change those who embraced the change were often scorned and ridiculed. The future would prove him right. Patience was a virtue he must embrace.

When his son got admitted into one of the prestigious universities in the city his joy knew no bounds. The fees were expensive but he had told his son to face his studies and let him do the worrying. He worked harder and produced more bags of garri.

He began to realise that no matter how much he toiled, he just had to find a way to augment his income. That was when his wife suggested he find a shop to rent in the city. They would have to boycott the middle man and sell directly to the consumers. It was hard at first. They did a lot of borrowing which took years to pay off. Eventually they started making profit. The only problem was that the school fees kept going up. The new world was going to be very expensive.

Salami jnr. did not know what to expect when he got to the university. Being one from the village, he found that his ways were very different from those who had spent all their lives in the city. He talked different and had no clue who most of the celebrities they liked to talk about were. The lifestyle was different. Women dressed differently too. They wore provocative clothes that were as distracting as they were disturbing. He had been brought up to believe he was not supposed to have any intimacy with any woman before his father and her father had approved and the dowry paid. It was different on campus. Most of his fellow students lived immorally.

The women found him attractive. His ignorance made him different from the others. Eventually he started dating one of the campus girls. They quickly learnt that garri was not one of his problems. It was cheap in the village but expensive on campus. Before he knew what he was doing he was neck deep in the lifestyle. He soon had lots of girlfriends on campus. His studies began to suffer. He managed to scale through to the clinical stage. If he had failed, he would have been withdrawn from medical school like many of his friends.

Clinical school was different. It was more hands on and they had to come to the teaching hospital at night after long hours of lectures in the daytime. He spent his free time wondering just who created such an evil system. Life in the village was far easier. His father advised him to stay focused when he complained. Life was not to be understood but overcome. He had no clue what his son had been up to.

It was during his final year in school that the inevitable happened. He failed his final exams. After years of near misses, he had come to develop a new philosophy that he was the bounce back kid. He had failed several times before only to pass at the final attempt. This did not happen. When he realised he had been withdrawn from medical school he went into a period of depression that lasted almost a year. His father had no clue that there was even a possibility of that happening. They would talk for hours about his graduation that he knew was never to be. He even feared the old man would have a heart attack if he knew. He kept it to himself and pretended all was well. Come graduation day he acted like he had graduated. They had a party in the village in his honour. The old man died proud believing he had at least achieved his goal.

One of his friends who had been withdrawn as well introduced him to a doctor who had an abortion clinic. Abortion was illegal at the time unless on medical grounds. The man was a gynaecologist and looked to recruit would be doctors to do his dirty work. Medical grounds for abortion could always be invented. He made a lot of money even though he battled with his conscience daily. He was brought up catholic and abortion was murder to him. They treated other minor ailments like urinary tract infections, sexually transmitted diseases, cold, malaria, typhoid fever, diarrhoea, and others. His boss had a simple motto: Don't try to be a hero. He always advised them to refer anything they could not handle to the hospital.

It was while he was working there that he met Madam Caro. She had come with five of her 'daughters' at the time. He had commented on how pretty they all were. They had been treated for various ailments. Two were pregnant and had to undergo terminations. He found this odd. Daughters in that part of the world found ways to cover up their bad behaviour. They would rather find a friend to confide in than talk to their mother. The fact that two would be pregnant at the same time and then come with their mother for a termination was strange. She was wealthy and paid well. Other 'daughters' were treated over time.

One day she asked him if he ever thought of venturing out on his own. He told her he would not mind if he could find the capital. She was more than happy to lend him the money if he would agree to be her family's physician. He had no idea just how large and diverse this family was. It was during this business deal that she did her research and realised he was not qualified. She did not mind. It worked well for her. He had treated her well so far. His level of experience was good enough for her, qualification or not. His secret was safe with her. No one was a saint.

He eventually opened his own practice with money he had saved plus a loan from her to make up the rest of the capital. He used to have some visitor from the licensing department in the early days. Madam Caro always had a way of getting them off his back. He was quick to learn that she was as dangerous as she was generous. One wrong move on his side could spell disaster for him. He learnt not to ask too many questions even when he saw some of her daughters with wounds that were suspicious of abuse. Once he attended to one of them who had what looked like torture wounds. She had eventually died. Madam Caro had advised that he dispose of the body promptly. He made out a death certificate with cause of death being pneumonia. The body had been incinerated. The guilt plagued his mind for years after this.

He did a bit of digging of his own and soon realised what she was up to. He also found out she knew a lot of powerful men in high places including the medical board. His plan was to train his son to be a doctor. As soon as he graduated and had his practicing licence he would take over the place and he would retire. That would be when he would terminate every link with Madam Caro.

Working without a licence was not easy. It was like driving a hired car. He had to make sure he did not make mistakes. He studied hard and polished his communication skills. Thus, he was more popular than some of the registered doctors in town. His son benefitted from his wealth of experience. He had never failed a class and this made him proud. He even benefitted from the Obaseki Foundation scholarship because of his performance.

He could not wait for him to graduate and become the first authentic medical doctor from the family. His own father had died years ago believing that his hard work had paid off. The man had died happy and proud. In a way, he had achieved what he set out to achieve. Without his sacrifice, he would still be in the village relying on garri to survive while the world moved forward without him.

He had met his wife at a dinner party in which he had been invited as a guest of honour. His status in the community meant lots of doors were opened easily to him. He chose carefully which of the doors he walked through. A wrong move and one inquisitive doctor would find out his little secret. She had overseen catering at the dinner. One thing led to another and they started dating. She married him believing he was a doctor. She still did. Not even his family knew his secret and he intended to keep it that way.

The work was satisfying. He liked the idea of helping end other people's suffering. Occasionally, he would go to the village with a team of overseas doctors to help those who could not make the trip to the big hospitals in town. They had a mobile surgery that was paid for by generous donations from people the world over. Men and women who thought they would die blind regained their sight. Women condemned to lives of seclusion and pain because they had an inexplicable growth in their belly had the growth removed and their social lives restored. Sometimes the impact of what they did brought tears to his eyes. He was given a title in appreciation for the good work he did. They called him The One Who Ends the Suffering of the Poor. The day he received the title he dedicated it to his late father and reminded those present how he was the product of a man many mocked and called The Owl.

Life was good. He had long lost any fear of being imprisoned. If he had not been caught over the years, it was unlikely he would get caught now. His only problem was Madam Caro. He went to work with a sense of purpose and satisfaction. They even had a psychologist who came around once a week to help the many lost teens caught up in the tragedy that was the current modern life. Nothing pleased him more than to help someone out of darkness and poverty. He tried to do for many what his father had done for him. It was his own way of giving back to society. At least eight people were in school on their way to becoming doctors and engineers because of his scholarship. His message to them was loud and clear: Fail a class and you lose your scholarship.

He was proud of his children. So far, he had managed to instil in them the discipline they needed to survive in a world he knew to be cruel and immoral. One wrong alliance is all it takes to destroy a life of hard work and his children understood this. It was for this same reason that he sometimes felt guilty about his role in Madam Caro's set up. If he could severe ties with her, he would. She had leverage on him and she knew it. His day of freedom was coming. All he had to do was sit tight and wait.

His office was spacious compared to a lot of others. It was decorated with accolades he had supposedly won. There was an enlarged picture of his late parents on the wall directly above his head. Many initially think they represent some NGO he was a part of. He always took time to explain, with a sense of pride, who they were and how he would never have been who he was without their foresight and sacrifice.

Many troubled teenagers had been made to gaze into the eyes of the late Salami senior. He would make them stand in front of the picture and tell them tales of how he had endured name calling and peer pressure just so that his son would have a better future. Most of the self-absorbed teens would stare speechlessly with a look of awe in their eyes. Sometimes he would stand in front of the picture and gaze into their eyes for hours. Sometimes memories and the realisation of the sacrifice they made would hit him and tears would come to his eyes.

When Jeff walked into his office he had just finished his little ritual. On this particular day, he had been strangely apprehensive, as if some impending doom was coming. He had called his kids to make sure all was well. No one reported any issues. He had learnt never to let his emotions get in the way and flashed his usual smile as he shook hands with the man on the other end of the table.

"Nice shirt," he said as Jeff sat. "Where did you get it? It's been rumoured that us doctors don't know anything about fashion so I take my clue from well-dressed clients."

"I buy from any shop. Not particular about fashion," Jeff said laughing. "Tell you a secret, let the wife do the shopping."

"I let her," Salami said. "That's what gets me into trouble. She is stuck in the eighties."

The two men laughed at the joke. Salami instantly took a liking to him. He could see how he had built a large following for himself. He wished he had not come for the reason he had.

"So," Salami said assuming a business-like attitude. "What brings you here? I don't think I have seen you before."

"I am a new patient doc," Jeff said. "I have this constant headache at the back of my head that I have had for years. Sometimes my vision gets all blurry and my eyes water. Seen a lot of doctors and done several imaging. Nothing has been found yet."

"Don't do any more," Salami said leaning forward, his hands on the table. "Those things can give you brain cancer. They are expensive too. Have you ever had migraine?"

"No."

He nodded his head and watched him for a while as if he was about to announce that he had just won the lottery.

"Tell me more about this headache," he said eventually.

Jeff went on to describe the headache. It was true that he often had these headaches that blurred his vision. He had been to two doctors who thought it was caused by two totally different things. The first made him do a CT scan while the other made him do an MRI. It was much later that he realised they got a percentage for every patient they referred for imaging. He still had the headache from time to time.

When he was through with his description the doctor invited him to sit up on the bed. He took his blood pressure, checked his temperature before listening to his chest.

"You have the heart of a twenty-year old," he said "I can tell you are someone who takes care of yourself. Keep it up."

Jeff nodded. He felt proud of himself. The doctor then proceeded to check his neck. He made him turn his neck in every direction, even made him twist the neck in ways he never knew were possible.

"You may return to your seat now," Salami said when he was done with his examination. "I think I know what the problem is. Those tests were a complete waste of time and money. These young doctors of today rely so much on tests. Clinical acumen, that is the key and that is why medicine is a form of art. The body talks to you if you know how to make it speak. You must know how to observe, feel for anything out of place."

"What do you think it is?" Jeff asked.

"I will show you," he said and picked up the I-pad on his table. His fingers moved swiftly across the screen like some computer wizard. He turned the I-pad to face Jeff.

"What is it?"

"Watch the short video," he said. "It is called cervical spine dysfunction. You can hold the I-pad. I'll let you watch while I enter some details in your file."

Jeff watched the video. It was a tutorial of some sort. A metallic female voice that sounded like it was about to hypnotise him explained the images that appeared on the screen. In the end, he felt like he was qualified to be a consultant of some sorts on the topic of cervical spine dysfunction.

"You need to see a physiotherapist," Salami said. "I know a very good one and I will quickly type out a referral letter. You will be good in less than a week and that's a promise. No money back guarantees here but you can count on my word. Get a new pillow too. Don't let the wife choose it."

They laughed again. Jeff rubbed the back of the neck as he contemplated how to approach the subject that had brought him there. The rapport they had developed in the short time he had known the doctor made it difficult. He cleared his throat.

"Have a cough too?" Salami asked.

"Yes," he lied.

"Hmm. Let me see. Open your mouth like a crocodile about to swallow a Kardashian and say 'Aaah!'".

Jeff tried not to laugh as he obeyed. A bright light from a surprisingly small torch was pointed into his mouth.

"Interesting," the doctor said.

"You see anything?" he asked.

"Your mother in law," he said jokingly. "Poor woman. What did you do to her? I think you may just have a slight cold. Throat is as healthy as a shark's. Ever heard the joke about the python with the sore throat? Never mind. If it gets any worse just come back. Anything else?"

Jeff shook his head and cleared his throat again.

"You smoke?"

"Used to," he said. "Gave it up years ago."

"Good for you," the doctor said. "Think of all the money you must have saved by not smoking. A dollar saved is a dollar earned."

He typed on his keyboard and stretched his hand towards the printer on the table. He snatched up the referral letter as soon as the printer spat it out, signed it and handed it to Jeff.

"Tell him this was your first visit here," he said. "He will give you a discount. I will see you again in about a week or two. Just call reception and make a booking. See you then."

"There's something else I came here for," he said.

The doctor's smile did not wane.

"Go on," he said. "By the way, would you like some water?"

"I'm fine, thanks," he said. He felt genuinely sorry that he had to bring up the topic. "I have this problem that I think you can help me with. It is about a girl I came to know recently."

Salami nodded, urging him on.

Jeff went on to tell him about his encounter with Ehi as summarily as he could. He gave the doctor some insight as to what really went on in the place and his plans to get Ehi out of there before making sure the place was shut down for good. He deliberately left out the fact that he knew he was not a registered doctor. He would bring it up if he faced any resistance. When he was through the doctor's response surprised him. He placed his hand on his forehead and wept. Unsure what to do he just sat there and waited for him to regain his composure. Eventually he reached for a tissue from the tissue box on his table and wiped his tears away. For a while he could not look him in the eye.

"I cannot tell you how hard I have tried to distance myself from that woman," he said when he was able to speak. "One of her girls died in this clinic. I believe she was tortured. Before her death, she had been my patient. I should have done something. You need to be very careful. I understand you are a teacher."

"I am actually a journalist," he said. "I just put that down to avoid any bias. Most people tend to treat lawyers and journalists differently. Everyone loves teachers."

"That's because they always carry on as if they are at war with everyone," he said. "I hope you are not recording any of this."

Jeff assured him that he was free to speak freely. It was just between the two of them. All he wanted was to see Ehi free. The doctor nodded thoughtfully and stood. He turned to face the giant picture on the wall behind him. For a while he just stood there with one hand on his chin and the other arm across his chest. Jeff wondered who the old couple were. The man looked like he had seen the days when dinosaurs roamed the earth a few centuries back. He had that many wrinkles. For some reason, he could not take his eyes off the man's eyes. There was something in them. It suddenly dawned on him that the weather-beaten face had eyes that could have belonged to Barak Obama. There was a certain hope that burned in them that was inexplicable.

Salami turned and perched on his desk.

"I have a son and a daughter," he began. "Every parent worries that he would not be there to ensure his kids attain a certain level of maturity and independence. I have prayed often that my life be kept until my kids graduate. Then I can die a happy man."

"You will live longer than that," Jeff said. "You will live to see your grandkids."

Salami nodded in acknowledgment of this common prayer.

"I am being practical," he said. "I will like to see them get married and have kids, my grandkids. But, I am just saying that if ever I were to die, let me at least die knowing they have the necessary skills and means to carry on. It is a cruel world out there. You should know. You are a journalist. I believe you have covered a lot of atrocities on this wicked planet."

"I sure have," Jeff said.

"All I do," Salami went on, "all my blood and sweat is for my children to have some degree of security if anything happens to me. I have seen a lot sir. When a boy or girl has no adult to protect him or her, he is at the mercy of every evil man and woman out there, and there are lots of them looking for the weak to oppress. It is for this reason that I started my trust fund. Not many know about it. They cater to orphans and widows. Most do not even know I am the one behind their school fees and bags of food now and then. Not just me, I must say. There are many good men out there. They donate generously to our cause. Good men and women are not as loud as the bad guys. Most of them want to remain anonymous. Excuse me."

He pressed a button on his intercom and asked the receptionist how many people were still waiting for him. He instructed her to squeeze them into the other doctors' waiting list. He stood and looked at Jeff.

"Madam Caro has dirt on me," he said. "She and the people she knows are very dangerous. I can tell you because I know some of them. They are quite powerful too. If you need a job in any ministry in this country she can get it done with a single phone call. That is how connected she is. Do not be fooled by her appearance."

"Then why does she not connect those girls?" Jeff asked. "Why not help them get meaningful employment?"

The doctor smiled. "Man is a queer creature," he said. "We have weird needs. Sick needs. I dare say she maintains this connection by what she can provide them. We carry on as if water, food, and shelter are the primary needs of man. Men need power, pleasure, and assurance or security. These are the primary needs. Wars are fought because men want to guarantee these needs. A man would choose these over any mansion or clothing. This is the underlying principle behind slavery and colonisation."

Jeff tried to understand him. Someone once told him that most doctors were deranged mentally and he was beginning to wonder if it was true.

"At the core of our being is something very strangely evil. Trust me on this. As a doctor people tell me things they will not tell anyone else. We have a psychologist here. They tell her even worse. Why do you think the adult entertainment industry is worth billions of dollars every year? Even drug dealers are becoming pimps. Many call it a deranged industry yet it thrives just beneath what we call the sane and decent world. What do you think would happen if the plug was pulled on this industry? Many will lapse into a state of depression. What does that tell you?"

Jeff shrugged.

"I have listened to Caro talk," he went on. "We are quite close, she and I. We do have dinner sometimes. She believes she is giving those girls hope. Initially it is easy to judge but when she gives you her own point of view it shows a certain version of truth that is as scary as it is disconcerting."

"And what exactly is her version?" Jeff asked. "What is her excuse for holding people in a state that is nothing short of slavery?"

"That many women and girls are abused in the comfort of their own homes," he replied. "That many babies are being thrown away by underage teens who have no means of taking care of them, teens that would be shunned by society if they keep the baby. That domestic violence kills hundreds of thousands of women every year and maims a lot more. That the only way to stop this is to balance the equation; give women a level playing field by empowering them in any way possible."

"Or enriching herself?" Jeff asked sarcastically.

"You need to be a bit more broad-minded," the doctor said stiffly. "I am not saying I support her. I am just saying that sometimes I feel they are better off where they are than where they would have been. It is a shame to society and no less shame to her. What do you do with a girl who runs away from home because she is being molested by her step dad?"

"Report to the police," Jeff said. "Get him arrested."

"And after they have arrested the sole breadwinner of the home what happens to the rest when they are left homeless and at the mercy of even more sinister molesters? Will you arrest him and endanger the rest or let him be for their sake?"

"Don't give me impossible examples," Jeff said. "Let us focus on this one problem."

"I am giving you real examples. I know those girls and what they have been through. I also know what they are going through. It is like the situation in Syria. There is no winning. It is never black or white when it comes to reality. All people know is how to judge. 'Abortion is evil,' they chant. Yet no one judges the hidden one responsible for the pregnancy. Stop fornicating and you will not need abortion. 'Prostitution is sin,' they cry, yet no one wants to take in the poor girl child in the street or even find out how she ended up there. When she gets picked up by women like Caro men like you judge her."

"Whose side are you on?" Jeff asked looking a bit confused.

"Why should it be about taking sides?" he asked. "Most of those men who go to her resort have their own daughters safe at home. They plunder our economy so that their children may have a good and secure future while they exploit the children of the unfortunates. Let's say you find a way to make her change her mind and let them go free, what will they do? There are hundreds of thousands of youths walking the streets looking for work. Would they join the rat race or what? The other day I placed an ad in the local newspaper for another receptionist. Do you know how many applications we got? It is ridiculous."

Jeff pinched the bridge of his nose and shook his head. The man was speaking hard truths that he had often contemplated himself. He had learnt that the only way to navigate the earth with his conscience intact was to adhere to his moral code and leave sentiment out of his decision making. Let God deal with those seemingly impossible situations that were made impossible by humans in the first place.

"I just want this particular girl out of there," he said. "I will take care of her."

"And I will help you," he said. "Provided I do not put myself, my business, or my family on the line. I will not take any unreasonable risk. I have come too far to crash. I hope you understand this. My children will not end up in the streets!"

"I can assure you that what I have in mind will not put you or your children in the street," Jeff said. "Listen to the plan first and if you don't like it we can modify it or you can walk away from it. It is a very simple plan but for it to succeed we need your help."

Salami looked out of his window. There was nothing but a brick wall and a hibiscus plant in view. He turned and sat on his chair. Jeff leaned forward and explained what he thought was a foolproof plan. When he was through the doctor leaned back and sighed heavily, a worried look on his face. Afterwards he did not speak much. He seemed numb even when they had their parting handshake, leaving Jeff wondering if he had other plans in his mind, plans that could jeopardise everything. He had not raised the topic of his registration status out of sympathy but he knew he would wield it as a weapon if necessary. He just hoped he would not have to.

When Jeff left, Salami sat on his desk and faced his parents. It was as if he sought answers in their ancient wisdom. The man he had just spoken to was not from the medical board, thank goodness, but posed as much of a risk nonetheless.

"What should I do?" he asked his dead father. "Should I go to Caro and report everything that has happened? Should I go along with what that mad man is suggesting? She can ruin my life if this goes wrong and she finds out. He on the other hand is the devil I do not know."

The eyes of his father pierced through his like it did when he was alive. The man stood for truth and honour. If it was him sitting on the desk, there would have been no doubt what he would have decided. The man put honour above even his family. He would rather die than tell a lie or support evil. In a way, he felt ashamed that he even asked. He felt ashamed that knowing the truth, he was contemplating the coward's path. Life was not as straightforward as it had been during the times of his father. His decisions could threaten the future of his family and that of others.

He decided he would pay Madam Caro a visit. It would be a cordial one. If the opportunity presented itself, he would find out if she was the one behind the kidnap of Jeff's friend. She hardly hid anything from him, not even her darkest fantasies, thoughts or deeds. Being her doctor, she knew he was bound by the confidentiality act. The fact that he was not qualified did not make it any less binding. Besides, she knew him to be a man whowas trustworthy. If she kidnapped Mason, he would find out. If he could, he would try to persuade her to let just this one girl go and save everyone the trouble.

He left the office and headed home. His stay at home wife was in the kitchen preparing dinner. The aroma of her chicken soup filled the air as he walked in. The two shared a passionate kiss before he settled into his favourite chair. She knelt on one knee and proceeded to remove his shoes and socks, a habit she had adopted from the day they got married.

"You look worried today," she observed. "What is wrong?"

"Just had a difficult patient," he said. "Had a good day before he showed up."

"I thought we agreed that once you walk through that front door you leave all your work woes behind," she said. "You are not being a good boy today."

He chuckled. She stood and undid his tie.

"Pardon me," he said.

"Your son called," she said. "He passed. Top of the class."

"That's great," he said without much enthusiasm. "I knew he would. Takes after his dad."

"Are you saying I did not play a part?" she asked.

"You know what I mean," he said. "Your daughter takes after you. She's good, but not top material. It's the DNA."

She slapped him jokingly on the cheek, picked up the shoes and headed for the bedroom. He admired her behind and thanked God for her.

"By the way," she said from the bedroom. "He wants to know if you will buy him that car. You promised."

"A promise is a promise," he said. "Besides, he has earned it. I think he can handle a car. He has handled himself well."

He closed his eyes and tried to meditate. Jeff's face kept popping up in his mind. Eventually he gave it up.

"I have to see Madam Caro tonight," he said.

"What for?" she asked. "Can't it wait?"

"We are thinking of expanding," he lied. He had rehearsed this on his way home. "Other business partners will be there too."

He waited for her response. She did not reply. She knew Caro as the one who provided most of the funds he used to set up his clinic. The two had never met. His excuse was that he did not like mixing business and family. He knew she had her suspicions and had once asked why she had agreed to finance his project. His reply had been that she had seen potential in his plans and as a good business woman had agreed to invest.

She returned to the kitchen. While she attended to the food he sat on the chair thinking. She was saying something about a friend of hers who had come visiting and the troubles she was having with her husband who was a serial cheat. He scarcely listened, replying only in monotones just to make it look like he was following the complicated story. Eventually he dozed off.

10

CHAPTER 10

From the clinic, he drove straight to the orphanage that had been referred to in Mason's report. He called Mason's partner Toby to see if Mason had been in touch. He had no clue what was going on so he updated him on the last phone call he had received from him. Toby was not happy that he had not called him immediately after the incident. He was a small man who looked like he had liked mathematics when he was in school; thick pair of glasses, front teeth that could have been a rabbit's and all. Time was very crucial. He gave him the licence plate number of the car that had been following Mason. He could sense the urgency in his voice when he promised to investigate it. He assured Jeff that they had contacts in the streets and some very strange places, the very reason they were the go-to company for kidnap cases.

"They chose the wrong person," he said angrily after their conversation.

He was confident he would at least find out which group was behind the kidnap. The way he spoke gave Jeff some degree of confidence that the mystery would be unravelled soon. He promised to call him back once he had something important before ending the call. Jeff drove on with renewed vigour.

The orphanage was right in the middle of a ghetto. He often thought it was not the best place to have it but what did he know? Someone may have wanted cheap land or some other advantage. There was a rusty gate hopelessly guarding the entrance. It was wide open. Apparently, they had no money to hire a security guard or a gardener to tend the garden and overgrown grass. He could tell that the children were being used to tend the place. It was none of his business. He was not one of those who considered children working as child abuse. Obese children spending countless hours on the couch was, to him, far worse. They needed the experience and exercise provided they also had the chance to play.

It was a two-storey building with a massive mahogany door that reminded him of the days he used to go to church with his parents. He knocked on the door and waited. A smiling girl who looked ten opened it.

"Good day, Sir," she said.

"Hello child," he said returning the smile. "May I see whoever is in charge?"

"Come with me, Sir," she said.

He followed her through a corridor that had various paintings that were obviously done by children. There were some photos of politicians on the wall as well as others he did not recognise. She stopped in front of a door with the word MATRON engraved on it and knocked.

"Come in," a thickset voice that almost sounded masculine said from within.

She opened the door and stepped aside. He walked in to see the fattest woman he had ever seen sitting on the other side of a very large table that looked centuries old. He could smell food in the air and could tell she had been eating.

"Welcome," she said wiping her mouth with the back of her hand. "Please, sit down."

He sat. She smiled.

"Would you like something to drink?" she asked. "Coffee?"

"I'm fine, thanks," he said.

"My name is Veronica. What brings you to our nice little orphanage?" she asked.

"I'm Jacob," he lied. "My wife and I are thinking of adopting a child. She's at home but I'll come with her next time."

"That's fine," she said. "Most of them are asleep now. This is siesta time. I'll get you some files and you can see what we have. By the way, what do you do for a living?"

"I'm a businessman," he said.

"I like businessmen and women. They are our biggest donors," she said as she struggled out of her chair. She walked to a set of cabinets behind her, opened one and brought out a thick file.

"This place is not run by the government?" he asked.

"We are a private not-for-profit organisation," she replied. "We do have some politicians donate something now and then. We are in no way funded by the government."

"Must be tough then," he said.

"It is hard," she said as she set the thick file down on the table. "Nothing is easy in life. We do manage to run things in a reputable way. People are generous. Some people more than others. Any particular age in mind?"

"Not really. Four years. Anything from four to twelve."

"Male? Female?"

"Can I have both?" he asked jokingly. "That way they can keep each other company."

"You can have ten if you want," she said. "It really is up to you."

He sensed that she was eager to get rid of as much children as she could. In a way, this saddened him.

"Really?" he asked.

"Sure," she said, her focus on the file. "Orphanages play a role in society but the best place for a child to grow up is in a family setting. The worst family is better than an orphanage. In places like Australia they have dumped the traditional orphanage system for a system that encourages foster homes. We plan to adopt the same system here. So yes, if you feel you can take care of ten kids then we will give you ten kids. We do not pay foster carers like they do in Australia. Things like this should never be commercialised."

"I used to think it was difficult adopting a baby," he said.

"It is hard," she said. "You look responsible. If I thought you were a criminal or some child molester I will not allow you take one of our kids."

"Looks can be deceiving," Jeff said.

"Not to me," she said. "I have the instinct. Trust me. Here. These are siblings. They lost their parents three years ago. They were brought here by some police officers."

He looked at the picture. They looked solemn.

"Their parents died in a car accident or what?" he asked as he looked at the picture.

"No. Murder-suicide. Sad case. Unfortunately, it is becoming common these days. People watch too much porn. Humans are oversexualised these days and it is starting from childhood. People are marrying for the wrong reasons. Lord have mercy. Father was a soldier. Mother was a stay at home. Man comes home one day from the north east where they were battling terrorists to find another man in his house. Three shots are fired. When the police came, they found three dead bodies. Thankfully, these three were in school at the time. The youngest was only a toddler then. Life."

Jeff shook his head. He had seen such stories in the news. Seeing firsthand the children left behind gave him another perspective on the issue. He could not take his eyes off the oldest. He looked eight. He felt like adopting all four.

"How come they have never been adopted?" he asked.

"Most people do not like the idea of breaking them apart," she said. "They also do not want to have the burden of raising four children. Things are hard out there Jacob."

He nodded in agreement.

"What sort of monitoring do you have in place?" he asked.

"What do you mean?" she asked.

"Don't you follow up on them to see how they are settling into their new homes?" he asked. "How would you know if they are being mistreated or abused."

She shrugged. "We do not have the resources to do that. I know we should but that is financially impossible. That girl who let you in, she needs a heart surgery before she turns twelve or she may die. Do you know how much a heart surgery costs? We have children whose parents died of AIDS. They have the virus and need antivirals every day of their lives. By the time we attend to all these do you think there is anything left to travel say a thousand miles just to check up on a child?"

"So, there is no follow up," he said.

"No sir," she said. "Ideally there should be. We just hope that most of those who come here do so because they want to make a difference."

Jeff was shocked. He turned to another page. The file was full of children without parents, each with their own story. He was quite impressed at how much she knew and remembered about them. He kept going back to the four siblings. He would have to discuss with his wife first but something told him he would be taking them home someday.

"You seem to have a heart for them," she said. "Take them. They are quite lovely kids, always looking out for one another. The oldest is like a father to the others. I wish you had come when they were awake. Most who have seen the chemistry between them preferred not to separate them. I keep telling them that one day someone will come who will take them all."

Jeff could tell she had a special relationship with the kids and was grateful for that. He had heard of matrons who were so wicked they had no business being around kids, especially kids who had been through a lot already.

"The youngest is everyone's darling. Not one person has come here not wanting to adopt her. Like I said, they must go as a family or remain here."

"What happens when they become adults?"

"They move on. We provide them with as much education as we can give."

"So, they go on essentially without any family?"

"We try to reconnect them with their extended families when possible," she said. "Sometimes this is hard. Some were babies left on doorsteps of strangers, their biological mothers untraceable. The scourge of terrorism is also producing orphans that have had their entire villages wiped out. It is getting scary out there Jacob."

Jeff shook his head. He felt someone was failing the children somehow. Their fates should not depend on the goodwill of strangers.

"If I want to trace someone I believe had been here before being adopted," he asked, "would that be possible?"

"What do you mean?" she asked.

"Let's say someone was adopted from here ten years ago and I want to find her biological parents, would that be possible?"

She thought about it.

"We have had mothers who abandoned their babies when they were teens coming to look for them. Life has a way of settling things. Some left their babies to die, got married years later or things got better and felt they needed to reconnect with their abandoned baby. Sometimes it is a result of guilt. Other times it is because they cannot have another baby. I am no judge but sometimes I believe people get paid in their own coin. We do try to trace these babies. Sometimes a DNA test would have to be done to verify things. If they have been adopted there is nothing we can do. I think there were only two cases where the biological mother got her baby back. One returned the next year and the child was still with us. The longer they wait the harder it is. As a rule, we do not disturb those who have settled into new homes. It would be too confusing and destabilising to their psyche."

"Fair enough. What if I just want to know, I mean out of curiosity?"

"Did you abandon a baby?" she asked. "Usually I deal with women. I will find it strange that a man would have abandoned a baby."

"I had a girlfriend who got pregnant back in the day," he said. "She did not tell me she was pregnant when we broke up. I heard rumours that she gave birth to a girl but gave her away."

"You men should stop treating us like we are garbage, seriously," she said grudgingly. "What do you mean by you did not know she was pregnant?"

"She did not tell me," he said. "I was just eighteen at the time."

"That's why you have to zip up if you know you are not ready for that kind of responsibility. What is her name? Write it down."

"He wrote her name down. It was a thought that just came to him. She typed on the keyboard and began to murmur as she waited for any results.

"These things are slow sometimes," she said. "So, you were once a naughty boy."

"Unfortunately," he replied. "You get wiser as you grow."

"Some get more foolish as they grow older," she said quite angrily. "It will amaze you what some old men of today are doing. There is no shame anymore on earth. Those who should be advising the teens are the ones exploiting them. My prediction is that at this rate we are going to be needing more of this sort of establishments in the future. There you go. Is this her?"

She spun the monitor around. Jeff choked as he saw her. He was shocked at how young she looked. They had been teens at the time.

"She did leave a baby with us. Congratulations Jacob. You have a daughter you have never met. Let's hope she has found happiness and a good father."

Her words stung like bee stings. He felt some pain in his chest as he stared speechless at the picture of the once girlfriend he had booted out of his life so casually. It dawned on him that there had been others besides her.

"I do hope you have learnt to treat women better," she went on. "I was raised by a single mum. I know how hard it can be. There is this ignorant guy called Sotomayor on YOUTUBE who goes on and on about how black single mothers are the cause of all of society's woes. It takes two to make a baby unless you go for a sperm bank. Men have a way of passing on the blame to us. I never dated a man. I wanted to become a nun. I guess my mother's experience turned me off. Unfortunately, I cannot help you with her baby's current address. It's possible they have moved from there."

"Can I see the baby's picture?"

"Sure."

She turned the monitor to face her and did some more typing before turning it to face him again.

"Here. Pretty baby."

This time tears welled up in his eyes. He could not stop looking at her. He wondered at how ignorant and arrogant he could have been then not to have at least considered the possibility that he was responsible for the pregnancy. He had smartly denied it, calling her a whore who slept with every man she met even though he knew she was devoted to him. The problem was that at the time she was just one of several. It was a game. The reality was staring him right in the face. His game had created real consequences."

"I need to find her," he said desperately.

"No. I do not think so. Drop it at once Jacob. I did warn you. That is a no. Don't even try."

She turned the monitor away from him.

"You are one of those people I feel life has dealt a backhand slap," she went on. "Your daughter has moved on. Move on too. It's been too long. You think she even knows you exist? She has a father now. Even your girlfriend cannot be told anything about her."

He nodded and wiped the tears from his face.

"I will come back with my wife," he said tiredly.

"You care to make some donation?" she asked.

"I think I will," he said. "You folks are doing a great service to society despite all your deficiencies. On second thoughts, I think I would like that drink after all. Coffee."

"Sure. I'll go get some. Try not to think too much about the baby. Just hope and pray that she is happy. Do for the kids of others what you want others to do for your kids. That is what life is all about. Do unto others as you want to be done unto you."

She stood and left the room. He quickly pounced on the keyboard. She had shut down the computer but he quickly restarted it and went to her recent places. He returned to the page. He took a picture of the baby quickly with his phone before writing down the name and last known address of her adopting parents. Next, he wrote down the address of his ex. He quickly logged off when he heard her heavy footsteps approaching but not before writing down the IP address of the computer. He knew how to access computers remotely.

"Here you go," she said setting down the cup of coffee on the table and placing a cheque book beside it.

He sipped the black coffee thoughtfully while she talked about how generous donations made a lot of difference in the lives of the children in their care. He wondered if he should ask her about Madam Caro. She looked like an innocent woman just happy with her job. He did not think she was the type to be a part of some evil network. She did care for children and he could see that she was genuine. If she erred, it was by omission and not commission.

"Do you know any Madam Caro?" he asked.

"Of course, I do," she said excitedly. "She is one of our most frequent donors. Lovely woman too. I wish there were more like her. If she had her way she would adopt every child in this place."

"So, she does come here regularly then?"

"She does. I would say at least once every three months at least. Sometimes she comes with couples from abroad who want a baby. She wants to see every child in a loving home and every deserving couple with a child they can love."

"That's nice of her."

"Why do you ask?"

"I heard the same. She actually inspired me to come here," he said.

"You know her then?"

"Not personally," he said. "I have heard of her good works. How much do I donate? Would ten thousand be enough?"

"Better than nothing," she said.

He set the coffee down and wrote on the cheque book, gave it to her then announced his intention to leave. They chatted all the way to the entrance where they stood and chatted some more. He promised he would be coming back with his wife. They would come in the morning or evening when the kids would be awake. She gave him a hug when he offered his hand for a handshake. It was like hugging a giant panda. He felt like telling her to lose some weight. She was a fat woman with a good heart. If she dies of a heart attack some naïve mind would ask why bad things happens to good people.

Once in his car he looked at his cell phone. There were seven missed calls. One was from his wife. He wondered what his boss may have been calling for. There was none from Mason. He called Nneka and was relieved when she answered. He had been secretly worrying about the kidnappers coming to their home.

"Where have you been?" she asked. "There was a strange car parked across the street from our house. It was there for over an hour and the occupant just sat there."

"Was he looking at the house?" he asked, his heart pounding.

"I could not tell. I did manage to get the plate number."

"Good," he said. "Good job. Send me the number. How are our guests?"

"The kids are playing outside," she said. "Their mum is in the living room."

"Why are you whispering?" he asked.

"I'll tell you when you come," she said. "Be careful."

He drove as fast as he could. It was the wrong time of the day to be in traffic. It was hot and people were in a hurry to go home. He cursed and wished he had air conditioning in his car. For some reason, he thought of Donald Trump's helicopter. The rich did have it easy in every way. The sweat poured down his face like running wax from a melting candle when he rolled up the window. When he rolled it down hot air mixed with fumes threatened to suffocate him. The air was so toxic it stung his nostrils and eyes. In the end, he had to choose the heat and the sweat.

The traffic jam was one of the worst he had ever been in. Impatient drivers blasted their horns, making him wonder why they did that. The traffic was in almost lockdown mode and no amount of horn blasting would make a difference. The noise only added to the irritation.

Gbenga called again. He ignored it. He was not in the right frame of mind to be talking to his boss. When the phone kept on ringing he decided to answer it for the sake of his sanity.

"Someone saw you in traffic," he said. "Thought you'll be saved the rush hour nightmare by working at home."

"Went out at the wrong time," he said trying to stay calm. He did not like the idea of someone calling his boss just to tell him he was seen stuck in some traffic jam. He even believed it was the boss himself who saw him.

"You should be at home working Jeff," he said. "You should be working same hours as if you were here. When are you going to finish it?"

"Do you mind if I call you later?" Jeff asked. "It's really a slow traffic and I need to focus."

"Relax," Gbenga said. "The slower the traffic the easier it is. You talk as if I have never been in a traffic jam myself. How do you think I get home every day? Just answer the question."

"You'll get it when it's done," Jeff said impatiently.

There was a pause on the other end. He instantly regretted his remark.

"I think your short stay at home has made you forget certain facts," Gbenga said after a while. "You seem to have forgotten where your pay comes from."

"I'm sorry boss," he said. "I've been stressed lately. There is a lot going on in my life."

"Life is hard," he retorted. "Deal with it like the rest of us do. A lot of people will shed blood and sweat to be where you are but it seems you fail to understand that I did you a great favour. I want you to return everything that belongs to the company in your possession tomorrow."

"Are you firing me?" he asked in shock.

"You are at least smart enough to figure that out," he said and ended the call.

He dropped the phone on the passenger's seat and grabbed the wheels tightly. A strange chill ran down his whole body as the reality of life without a job and its financial implications hit him. Suddenly it seemed the world had stopped for a few seconds. In that moment, all he could hear was the pounding of his heart as he struggled to get air into his lungs. He honestly thought he was having a heart attack. Eventually he managed to take a deep breath and the world started moving again. He wanted to go home, lie down, close his eyes and never wake up again.

A hundred thoughts came to his head at once. He lost his focus for a second. In that split second, he had no idea how he rear-ended the car in front of him. It was not just any car but an almost new S-Class Mercedes he had admired a short while back. It had been to the right of him. How it ended up directly in front of him beat him.

The car stopped and the driver got out, a young man in his early twenties in a pair of beach shorts and a T-shirt with a thick gold chain around his neck. Jeff shook his head and crawled out slowly. The horn blasting intensified. He felt as sorry for them as he did for himself. The traffic situation was going to get worse because of the accident and that was the least of his problems.

"You gat to drive carefully man," the young man said. "I just shipped this Benz from Germany two weeks ago. I hope you do have insurance 'cos it ain't cheap. Gees!"

Jeff apologised. In different circumstances, he would have found his attempt at the American accent hilarious. He knew exactly the sort of person he was dealing with. He had seen his type before. He was part of the new generation of youths who were weaned on hip hop, had found new money and were intoxicated by it. He was not going to beg his way out of the situation. They had no concept of human kindness. He apologised again.

"I accept your apology man," he said. "Fact is, that ain't gonna fix this car. You know what they gonna say? They gonna say they need another bumper shipped from Germany to replace this one. Ain't no patching job on this car so you better start calling your insurance or your bank 'cos am calling the cops."

Some drivers took time to hurl abuses at them for making the traffic situation worse. Others looked at the scene curiously. Some even had pity in their eyes for him. They knew exactly the type of trouble he was in. It was the type of accident every poor driver prayed he never got into. He took out his phone and called his insurance. After five minutes of listening to various number options a metallic female voice asked for his name, address and date of birth. He told her as calmly as he could. Young money was on his phone presumably calling the cops.

"I will transfer you now," she or it said.

He shook his head. After few minutes of listening to the most nerve wrecking music he had ever heard another female voice asked him for his name, address and date of birth. It sounded human this time.

"Don't you all work together?" he snapped.

"Sir," she said mechanically, "please give me your name, address and date of birth."

He gave it to her.

"What is your policy number?"

"How am I expected to remember that?" he asked.

"Can you spell your surname for me?"

He swallowed hard, closed his eyes and spelt it out while rubbing his temple to dissipate the headache that was coming up."

"Thank you, sir. By the way, how is your day so far?"

"Take a guess. Terrible. Hope you don't make it worse."

"Sorry to hear that," she said. "That's why we are here. At times like this we do have your back."

"I do hope so," he said.

He could hear her typing rapidly on her keyboard.

"I don't think your policy is active," she said.

"What does that mean?" he asked.

"You missed your last two payments," she said. "Per our policy that made your account inactive."

"Then activate it," he said. 'I just had a car accident. What am I supposed to do?"

"Sir, it is your obligation to ensure your premiums are up to date," she said. "I can activate your account but you will not be covered for anything until after a month."

"Are you kidding me?" he asked. He felt like his head was going to explode. He wanted to get away from the heat and the noise. He knew he had to stick around until things were sorted out.

"That is our policy," she said. "Next time just make sure…"

"Next time I'll try a different company."

"It's the same everywhere," she said calmly.

"Don't tell me you don't have insurance," the young man who had finished his call said. He had no idea when he came to stand beside him.

"May I speak to your manager?" he asked the lady on the other end of the phone.

"I am not supposed to do that," she said.

"Why not?" he asked.

"Company policy," she replied. "We don't even work in the same office. I just manage the company's calls."

"Well I need to speak to someone who can clear this mess up," he said.

"You are speaking to me. We follow our policy. Even the manager cannot go against the policy."

"What are you, robots?" he asked angrily.

"Sir, I am just doing my job. I wish I could help you. Is there anything else?"

"Yes," he said. "Get me your manager. I have just been in an accident and I need the damage covered."

The line went dead. He could hear sirens in the distance and wondered how the cops were going to make their way to the scene through the heavy traffic. He did not have to wonder too long. They came through the African way; with whips, pepper sprays and batons. How the space through which they passed was created was a mystery to him. Drivers parted in a hurry or risk being manhandled by the cops who looked like they had just returned from a military drill in hell.

"What's going on here?" one of them asked.

"Licence and registration," another asked.

They instantly became friendly with the young man who gave his name as Akpu. The cops got carried away with the beauty of the car. Their leader ended up chatting with Akpu about business and how he could hook him up with some young money. He overheard him complaining about his salary as a cop. In the end, they exchanged business cards. Jeff was treated like the proverbial bad son. They wanted to know what he was thinking when he had the accident. One of them asked if he didn't know he should have given the expensive car a good distance.

"Fear no even catch you," he said. "You see nice car like this and you want follow am do bumper to bumper. Oya, go sell your papa car come repair am now. Shame no catch you say na young boy wey dey drive the car."

"The idiot no even get insurance," another said. "We suppose take am go lock for prison for at least one month."

He knew not to say anything. One wrong word and they would pounce on him like a group of thugs. He had seen it happen. They took his licence and drove off, advising him to report to their station later. Akpu promised to call their boss the next day. He was allocated a cop car to help get him through the traffic situation. They were friends already.

"Go find the money and get this fixed quickly," he said. "This is a dent to my pride. Now I must drive this beauty with a dented bumper for who knows how long? Just get the money and let me fix her up asap."

He got into his car and drove away, following the cop car with its loud sirens closely behind. Jeff got into his. He drove behind Akpu's car slowly and carefully. He could see other opportunistic drivers behind him.

When he got home it was already dark. Nneka was sitting in the living room. The recent events had brought them closer.

"What happened," she asked. "I was worried. You did not pick your phone."

"I was in an accident," he said weakly.

"Goodness!" she exclaimed. "Are you alright?"

He nodded.

"The insurance company said I am not covered," he said. "Of all cars I had to bump into it had to be this new Benz with a driver who looked like he was some underage drug dealer. I could have bumped into one of those beat down taxis and no one would even notice any difference."

She sat beside him and placed a hand on his shoulder.

"Get some rest," she said. "The sun will still rise tomorrow, remember? Are you hungry?"

He felt numb. He shook his head. She went to the kitchen anyway. The reference to the sun was a phrase they used to cheer each other up when things went south.

"The kids are in their room," she said from the kitchen.

"Where is Becky?"

"Went out. I have no idea where. Just told me she may be coming back late. You remember that car I told you about?"

"Yes?" he asked scarcely listening. She returned with some yoghurt in a cup, handed it to him and sat. She always knew exactly the sort of food he would need in any situation. To think that he ever contemplated divorcing her amazed even him.

"I think it was here for her," she said. "I saw her acting all strange and sending text messages all through the period the car was there. Whoever was inside wanted to see her."

"Remember what we used to say about speculation and gossip."

"You know me. I would not have told you if I did not think it was true. Before she left I overheard her talking to someone over the phone. I know Mason is your friend but I think his wife is having an affair."

"Don't go there," he said.

"It is what it is. Her husband is nowhere to be found and, where is she?"

"She may have gone to see a friend," he said. "She is an adult. She is under a lot of stress. Perhaps she needs some distraction."

She shook her head.

"I am also an adult and I know what I heard. She is in their house with whoever was in the car."

Jeff scarcely listened as she went on. He was too stressed himself to worry about another man's problems. If she was having an affair, so what? He was nobody's moral police. If a private detective had no way of knowing what his wife was doing behind his back, then that was his problem. He ate a little bit of the yoghurt then set the cup down. His appetite was gone. He was trying to figure out just what he was going to do when the bills started pouring in.

Gbenga was a man who prided himself with being approachable and friendly. The truth was that he was quite the opposite. Begging for his job was an option but knowing his boss very well he knew the chances of getting it back was close to zero. Many had described him as a psychopath who made erratic decisions. He had never been known to back down from any decision even if it cost the company money.

He did not want his wife being part of the stress. He hoped somehow he would find something before things got so bad she noticed. Going back to his freelancing days was an option. With every youngster becoming a self-proclaimed journalist and with more and more people turning to alternative media for their news source life was becoming harder for the conventional journalist. He thought of opening a YOUTUBE account. He could even start blogging.

She eventually stopped talking when she thought he had fallen asleep. He just had his eyes closed. She got a blanket from the room and covered him before going to bed herself. When she was gone, he focused his mind on the events of the day and the future. Akpu would have to wait till he got money for his imported bumper. It might take the next ten years. There was just nothing he could do about that. Ehi still needed to be rescued and not even all the trouble in the world would slow him down. It was going to be harder without much funds but he was not backing off.

His thoughts eventually shifted to the issue at hand. Where in the world was Mason and who had him? Madam Caro was the only one he knew who had the necessary link to cops. If the cops were involved, then he had no doubt she was involved. The question would then be who amongst the top cops she knew to be able to pull off such a thing. If anyone would know, itwould be Robert. From Mason's report, Robert was like her personal secretary. He knew almost all her activities. He decided he would have to pay him a visit. He had to be careful. If they already knew of his link with Mason, he could be walking right into their hands. So far, he had no idea what they had or had not figured out. He had to take the risk. Besides, he needed to see Ehi again.

CHAPTER 11

It was ten in the morning. Madam Caro was in the VIP section of the resort putting finishing touches to the planned new site in India with her guests when her phone rang. She excused herself. They were all busy people who were well connected and she was not the first person to excuse herself to take a phone call that morning. No one complained. Whoever made the unwritten law that no one should make or receive calls during meetings was, in their eyes, a politician and not a businessman. Businessmen understood that some things cannot wait. She went to a different section of the room and studied the number on her ringing cell phone. It was not one she recognised. She answered reluctantly and suspiciously.

"Hi sweetheart," an excited male voice said. "I told you I'll be back."

Her heart began to race. Not even a hundred years apart would have made her forget that commanding voice.

"You?!" she cried in anger, frustration, joy, and excitement.

"It's me baby," he said. "I'm back."

"Where on earth have you been?" she asked. "Not even a call? Where are you?"

"I'm in town. Listen, we have to talk but not over the phone," he said. "I will explain when I see you. Where are you?"

"How do you know I even want to see you?" she asked. "What if I'm married?"

He laughed.

"Don't be ridiculous. Tell me where you are and I'll be there."

"How did you get my number?"

"Come on now, this is your old number. You never changed it. If I drop this phone you may never hear from me again. You want to give me an address or not?"

"I will send someone to pick you up," she said. "I live out of town. There is no address."

"That explains it," he said. "Ikoyi hotel. Tell whoever is coming to call me when he gets to the lobby. I do not want anyone knowing I am in town. My life depends on it. Do you understand?"

"No, I don't," she said. "You still have not explained to me why you never called me all these years. You had my number and never lost it apparently."

"I was in jail," he said. "Wait till we meet and I will explain. You never know who is listening."

"Do you know you have a son?"

There was silence on the other end. She could hear his breathing. Men!

"I have a son?" he asked eventually.

"Yes."

"We have a lot to talk about. See you soon."

She stared at the phone in her hand confused and happy. Suddenly she became self-conscious. She had been young and shapely when they had last met. Now she was fat and, in her eyes, not as pretty as she used to be. What would his reaction be when he saw her? One of disgust and revolt? She wondered if it was even wise to bring him there. She had a house in town that only those who were considered family and true friends knew about. Robert was the only one from the resort who knew about it just because someone had to run errands there. Perhaps it would be safer to take him there. She called Robert and gave him specific instructions on how to get to the Ikoyi hotel and what to do when he got there.

"Do not say a word about me when you get there," she warned. "If he asks you any questions just tell him you do not know. Your duty is to drive me around and nothing else. If he asks what it is I do, tell him I am into wholesale importing and exporting."

Robert nodded. She doubted his intelligence in such matters but had no alternative. She could not go herself with her Indian partners there and did not want the others knowing about her personal issues. As soon as he was gone she returned to the meeting. She found it hard to concentrate on what was being discussed. He had not asked about the money. She was torn in two. On the one hand, she wanted to believe he had some genuine reason for not calling her all those years. On the other hand, she had come to distrust men.

She would use the money as a leverage. If he was back because things had gone wrong in his life and he saw her as a mere old chic to run back to then he was mistaken. He would not get a dime of his money. On the other hand, she yearned the brief love they had shared together. For some reason, all her relationships had been a disaster because she compared all her experiences to the one brief mind blowing encounter she had had with him. Even her friends thought she was unrealistic and unfair to her subsequent lovers. If he had stuck around, she would not have rated him that highly, they say.

The meeting ended way past midday. It ended well and documents were signed that she did not bother to read. In their circles documents meant less than words. Matters were hardly settled in court and they all knew this. They would start work in a week. Once the building was completed she and her team would take over the running of the Indian business. International guests were the target, specifically the Chinese and the Saudis. They had already estimated the profit to be in the millions and had toasted and drank to that.

As soon as they left she called Robert and asked him to take her to her house as fast as he could drive. On the way, she wanted to know what he looked like and if he had asked any questions. He told her he was quiet throughout the drive from the hotel. The only question he asked was who he was to her. She smiled. The jealousy was good even though she thought it a bit demeaning that he would even assume she would date someone like Robert.

"What do you think of him?" she asked. She had considered the wisdom of this question to someone in Robert's position but could not help herself.

He shrugged.

"He looks like a decent man," he lied. "Is he your new man?"

"Mind your business!" she snapped. "And not a word of any of this to anyone."

"Yes ma," he said, his eyes on the road.

She was too engrossed in her own thoughts to realise he was in deep thought. He knew he had seen the face somewhere. There was something about the sharp eyes that was familiar. He just could not give up the thought. On her part, she toyed with the idea of calling him. She did not want to seem too excited. He was, after all, a man who had abandoned and ignored her for more than a decade. She was not supposed to go rushing back into his arms like he was coming back from some noble war in Iraq or Syria. Who had he dated all those years? Had he got married? Was he back because he was recently divorced? She had heard about how marriages in the diaspora never lasted and how the law meant a man could lose everything in a divorce.

She tried to tell herself that it did not matter. All that mattered was that the one man she had ever loved was back. She must not ruin her opportunity at rekindling what to her was true love. She would play the role of the angry and dejected lover but only briefly. She had come to know that playing hard to get was no longer as powerful as it used to be. Something mysterious was happening to the male species. It was possibly the fact that women had made themselves too readily available. She felt that women were becoming masculine and men feminine. She blamed the new trend in the romantic world on Hollywood and the porn industry. The mystery that used to be the female body had been blown wide open by cheap and immoral men and women who only knew about money and little else.

She tried to picture what he would look like. If he had been in jail, then he may look muscular. She would like that. She liked smart men who were fit and strong. A lot of the men she had dated had been weak. This was partly the reason she had dated them in the first place. They had thought their money was enough to win her over when all she wanted was their money. Many had been too eager to abandon their wives and children to be with her. Initially she had let them do that. Many had signed divorce papers only to find that she had absconded with a large chunk of their wealth. When she turned thirty she had a near death experience which frightened her. After the experience, she vowed never to date married men again. She believed a particular woman who had threatened her for cheating with her husband had been responsible for the accident that almost left her crippled. She had been in the hospital for over three months. That was when she gained a lot of weight, weight that she never had the motivation to lose.

She started dating younger men who were single. The fact that they found her attractive and preferred her to those closer to their own age group was a boost to her self-esteem. They gave various reasons for preferring her. Most believed the women of their time were self-centred, mannerless, lazy, and arrogant. She knew she was all that when she was younger. It was easy to be arrogant when you had beauty, youth, and a hundred men willing to die for you. The humility comes with the passing of time and the fading of beauty.

There was a time she used to make heads turn. Then she would wear the skimpiest of dresses and the highest of heels. She was one of the few with exceptional beauty and a great body to go with it and she had been unapologetic about it. Even some women envied her. Many wanted to be her friend. Unfortunately, she learnt not to trust women before she learnt not to trust men. It was a human problem.

When she first met Osun she immediately knew he was different from every man she had ever met. There was something in the way he looked at her that was unnerving and exciting at the same time. She described it to her friends as the look of a lion admiring a pretty deer. He exuded confidence.

She suspected from day one that he had criminal tendencies. He was always watching his environment as if he expected someone to jump him at any time. When they dined he never sat with his back to the entrance. She immediately suspected he was into something shady. At the time, he had a lot of money to spend. He had access to thousands of dollars at a time she considered herself lucky when a man gave her a hundred dollars. He talked like he knew exactly what he wanted in life. His sweet talking was mesmerising and she could listen to him all day even when she knew half of what he said was all made up nonsense.

Their relationship progressed quite quickly. Within a few days, they were as inseparable as siblings and knew most of each other's secrets. It was his honesty to her even though he was not an honest person at all that won her over. She learnt from him that being a crook was like being a lawyer or an engineer. It was something you do and not who you are. He was a crook because he had to survive. When he handed her the money before his trip she had tears in her eyes not because of the money but because of the trust he had in her. She had pleaded with him not to go. She had seen men and women who went abroad thinking things would get better only to return years later broken and as poor as they were before they went. Home is where you get your respect. Once you are a foreigner in another land you are treated differently. They had enough money to start a genuine business and a family with.

He had his mind made up. He had gone too far to change his mind. He debunked all her arguments about home being the best place to be and gave the example of the kidnapped Chibok girls. The irresponsibility of the elite politicians who, in his eyes, were nothing but crooks, had reduced not just the country but the continent to a state of ruin and ridicule. He gave the example of the thousands of men, women, boys and girls who die every year trying to cross the Sahara or the sea to Europe. Desperation was something she had not experienced. Desperation was being without hope. It was desperation that drove thousands to make journeys that they knew could cost them their lives. When men and woman had come to a point of desperation, they would do whatever it would take to survive, including joining terror groups and gangs.

He did not like talking much about his childhood. It was locked away behind an impenetrable iron curtain that not even the best psychologist could reach. She suspected that somewhere behind that curtain was the key to unravelling his mind. There were times when he would sit down for hours smoking cigarette after cigarette or weed. During those times, it would seem as if a dark energy had come over him. Once it had passed he became his usual self again.

Her heart started beating faster as they drove through the gate. She looked at her face one last time in a mirror she had in her bag and retouched her makeup before exiting the car. She tried to walk casually even though she wished she could run.

He was in the sitting room watching Aljazeera news when she walked in. He stood and smiled at her. It was as if he had not aged at all. She forgot about her pride, self-esteem and all the hard questions she had prepared in her mind. Those would come later. She gave out a cry and rushed to hug him. They hugged tightly for what seemed like hours while she cried and shuddered.

"Look at you," he said when he managed to disengage himself from her tight embrace. "Come, I have something to show you."

"You have an accent now," she said laughing.

"Inevitably," he said as he led her to the sofa where they both sat down. "You still have that ring I gave you. Amazing."

"What did you expect me to do with it?" she asked.

"I have a better one for you," he said reaching into his pocket and producing a red box. He opened it. In it was the most magnificent diamond ring she had ever seen. "Hold out your hand."

She tried to resist. He still had his way of talking to her as if she was his kid sister and expected no opposition. She was, after all, not that naïve young girl of years ago. She was a powerful and rich woman with dozens of employees.

"Don't you think we should talk first?" she asked.

"How will the ring stop us from talking?" he asked. "Come on babe."

She stretched out her left hand. It trembled as he slid the ring into her ring finger that was already crowded with rings. Her other hand was over her mouth in shocked excitement.

"Beautiful," he said admiring the look of it on the finger. "Perfect. Now we can talk. By the way, do you have any drink in this house? I'm thirsty."

"Beer?" she asked.

"Water will be just fine," he said.

She wondered if he had undergone some New Age reformation as she went to fetch the water. From the look of the ring she could tell he had done quite well. He looked wealthy. He did not look like someone out of jail. She got some water from the refrigerator and returned with it. He drank like a camel in the desert and asked for more. This time she got a whole jug full of water and set it on the side table beside him.

"How was jail?" she asked. "You look too good to be coming from jail."

"Jail was jail," he said. "Nothing good about it except that you stay physically fit. Makes you tough mentally too. Finally started reading books. Found out they are not as bad as I used to think they were. Knowledge is power. I should have read more as a kid."

"When are you going to answer my question?" she asked.

"Can we just enjoy the moment?" he asked a bit impatiently. "I know you have a lot of questions. I have a lot of questions too. We are going to talk. This is just not the right time."

"When?"

"Tonight," he said. "Come here."

He tried to kiss her but she pulled away.

"It's been ages," she said. "The last time I let my heart lead me I ended up with a broken heart and a son who wants nothing to do with me. We need to talk."

"Okay," he said raising his hands in surrender. "Where's my son?"

"We will get to that," she said. "Let's talk about you and I first. You cannot tell me they don't have phones in jail. I need a good reason why you never called."

Osun sighed.

"Do you have a smoke?"

"No." she said. She had forgotten he was a chain smoker.

"I know this may sound funny but I was protecting you," he said before taking another sip from his glass of water. "I knew they were monitoring my calls. I could not risk letting them know you. The people I am talking about have their tentacles everywhere, even here."

"Which people?" she asked.

"You see why I said we should leave this for later?" he said. "It is a long story and for it to make any sense at all I have to start from the very beginning. There are still stuff too traumatic for me to talk about. Can we leave this for now?"

She could tell he was beginning to perspire and his breathing had got quite fast.

"Tonight," she said. "You must take me to a very nice restaurant and date me all over again. I need to know that I still have a place in your heart."

He nodded. There was a distant look in his eyes as if he was recalling some very frightening experience. She drew close to him and put her arms around him. He did not respond. He just sat there staring at the wall, a blank look on his face. She eventually disengaged. Her mind was as busy as his. It was not particularly the reunion she had hoped for. There were too many unknowns for her to settle right into his life or allow him back into hers. She was happy to see him and still felt like no other man ever made her feel when she was around him. Once he had cleared the air of every uncertainties she was sure they would have a wonderful time.

"Robert?!" she called.

He came into the living room. He had been standing outside and had overheard everything. He had also remembered who the mystery man was. He knew people who would pay good money for information regarding his whereabouts. He had already devised a plan that would solve his financial problems. He needed to be free to roam the earth once more. The people who wanted him dead may want their old foe dead even more. If he could trade his freedom for the information he knew they wanted more than anything else, then the biggest nightmare of his life may not be as impossible to resolve as he had imagined. All his plans involved running away from the country and never coming back. He knew the plan could have serious implications when he started having kids. Home would always be home.

"Why are you staring at him like that?" she asked. "You like to embarrass yourself all the time. Go to that Calabar restaurant and get us some garri and afang soup. Hurry up."

"Yes ma," he said and left.

"I hope you still remember Mama Calabar?" she asked.

"She still alive?"

"Very much alive and her restaurant is still there," she said.

He smiled as he remembered how they used to have their lunch there. His favourite was her vegetable soup. It was a delicacy that brought the wealthy from even other states.

"I have asked my driver to get us some food from there," she said. "Your favourite."

"You really know the way to a man's heart," he said.

"I try to teach these young girls of today," she said boastfully. "They think it's about going to the gymnasium and starving to death to maintain an impossible figure. They don't even bother to ask the men they claim to be doing all that for what they really want."

"A man's heart is through his belly," he said resuming his usual jovial attitude.

"I'll give you some good massage once we are done eating. I'm sure your flight was stressful."

"Muscles do ache," he said. She had no idea he had been in the country longer than he was telling. "I'm really gonna need that massage."

"Do me a favour and lose that accent," she said grimacing. "You are back home now."

"I'll try," he said grinning.

"I'll go take a bath," she said standing. "Feel at home."

"I am at home," he said.

She found herself humming to herself as she went, something she had not done in years. He observed her behind for some time, leaned back to rest his head on the sofa, closed his eyes and smiled. He had not felt this relaxed in a long time. He wondered what life would have been like if he had remained and married her.

Ever since he left the country he had never felt relaxed. There was always some issue that needed to be tackled. It had been one problem after another. Sometimes he believed karma was paying him back for what he did to his friends. Being abducted and tortured was the last straw that broke his back. He still had flashbacks of the most horrific moments. He wanted nothing short of revenge on the culprits but first he must bide his time and do their bidding.

Life in the west was wild and free. They had freed themselves from the shackles of culture and religion and were led by the pleasures of the flesh with no restriction whatsoever. Even he found the feeling strange at first. He eventually unshackled himself. He dated any girl who caught his eye. She was far from his mind while it lasted. The night life was surreal. Nothing wastaboo and he wondered why some extremists believed they were a Christian nation.

He hooked up with a bunch of crooks who dealt drugs and any contraband that was in high demand. They lived life on the edge knowing that death or prison could come at any time. It was the thrill of his life while it lasted. He was always high on adrenaline or some other drug. There was no dull moment with them and the cash and the women flowed like a wild river. Something kept telling him it would all end badly. He tried to dismiss the inner voice as the remnants of his conscience, a conscience hard wired on a culture that believed in reward and punishment for deeds done. If his conscience had been as loud as a sonic boom while in Africa, it was a mere whisper in comparison in the states.

When it ended, it was abrupt. He was sleeping on his couch after another typical night of hard partying and booze when some evil looking men barged into his home. What seemed like a hundred flashlights almost blinded him. His hands were tied and he was led into a waiting car. Thinking they were cops, he knew jail was inevitable.

"Do you want to join me?" she asked from the shower.

"I'm too tired," he lied.

"Remember how we used to shower together back in the day?" she asked.

"Those were good old days," he said nonchalantly.

"We still here," she said. "There's time to revisit the good old days."

He did not reply this time. He was thinking of the best way to approach the issue of his money. He needed it badly. The diamond ring she was wearing was stolen property. It was marked which meant there was no way it could be sold. The last thing he wanted was for her to think he was only back in her life because of it. If he had come to learn one important fact it was that women were no fools and do not like being taken for a ride.

CHAPTER 12

Jeff woke with a start. He thought some bright light had flashed in his eyes just before waking up. He heard a car door slam shut outside and went to the window to see who it was. He was just in time to see Becky leaning into the window for what he assumed to be a kiss from whoever was in the driver's seat. He shook his head and went back to the sofa. It was almost ten. When she walked in he could tell she had been drinking. Her voice was high pitched and she had a slight stagger to her gait.

"Where have you been?" he asked.

"Not even my husband asks me such a silly question," she said rummaging in her bag for something. "Have you found him yet?"

"No. You need to be careful," he said backing off tactfully. "Until we figure out who is behind this we all have to be very careful."

She laughed. "You are the one who needs to be careful. Does your wife know about the girl you were planning to marry? My husband has been in this business for years. How come it is now that he decided to help you that he gets kidnapped? You should know who the kidnappers are. Until he gets back I will advise you to keep your nose out of my business. I have a home. I am not homeless, thank goodness."

Jeff was too stunned to say anything. Mason had assured him that he had kept the whole thing private. He had obviously lied. He wondered who else knew about the plan and if it was not jeopardised already.

"Can't talk anymore?" she asked mockingly. "Go find my husband. I don't care what business you have with that Ehi or whatever her name is. That is your wife's business, not mine."

With that she left and went into her room. He laid there for a while, too stunned to move. She obviously knew too much. He had always trusted Mason to be professional and was beginning to doubt the basis of that trust. He knew women talked to each other. She could discuss it with his wife who may in turn misinterpret the whole thing. Worse still, she could discuss it with the wife of someone who patronised the resort. He had kept it secret from Nneka for that same reason. To discuss it with her would mean either lying or explaining how he came to find himself in Madam Caro's resort in the first place. The time would come when he would tell her what she needed to know but he knew it was still premature to talk about it.

The time was eleven-thirty. He picked up his car key and left. He had overslept by an hour but was not too worried. He knew he had to see Ehi. The doctor had sent him a message that evening. The implication of the message was that things needed to be speeded up or Ehi might find herself in India or Dubai in less than a month's time. It was a short message. Unfortunately, the doctor's phone was unavailable for clarification. His deposit was running out and he had no idea where to find the money to extend it.

The night was cold and he struggled to keep his eyes open, yawning repeatedly as he drove. All the troubles that were springing up in his life threatened to drive him crazy. He tried not to think too much, to follow the advice he had given too many of his friends who had lost their jobs. He had looked up the car he had hit. The young man had not been lying. The entire rear bumper needed to be changed. It had electromagnetic sensors that may not function properly if a new one was not installed, making the owner liable for any accident that might happen after any damage no matter how minor. Apparently, just having bumpers that simply looked nice was no longer enough for some humans. He strongly believed the devil's meanest demon was on his case. There was no other way he could explain the recent chain of events. It had been a long time since he worried about money and it was not a good place to be.

Caro's place was as busy as ever when he arrived. He found a vacant table with half eaten plates of food and empty beer bottles on it and sat. He even mused at the idea of applying for a job at the place. They obviously needed more hands. He looked around and spotted the doctor. He was surrounded by three gorgeous women who looked like they were models. He must have said something about him for they turned and looked in his direction before he cautioned them and they looked away hastily. One of them stood after a while and walked past his table. She dropped a folded piece of paper on the table as she did. He unfolded it. The word TOILET was scribbled on it. When he looked for Doctor Salami he was no longer there. He hurried to the toilet wondering just how unthoughtful the man was. He could have just called or sent a text.

Salami was washing his hands when he arrived. He proceeded to do the same.

"What's up?" he asked.

The doctor placed a finger on his lips and pointed to one of the doors. They had to wait for the occupant to finish his business. They waited.

"They are taking some of the girls to India and some to Dubai," he said when they were finally alone. "She said she would be sending her most troublesome girls over there to ease her headache. I will oversee the final medicals, HIV tests and all."

"You think she is on the list?" Jeff asked.

He nodded. "We need to act fast. I saw her today. She misses you. If I did not know better I would think the two of you are in love. Maybe I don't know better. Just make sure you know what you are doing."

"I'm just trying to get her out of a difficult situation," he said. "Nothing personal."

"That might not be her point of view," Salami said. "Anyway, I will try to be as uninvolved as I can. In a few days, she would feign illness. I gave her a pill that will make it easy for her. It is something we give to alcoholics called disulfiram. Robert will raise the alarm that she is very ill and at the point of death. Madam Caro will do the obvious and send her to me. We will conveniently declare her dead. If she lives up to her reputation she will mourn her financial loss but will want to have nothing to do with her body. If this happens, you will be free to come pick her up."

"How will you convince her that she is dead?" Jeff asked. He was beginning to perspire profusely. The plan was becoming real and this made him anxious.

"Leave that to me," Salami said. "Just promise that when this is over I will never hear from you again. I'm doing this for my son and not you or even me."

"You have my word," Jeff said.

"I will give you a call when everything is ready," he said.

"What happens if she decides she wants to see her body?" he asked.

The doctor shrugged as he grabbed some paper towel to dry his hands.

"That will be most unfortunate and uncharacteristic of her," he said. "I do hope that does not happen."

With that he put on his professional smile and left. Jeff shook his head. On the one hand, he thought the idea to be brilliant. On the other hand, he wondered if he could not have come up with something less complicated. He left the toilet feeling drained. A visit to Ehi was just the right thing he needed. He thought of what the doctor had said. If he fell in love with her it would be the most complicated thing to ever happen to him. He did love her but it was pure love, the type he would have for a sister or daughter.

He headed for her room. Jack looked up from the Men's Health magazine he was reading to see who he was. He picked up his phone and began to dial. He did not bother greeting him this time around. He knocked on the door and opened it. An ecstatic Ehi jumped on him. It was becoming her habit.

"You are so cruel!" she cried. "How could you leave me by myself for so long?"

He observed that she sounded exactly like the girls he had dated in the past.

"I have been busy," he said. It was his usual excuse during his playboy years. This time it was the truth.

"Too busy to see me?" she asked accusingly. "It's been weeks."

"My apologies," he said before sitting on the only chair in the room. She sat on the bed.

"The doctor came to see me," she said. "I am really scared."

"Do not be," he said as reassuringly as he could. "Just focus on the plot. You will feel ill for a short while but that would be it."

"What if I die?" she asked, her eyes as wide as saucers.

He shook his head. He wanted to tell her everything that had gone wrong in his life since their last meeting. He wondered if she was too young for such. He sometimes forgot her age. It suddenly dawned on him that he needed someone to talk to. Lots had happened and he was bearing the burden alone.

"You look worried," she said. "Judging from the look on your face I guess I do have a lot to worry about."

He shook his head again and managed a smile.

"It's not the plan that's making me worried," he said.

She came to sit on his laps. He immediately felt a sudden urge to grab her by the waist and kiss her passionately. His heart pounded in fear. He was shocked at how easily his old nature could rear its ugly head. The naughty boy was not dead, just suppressed. With all the internal will power he could muster he resisted the urge. He was not sure if she was being an innocent childlike teen or an expert in seduction. Obeying those urges would merely make him the monster he did not want to be again. If he gave in, then he had no moral ground to continue his mission. It was that simple to him. He wished he could tell her that he was, despite all, a mere man. The safest thing to have done would have been to ask her to sit on the bed. That would have spoilt the innocent trust they had in each other. He let her be and bit his lip instead.

"Talk to me," she said, her lips close to his ears. The sound of her voice so close to his ears unnerved him in a way that both shocked and surprised him.

He told her about his job loss. He was essentially unemployed and was living on his savings and scrambling for freelance jobs the way he used to shortly after his graduation. It was not a good way to live. He told her about the accident that would take a huge loan to fix, a loan that no sane bank would give him considering his circumstance. He told her about Mason's disappearance. She listened as he spoke, genuine concern on her face. When he was done, she stroked his cheek.

"You are falling apart," she said eventually standing. "Have you read the book Things Fall Apart?"

"Sure have," he said.

"Remember all you told me the first day we met?" she asked. "You gave me a lot of hope. I now see the world in a different light. You should cheer up and believe it will be alright."

He laughed. It was ironic that she was now the one doing the encouraging. In a way, he was proud of her. She had come a long way from the frightened and disillusioned girl he had met. She sat on the bed and folded her arms across her chest.

"There is a lady who comes here," she said after a brief period of silence during which either thought over the whole situation. "She is pretty. Stands out easily from the rest of the crowd. We call her Red Ivy. She likes to dress in red and is as poisonous as Ivy. Very pretty but very deadly."

"How so?" he asked.

"She comes here to lure men into her den," she said. "Some think she is an accountant. Some think she is a lawyer. She would give them her fake business card and arrange a meeting. Most of the men have no interest in her professional services. You know what men are like when they see a pretty woman. What they do not know is that she works with a group of very bad men who specialise in kidnapping."

Jeff remembered the pretty lady in red he had almost lusted after.

He wondered what would have happened had he followed through with things.

"I think I have seen her," he said. "She has quite a disturbing stare."

"We call it Medusa's look," she said giggling. "Few men can resist it. Look."

She stared at him steadily until he got uncomfortable.

"Will not work on me," he said. "Stop it."

"It's because you know me now," she said. "Madam Caro taught us the look. She said it is a woman's way of inviting a man into her personal space."

"Interesting," he said.

"I think she and her gang may have something to do with your friend's disappearance," she said.

"What makes you think so?" he asked.

"They operate with a police car. Usually they would stalk their victim once she has confirmed he has the type of money they are looking for. They would follow him in their police car, pull him over at a convenient spot and then forcefully take him to their den. Once the ransom is paid they threaten him to never reveal any detail to anyone. They are quite scary. Most of their victims never talk about the ordeal."

"Why don't they get her arrested?" he asked.

"The victims have no idea she was behind it," she said. "It is hard to link the crime to her and that is why she can do the same thing repeatedly."

"How come you know about this in so much detail?" he asked.

"Robert told me about them," she said. "Would you like some coffee?" He shook his head.

"Same Robert who works here?" he asked.

"Caro thinks he is dumb but he is not as dumb as she thinks he is," she said. "She says a lot of things she should not say when he is there. He knows virtually everything about her. She trusts him. She thinks he is stupid and so feels free to discuss things she should not in his presence. Caro does not trust people that much. She does not trust men at all. You can say she trusts him to be stupid enough not to make much sense of her conversation."

"And how would she know about this gang?" he asked.

"Her son is part of it," she said. "Some say he is even the gang leader. They are estranged but she keeps her ears open for news about him. Knows some cops who give her feedback."

"You mean the cops are aware of these thugs?"

She nodded. "How do you think they have access to a police car?"

"I thought it may be a fake police car," he said.

"There is an inspector who comes here," she went on. "His name is Dele. If you can talk to him he may be able to help you."

"What if I become a target?" he asked. "I can't just walk up to a police inspector and tell him I know he works with criminal elements."

"I have information that you can use against him," she said. "When you work underground you tend to know a lot that folks like you who work in the normal society of seemingly innocent folks know nothing of."

"Are you asking me to blackmail him?" he asked surprised.

"Just an arm twister," she said. "How else do you think a man like that can be reached? He is a crooked and arrogant man. Such men only care about themselves."

Jeff shook his head. He knew he could easily get arrested or even killed.

"Robert has video recordings of him," she went on. "He says he plans to use it when he is ready to leave the country. Caro keeps video records of important men in her room. He believes he can use the inspector's influence to make his police file disappear. Caro refused to help because she wants him to remain here."

"Really?" he asked.

"He plans to start a new life," she went on. "He is more scared of the thugs after his life than the cops. He has figured out how to sort out the cops. The crooks are harder to deal with. They want his life for the life of their gang member he took years ago. He says once he has figured out how to get them off his back he would leave. He is tired of Madam Caro's insults."

"Why would he tell you all this?" he asked.

"He loves me," she said.

The statement took him by surprise and shocked him to the core. He was taken over momentarily by jealousy. Never in his wildest dreams would he have suspected it.

"You look like you've just been stung by a bee," she said laughing. "I said he loves me. I did not say I love him. He is a nice guy. Forget about the face. Inside he is more a man than all the millionaires who come here put together. He has never for once disrespected me. On the contrary, he is the one who protects me from men like Musa."

"The man is a murderer," he said emphatically.

"He killed a man once," she said. "That does not make him a murderer. I do not think he will ever kill again."

He shrugged.

"You seem to trust him," he said.

"I do not trust him," she replied. "I do not distrust him either. He has finally found a way to get the thugs off his back."

"How?" he asked.

"A man arrived the country a few days ago," she said. "This man is wanted by some key members of the gang. He robbed them of a lot of money and fled with it abroad. They have vowed to assassinate him if he ever set foot in the country again. He sneaked in thinking no one would know."

"Why would he even come back knowing he may be killed?" he asked.

"Some men think they can outsmart everyone," she said. "I'm not sure why he came back. Perhaps he got homesick. All Robert knows is that he is back and the information could be used to buy his freedom."

"And how did he know this?"

"He is Madam Caro's boyfriend," she said.

It dawned on Jeff that she must be talking about Osun. His jaw dropped and he stayed speechless for some time.

"You know who he is?" she asked.

He nodded.

"Well I hope you won't tip him off," she said. "I would not have told you if I knew you knew him. Robert would be mad. He told me in confidence."

He shook his head.

"Your secret is safe," he said thoughtfully. "How come he trusts you so much."

"Robert?"

"Yes."

She laughed. He wondered why she was acting out of character. He even wondered if she had been taking some drugs.

"I told you he loves me," she said. "He is not handsome and is certainly not rich. The only thing he has for me are his stories. He is my big brother in this place. Protects me from men like Musa."

"You do talk a lot then?"

"Now and then. Not a lot. You want some whiskey?"

"No, thank you," Jeff said. "How come you have whiskey?"

"The doctor advised that for the drug to work I will need to get some alcohol into my system."

"He is crazy," he said.

"Thought so," she said. "The whole plan is crazy. He is the doctor. He must be smart. He's here today meeting with some folks from Romania. They have this thing going on that is worth some millions if all goes well. Research, he calls it. He has taken a down payment and has to deliver."

"Where is that whiskey?" he asked.

"Under the bed," she said. "Want some?"

"I need some," he said.

She shrugged, reached under the bed and pulled out a bottle of whiskey. She handed it to him.

"Grab a glass from the drawer," she said.

He opened the drawer and took a glass. She watched as he poured himself a good measure and took a sip.

"You plan on getting drunk?" she asked.

"Why?" he asked.

"A lot of these men drink to get drunk," she said. "Silly thing to do if you ask me. What's the point of that?"

Jeff shrugged. "To give themselves a reason to justify their actions I guess. They want to be able to blame whatever they do on the alcohol. Or maybe to numb their conscience. Most people know what they are doing is wrong but do them anyway."

"What's the point of having fun if you are not sober enough to enjoy it?" she asked. "And what's the point of being a grown up if you need something to blame your actions on?"

"You may not understand this but people never really grow up," he said. "We simply grow bigger and more independent if we are fortunate enough to have a job. A stupid teen will become a stupid adult. That is why our economy is in shambles. We are ruled by teens who have grown up with the same teenage stupidity and find themselves in charge of a nation."

"May I have the bottle back?" she asked.

"Why?" he asked.

"Isn't that enough?" she asked. "I don't want you getting drunk."

He laughed. "The last time I got drunk was years ago. Don't worry about me."

She took the bottle and returned it. He continued sipping his whiskey. She watched him as he drank. Suddenly she laughed.

"What's funny?" he asked.

"Are you seriously telling me that all those grown-ups down there looking like they know what they are doing are nothing more than big kids? That's funny and scary at the same time."

"Not all men are like them," he said. "Most. To be an adult means being responsible not just for yourself but for whatever and whoever you have in your care. I know you don't know much about history and politics but most of our past leaders including local government councillors have looted funds meant for the country. They have used these stolen funds to buy cars, build unnecessarily big houses, maintain numerous mistresses, and travel the world. If you are a kid and find yourself in charge of millions of dollars, wouldn't you do the same?"

"I'll buy whatever toy I want and eat lots of ice cream and candies."

"They do all that as well. If they are adults, then what are they doing downstairs when they have families at home? That is why we do not have good infrastructure in our country. That is why too many orphans are left at the mercy of exploiters. That is also why a lot of kids grow up to become armed robbers and terrorists. If all the money those men and women steal from us was invested where they were meant to be invested, things would be much better. Our wealth from the oil boom was spent irresponsibly. Now the price is down everyone is complaining like kids who suddenly had their weekly allowances slashed."

"Why don't the real adults run things then?"

"Politics is a dirty game," he said. "Those who don't like playing dirty simply get out of the way. It's like you are wearing very clean clothes and you come across a group of people throwing mud at each other. What do you do? Unless you don't mind getting dirty, you will get out of the way as fast as you can and let them play dirty. People get killed in the game of politics."

"Why is it called a game then?" she asked. "Sounds like serious business to me if it can get you killed."

He shrugged and took another sip.

"A lot of things do not make sense on the outside," he said. "You might as well start understanding this while you wait to get out there. It is no free ride. Life is tough. One thing I want you to understand is that no matter how tough things get, you must never use that as an excuse for wrongdoing. People suffer when we do wrong even when it is not immediately apparent. Every one of those married men downstairs has a woman at home who is being neglected and wondering where they are. Be honest and work hard. Money is not as important as we are made to believe it is in this country."

"What if I choose to go into politics?" she asked laughing.

"Nothing wrong with that," he said. "Many have gone into politics with noble ambitions. The problem is that no matter how noble our ambitions are, without discipline and selflessness, the love of money will always take over. Lots of corrupt businessmen have money dedicated to politicians who are willing to take it so they can get some business advantage. The temptation is huge. The first lesson you should learn then is that it pays to be selfless."

"I might become a lawyer instead," she said more seriously.

"It is the same rule," he said. "Money is the currency for trade. Wherever money is involved, greed can be born. You must develop character before pursuing money. Your principles must be sound before you go out there. In the end, we all die. Believe it or not, after death every man and woman who ever lived must face judgment. God, the creator, will hold us accountable for our actions."

"If that is true," she asked. "How come they are not scared of him."

He drained the last of his whiskey and shook his head.

"It is complicated," he said. "It is easy to be lost in the moment. Some don't even believe God exists. They think we evolved from apes. It is a complicated and stupid theory."

"I would have preferred it if God delivers his judgment more instantly," she said. "If you steal, some angel or even demon should come and whip you or something."

"We do get our reward here as well," he said wiping his mouth with the back of his hand. "The problem is that many do not even know when they are being punished or rewarded."

"I would like God to punish Zudock," she said angrily. "I would like him to punish every man who ever came into this place to exploit us. Every man who has ever taken advantage of a child should die. Do you know what they do to children in India, Nepal or Vietnam? Ask Robert. They are dying of AIDS and no one cares, diseases transmitted to them by adults. He plans to help them when he gets out of here. He is going to leave here very rich. I hope he succeeds."

"That would be nice of him. You must not say such things," he said. "Let God do the judging. We must love even our enemies. That is the teaching of Jesus."

"Who is Jesus?"

"He is the son of God," he said. "I will explain all these when we meet again, hopefully on the other side. When we hate, we poison our hearts. That can lead to all sorts of vengeful thoughts and even mental illness. Keep your heart pure."

"Why should we not hate those who do us bad?" she asked angrily. The look on her face frightened him. It was a murderous look that should not be on the face of someone her age. He walked up to her, sat beside her and placed his hands on her shoulders.

"Listen to me," he said. "People do change. Many, too many, walk in darkness. Think of Jesus as light. When you encounter him, you encounter light and life. Suddenly it seems like someone turned on a light switch inside you and you begin to see. Things you used to do and value begin to look as dark as they really are. Many people are in darkness. Jesus came to save us all before we die. It is our duty to tell them about him, not to judge them or wish them harm. You must understand this. We don't know why people do what they do, what they are going through themselves. Only God knows our hearts. That is why only he can really judge fairly. What if I was punished for my dark past? I may not even have known you."

"What happened to him?" she asked.

"Who?"

"Jesus."

"He was murdered."

"Really?" she said. "I thought you said he was God's son? How could they murder God's son?"

"God knows best. He rose from the dead on the third day," he said. "That is the evidence that he is the son of God and our saviour. That plus all the prophecies about him and the miracles he did. He died, but he lives. Every man or woman who encounters him becomes a different person with a new life and a new hope. You begin to see things differently. You begin to hate evil and to love good. It is the most wonderful experience you can ever have."

"How come everybody is not having it then?" she asked sarcastically.

"Because some people want to remain in their sin," he said. "Some people want things that are contrary to God's will. They do not want to give sin up. When you reject God's salvation you simply say you wish to remain in Satan's bondage. Trust me when I say that the devil does know how to keep people preoccupied with distractions. He will give you anything that will keep your heart away from God. That is why places like this exist."

"So, we are Satan's tool on earth," she said broodingly.

"You are not here of your own will," he said as tenderly as he could. "God knows when you are willingly going against his will and when you are not. Let us focus on getting this thing done."

He looked at his watch. He had been there for over an hour.

"I have to go now," he said. "Stay focused. See you on the other side."

"I hope it all works out," she said wearingly. "I cannot go on living like this. My life should be so much more than this. Imagine those who died knowing no other life."

He thought of telling her about Caro's plan to take some of them to

India and Dubai but decided against it. She had enough to worry about already.

"I will pray for you," he said as he got up. "I know it will all end well."

"I will pray for you too," she said managing a smile. "I think you need help as much as I do."

They hugged briefly. He was worried about the look on her face. She looked resigned. He paused by the door briefly to wave. She was sitting on the bed, her gaze directed at the floor. He closed the door gently. Jack was engrossed in his magazine but he had an uncanny feeling that he was just pretending to be reading. Ever since he arrived he had been having an uncanny feeling that he was being watched.

Downstairs was as busy as ever. The doctor was still there with his women. This time there was a white man with them and they were looking at an open file on the table while the girls talked amongst themselves. He guessed he was the Romanian Ehi had spoken of.

He saw her sitting by the bar. She had a different dress on but it was still red. He looked around for a suitable place to sit. He found an empty chair by a table beside the one the doctor and his friends occupied. A man who looked drunk was sitting at the table by himself. He pretended he had not seen her and walked to the table. He excused himself and sat. The man stroked his long grey beard and nodded. He signalled to a waiter and ordered some lemon and lime bitters then took out his phone and checked his email. He could hear what the doctor and his guests were saying. He could not help eavesdropping.

"These figures show that the unfavourable factor is more common in the men between twenty-five and thirty," he was saying. "Take them out and we have a more favourable outcome."

"That will be wrong, sir," the doctor said in protest. "We have been through this. Data is supposed to be interpreted, not manipulated. It is the same with what you suggested with the women above sixty."

"You really expect me to go back to the sponsors and tell them that after spending hundreds of thousands of dollars on this research, they will have to pull their product?" he asked.

"I have done my part," Salami said. "You paid me to do honest research. This is the outcome."

"We will pay you to do it again," he said. "This time around make sure you know who to exclude."

Salami sighed.

"I'll see what I can do," he said.

"Do you agree then?" he asked.

"I said I will see," Salami replied a bit impatiently. "Just leave it at that."

The man laughed.

"You will get the cheque tomorrow," he said. "We have lots of research coming up. Africa and Asia are valuable to our business. The pocket that funds them is deep. You did well the last time. People were happy and our share prices went up."

Jeff looked up from his phone. She was staring right at him. Even though he was prepared for it he still found it unsettling. Coming from a woman that pretty made it harder to resist. He acted rattled and looked around as if to see if he was being watched. Inspector Dele was on the other side of the room with two men who looked like cops.

His drink came. He took his time. The woman had singled him out and there was no need to rush. The next time the waiter walked past he asked him to invite her to his table. He watched as he delivered the message. Without taking her eyes off him she smiled, finished her drink, picked up her hand bag and cat walked to where he was. Her evening dress was a tight fit and every curve in her figure was accentuated. He clenched his teeth. The kidnappers had chosen carefully and thoughtfully. Few men would be able to resist such beauty and elegance.

"Hi handsome," she said in surprisingly good English.

"Hi princess," he replied. "I couldn't help noticing you sitting there all by yourself. The name's Jacob."

"Antonia," she said extending her perfectly manicured and ring laden hand. He shook the hand.

"So," he said shifting nervously in his chair. "What are you doing here all by yourself."

"Looking for some excitement," she said. "I work hard during the day with hardly any time to unwind. It's a lonely world when you are a professional woman in a highly competitive industry."

"What industry would that be, if I may ask?" he asked.

"Insurance," she said without hesitation. "Do you have your house and your life covered? I can sell you a policy if you want. Business can go very well with pleasure."

"I actually do not have any life insurance," he said laughing. "Who does in this part of the world?"

"You will be surprised at how many people who do," she said. "Mind if I smoke?"

He shook his head. She took out a packet of cigarettes from her bag, selected one, placed it in a holder and lit it with a lighter. He watched as she puffed smoke into the air while watching him from the corner of her eyes, a wry smile on her face. For someone who moved in the circle of crooks, she did act with elegance, he thought.

"We can go to my place," she said. "You can relax while I get the paperwork ready. All I would need is your signature and credit card details. Bank details if you prefer. Once done we can then get down to the other side of business."

"Sounds good," he said. "The only problem is that I have to be at work in an hour. How about we meet tomorrow?"

"What kind of work do you do at such an unholy hour?" she asked looking disappointed. He saw the façade disappear.

"I oversee the graphic design for a media company," he lied. "Tomorrow's issue needs to be printed this morning. We distribute them nationwide and they need to hit the shelves before sunrise. It is hard work but it pays."

He could almost hear her brain move as she tried to figure out if he was worth the effort. She reached into her bag and produced a business card.

"Meet me tomorrow then," she said. "Seven O'clock. The address is on the card. I work from home sometimes. Be on time, I hate being left waiting."

He took the card and without looking at it placed it in his pocket.

"I will be there," he said. "I too do not like being disappointed."

He stood. She looked worried and a bit disappointed when he announced that he had to hurry on. When he got to the exit he looked back to see she was already working her magic on the man with the long beard. He wished him luck before stepping out into the cold night.

13

CHAPTER 13

Ani lit a roll of marijuana as he sat on the mound of earth that was once his good friend's beautifully decorated grave. The flowers had died and the tree they had planted in his honour had not thrived. The superstitious would say it was a sign his soul was languishing in hell. Weeds had overtaken everything. He felt a bit sad that someone he knew and shared life with was now just bones beneath the earth. He tried not to think about stuff like heaven and hell. The latter scared him to death.

He reminisced on the past as he smoked his joint and waited for his guest to arrive. He had chosen the site because it had been years since he went there and it was in a secluded area. He also wanted the seriousness of what had happened years back to be driven home. Esu, the man Robert had killed, left behind two kids from different women. He remembered sitting them on his laps and promising them that he would do whatever it would take to make sure they got the education their father had joined a gang for. They did not know their fees came from the proceeds of crime. He had not kept the promise and he still felt guilty about it. The two boys had eventually dropped out of school and were now small time crooks themselves, something their father had tried to avoid. The cycle continues.

He had not been very close to Esu. Smallie was the one he had been close to. Too many of his childhood friends were dead or in jail.

Interestingly, none of the kids they used to mock as being nerds were dead. He had thought about it and concluded that something must have been wrong with their own line of reasoning. They had joined gangs for quick money and women. He should have just waited and listened to his primary school teachers.

Thinking about it now he realised that they were merely being used by the older gang members. They were the ones who made the real money. It was for this same reason that they went ahead and formed their own little group. It had failed because of Osun and his situation was worse than what it had been; in a gang running errands for those much younger than he was. He could have been higher up in ranks had he stuck to his original group. Life was unpredictable.

As he waited, he remembered Smallie's interesting views about life and the reasons he gave for his life of crime. He wanted to move his siblings away from the ghetto. He was the sacrificial lamb who would take the sin of poverty away from the next generation. He wanted them to be accountants or engineers, anything but crooks. He would make sure they did their homework and gave them a beating if he heard they missed even a day of school. For a man who had been a truant he was quite strict. He had been a bit harsh on his siblings but the world was equally as harsh. To prepare for the real world meant enduring some serious disciplinary measures as a kid. His own mother had been soft on him. He often wondered if that may have been his undoing.

He laid on the grave still smoking his joint and gazed at the intensely blue sky with the clouds hurrying across. He remembered when he was a kid and would stare at the clouds until it seemed he was the one moving. It was Smallie who taught him the trick they dubbed space travelling. He considered the earth a spaceship travelling through space. Sometimes they would lay for hours until they slept off. He missed his old friends minus Osun. The new crew he had decided to join was made up of mostly ruthless youngsters who, as far as he was concerned, had no souls. He only joined out of desperation. Everything was going corporate, including crime. It was no longer profitable to go solo in anything. He got better pay too.

He sat up when he heard a car approach. It was a nice white Toyota Prado. For a split second his criminal instinct kicked in and he thought of hijacking the car. He calmed himself down. He had to focus on the main price. He was there as an emissary and had to deliver. He watched as Robert alighted from the car. Rage seized him as he recalled the brutal manner his old pal Esu had been murdered. To be beaten to death was one of the worst ways a man could die. It was a death that was as painful as it was humiliating. He had been wise to run away. Too many wanted him dead in the cruellest of ways. If he had been caught it would have been terrible.

He stood and walked towards him. There were no smiles and no handshakes. They went straight to business. He had his knife in his pocket and was sure Robert had also come armed. There was a bulge underneath his T-shirt that he suspected to be a gun.

"Did you bring the money?" Ani asked.

Robert produced a brown envelope from the back of his jean pocket and handed it over. It was the money that secured the meeting. He put it in his rear pocket. He had inflated the amount. Half was his and no one would know.

"So," he said. "You think say you see Osun."

"Sure," Robert said. "I know where he dey. I fit tell you if I am guaranteed safety and freedom. That na the deal."

"I go talk to the others," Ani said.

"I think say you don already talk," Robert said.

Ani shrugged. Each man tried to look as tough and unafraid as the other.

"We don talk. Some think say your offence dey too unpardonable. Others think say Osun na price big enough to consider your proposition. You understand say what you did was too cruel. Him grave dey just behind me."

"Na self-defence," Robert said.

Ani shook his head.

"Everybody call you Monkey Face back then," he said. "We all get our own nicknames. No one kill anyone for name calling. Na tradition. Na you throw the first punch. Even when he dey down you continue to punch am. We no dey fight like that. That is why some still think you need to die, including me."

"I been vex during the time," Robert said. "I no agree with the name. If someone no like any nickname you suppose stop."

A surge of rage went through Ani as he spoke. He almost pulled out his knife. He clenched his fists and let the feeling pass. He knew he would be no match for him. He shook his head and proceeded to light another joint.

"Give me the details," he said after taking two puffs.

"I need your word say you go honour our deal," he said adamantly.

"I go get back to you on that," Ani said, his feet were beginning to hurt. He was supposed to be on insulin but he just did not have the time to be injecting himself every day.

"Then until I get assurance I cannot divulge anything to you," Robert said.

They had a brief face-off after which Ani walked away to make a phone call. When he returned, he had a wry smile on his face.

"Some folks really go like to see you bleed," he said. "They say they accept your deal."

"All of them?" he asked.

"I believe the boss fit talk for everyone," he replied.

Robert returned to the car. He sat on the driver's seat and sighed heavily as he considered what he was about to do for the last time. Betrayal was not something he liked. He too had heard of what Osun did to his friends and disagreed with it completely. He had also seen how Caro had changed since his arrival. The woman was acting like a teenager in love and despite her treatment of him he was happy to see her that way. She had also become nicer to everyone. He realised it was her frustration that was making her mean. The fact that he was about to take all that away put a huge burden on his conscience. In the end, he rationalised that it was his only ticket to the life he had always dreamt of. His family could not keep hiding forever even if he left the country. There was also the issue of trust. He was not certain he would be left alone after the deed was done.

He took out the piece of paper on which he had written the address minus the house number from under the seat and returned to Ani. He handed him the paper. Ani smiled as he looked at it. It was a very cruel smile that made him almost rip it out of his hand. He did not want to know what a man with such evil intent planned to do to Osun. He had a distant look in his eyes as he stared at the paper, even forgetting that he was there.

"House number sixty-five. I need to go now," he said. "I hope we no go see each other again. If you see me for street just pass by. No bother to greet me."

"The score go settle if we get our man," Ani said. "I believe my business with you don end. Good luck."

Robert did not like the way he said it. There was insincerity in his shifting eyes. He watched him for a while before walking away. He had plan B in place. If they ever considered coming for him after that day, he would have no choice but to fight back. He was done running from his past. He already knew where the leader of their gang hung out.

He realised his hands were shaking when he tried to start the car engine. Ani had not moved. As he drove away he could see him still staring at the piece of paper and smoking his weed. He drove fast. There was no time. He had less than two hours to return to the resort. He had chosen that day to meet with Ani for a reason. His own plans were at the final stages. The car rattled and groaned as he drove through the bush without regard to its wellbeing. He just wanted to be back at the resort on time. Once Ehi was gone he may never see her again. That must never happen. When he re-joined the dirt road, he stepped on the gas.

He drove like a demon out of hell and left a cloud of dust behind him. Villagers on foot and motorcycles coughed and cursed as he drove past. He wished he could slow down but there was important business to be attended to. When he eventually turned into the highway he pushed the throttle to the floor. His heart beat madly as the speedometer reached 200. He only slowed a bit when he came close to town. That was when he noticed a red Hyundai ix35 following. He knew Ani must have alerted the driver whom he instantly recognised. He was not fazed. He was only disappointed that the old crooks had thought they could eat their cake and still have it. He always knew there was a possibility that this would happen. The lust for vengeance was too intense to pass up. His assumption was that they wanted to know where he was staying so that they could pay him a surprise visit. Their blood still yearned for revenge. They probably did not take him during his meeting with Ani because they also needed to get Osun as well. They wanted to have the address first. Greedy and unforgiving bastards, he thought.

The fact that his conscience would have to bear the burden of another murder weighed on his mind for a while as he drove. Eventually he decided he had made a big mistake. Without thinking he called Osun. He advised him to get as far away from the house as he could, lying that he had overheard street talk about a hit squad heading his way. Surprisingly he did not panic.

"We will talk when you get here," he said. "Come here right now if you know what is good for you. Don't even try to be smart about it, I am not Caro."

He ended the call. He was as confused as he was scared. He thought he would have wanted to know how much time he had. He really did not want to be anywhere near Caro's house. He wondered if he should have just let them get their man. Something told him he was in a deeper hole than he had been in.

The Hyundai tried to stay undetected. It allowed two cars between it and his Prado. He tried not to look at the rear-view mirror too many times and put on a pair of goggles to conceal his eyes. He had watched movies and seen how most people drove through red lights to lose a tail. The problem was that in Lagos most of the traffic lights were out of operation. He did not want to make any sudden move until he was sure he would be successful. As far as he knew they did not even know he had detected them.

He drove as casually as he could. His tail seemed to be in no hurry. He could see he was making a lot of calls and assumed he was giving feedback to whoever his boss was. His chance came when he got to a busy traffic. Without warning he crossed over to the other side of the road and then made a sharp turn into a side street and stepped on the gas. He turned into any street he could find before turning into another major road. He knew the driver of the Hyundai would have no chance even if he was a pro and was not surprised when he did not see any sign of it.

He shook his head when his cell phone began to ring. It was Caro. He ignored it. When he was sure he was safe enough he called her. She wanted to know where he was. He told her he was stuck in traffic. She had an appointment and was running late. She yelled at him to return to the resort immediately.

He did a U-turn and headed to the house hoping there would be no nasty surprise waiting for him. He was not going anywhere near it if he saw anything suspicious. He would get Osun and be out of there as fast as he could drive.

It took him a good thirty minutes to get there. He approached the closed gate cautiously but relaxed when he heard Osun talking loudly over the phone. When he entered the compound, he held out a finger as he continued his call, indicating he should wait. He knew Ani and his people planned from the onset to capture him alive. He winced as he imagined the extent they would go to exact punishment if they did get him.

After what seemed like ages he eventually ended the call and beckoned to him to follow him inside. He did not speak but it reminded him of the days when he was summoned to the principal's office after a fight.

"They would be here any minute," he said anxiously. His pounding heart made it almost impossible to speak. Osun smiled.

"Robert," he said looking him squarely in the eyes. "Do I look like I am incapable of taking care of my problems? Let's go inside. Stay calm."

He followed him inside without any further ado. There was an almost empty bottle of vodka on the table and a small mirror with suspicious powder traces on it. Osun grabbed the bottle as he sat and took a quick gulp then cleaned his mouth with the back of his hand. He proceeded to place his phone on the table. It was abuzz with activity but he ignored it.

He leaned back, closed his eyes and sighed heavily. A panicking Robert was certain a busload of evil men was on its way to the house. He thought of getting up and leaving. The man was not his boss in any way.

"Death is not to be feared," he said, his eyes still closed. "Dying is easy. Living is the hard one. Get your act together. Your fear is a distraction. Wait here."

He went to the bedroom. Robert hurried to one of the windows and peeped through the curtain when he heard a car screech to a halt outside. Men who looked like they were black ISIS soldiers were coming in through the gate. He thought of bolting through the back door. Osun emerged from the room with a pistol in his right hand.

"Relax," he said. "Those are my people. You killed Esu. That must have taken guts. Tried his bullying shit on me too. What happened to your gusto? Caro destroyed your manhood? Women like that will destroy you if you let them. That's why you need to be as cunning as a snake when it comes to them."

He had no idea how to respond. He just stood and stared, paralysed by fear and confusion. The fact that Osun was playing Caro all along was his least concern.

"You know how to use a gun?"

"No," he lied.

"Really?" Osun asked in surprise. "Every kid in The States knows how to use a gun. May not be a good idea giving you one then. Go back to Caro before she decides to come looking for you here. Not a word about any of this to her."

Someone started knocking on the door.

"Let them in," Osun said. "Those are my men. They are here to fight for me. Which do you think is stronger, pride, or the quest for vengeance?"

He went to open the door not knowing how to answer.

"Boss!" several men hailed as they poured in.

"Have a seat," he said. "Scorpio, go to the fridge and get the men some drinks. Drink minimally guys. We need to stay alert. They'll be here any moment."

"Is this the guy?" he heard an angry voice ask.

"Sure," Osun said. "Beat the shit out of the bully. Used him as a bait. They'll be here for sure."

He had never seen any of the men before. Some shook his hands for being able to stand up to a bully even though it had been decades ago. They all knew what oppression was. Most of them were from the Niger Delta where they had been neglected for decades while the oil that fed the nation was being sucked from their land. They considered this bullying of national proportions.

"You may leave now," Osun said. He gave him a letter in a sealed envelope. "Give this to Caro if I die. Some lives depend on it. I will call you later if I survive. Still have some use for you so don't go disappearing on me."

He left gratefully and eagerly. When he got outside, he saw some men offloading boxes from a bus. He got into the Prado and sped away. He only relaxed when he had a good distance between him and the house. He did not know what Osun planned to do but he did not intend to stick around to see.

When he was finally able to relax, he took out his cell phone and called Ehi. After almost ten attempts he gave up. He needed her to take the tablet in a place where she would be seen. Once she got ill they would have to call the doctor who would then have to send his ambulance. It would take at least fifteen minutes for the pill to act. If he got lucky he would arrive there just in time to go with the ambulance. They would have to coordinate everything perfectly.

He drove like a maniac for some time before trying her number again. This time she answered sleepily.

"I don dey try your number," he said.

"I was asleep," she said yawning.

"Go downstairs where people go see you and take the pill. I go arrive soon."

"I'm scared, Robert," she said.

"No think about am. The doctor go take care of you. I go call him now. Just do it."

He ended the call. He thought it best not to give her any opportunity to back out. Next, he called the doctor.

"Has she taken the pill?" he asked.

"About to," he said impatiently. "If you don't hear from them just send the ambulance. I'm on my way there."

"Won't she be suspicious if we arrive too quickly?" he asked. "You should have been there. Where are you?"

"Suspicious of what?" he asked. He wanted it over and done with. He had his own personal plans to focus on. As far as he was concerned he did not plan to be there to deal with her suspicions. Next, he called Ehi to see if she had taken the pill. There was no answer. He stepped on the throttle. He tried not to think of what he would do if she died. He would snuff the life out of the doctor with his bare hands.

He was tired of running from his past and living like a fugitive. He hoped to start afresh. To start afresh would mean a lot of money. He did not consider taking Caro's money as theft. To him it was reparation for all the emotional abuse he had endured. It was a word he had heard when a now dead politician was campaigning for some compensation for the years of slavery blacks had suffered centuries ago.

It took him less than thirty minutes to arrive the resort. He had driven the Prado like it was a race car. The ambulance was parked in front of the resort and a twitching Ehi was being carried into it. Caro was on her phone but managed to bark orders at the same time. He was shocked to see how unwell Ehi looked. She was completely unconscious and her eyes looked like they had rolled into her head. He knew there was no way she could fake that.

"Where have you been?" she asked when she was through with her call. "Where did you go with my car?"

"Traffic heavy," he lied.

"And where is Osun?" she asked. "He has not been answering my calls."

"He dey house," he said. "After I come out from traffic I say make I hurry come back."

"You need to take me there now," she said. "I'm not even sure he has eaten anything all day."

"I been buy food for am," he said. He knew there was no way he would be going back there. He went to the back of the ambulance. A profusely sweating Salami winked at him but he could tell the doctor looked worried. He wondered if anything was wrong. He did not like the look on his face.

"I'll go get some items from the house," he said. "Wait for me."

"That would be suspicious," the doctor said. "Let her ask you to come first. You know where to find me if she does not."

He paused long enough to see him insert a needle into her vein attached to a bag with clear fluid in it. He thought his hands shook as he did so. By this time, she had stopped twitching and was completely still. She looked like she was dead. Salami checked her pulse. Caro came to see what was going on.

"Is she still alive?" she asked. "Is she even breathing?"

Salami wiped the sweat from his face.

"Barely," he said. "I have to go back to the clinic quickly. She might need to go to a hospital."

"How many times have we been through this hospital nonsense?" she asked angrily. "Aren't you a doctor? Take her to your clinic, please."

He shrugged and advised the driver to take them to the clinic as quickly as he could before he shutthe door. The ambulance sped off, sirens wailing as it went.

"And you, Robert," she said turning to him. "Go get me my stuff while I get ready. You will be driving me to my house. I want you waiting in the car and ready by the time I come out."

He nodded. He hurried to his room where his bag was already packed and ready. He grabbed it, hurried outside and threw it into the back of the Prado. Next, he went to Caro's room. He could hear her talking on the phone. He left. He wanted her to be in the shower before he went in. He kept returning to her door to listen. When he eventually heard the shower running he opened the door gently and went in. He knew exactly where the items he wanted were. With the swiftness of a soldier he grabbed the things he needed. He had always known of the bags of money she kept under her bed. He also knew about the memory sticks she hid in her wardrobe. He tore off more sheets from her cheque book and took some gold rings and chains. The gun he had carried with him to meet Ani had been stolen from her that morning. There was also a misleading map in his room with a mark on a state he never planned to visit.

No one questioned him when he returned to the car with the bags. They assumed he was as usual running some errands. He took one last look at the resort that had been his home for years before speeding off again in the Prado. He did not look back.

His plan was simple. He would check himself into a hotel and lay low for a while. During this time, he would create a false identity for himself and use the details to open a bank account where the money would be deposited, preferably one that he could access from anywhere in the world. He had done his research. A known banker who frequented the resort had told him about the wonderful world of internet banking. Salami had told him about cheap plastic surgery in Thailand or India. He also knew about Cuba and Brazil. He would blend in quite easily in Brazil. The future looked better than the past. All he needed was to convince Ehi to come with him. With her by his side he would never be unhappy again.

The hotel he chose was on the outskirts of town. He chose a room that had its window facing the entrance. He needed to see everyone and everything that came in. It was a two-storey building and the room he chose was on the top floor. He ordered a meal and some cold beer. He ate like a horse after a race and even managed a short nap. When he woke up it was already dark. He drove into town, left the Prado in front of a shopping mall that had a car hire service and rented a car. He drove quickly to the clinic.

Ehi was stable but unresponsive. The tired doctor wanted desperately to go to sleep but was afraid to leave her unattended. He was worried about her dying in his clinic though the worst seemed to be over. He was yet to contact Jeff. He still could not bring himself to make the call to Caro and declare that Ehi had died. Lying was never one of his talents. Robert told him not to worry about Jeff, he would inform him at the right time. He advised him to go and get some sleep but advised him to call Caro before doing so. He would stay by her side and inform him if anything of concern happened. The reluctant but grateful doctor agreed. He explained the alarm system to him and what to do if it went off accidentally.

He sat by her side and held her hand. He had never felt more relaxed since the day he started his fugitive existence. He felt the scar on her wrists. He still remembered the night he had bandaged the wounds. That was to mark the beginning of their friendship.

He sat back on the chair and tried to think. As far as he knew there was no reason Caro, Ani or Osun would want to come to the clinic. He began to feel a certain uneasiness. His mother had always taught him to listen to his instincts. He got up and paced the room for a few minutes. Eventually he made up his mind.

14

CHAPTER 14

The kidnappers' den was deep within the jungle. It was far from the resort but located within the same jungle. The jungle was often the final refuge for those pushed away from the hustle of city life. It was also the perfect hide-out for those with bad intentions for society. The men and women who took refuge there had various reasons. Some were on the run from the law. Some found the city too noisy, congested and expensive. Without a job to pay for the rising rent in the city, they simply moved into the jungle where it was at least free to live in. Modern man had yet to extend his greedy tentacles into the unexploited territory.

Some were involved in the marijuana growing business. They planted their herbs amongst the vegetation. Rainfall was reliable and all they needed to do was guard their investment from thieves and law enforcement officials. They would kill to do so. The plants thrived so well that they were sometimes found in places where no human ever planted them.

The jungle was vast. Even the officers of the law knew to stay close together when they ventured into it. This happened only rarely and were often futile exercises. Most of the time the criminals they came for would not be found and not surprisingly. It was that vast. The human elements blended quite well with the thick vegetation and unless you had an informant or a guide, chances are that you can drive or walk around for hours without encountering a single soul. They were there nonetheless, just hidden from sight. Oftentimes they would track phone signals of kidnapped people to a tower close to the jungle. From there the trail would go cold and there was nothing else they could do. It was usually at this point that the victim's relatives would have to pay the ransom money or contact Mason's firm.

Akpu, the man whose Benz Jeff had damaged, had made the jungle his second home. He had arrived there during his teenage years. He had been in and out of jail prior to his arrival and was tired of it. One day, at a night club, he was approached by a man who offered him a job in his 'business enterprise'. Per him, they had lost a valuable member of their team and needed a replacement quickly or they would lose out on a new project which was worth millions. The amount of money involved was what attracted him. Prior to that encounter he was used to deals that netted in a couple of tens of thousands at the most which he usually spent in less than a week. He did not like being out of money which was the main reason he was often in trouble with the law. When he ran out of money he did silly things and made stupid mistakes.

The man in question was no poser. He had everything Akpu had ever lusted after; money, designer clothes, fancy cars, and women. His clothes were always top range designers' and his fleet of cars spoke for themselves. When their business relationship went further and he eventually invited him to his home, Akpu was stunned. The mansion was something he could not wrap his brain around. He could not fathom how any man could own so much in a world where all he had ever known was stress and poverty. He had to steal every reasonable dime he ever spent which to him was not fair. Stealing was hard work unless you are a politician.

The man who preferred to be known as Ivory made him sign a few documents that he had not bothered reading. What could he lose? He was worth just the skin he inherited from his irresponsible mother and, as far as he was concerned, a coward of a father. He had rejected his birth name and adopted the name Akpu to signify his severance from his parents. He put ink to paper and did not protest when he was told his picture and finger prints would be taken and kept. He did not want to risk losing the opportunity of a lifetime by asking any wrong question.

Ivory disclosed to him that he started out selling ivory at the Federal Palace Hotel to tourists. His boss at the time was a stingy man known as Big Ben. He only survived because he managed to contact the hunters themselves and quietly carved a healthy niche for himself without Big Ben knowing. The ivories came from all around the continent. Business was good but really picked up when, for whatever reason, some silly international body that was not even based in Africa decided to outlaw the trade. That was when the price went sky high. It was every ivory dealers' wish come true. When the Chinese moved in some time in the seventies everyone cheered. Business was good even though risky. The overlooked stuff was worth more than its weight in gold. He could not understand why anyone would worry about dead elephants in a world where human lives were worth a dime a dozen.

Big Ben was later arrested somewhere in East Africa where he had gone to conduct business. He believed he was either dead or in jail somewhere in Tanzania. He did not miss him. He continued with the trade and made himself a decent amount of money. That was until the cops started looking for men like himself who traded ivory. At the time, it was worth a thousand dollars a kilo. He was more generous than Big Ben and paid his hunters and smugglers well. They alerted him that he was under surveillance because of his generosity. He packed up and went underground. Business slowed. There was too much bribe to pay to survive and he decided the risk was not worth it anymore. That was when he met the man who introduced him to the world of kidnapping.

Their first victim was an ivory dealer who was a rival and had snitched on him just to eliminate competition. The family had no idea what to do and quickly paid the ransom. At the time kidnapping was unheard of and cell phones where not even made. Tracking was impossible and they conducted business from pay phones. Life was easier then. Technology had made things difficult but not impossible for the average criminal who worked as hard, if not harder than any equally crooked politician to survive.

They liked the amount of money they made from this first job and how easily they had made it. He learnt that the rich only give their money to pretty mistresses and their own children. Every other person did not matter except those who had a gun to their head.

Ivory painted a picture of a lavish lifestyle. He would have loved to quit. He could afford to quit if he wanted. He just liked the idea that he was creating employment for the next generation of young crooks and taking from the crooked rich what rightfully belongs to the masses anyway. No rich crook should feel at ease.

Kidnapping was not just about money. They were like hired assassins. Sometimes people hired them to kidnap a business rival or political enemy. They hardly ever killed but often left their victims financially handicapped and emotionally damaged for a while.

Akpu liked what he heard. If he knew where his father was he would have liked him kidnapped. He was surprised at how organised the enterprise was. They had men all around the world. They even had a website in the dark web. Soon he was counting his own millions. They did not know it yet but he was plotting his escape. He was smart enough to know that the only way he could leave was if he died. That was clearly stated in the forms he had signed without bothering to read. Not that it would have mattered to him at the time he signed it if he had known. They were essentially a gang. That way Ivory maintained control over the men and women who worked for him. They were his soldiers as he liked to say.

If he did not maintain an iron grip control over them they would each venture out on their own. It was far too easy to form a kidnap gang. He liked to use Libya and Iraq as examples of what happens to any group or society when the strong man is removed from the scene. Society needs strong people at its helm, whether good or evil. A dictator was far better than a thousand independent rebels. There should always be someone at the helm of affairs who could be negotiated with.

Ivory hardly came to the jungle. He left the running of his affairs to Akpu who in turn left the dirty side of things to other men and women he had since recruited. Some were old enough to be his parents. In a country plagued by poverty and turmoil it was not difficult to find recruits and they were quite grateful for the opportunity to serve for a fee. They considered themselves better than the politicians and corrupt law enforcement officials who stole money even though they were employed. They did what they did because they had no other source of income. Each of them was now worth millions. They would have quit a long time ago and made way for younger people if not for their boss.

Ivory always encouraged his employees to be generous. They were encouraged to send their relatives to school and help the poor who had no one to help them. Wealth was no use if it did not create wealth in others. The whole set up was like a religion to them and they considered him some sort of guru. He even organised seminars once a while during which they were taught life's survival lessons such as how to make a budget and buy lucrative shares.

Akpu sat on a tree stump that had a cushion placed over it. The Lady in Red, as she was known, was sitting in front of him. If she had been a man she would have been tied to a tree and flogged like a Saudi crook. He knew her body was vital to her craft and did not want to cause any unwanted wound. She looked baffled. The other men had since lost interest and were drinking all sorts of drinks and waiting for some action. She had always delivered and that was also one of the reasons she was being spared a heavy punishment. One lapse in a while was acceptable.

He tried to piece together what could have happened from her narration which he had no reason to doubt. Their foolproof plan had always worked.

He lit two joints and offered her one. She declined.

"Do you think the man has figured you out?" he asked.

She shrugged. "It's possible. How else can you explain it? Perhaps he noticed something odd and decided to bail."

"Maybe it's time we found a replacement for you," he said thoughtfully. "It's so hard finding someone as pretty and as smart. Such a combination is so rare. Lucy is pretty but not that smart. No one would ever believe she is an insurance agent. She talks and acts like a ghetto girl. You reckon you can teach her how to speak like you?"

"She needs to listen to BBC radio often instead of those silly FM channels that play nothing but ghetto music and hip hop," she said. "I've told her that. It takes practice and dedication. All she does is watch home videos and associate with crooks. You will have to find someone else."

Akpu shook his head. He smoked his joint in silence for a while. When he was done, he lay on the ground and gazed at the huge trees and the bit of sky he could see through the foliage.

"Tell me what happened again," he said. "Let me rethink your story through the mind of cannabis. Do you know these things sharpen your brain?"

"Just before they kill the brain cells. How many times do I have to say it?" she asked.

"This will be the last time," he promised. "Now I've got some weed in my brain I want to hear it again. That is what Sherlock Holmes used to do. Did you read that book I gave you? Every crook who wants to be successful must read such books."

"Yes, I did," she said. "He is not real, just some fictitious character."

"He was real," he insisted. "Was a genius too. So, what happened? Start from the very first time you met. Don't leave out anything, no matter how insignificant."

"I met him at the resort," she said. "First time I tried my spell on him it did not work. He looked like he was troubled at the time. He was too stressed to party."

"And that has never happened before?" he asked.

"Never."

"Was he alone?"

"Yes."

"Carry on."

"I will if you let me."

"Don't be rude," he said.

"He does not come there too often," she went on. "I know because I try to look for him."

"You were mad he rejected you the first time," he said laughing.

"Don't be ridiculous," she said. "This is business. He is not close to my type in the real world. Anyway, the few times I saw him there he seemed to be always busy. On that night, I managed to hook my fangs into him and we agreed to meet the next evening. I gave him my business card with my address and phone number on it."

"Did he act strange or suspicious?"

"No," she said. "He seemed to believe what I told him. I told the boys about him and gave them the usual details. He arrived on time the next day. We drank. Or rather I drank, come to think of it. We talked business. He was all charming and respectful. He did not try anything and we kept it professional. He wanted life insurance and I gave him the usual fake form to fill. He did. I should have it at home."

"Why didn't you tell me this all along?" Akpu asked.

"You did not ask," she said.

"That's because I did not know you met him as an insurance agent," he said. "I need to see that form. Let's hope he did fill it honestly. Go on."

"He filled the form. We chatted for another thirty minutes or so."

"About what?" he asked a bit jealously.

"Every day stuff. Politics, business...he seemed quite knowledgeable. I must say he would have been a great friend had the situation been different."

"The next thing I'll be hearing is that you want to settle down and get married," he said sarcastically.

"The day will come," she said. "I can't remain in this business forever. You should know that."

"What would happen to me when that day comes?" he asked.

"You are not serious about settling down," she said. "The thing about us women is that when a man is not serious we simply move on like Oprah did. I'm not going to look this stunning forever. I seriously believe in family and you know that. I want to have kids and grandkids. I want to grow old and watch my grandkids play in the fields. Money is not everything."

"Money is everything. Let's leave that talk about family. So, you chatted about how to end the war in Syria. What next?"

"Stop being sarcastic," she said. "He asked to use the bathroom. Afterwards he left."

"Through the front door?"

"Yes. How else would he have left?"

"Our watcher said he never saw him leave. You did not alert the men. Were you drunk?"

"I may have had a few drinks but I was certainly not drunk."

"Why didn't you alert the boys?" Akpu asked. "I suspect he slipped something into your drink."

"I don't have to alert them. It's their job to be vigilant. I did my part. They should have done theirs," she said stubbornly.

"He did not walk out that door. Did he spend the night with you?"

"You've asked me that before. No, he did not. Why would I hide it from you if he did?"

"You do know this is serious, don't you?" he said sitting up. "If Ivory hears about this it will be a problem for you, for us. That man looks like he is unto something. I am worried about what his end game is. He obviously sneaked out the back. That means he knows our modus operandi."

She shrugged. "Have you thought of an easier explanation, like your men not being vigilant?"

"He arrived in a truck," he said. "What rich man drives around in a truck? When our men went to the parked truck after hours of no show they found it empty. Turns out it was from a car hiring company. The person gave fake names. Ivory is yet to know about this failure but, I dare say, if we don't solve it before the last ransom comes in I will be forced to tell him. I really am worried."

She considered what he said thoughtfully.

"I did not sign up for this," she said eventually. "I did my part. If I am expected to take the blame for someone's incompetence, then I think I need to stop."

"It has not come to that yet," he said hastily. "You just need to lay low for a while. We need to alter your appearance a little bit. Maybe you need to stop wearing red. Black maybe. Get me the form he completed when you get home. He may have been dumb enough to have put down his correct details."

She stood and left without a word. The men stared as she walked to her SUV. Being in the forest for days on end meant limited contact with pretty women. No one whistled or made any lewd remark. The last time someone did he was made an example of. They knew not to mess with her.

As soon as she was gone Akpu went into his thinking mode. He had a sense of foreboding. All the years he had been in the business he had felt in control of things. For the first time, it seemed someone had outsmarted them. The fact that he did not know what was going on made him feel uneasy. He called one of his men named Edward. Edward was a hulk of a man who spent his days working out. Even in the jungle he had a makeshift gymnasium made of heavy logs of wood and stones. He was the man they sent when someone needed a beat down.

"Keep a close eye on her," he said. "I want to know every person she is talking to or visiting outside our circle."

"Sure," Edward said.

"Report straight to me and not a word of it to anyone," he said. "I don't want them thinking we spy on our own. This is an unusual circumstance."

"Sure. Understand," he said.

"Did you guys fall asleep in the car? I need the truth," Akpu asked.

"No way," he said feigning a hurt look. "We were awake all the time. It is the way I said it was. Trust me."

Akpu nodded. He believed him. He had another theory.

Edward went to his car and drove away. He stood, stretched and decided to take a walk through the jungle. It was something he liked to do when he was stressed. The jungle took his mind off his troubles. The huge trees, exotic flowers and strangely coloured butterflies were all captivating and relaxing. He often wondered why humans chose to cut down the trees to build cities made of nothing but concrete and metal. He liked his house and his suburb but he felt it was devoid of soul.

Top on his thinking agenda was the mystery man who apparently knew their modus operandi. He believed Red Ivy was unto something or someone was unravelling their operation, someone who understood how they worked. He did not like the unknown. He had watched enough of crime shows on television to know that some law enforcement agencies could survey a group for years before pouncing. He wondered if Inspector Dele was in on it. It was possible he was being forced by some forces higher than him to smash their gang. He concluded that whoever was behind it had to be someone outside of the inspector's department. He suspected it was linked to an operation they had done the previous year. They had kidnapped an American and a Dutch citizen. Both men worked for the oil company Chevron which had paid up quickly. Perhaps Interpol was after them.

He eventually stopped thinking about his problems and instead focused on the marijuana plants that littered the forest. He already had plans to build a makeshift factory for the drug Ice. Since it made its debut in one of the night clubs in the city known to be frequented by tourists from Asia, he knew it was the drug of the future. He had contacted a Chinese chemist who promised to send one of his men to teach him the process of making it. They planned to use the factory as a gateway to the rest of the continent. His projection was that they would not have to kidnap any one once the factory was fully operational. He wanted to be the boss of this new operation and he was already thinking of how to severe his contact with his boss. It was going to be a messy severance. So far only a few trusted men knew about this plan. Men were going to die.

When he was through with his walk he returned to their makeshift camp and held a brief meeting with the rest. The main item on the agenda was focus and diligence. He was still talking when the bus he had sent off earlier with some men arrived. The driver and some of its occupants literally jumped out. Their clothes were blood stained. When Akpu went closer to see what was happening he realised there were more men inside too hurt to move. Some were completely motionless.

"We walked into an ambush," the driver said. He was afraid, an emotion that he had never seen in any of his men in a long time.

"What happened?" he asked.

"Monkey Face must have double crossed us. He knew we were coming," he said rubbing a bruised lump on his head. "It was a blood bath. Some of our men are still there. We need to send reinforcements quickly."

Akpu looked at the horrific scene in the bus with shocked disbelief. Suddenly he went into a fit of rage. He did not know Osun personally but had heard of his sin since childhood. He was the face of backstabbing in the world of crime. Ivory had known Osun. He was the mastermind behind the move to capture him alive so he could pay for his crimes. Smallie had been Ivory's nephew. Despite his rage, he knew sending any more men would be catastrophic. They had to count their loss in humility. He called Ivory and braced himself as he delivered the news.

15

CHAPTER 15

Jeff finally dragged himself out of bed. It was almost nine and he had laid on the bed wide awake since six-thirty that morning. He kept promising to get out of bed at a certain future time and kept breaking his promise. All his motivation was gone and he felt like he weighed a ton. It was his need to go to the bathroom rather than his zeal for the day ahead that finally conquered his fatigue. Wearily he dragged himself to the toilet and emptied his overfilled bladder. He decided to use the opportunity to brush his teeth and wash his face. There was not going to be any showering. He did not have the time or strength.

The kidnappers had finally called. They had contacted Mason's wife the previous night and she had broken the news as if she was announcing a birthday party. He still remembered the look on her face when she asked rhetorically where they expected her to get half a million dollars. She had laughed hysterically, as if it was the joke of the century. He did not recall any concern for the man that had been in captivity for days. Women.

She had moved back to her house with the kids 'for more personal freedom'. He suspected she needed more space for her affair which she no longer tried very hard to hide. He felt sorry for Mason and wondered if he knew. They had talked for over an hour trying to figure out how to raise the fund. In the end, he promised to speak to Gbenga for a loan. He knew this was an impossible request. It was one of the reasons he was reluctant to get out of bed. The thought of going to the very man that fired him for help was humiliating. Mason was not a full-time staff but he knew of his contribution to the success of the investigative journalism he and others in the company enjoyed.

He had other people he wanted to see. The file Mason had given him contained an address which he believed was the dwelling place of Ehi's biological mother. He knew the area very well. It was the dwelling place of the rich and powerful. Every house had its own private security detail and he still had not figured out how he was going to get through to her, if she was indeed the one.

No aspect of his plan for the day was exciting. He knew he had to get it over with as a matter of duty. He owed it to her. He was still not sure if the doctor was being honest when he said he did not know where she was. He believed Robert had eloped with her. His fear was that Madam Caro had got wind of their plan and had them both in some torture room in her resort. Dr Salami was either a good liar or a good actor. According to him, Caro had called asking if Robert was at his clinic. Apparently, he had stolen a huge amount of money from her. She would not disclose how much but from the way she sounded he believed it must have been huge.

Nneka was not in the kitchen when he finally got out of the room. The house was eerily quiet and he had this negative feeling that something unfavourable was about to happen. After he lost his job she had taken up teaching in a nearby private school. She taught the kids mathematics and English. He did not like the idea but there was nothing he could do. She had also since come up with the grand idea of reaching the rough neighbourhood kids through her teaching and had plans to start organising some after school science classes for those who could not afford it. She had never been so enthusiastic about anything in a while and he was happy for her. His own life on the other hand was fit for a movie that could be called Bad Luck Fellow.

He made himself a cup of coffee and some toast. It was while he was eating that he began to have a strong urge to visit the mystery man by the lagoon. He no longer regarded him as a mystery man. Human beings with their greed and selfishness were the true mystery. He was just a simple man who had decided not to live by the norm. The norm was survival of the fittest. All week he had been trying to shake off the thought of him but it stayed on like a bad habit. He decided then that he would visit him that morning.

After breakfast, he dressed up simply, got into his car, patiently coerced the engine to start and drove away. While he drove, the same thoughts plaguing his mind continued. He wished someone would teach him how to switch his worrying mind off.

The Ethiopian was all by himself when he arrived. He was sitting on a stone and looking in the direction of the sun. He wondered if he was some sort of sun worshipper.

"I was wondering how long it would take you to come," he said without turning. "Sit."

"Good morning," he said. He looked around. The only place he could sit on was the ground. He made himself as comfortable as possible.

"The sun has intrigued the ancients since man walked the earth," he said. "Not surprising why many saw the sun as the source of life and chose to worship it. It is in a way a source of life."

"You worship the sun?" he asked.

He shook his head. "The sun, the moon, the stars and the so-called planets...they are all mysteries in their own rights. The greatest mystery of all is the one who brought them to be. The sun in all its glory is nothing but a ball of energy. It is devoid of soul. You cannot worship that which has no life. How have you been?"

"Stressed. Burnt out," he said candidly.

He smiled. "It is always tough when you are on the right path. Unfortunately, many decide to quit when things get tough. It is also toughest when you are closest to victory."

"Right now, I feel it is toughest when you are closest to annihilation," Jeff said. He too was staring at the sun. He could see the dark spots on it quite easily and had often wondered just what they were. The explanation in the science books and sites did not make sense to him. Someone had suggested that aliens lived in the sun and the dark spots were the entrances to secret bases.

"Many have died fighting a just cause," he said. "The path to righteousness is stained with the blood of the righteous. Look at history. The wicked always count on the fact that men and women will always choose their own safety over any cause. Therefore, they resort to threat and blackmail when bribery and coercion will not work. In every generation, there will always be those who will not count themselves greater than the just fight they have chosen to fight. They will rather die than succumb to the violent tactics of the evil ones."

"But why?" he asked earnestly. "Why would a powerful God allow his own to suffer so much? Why do we feel like we are weakest when we try to do that which seems good? I used to feel invisible when I was deep in darkness. Hardly had any bad day. Since I turned my life around it has been one issue after the other. I used to just do things, just live, you know. Now, I must think things through as if one false step on my path will send me straight back to the paths of hell. This is not fair."

"This is the realm of man," he said. "What is permitted by mankind is what will be. God has his realm and has given mankind this realm to hold and shape. It is what we make it. Remember what the Messiah said, 'What you bind on earth, is bound in heaven. What you set free on earth, is loosed in heaven.'

"Life is full of challenges and trials. Some problems are because of the mistakes we have made ourselves. Some are there so that we can come out wiser and better individuals. In it all, we can only make accurate sense of the situation when God has his proper place in our lives; when we view the problems from God's view point. He alone gives meaning to life's ups and downs.

"Unfortunately, many try to take shortcuts out of their problems. When you take shortcuts; easy routes, out of your problems, you miss the lessons of life and the purpose of the trial is lost on you. You miss the knowledge of God, the intimacy with God who reveals himself in our trials as the God who delivers and loves.

The undergraduate who chooses to go out with married men or women because of financial difficulties, the man or woman who chooses to rob or work in the adult entertainment industry, the drunkard who must drink to forget his sorrow...all have chosen shortcuts and so have missed the glory that is the crown of all those who seek and find God in their situation.

"Friendship with God grows when you win battles together with God. Those who try to find fraudulent solutions to their problems soon discover that shortcuts only take them deeper into trouble, for they must face the trial that is only there for their own good. In life's situation, never consider evil as an option, for you will only worsen life for others and yourself.

"Problems will end one day. Grief ends. Nothing stays permanent. That is the purpose of the current life under time. Tears dry. Wounds heal. Lessons learnt and character formed outlast the problems. Remember this and you will begin to see the world in a different light."

Jeff sighed. Nneka had told him something similar.

"Forgive my questions," he said humbly. "I understand what you just said. How easy it is to focus on this temporal world and forget the big picture."

"You should look for answers," he said patiently. "God wants us to ask when we do not understand. Do you know the most common question I hear from people? Many ask me questions believing that I am somehow closer to God than they are, that I will have got all the answers to all the questions from him. I still ask. We are as close to God as we choose to be. Most people want to know why there is so much evil on earth. They want to know why a supreme being would allow so much injustice to prevail."

"I ask that question every day," Jeff said. "It does get to me when babies and children are involved. They are supposed to have guardian angels. Do they stand by and watch when these innocent ones are being abused or killed?"

"Let us take a walk," he said. "We will talk as we walk. Let us walk this talk."

The two men stood. The Ethiopian looked self-assured and relaxed. Jeff looked hopeless, tired and angry. He let the Ethiopian set the pace. It was a very slow one.

"To God there is no difference between the end and the beginning. He sees the end from the beginning," the Ethiopian said as they walked. "The baby is the man and the man is the baby. A nation and a family are the same. We deal in numbers, quantity, he does not. Past, present and future are not to God what they are to us. Did he not say to the prophet that by the time he was formed in his mother's womb he was already known? To understand God, we must realise that most of the emotions and sentiments humans are plagued with do not apply. Pain, death, time…these are not to God as they are to men. When you begin to realise this, you begin to see things differently."

"The pain is real for sure," Jeff said. "Suffering is pain."

"And pain serves a purpose sometimes, just like joy and pleasure. Sometimes pain is meant to deter the same way pleasure is meant to inspire and encourage," he said. "I will give you an analogy. When a man or even animal dies violently, we are left with the graphic image and memory of his manner of death. Few can fathom the fact that at death, it ends. It does not matter if it took that man a second or a week to die. Once he died, his pain and torture ended. Nowhere but in the memories of those left behind to ponder his death does the pain exist. Nowhere in the universe or time does that pain exist. It is as if he never even had any pain."

Jeff nodded even though his forehead was creased in thought.

"Most cannot get past the painful end," the Ethiopian said with understanding. "They want to think that his period of suffering has to count. That to declare it null is to disregard how much he suffered. But it is what it is. We abide in time. It is hard for us to contemplate an existence out of time. The good thing about time is that every event and experience ends. The bad thing about it is that we all die and every good experience must end. This to many is the curse of love."

"It is a great curse," Jeff said. "We love to die. Those we love we must leave or they must leave us. We are all on death row. It all seems so sadistic."

"Do not get distracted by your emotions" he said. "Why does God allow evil? He does not allow evil. He allows humans. Humans choose evil. Humans choose good also. What is good and what is evil? Who is good and who is evil? These are not mere things that you can just remove. Let us for instance imagine a world without evil. It means that we will be bound by nature to do what is right. What would that make us?"

"Angels," Jeff said managing a laugh.

"Robots," he said. "Angels are not beings with no capacity to choose to do evil. They are beings who are subject to the will of the almighty. They accept his authority and understand his love. Having no option of evil is not being good. Having the option of being evil but choosing to be good, that is good. You see, the concept of good and evil is not understood by men who ask why an almighty being would allow evil in his creation. To understand good and evil you must understand that God wants men and women to be good when there is an option of the opposite. Every evil that exists on earth does so because a man or woman decided to act contrary to God's will. That same man or woman has the ability and opportunity to change every day the sun rises."

"He knows the end from the beginning," Jeff interjected.

"Not when human decisions are involved," he responded. "Actions can be deduced when the level of devotion is known. You can tell what a rapist will do when left alone with a woman. You can tell what a thief would do when he stumbles upon an open safe. That is deduction. We have a choice to change every single day of our lives. The good becomes evil and vice versa. If God should remove 'evil', who will he remove? Those who are evil today but may repent tomorrow? Or those who are good today but will renounce good in the future? The first shall be the last."

"What about justice?" he asked.

"There are some who become so evil that God judges them while they are still alive," he replied. "They ignore warnings and march on with no intention of changing. How he decides about these matters is for him to know. I am just a messenger. Sometimes I am sent to deliver a warning to someone. Sometimes they listen, oftentimes they don't. Usually this happens when judgment is near. He decides. Good and evil are not absolutes. The real battle is between darkness and light. Just like the angels, humans have the choice to live for God or for the devil. Whether humans realise this is another issue. Ignorance is not an excuse. People must seek the truth."

"Some have found truth not knowing that the truth they have found is a lie," Jeff said. "It is confusing really."

"To you," he said. "God himself declares that he has given humanity everything there is to give that they may know him. Even creation declares the presence of the maker. One thing I know is that God is just and fair. He reveals himself to certain people. Any man or woman who seeks God wholeheartedly will find him. The problem is that our quests are often tainted with some selfish ambition or need. When you search for God with all your heart, you will find him. That is his word, and he never lies. It does not matter if you are in the heart of Arabia or close to a church in England."

"And Christ?"

"What about him?"

"Many cannot bring themselves to believe that he is the only way to God. There are a lot of good men out there who do not necessarily believe in Jesus Christ."

"'No man comes to me unless the father himself draws him near', were the words of Jesus. If you are really 'good' you will be drawn to Christ. The spirit realm is definite. When God sets a standard, it is set. There is no loophole. Cornelius was a pagan Roman soldier who met God's criteria. God sent Peter to teach him about Christ Jesus. It is like that. Now, let us talk about the days ahead."

"The days ahead," Jeff mused. "I wish tomorrow will never come. I see nothing but doom and gloom. Nothing is working in my favour."

"Mind your words," he said. "It is the end that matters. When you are in battle you do not focus on anything but the battle. Fight the good fight of faith. You have asked why God allows evil on earth. God often sends men and women to fight good causes. Guess what? Many choose to remain in their tiny world of selfish ambitions than respond to the call. Some respond but backout when the stakes seem high. You must consider yourself small but useful. Your life should be considered worthy of sacrifice to the higher cause. Those who understand this have found true freedom. Freedom is not to live with no responsibility. Freedom is to be lost in responsibility with no fear or want except to fulfil the higher calling. The one who sent you will provide. 'If I perish, I perish', Esther said. She did not perish. I will not beguile you. There are some who have perished."

"Am I going to die?" Jeff asked. He had a look of concern on his face. The Ethiopian stopped and faced him.

"Does it matter if you die or not?" he said. "What matters is that you dedicate your life to your calling. Move forward with no fear. Let nothing matter to you more than your calling. Whatever you hold dearer will be used to discourage you. If you perish, you perish, so what? We only have this one life to get it right. At the end of your life, what happens to all the pain and the gain? The rich and the poor shall perish one day. They shall stand the same on the other side. Wealth will not be their difference. Christ will."

"If I perish I would like to know that it counted for something," Jeff said.

"It always counts," The Ethiopian said. "Many died not seeing the end to their fight. Let he who calls decide on issues like that. You focus on the battle. If you are to die, then you are to die."

"If I am to die then I must die knowing it was worth it," he said. "He who calls should protect me to the end. I don't mind dying afterwards."

"No one dies after battle except a death unrelated to the battle," he said. "Jesus had twelve disciples. All but one died violently. Is the cause dead today?"

"Seems like it is finally dying," he said sarcastically.

"It lives," the Ethiopian said with enthusiasm. "Thousands of years later it still lives. There are many who have vowed to see an end to it, men like Aleister Crowley. We live in dark times. We live in beautiful times. It all depends on who you are and what you see. Fear not the evil one. I have faced him and I still stand."

"You should have been given this battle," Jeff said jokingly.

"I have mine. This is yours. Do you think this is about one girl? You think your battle ends with her rescue?"

"No?" Jeff asked a bit worried.

"On your shoulders lie a task so great that even you will shudder when you know the full extent of it."

"You know?" Jeff asked. "Tell me."

"A step at a time," he said. "The forces at play here have higher goals. Humanity has different strongholds aimed at weakening it and enslaving it to the evil one. I will give you a clue. Cathy O'Brien."

"Who's she?"

"A clue. The system that held that girl captive traverses the globe. It goes beyond what you can ever imagine. The same people who ask why God allows evil are quick to embrace the path of darkness and slow to act when called upon to usher in light. When you are done, you will understand what I mean when I say that our lives matter not except to lay it down to a calling we have chosen to believe in. Go forward. Have no fear. Have no price. Seek for no personal gain or glory. You are but a tool in the hands of he who sees further than any man or woman. Let him guide you. If you perish, perish. Death is nothing but a transition. Be dispensable. Be like the bees who go around gathering honey without realising that without their seemingly simple role life as we know it will never be the same. You never know the full extent of what you do unless your eyes are opened to see."

Jeff nodded. He was still afraid. He feared for his wife. He feared for his life. He knew that whatever happens, he would never let his fear get the better of him. He would see to it that he fights to the end, whatever that fight might be and whenever that end may be. From the look on the Ethiopian's face he knew there was danger ahead. He was warning him. He was encouraging him. He had lived a long time serving himself. Nothing good had ever come out of it. It was time to do things differently. When he took the vow never to live selfishly again he had meant it. For better or worse, he was marching on. Like the marriage vow he was going to stay to the end, come what may.

They continued their walk. The Ethiopian kept on talking but his mind was engrossed in his own thoughts.

"If she was lying," The Ethiopian was saying when he switched his mind back to reality. "She would have been arrested or sued."

"Who?" he asked.

"Cathy O'Brien," he replied. "You have allowed your mind to wander. Always pay attention. The answers we seek often comes at a time when we are not looking for answers. She claims to have been abused by many top-ranking US officials including Hilary Clinton since she was a kid. That is a damaging claim. If she was lying, why has she not been sued?"

"Perhaps they don't even know about her claims," he said. "Perhaps they feel silence is the best reaction. Sometimes we bring up dirt when trying to clear our names. Take Nigella for example."

"I have never heard the name," he said. "Do your own research as a journalist and come to your own conclusions. No offence is as bad as that done to the defenceless. Those who prey on children are among the worst of humanity. You need to understand that the people behind these crimes are powerful in a human sense. One thing I know is that the powerful of society do not like their true nature uncovered. They love their corrupt activities but want it hidden from the public. They will come at you with everything they have. This is why I have told you to consider yourself dispensable. Some are known to be humanitarian but are in truth predators. Some have a reputation of being honourable when, in fact, they are deplorable. They have no shame in their acts but will rather kill than have their true nature exposed. You need to know this.

"The devil works his evil acts through humans. Light always conquers. The righteous are as bold as a lion. These evils go on unchecked because most people cannot be bothered about what happens to the weak of society. It is only when the advantaged or strong of society are directly affected that they try to alert others. The ancient demons did not die, neither did humans stop dealing with them. They are alive and being worshipped by many today for gain. They merely adapted to suit the world of today. They murder children. They love to defile whatever is pure in God's eyes. They were sacked in ancient times because of their wickedness. We keep running back to them again and again for gain then turn around to blame God for the actions they perpetrate through us.

"It is worldwide, this problem. God does not do nothing. He works through men like you. There are many like you the world over. Some did not respond to the call, preferring their selfish ways. Some responded but quit when threats were made and fear set in. The evil will stop at nothing to preserve their way of life. They have placed themselves in what they think are places of power. The true power belongs to them that have the Spirit of the one true God. That is why they who fight them must value nothing of this world over the cause they have chosen. It is God's fight. He is with you. Just follow his directions even when you feel like turning back."

"How will I know he is with me?" he asked genuinely. "How can you tell me he is with me if I can die in the process?"

He smiled. "His ways are different from our ways. The death of Christ makes no sense to many. Humans are used to conquering by force. The concept of the cross makes no sense to them. You read the book of Enoch. The Holy One, the one that 'was as a son of man' was meant to die 'but not for his own sake'. Unsaved humans can see no sense in a crucified saviour. The disciples were murdered but one, yet he was with them. He is with you, rest assured. Doors will be opened that you will have no idea how they were opened. Walls will disappear. The divine will always help you out when you need help. You will have no doubt as to their presence. Walk in faith. Let God be God. And never settle for the mundane when the heavenly is calling."

He stopped walking when he got to a spot by the bank of the lagoon with two wooden chairs and a makeshift shade made from bamboos and palm leaves.

"Let us pray," the Ethiopian said. "Kneel and close your eyes."

He knelt and closed his eyes. The Ethiopian remained standing. He could tell from the direction his voice was coming from. He could not understand a word he said. It sounded like he was speaking Aramaic. When he was through he asked him to open his eyes and helped him up.

"What language was that?" he asked.

"The language of the Spirit," he replied. "We speak in tongues when we are lost for words. We let the Spirit pray for us. It is the privilege of every child of God in Christ."

Jeff did not know what to say. He remembered coming across a student group one night. They had all been praying behind one of the hostel blocks in very strange languages. At the time, he had been with a friend and they had laughed, calling them drunk lunatics who had no life. Back then having a life meant sleeping around with girls and getting drunk at parties.

They walked back in silence. They parted with a handshake and an embrace. He felt strangely calm when he got to his car. He knew there was not going to be any more procrastination. Whatever needed to be done had to be done on time. It was time to pay the one woman who could unravel the whole drama of Ehi's childhood a visit.

He drove towards the suburb where she lived and tried not to think about his dwindling finances. Freelancing was no longer as easy as it used to be. YOUTUBE and the internet meant stories were heard before the major news media published them and he did not have the means to go after the big news. He would need to travel to Russia, the United States and the Middle East for those. Men like Alex Jones became popular after he captured the bizarre video of the elite of society behaving like they were some ancient Babylonian sect at the Bohemian Grove. Since then he had carved a decent niche for himself and had become a big time independent YOUTUBE news mogul.

The house was as expensive as Mason had described it. The suburb was eerily quiet with scarcely a child in sight. Each house was a magnificent piece of art. It seemed they sought to outdo each other. They all had high walls and gates that would keep any prison safe.

The security man came to meet him outside the gate. He wanted to know what business he had there. He had a frown on his face as he assessed his beat down car.

"I am here to see your boss," Jeff said.

"And you are?" he asked.

"I am a journalist," he replied.

"Nobody is home," he said.

"Tell her if I don't see her now I will be forced to publish the information I have tomorrow," he said. "I will also mention the fact that I would not have published anything except for the fact that you will not let me through to see her."

"What news?" the man asked looking a little concerned.

"That is not your business," Jeff said.

The man thought for a moment.

"Give me a second," he said and went back to his post. Jeff could see him making a phone call. Afterwards he peered through the window, wrote down what he believed was his licence plate number before opening the gate. He came over, gave him a visitor's book to complete before ushering him in.

He parked the car in front of the house and walked up to a huge door with a brass knocker attached to it. He pressed the buzzer and waited. Moments later a very pretty woman in her thirties opened the door smiling like he was a lost brother. He could tell she had spent some time in front of a mirror before answering the door.

"Come on in Jeff," she said. "Make yourself comfortable."

He walked in after her and sat on a chair that was so comfortable he almost wished he could take a nap on it.

"Whiskey?" she asked as she poured herself a good measure from a bar on the corner of the massive room.

"No, thank you," he said.

She took a sip before sitting on the chair directly opposite the one he was on.

"So, you are a journalist," she said. "What exactly have we done to warrant the visit of a journalist? We are just simple people. My husband would not have handled it nicely and I hope you conclude whatever business brought you here before he comes back."

She looked at her wrist watch.

"You are Mrs Johnson?"

"Yes," she said. "I am quite popular around here and I wonder why you should ask. Who directed you here?"

"I was doing some research about a woman called Peggy Manuela," he began but stopped when her smile vanished and her facial expression turned cold as ice.

"Get up and leave my house right now," she said standing and pointing to the door. "You want to destroy everything I have worked hard to achieve? You journalists only know how to pry into other people's lives and tear homes apart."

Jeff stood. He was quite shocked by the abrupt transformation.

"I thought I should give you the chance to narrate your own side of the story before deciding if I should go public or not," he said. "I was just being considerate."

"Do you know what my husband will do if he knows about my past?" she said, her hand still pointing at the door.

"Imagine what he will do if he learns it from the papers," Jeff said.

She softened a bit and lowered the arm. There was spite and panic in her eyes as she looked at him.

"Sit down," she said uninvitingly and sat. She gulped down the remainder of her whiskey and began wringing her hands. For a while she just sat there in deep thought. Eventually she looked up at him.

"What exactly do you want?" she asked. "Is it money? I can pay you whatever you stand to gain from publishing whatever it is you have in mind. My past must stay in the past."

Jeff smiled. He did feel sorry for her.

"You had a daughter," he began.

She clutched her chest and began to sob. He had not envisaged such a reaction and did not know what to do. He averted his gaze and let her sob. When she had regained her composure, she excused herself and went to her room to refresh herself. It was a more subdued woman that emerged. All the arrogance of status and wealth had evaporated and her real personality had come through to the surface. Without any prompting, she gave him her own version of events.

"I was young and stupid," she began wearily. "I had parents who were strict. They wanted me to go to college, be a good girl and eventually become a lawyer. I was a straight A student until I met a man called Linus. I met him at a club I had no business being in at my age. There was this girl at the time. She was from a broken home and my mum did not like her at all. She showed me the wicked world of night clubs, drugs and all. I would sneak out of my room to attend some wild party in some ghetto part of town. Sometimes we would go to some night club where dark and immoral stuff happened. I began to change. I became a rebel.

"I met Linus in one of these clubs. He was as charming as he was handsome. He was wealthy too. He told me I would never have to work if I stayed with him, that he was that rich. We were heads over heel with each other and in my mind then nothing could go wrong. He swept my naïve feet off the ground. Looking back now I could see how silly I was. I would sneak out to meet him. My mum found out but was too scared to tell dad. He was a man that believed strongly in the old ways. He was all Moses, ten commandments, fire, brimstone and all. Linus became more and more demanding. He would want me to spend a weekend with him sometimes. I knew that was pushing it too far. When he threatened to discontinue the relationship, I decided I had to run away from home. He had been urging me to move in with him. He was tired of all the hide and seek romance as he had put it and was no teenager.

"The day I arrived his home with nothing but a small bag with some clothes in it he went into a fit of rage. I should have informed him before coming, he said. I thought he would have been pleased. There was a woman in his home at the time and he managed to convince me she was his cousin. She stayed with us for a week before leaving. He was acting cold. Whenever I confronted him about it he blamed it on some stress he was having. I reminded him it was his intention that I moved in with him in the first place. I thought of returning home but was too scared. What was I going to say? Where would I tell my father that I had been?

"Sometimes he would be back to his former self. We would laugh and play and go shopping. The problem was that he always had this dark cloud hanging over him and no matter what happened he would go back into his shell where no one could get to him until he emerged. I later learnt he was using cocaine. I Are you recording this?"

"No," Jeff said wondering why she was telling him all that.

"He had friends who were nothing like him," she went on. "At least that was what I thought. I should have known that birds of the same feather flock together. I mean these were men who owned brothels, strip joints and night clubs, those sorts of shady businesses. He claimed he was into wholesale. He imported electronic gadgets from China and sold to various retail outlets. I believed him. Sometimes he would go on business trips to China or Thailand. He would be gone for weeks. One of his friends would always visit when he knew he was out of town. He kept offering me money to strip in one of his joints. He is dead now. Died of a heart attack. Life gets us all in the end, doesn't it? Anyway."

She stood and walked to the bar where she poured herself some more whiskey. She decided to stay there.

"Turns out Linus was a drug dealer. The house was raided one evening. Nothing was found there but he was taken away anyway. I was taken away too and interrogated. They told me about his dealings, how he recruited young girls and promised them the holiday of a lifetime. He would give them money for shopping abroad and pay for their accommodation. They would go without knowing they were being used as drug mules. Some came back without knowing what they really went there for. Others were caught. Some are still in prison as we speak. I don't know if I would have been involved or he really meant it when he said I was his sweetheart. I will never know."

"Where is he now?" Jeff asked.

"Prison," she said. "I was let go when it was confirmed I had no knowledge of his illegal business. It was during his trial that I realised I was pregnant. I had thought the stress was affecting my menstrual cycle. Pregnancy was the last thing on my mind. By the time I knew, I was almost five months. He was sentenced to thirty years in jail. He was full of joy when he learnt I was pregnant. He asked me to wait for him, that thirty years was nothing and he may even come out before then if he was paroled. He really knew how to sweet talk. He convinced me to keep the pregnancy. After I gave birth I had to do a reality check. My daughter would never know her dad. She would be thirty when he came out. I would be forty-six. I decided to pay him one last visit. I told him I planned to give her up for adoption. He went into a fit of rage and threatened my life and that of my family. I was not going back. The spell was finally broken.

"I gave the child up. The rest is history, or so I thought. I since went back to my parents. Dad was a changed man when I came back. He was much softer. I learnt he had a major stroke during my absence. I suspect I was the reason for that. I knew then that he really loved me. That he had always wanted the best for me. I did not tell them about my pregnancy. As far as they were concerned I was the prodigal daughter returned home. I returned to my studies. I returned to making good grades. I went to university, studied Architecture and graduated. I met my husband there and we got married soon after graduation. We have two beautiful children. I do think about her sometimes. Unfortunately, I cannot undo what has been done. I signed away my right as a parent."

"Wouldn't you like to know where she is now, how she has been faring?" Jeff asked.

"I was told she would be adopted to a responsible family," she said. "When I signed the documents, I was told I was never to ask about her or try to contact her. That it would be traumatising to her and her adopting parents. Do you know where she is?"

He nodded.

"Where?"

"I don't know if I should tell you," he said. "Let's just say that she has had a very hard life. Whoever told you she was going to a responsible family lied to you. That girl has been mistreated from birth."

She placed a hand on her mouth, a shocked look on her face.

"I have always justified my actions thinking I did what I did to give her a better future," she said. "I had no idea."

Jeff stood.

"I have to leave now," he said. "I am still investigating. Those responsible for this will be brought to book. I can't tell you too much right now."

"What happens to me?" she asked. "My husband must not know about this."

"He would not know," he said. "You did what you did in good faith. I can't blame you. My only problem is that you still think of your reputation and your status more than your own daughter. Out there is a girl who came into this world out of no doing of hers. She has been let down and betrayed by all of us. Evil people have taken advantage of her literally from day one."

"What has been going on with her?" she asked, her face contorted in grief and distress.

Jeff wished he could tell her that she was in good hands now just so that he could put her out of her misery. The truth was that he had no idea.

"I will keep in touch," he said. "She is fine, thanks to a few good men still on this planet. I have to go now."

"Wait."

She walked through one of the doors. When she re-emerged moments later she had an envelope in her hand.

"Take this," she said.

"What is it?"

"My contact details and a picture I took of her just before she was given away," she said. "I will very much like to see her again. My husband however must never know. If you ever need my help do not hesitate to call me."

Jeff nodded. They shook hands before she saw him out. Once in the car he became very emotional. She had a striking resemblance to her. He felt like he was talking to an older version of her when he was talking to her mother. He could see where the good looks had come from too. He was more resolved to find her and vowed to never rest till she was found.

He opened the envelope. There was a black and white picture of a baby lying on a piece of cloth. As he looked at it he tried not to cry. Of all crimes against humanity, none was as touching and cruel as that done to the innocent. He still could not understand the minds of those who preyed on such. They were evil and he would have no problem exposing them and bringing them to justice. She had scribbled her phone number on what appeared to be a piece of paper. He added the number to his list of contacts and was about to discard the paper when he realised it was a cheque book. He looked at the figure in disbelief. For a moment, he thought of returning it. Eventually he decided he was going to keep it. He would need every resource he could get to make sure the story had a happy ending.

He decided to put everything on hold and drive straight to the bank. For weeks, he had simply ignored his bills and the letters were left unopened in a drawer in his bedroom. They were locked away like the nuclear waste in the ground that earthlings chose to forget with no clue what would become of them. He managed to find a reasonable spot to park his car, hoping to be out of the bank before getting a fine for illegal parking. The banking hall was busy. Most were trying to get money out of their bank accounts. Few were there to deposit anything. He joined the short deposit queue and was standing before the teller in no time. She took one look at the cheque, one at him, another at the cheque then called one of her colleagues who was sitting idly at a desk behind her. He came to have a look.

"What is your profession, sir?" he asked.

"What does it matter?" Jeff asked. "The cheque is authentic, that's all you need to know."

He made a brief phone call, smiled as he apologised and instructed her to proceed. Several seconds later he got the alert. It was like a weight had lifted off his shoulders. He could focus on the task at hand and not have to worry about debts. The first thing he would do when he got home was to open all the envelopes and settle his bills. He marvelled as he recalled the words of The Ethiopian. In bed that morning he would never have believed if anyone told him that before the day ends he would be able to pay his bills. Life.

His phone began to ring. It was Mike. The two had not spoken in weeks and he was surprised. He looked at his rear-view mirror to make sure no cop car was behind him then answered the call.

"What's up?" he asked.

"It's been a while man," Mike said. "I'm going there tomorrow night."

"Where?" he asked.

"Where else, Caro's."

"Didn't you hear I lost my job? I've got no money."

"I'll pay for it," Mike said.

Jeff shook his head. "Maybe rent money would be more reasonable."

"You don't want to see your friend Ehi?"

"Nothing I can do about that," he said. "No money means no money."

There was a certain hesitation before he went on, making Jeff wonder if he was being genuine.

"When was the last time you saw her?" he asked.

"About the last time I saw you," he replied. "Are you going to loan me some rent money or not?"

"If you agree to come with me tomorrow," he said.

Jeff thought he sounded different. He could tell something was not right. He hesitated.

"Sure, if that's what it would take to stop me from being homeless."

"I'm sure it's not that bad," Mike said.

"It is that bad," he said. "If you had behaved like a friend and bothered to find out how I am doing you may have known. I gave Caro virtually all of my savings."

"And I still don't understand why," he said. "Especially since you are not taking full advantage of your investment. I would be going to see her everyday if I were you."

"She is a human being, not an investment," he said angrily. "It's not for you to know why. Men like you will never get it."

"Meaning?"

"Meaning you still don't think of women as humans. They are just items that exist to satisfy your lusts."

"Hey, I never judge you. Don't judge me. I did not make the world what it is. You are the one who wants to bind your conscience to some religion that was created just to get Negroes domesticated. You are coming or not?"

"Will you loan me the money or not?"

"How much?"

"Fifty grand."

Mike hesitated. "Ok."

"See you tomorrow."

He dropped the phone on the passenger seat angrily. He knew Mike was unto something. He even wondered if Caro had set him up to make the call. For all he knew, someone may have figured something out and he may be walking into a trap. His most logical reasoning was that they had uncovered the plot. Ehi was in Caro's hands. The thought of it made him extremely angry.

CHAPTER 16

Inspector Dele dropped his wife and two sons off at their family owned stationary business. He had convinced his wife to open the business in her name years back. She supplied the company that supplied all the stationaries to the police stations under his jurisdiction. She opposed it at first, believing it was fraudulent. He managed to convince her that there was nothing illegal about it. She was a devout catholic, the type who would lock herself in her room and pray in front of Mary's statue with her rosary beads for hours.

He had agreed to become a catholic when it became clear that her parents would never allow her to marry anyone outside their faith. He had lied that he was one. It was not a complete lie. He had been baptised as a child by his parents, or so he was told. He could remember vaguely scenes from masses they attended when he was a kid. The church was one attended by mostly affluent members of society and his memories were those of marble walls, golden cups that everyone was made to drink wine from as well as priests dressed like royalty.

His father had wanted him to be a priest. At the age of twelve he had considered it his goal. Three years later he discovered the lusts of the female flesh he had been warned repeatedly about and all his divine dreams were immediately swapped for more immediate mundane ones.

He could never get enough and quickly realised the key to the world of pleasure was money.

His father succumbed to his mother's pressure and abandoned his ambition for him to attend a seminary. It was better he went the way of the world than to disgrace the family by breaking his priestly vows like some had done. He agreed to get him a place in the police force where he was already a key figure. He went to a police college. Upon graduating he was given a good rank and from there his career, catalysed by his father's influence, went from glory to glory.

His father was a no-nonsense man who was known to be honest and loyal. There was no bad word from anyone except crooks against him. The only people who loathed him were those on the wrong side of the law. He was the opposite, a fact that worried him initially. He had hoped to be a man of reputable character like his dad. Scandal after scandal trailed him until he stopped trying to impress anyone. Once he decided it was not possible to have a good reputation and enjoy life at the same time he went for the fun part. Who would remember his deeds or those of his father centuries to come? He was a secret agnostic. He hoped there was no God and that the tales of a fiery furnace where sinful men like himself would roast forever was some fictional tale spurned from the mind of a deluded Greek. He hoped to slow down one day, maybe when he was old and impotent. An old man once told him that the urges never really go with age. He still did not know if this was a good thing or a bad thing.

On his way to the office Madam Caro called. She wanted to know when he would be there. There was an urgent matter. He asked her to be there in an hour knowing he would be there in less than thirty minutes. She would not say why she wanted to see him so urgently. She was the one person in the world who disregarded every protocol when it came to making appointments.

The reason was clear. She had dirt on him, the sort of dirt that could destroy his career and family. As long as he did her bidding, he was safe. There were times when he had thought of placing a hit on her. The problem was that they served each other well in a perfectly symbiotic relationship. Wrecking his career would not help her in any way. Having some degree of control over him was more beneficial to her. Sometimes he wondered how many more like him were being manipulated by her. She had convinced very influential people to do things for him that he had thought impossible.

She was already waiting for him when he arrived. His secretary made a face when he arrived and he smiled knowingly. She had sent him a message to let him know Caro was there. She had real tears in her eyes when he walked into his office. He feigned concern.

"Can you believe what that ugly faced fool did to me?" she cried before he even closed the door.

He locked the door behind him.

"Who?" he asked.

"Who else? That ape-faced man called Robert!" she yelled. "He virtually emptied my bank account and took some of my cash from home. I need you to find him as soon as possible. Bring him to me when you find him. No wonder God gave him a face like that. It was to warn people to be wary of him. I try to be good to everybody. That has always been my undoing."

"He has to be arrested if...," he began.

"I want to deal with him myself!" she cried angrily. "I took him in when he had nowhere to go and sheltered him all these years. This is how he repays me!"

Inspector Dele pinched the bridge of his nose. She sounded like a coal powered train when she was yelling and the sound of her voice pounded his ear drums with such force his head ached.

"Alright," he agreed just so that she would stop yelling. "I will hand him over to you when I find him. I will assign some men to it as soon as possible."

"Put at least a hundred men on this one," she said. "He needs to be found quickly before he spends it all."

"I will," he said. He knew he could only afford two men but there was no point upsetting her further. "Anything else? Do you have any photos of him?"

"Who takes photos of such an ugly face?" she asked. "You want my camera destroyed? You know what he looks like. Find him quickly before he spends all my money!" she said.

He picked up the phone and spoke to one of his trusted officers. He gave him the name and a description of the man.

"Get at least a hundred men looking for him and get him fast," he said.

The officer began to complain about how he was going to find that number of men and if it was even necessary.

"Make it two then," he said.

Madam Caro looked satisfied thinking he meant two hundred. She stood.

"It shouldn't be hard to find him," he said. "Just go home and relax. Once we get news I will personally call you. I might even come over tonight. Don't be surprised if he is with me."

"In that case, I will be glad if he comes in handcuffs. Bring along some pepper sprays and a stun gun."

She strolled out of her office. He felt sorry for Robert and wondered how stupid he must be to think of stealing from a woman like her. He did not wish to be there to see what she would do to him. He opened his drawer and took out a bottle of aspirin, popped two into his mouth and washed them down with water from a bottle the secretary always placed on his desk at the beginning of each day. He would have preferred beer but some rules were better respected.

He hoped Robert had not left the country. He had always known the man was not as stupid as Caro believed. No man was. The only thing that made humans foolish was love and he was not in love with Caro. In a way, he was not surprised. He had chatted with him on few occasions and knew he had big dreams, the sort of dreams that could not be achieved under his circumstances or wages. Something told him he had already fled the country. He had always dreamed of starting afresh in a distant land. He had even helped explain to him the process of obtaining a passport and applying for visa. Australia or Brazil was his likely destination. It was their secret and not even Caro deserved to know.

After a while they had got close enough to discuss embarrassing issues. Robert wanted love. He could not blame him. With a face like his and no money to supplement his features he doubted he would be a hit with the ladies. He urged him on even though he did not think he would have any success. Robert knew he would need money to change his fortune. Life had dealt him a bad fate, or rather a bad face. He would have to find a way to change his fortunes and the only way he could think of was to be rich. At the time, he had no idea what he had meant but now that Caro's money had gone missing he realised the ugly-faced man had been planning the hit for years.

They had agreed he would help him steal whatever evidence Caro had of him if he would wipe his criminal record clean. He did not know it at the time but there was no meaningful criminal record that would effectively stop him from applying for any visa. The record system still belonged to the colonial era when paper files were used. The only record of his crime was in some file in some local police station. He would be surprised if the writings in that file would still be readable. No red light would flash when he applied for his visa. Robert had no way of knowing but he saw it as his own leverage. The agreement was that he would help him wipe his record clean if he would obtain the little memory stick Caro kept somewhere, a stick that contained his sins. It was her blackmail tool and she had got too many favours from him because of it. He would have called him if he had taken the sticks. It was possible he had figured out he was of no use to him.

He sat at his desk and stared at his calendar. There was nothing to do. Most of his subordinates did stuff that he should be doing. He could go on a vacation for months and things would still function smoothly. He had adopted a simple signature that his secretary could sign in his absence. She signed most documents when he was not around. No one needed to know this. She read them at least before signing which was safer. He would be the first to admit that the public sector had more people than it needed.

He did not delude himself like the overzealous new commissioner who believed crime could ever be wiped out from society. If it was about resources and dedication, the United States would have wiped out crime and terror. The truth was that humans were by nature prone to evil. Organised crime was better left alone. Whenever he became chief he planned to use his experience to control crime, not stupidly try to eradicate it. He preferred crooks he could see to those he could not. People like Caro and all the other crooks he knew represented crime. He would rather have people like that controlling the underworld of crime than hundreds of ruthless youngsters with no ethics. Knock the bosses out and what you get is chaos. The middle east was a classic example of this and he was already preparing a presentation on this. Crime could exist side by side with the law. Welcome to the new age.

He was almost dozing off when his secretary knocked. She popped her head through the door to announce that a man wanted to see him, a journalist. The word journalist took all the sleep from his eyes and he became immediately alert. His father had almost lost his career because of an interview he had done with a journalist. He had bared his soul and given his honest opinion about sensitive issues during the interview. Not many took it well, especially many from the high ups in government. They had wanted his head. They demanded his resignation but the man was as stubborn as Trump. Public opinion was in his favour. Like Trump, he had many secret admirers who showed solidarity in the form of street protests. This was a man who had managed to get the figures down when it came to crime.

"Do you think I should see him?" he asked.

"Better to have them on your side," she said. "Just be polite and say as little as possible."

"Get us some tea once he has settled in, that Chinese tea that makes people drowsy."

"That stuff is supposed to be for sleep," she said giggling.

"Exactly," he said. "Chinese tea for the journalist, Indian tea for me. Please don't mix them up."

"I'll send him through."

He braced himself, cleared his throat in advance and waited. As soon as the man entered the office he was all smiles.

"Welcome, gentleman of the press," he said rising to shake hands with his unwelcome guest. "Have a seat. I believe you already know me or you will not be here."

"Jeff," Jeff said as he sat. "I am a freelance journalist."

"Is there anything as freelance?" he asked. "All journalists sell their story to some big media company. Who buys your stories?"

"The internet has changed all that. Now we can publish our story directly to the people. That way we are not obligated to change anything the big boys do not want. It is a whole new way of doing things."

"Not sure I like anything from the modern era," Dele said. "I am always for old school. I like things organised. The idea of everyone running around doing their own thing kind of worries me. I prefer corporations. The bigger the better. One CEO rather than a hundred small entrepreneurs. A king rather than presidents."

"It is for the good of democracy," Jeff said.

"I'm not a Democrat," Dele said and laughed. "I am a Republican. Show me one country in the world where democracy is practiced."

"The United States."

"Do they pay tax?" he asked.

"Yes," Jeff said.

"And they really like paying tax and high mortgage rates to the big banks?"

"I guess so," he answered.

"No, they don't," he said. "No one does and that is how we know it is not government of the people or for the people. Anyway, tea?"

"No, thanks."

"Come on," he said. "You are my guest. It is rude to refuse things from your host. Have some tea. We are not at war."

"Okay then," Jeff agreed reluctantly.

Dele pressed the intercom button and instructed his secretary to get two cups of tea. They chatted more about politics and the economy while they waited. Eventually she arrived with the tea and set a cup down in front of each person. Before she left she shared a secret smile with her boss. He struggled to keep himself from laughing as the journalist took his first sip.

"So," he said after taking a sip from his own cup that almost singed his lips. "What brings you here?"

"I am here to ask your help," he began.

"That would be a first," the Inspector said. "I never knew you folks ever ask for help. Go on."

"I am not here as a journalist but as a human being. Whatever we discuss here will not be published. Everything will be confidential."

Dele nodded and grunted. He knew it was just a trap to get him to trust him and run his mouth. He leaned back and listened as the journalist turned humanitarian talked about Caro's club house and how he needed the police to investigate what he believed to be gross abuses of the fundamental human rights of people he believed were being held against their will. He wanted the girls rescued, the place shut down for good and the perpetrators brought to book. He might as well be asking Trump to arrest Hilary.

He could not help thinking of Madam Caro as he talked. The woman had threatened him with exposure numerous times. She always did it subtly but a threat was a threat. Now this journalist was asking him to shut the place down like it was some bakery or bottle shop by the corner. What did he know? Was he aware he was a member of the same place he spoke about? Perhaps he had come to confirm rumours. He could not be sure. He had to be careful.

"This is a very ugly situation," he began when Jeff was done. He weighed his words carefully as he had promised himself he would. "If this place exists and for the purpose you insinuate, then I think we as the police ought to do something drastic about it."

Jeff nodded. He was impressed.

"Right now, I have a lot of cases on my hands. The Boko Haram folks are infiltrating society and trying to blow us up at every chance they can get. The only reason we are not seeing bomb blasts every day is because we are working around the clock. Resources are ..."

He paused. He had wanted to say, "Resources are thin," but did not want anyone accusing him of undermining the might and capability of the police force.

"Resources have been assigned according to priority," he went on. "People above me determine what is important. We have a division that deals with human trafficking and abuses of human rights. I can assure you they are working on this as we speak. Sometimes it seems as if we are not doing anything when in fact we are busy behind the scene gathering evidence. Sometimes we get our men to infiltrate these sorts of places to gather intel. This might take years. We like to go after the big fish. My experience has taught me that unless the big fish are netted you waste time and effort going after tiny ones. An organisation needs to be uprooted and destroyed. There is no point shutting down a branch only for it to pop up somewhere else under another guise."

Jeff was beginning to look frustrated as he listened to him. He was beginning to sound like a politician in his ears.

"Sir," he said. "I understand the urgency of the other issues but I think we ought to prevent more deaths while investigating terror. We are all citizens. Every life matters."

"Meaning?" the inspector asked. "Are we talking about human rights abuses or murder?"

"Both," Jeff said. "I have heard rumours of some of the girls being tortured to death. Horrific abuses go on there as we speak. I have cause to believe that a certain Ehi died there recently. Either she is dead or she is dying. Just send someone there and do not leave any room unsearched. I'm sure if you ask one of the staff there in confidence they will confirm it. What do you think happened to the Chibok girls? Some have been found with child. War on terror must also focus on the roots of social break down. The underprivileged are the ones these predators focus on when they need to recruit more foot soldiers. Social justice is eventually part of the war on terror."

Inspector Dele bit his lower lip, a habit he adopts whenever he was in a contemplative mood. He did not like what he was hearing. He normally went there for fun. The girls wanted money, he wanted fun and that was supposed to be it. He knew some of them to be underage but, in his thinking, underage girls were sexually active in the larger society anyway. What was the crime? Now he was hearing about abduction, abuse and murder. That was an entirely different issue.

He knew he had to investigate. If he did not, someone else would certainly be contacted. The young man was not the type to let go easily. The ball had to stop in his court. If one of those overzealous, self-righteous officers got wind of this his involvement might be discovered. There were other officers and top figures in the mix. If this got out a lot of careers would be destroyed and any prospect of him being chief would become a mirage.

"I'll see what I can do," he said. "keep this all quiet. If anyone gets wind of this, they might be alerted and Caro will simply relocate. That would help no one."

Jeff agreed with him.

"About this girl, Ehi, how are you sure the rumour is true?"

"I have my sources," Jeff said. "Unfortunately, I cannot reveal them.

I'm sure if you ask some of the men working there they will tell you. You may ask Madam Caro herself."

Inspector Dele nodded, a look of genuine concern on his face.

"I have a daughter," he said almost absent-mindedly. "She's just fifteen…"

He stopped, wondered why he was saying such a thing and smiled nervously.

"There's an orphanage in town," Jeff said. "It is linked to some religious NGO. If you check it out, you will discover that many of their adopted children are unaccounted for. Madam Caro adopts children there from time to time. It might interest you to know that she only adopts girls. Not a single boy. There is no proper documentation of these kids and no follow up to see how they are doing in their new homes.

Dele's jaw dropped in genuine shock.

"Are you sure of all this?" he asked.

"I am a journalist," Jeff said. "I do my homework before laying accusations. I am sure you are paid taxpayers' money to investigate such things for yourself. Don't take my word for it. I'll be leaving now."

"Wait a minute," the inspector said hastily. "You must not publish any of this."

"Not yet," Jeff said. "I'll wait for some reasonable amount of time then…"

He let the words hang. The inspector got the message.

"We will do something," the inspector said emphatically. "I only need time. I want you to understand that while we are carrying out our underground investigation it may seem as if nothing is happening. We all need to be patient."

"I might not be as patient as you may wish me to be," he said standing. "Try to act quickly. It did not take me much time to dig out what I now know and I am just one person with limited resources. Let's not play politics with this inspector. I'm all for the girls. Good day. Thanks for the tea."

"One last question before you go," Dele said. "How did you gain access to the club house?"

Jeff smiled.

"I'm just good at what I do, inspector. Everything is on a need-to-know basis. Good day."

"Have my card," Dele said offering him his card. "Call me when you have any new information or want to speak to me. We are in this together, okay?"

Jeff took the card, handed him his, thanked him and left. As soon as he was gone Dele picked up his phone and called his chief investigating officer, a man named Tayo. He had an impeccable record and he needed men with clean records for a change. In less than no time he was in his office. He handed him the phone number to Robert's mother.

"Get me all the numbers that have contacted this number in the last month," he said. "I want it on my desk before the end of the day."

"May I know what this is about?" Tayo asked.

"Not now. By the way get me four good men. I want you to handle an investigation into an NGO. We may be laying negligence charges so be careful not to mess up your evidence. Trafficking is involved."

"Drugs?" Tayo asked, his eyebrows raised in surprise.

"Children."

"Goodness! An NGO?"

"I'll brief you as soon as the team is ready. Keep this close to you and your team."

"Sure. Anything else?"

"Get me those numbers as soon as you can."

He nodded and left, leaving Dele to think about his conversation with the journalist and the possibility of a disgraceful end to his career if he was ever exposed. He needed to find Robert fast.

Less than an hour after he left, Tayo called. He had the list. Dele was surprised at how fast he had got it. He had forgotten the man was a computer wizard. While his mates played around with women he chose to spend his money and time attending professional developmental courses. When he spent five thousand dollars of his own money to attend a security conference in Israel many thought he was crazy. He returned and, at the recommendation of the Israeli chief of intelligence, was appointed head of the investigative division. This meant tracking down suspected terrorists as well as kidnappers using mainly what he termed cell phone and computer signatures which he could pick up by analysing data using a software only he understood.

"Can you fax it to me?" he asked.

"Right away."

His fax grunted and buzzed shortly afterwards. It spat out two sheets of paper. There were hand notes on the second one and a map with some numbers on it. Dele immediately suspected three of those. He called the first one. It was a rude teenager who thought he wanted foreign exchange. The next was a man who did not even speak English. The third one was Robert. He grinned as the startled man wanted to know how he got his number.

"You forget I am a cop," he said laughing. "You have really been naughty, Robert. What do you want me to do now? Madam Caro wants to eat your heart while keeping you alive so you can watch her eat it."

"Sir, abeg..."

"You stole too much Robert," he said. "By the way, I know where you are. My men are watching you. I need you to meet me. If you try to be smart, I will make sure you get delivered to her. Play nice and you can leave the country peacefully."

"Where,sir?"

"Don't call me that," he said. "I pay my taxes and did not steal anyone's land. Meet me at the Golden Gate Restaurant tonight at seven sharp. Did you get that memory stick?"

"Yes."

"Then how come you did not bother to call me?"

"I no sure if you go tell Madam Caro," he said.

Inspector Dele tried to hide his excitement. If he could get the evidence Caro had been using against him for years now it would be the end of her hold on him. He knew with journalists sniffing around it was only a matter of time before the whole thing came into the limelight. Heads were going to roll. Men, married and in high positions, were going to be exposed big time. He did not want to be on that list. His wife was a responsible member of her church who believed his late nights had to do with hard work.

"You still planning on going abroad?"

"Yes."

"Meet me there. Seven. Don't try to be late. I don't want to involve your mother yet. Don't make me."

He ended the call. He hoped he had sounded confident and tough enough. The problem with illiterate folks, he had discovered, was that it was easy to scare them. The truth was that he had no idea where he was. With Tayo's help he could easily find out. He did not, however, want the righteous man too deep in his personal affairs. The trouble with honest men was that you could hardly trust them which was ironic. They had this unique sense of responsibility that made it imperative for them to report any crime even if their own parents were involved in it.

17

CHAPTER 17

Robert lost interest in the food he had ordered from the small restaurant downstairs via room service. The Inspector's call had come as a huge shock. Sweating profusely, he remained on the chair by the small table and contemplated what to do. The visa was due in just a few days. He had paid an agent to handle everything including flight and accommodation. His passport was under a different name.

Ehi lay on the bed still drowsy from the drug he had mixed into her drink. He needed her in that state until all was set. He knew she could be stubborn when she wanted answers. As far as she was concerned, Caro's men were looking all over the country for her. Her life was in grave danger and he was the only reason she was alive. Once she had asked about Jeff. Her admiration of him made him jealous. He wanted her to love him.

Sometimes when she slept he would sit on the edge of the bed and watch her for hours. She was a piece of art. Her face was the prettiest he had ever seen. He would afterwards lay down beside her and dream of them together in a remote location with no Caro and no evil men. Sometimes he would picture them strolling along the beach with their two kids, a boy and a girl. It was a peaceful scenery and he would often fall asleep.

He wanted to rest. He needed to rest. Ever since he became conscious of his existence as a person he had never known rest. As a kid and then a teenager he was either fighting off bullies or worrying about the next day. Life on the run had not been easy. Living almost like a fugitive was tiring. Madam Caro treated him like a slave and used him as her servant, chauffeur, waiter, and thug. He regretted the things he had to do to the girls in her resort. Before he met her, he had watched movies about the slave era. He remembered someone asking why the slaves never tried to fight back. When he found himself under Caro's control he began to understand why. It was the feeling of being trapped in a system that had no mercy. He had resigned himself to fate. The machine around those slaves was as complicated as it was evil. It was the same for him. Cops were after him. Crooks were after him. The only way to survive was to hide like a rat while planning a way out.

He had always dreamt of a world with no evil, pain, shame or embarrassment. It was a utopia he knew could only exist with privilege, a privilege that only the wealthy could afford. The wealthy carved up the planet and insulated themselves from its evil. He knew many owned private islands. In his eyes that was wrong. How could one man own an entire Island? Who put the price tag on the island and based on what? For a world that may exist forever, what was the valuation factor based on? The child of the poor man was doomed from birth. To protect what they owned, the rich had to enact laws and policies that made it even harder for the poor to amount to anything. Even when a poor man rose in ranks, they invited him to switch loyalties. He was now rich and must take sides with them.

That was why, in his opinion, crime and the underground world would always exist. Most people he knew wanted to leave the life of crime and the ghetto. They wanted to give their kids what they themselves never had. While the world sing John Lennon's peace song the facts remain; mankind is inherently selfish. He did not want his daughters having to live like prostitutes or his sons surviving on crime. That was his justification for what he did. Caro had more than she ever needed. In his eyes, the money did not belong to her in the first place but to all those girls she was robbing and abusing.

He could see the end within sight. It was just within his reach. All he needed was his visa. He had dreamt of the day he left the country. He could see the ground and the houses get smaller and smaller as the plane made its ascent into the sky. He could remember how excited he had been. He was saying goodbye to an old life where all he had ever known was pain. Ehi was beside him and she was beaming like a happy kid. They were both leaving their sorrows behind and looked forward to a happy future together. It was a sense of peace that he never experienced before in real life. When he woke from the dream he almost cried in disappointment.

He stood and began pacing the room. He wondered if he should move to a different location. He still had no idea how Dele had found his new number. He had no idea if Caro was with him. He knew what she would do to him if she ever laid hands on him. The other men who worked with her were beasts with no soul and no conscience, the types who would beat a girl to stupor and then joke about it afterwards. He was no saint but he might as well be when compared to them. There was no way he was going to meet him without a gun. If Caro and her demons were there, he would rather die fighting and he would not die alone.

He had no idea where she got her thugs from. From the discussion they had from time to time, he knew they had grown amidst violence and abuse. It was all they knew. He was fortunate to have a mother who at least tried to raise him to be a responsible man. He had sometimes wondered what he would have become had he had a different mother. The thought of himself being like them with no conscience and no atom of human kindness was alarming. What frightened him was not that he could easily have become like them, but the fact that he would never have known he was even like that. It would be his life. The world was truly a jungle as Musa would say.

Ehi eventually woke up at around five-thirty. She sat up and complained of a headache. He gave her two aspirin tablets and a glass of water to go with it. He felt guilty for having to drug her but felt there was no other way. It was a necessary act to ensure their survival. In a few days, they would be out of the country. He had not told her of his plans yet and had no idea how she would react. He hoped she would understand that it was for her own good as well. If Caro ever found out that she was alive a lot of people would suffer, including Jeff and the doctor. The best way would be to leave quietly.

"I need to use the bathroom," she said. "Has he called yet?"

"No," he said impatiently. He wished she would forget about him.

"Why can't I call him?" she asked weakly.

"Our priority na to stay alive," he said. "Go take your bath make I get you some food and something to drink."

"Does he know I am here?" she asked.

"Yes, he sabi," he lied. "Caro suspect say something no right. She dey monitor the man. We need stay here until the visa ready."

"Visa?!" she asked. "To where?"

"Just go take your bath. I go explain later."

She stood, swayed a bit and then staggered to the bathroom. He hoped the drugs would not have any lasting effect. The rogue chemist who sold it to him had guaranteed there would be no issues. He had believed he was using it on a reluctant date. Once she was in the bathroom he resumed his pacing. He could not afford to leave her alert and awake when he goes to meet the inspector. He called the reception and ordered more food and a bottle of malt. The food arrived while she was still in the bathroom. He got what was left of the drug and mixed it in with the soup. He would have to get more on his way back from the meeting.

She came back looking fresh as a daisy from her bath. She had nothing on but a bath towel around her and another wrapped around her head. He gaped as he watched her.

"I need clothes," she said.

"Check the wardrobe," he said trying his best to stay calm. "E get some new clothes inside. Hope them be your size."

"Does it matter?" she asked. "It's not as if I am going anywhere."

She opened the wardrobe, held the clothes against herself as she sized them up in the mirror before asking him to excuse her. He went into the bathroom and waited. She removed the label and was about to drop them inside the bin when she noticed the empty packets of what looked like drugs. She hesitated, reached in to get them but changed her mind. After changing he returned.

"I get meeting by seven," he said. "You need stay inside this room. If they see you na trouble for both of us. Eat your food and watch TV. Will come back quick."

She shrugged. "I'm used to staying in my room. That should be easy. Where are you going?"

"To meet the travel agent," he lied. "Eat your food."

"I'm not hungry," she said. "Later."

"When I return, we need yarn," he said hardly looking her in the eyes.

"About?"

He hesitated. "Our future," he said. "No be small journey we dey go. We fit no return for many years."

"I want to go to school," she said. "I want to be a lawyer."

He sighed. He had not thought of school for her. As far as he was concerned they would settle down and have a family. He wanted children. He had enough money to take care of everyone for a long time. That would have to be addressed too. Without responding he went to the bathroom to get ready.

He left at six after reminding her to stay away from the window and to leave the curtains drawn. If anyone should knock she must not answer.

He hailed a taxi outside the motel. He was wearing a suit he had bought for the trip. The inspector's call meant that he had to take it out of its wrap prematurely. The gun was in the inner pocket beside the memory stick he had copied the video into. The original was in one of the bags with Caro's money in it.

"Where, Sir?" the taxi driver asked.

"Golden Gate," he said.

"That place far well," the taxi driver said. "E go cost you a lot."

"Just go," he said.

He knew the drive was going to take at least an hour. Traffic in Lagos was a nightmare after four in the afternoon. He leaned his head against the seat and closed his eyes. The fear of an ambush was real. He was not too concerned about himself. If he died it would be an end to his troubles in a way. He was more concerned about what would happen to Ehi if he did not return. He hoped she would find the money and figure out what to do. Maybe then she could call Jeff. He was a good man, the best he had seen so far. He was the only person in the whole world he knew of who would treat her well. All the men he had met so far were selfish and untrustworthy, men who could not even honour the vows they made to the women they singled out from the rest and decided they would love and cherish. Jeff was different.

He hoped the meeting would go as planned. He would give the inspector what he wanted and he would be on his way. Knowing him, he would want a share of his loot. He was prepared should that be the case. If he demanded more than what was discussed, then he would have to switch to plan B. Plan B was something he would rather not have to do. No one was going to snatch his dreams away from him now it was almost within reach.

The taxi driver tried to draw him into a political debate. He was in no mood to talk. It was not his business if the president of Gambia decided to stay beyond his term in office or if Trump lasted four years. He just wanted to get on with his life. It was not the president who had taunted him about a face he had not chosen. It was not the president who got his mother pregnant and disappeared. Eventually the driver turned on the radio and tuned in to BBC. He could not be bothered with the news.

They got to the restaurant at a quarter to seven. He had heard about the place. A plate of food cost a fortune there. He could not blame the men and women who ate there. They lived in their own reality. He lived in his. If they earned their money legitimately why should he care how they spend it? Lots of poor folks spend the same on alcohol and weed. They were equally guilty if ever there was any crime committed. He knew of thieves who had handled millions but were still poor and still stealing in the name of survival.

He paid the taxi driver and walked in. A waitress ushered him into a table for two. Never had he been treated with more respect. It made him feel like an impostor. He was asked if he needed a drink while he decided on what to order. He asked for a coke. It cost more than ten times what it would cost in a regular shop. He wanted to know why. The explanation did not make sense to him but he ordered one anyway, vowing it would be the only thing he was going to taste there that evening. He did not understand why any would feel sorry for a rich man dying of diabetes. It was a self-imposed illness as far as he was concerned. He had seen firsthand how they eat. They were gluttons.

While he waited, the place that was almost empty when he arrived started filling up. Dele did not show up until seven-thirty. He spotted him and made his way to the table.

"Look at you in a suit," he said laughing. There was mockery in his tone.

"No be small," he said. He was learning to ignore such statements and wished he had known how to years back.

"Did you bring it?" he asked after sitting.

"Partially," he said.

"What does that mean?" Dele asked.

"I get copy. I give you the original you leave me alone. The other one na sure banker."

"You mean guarantee," Dele said laughing. "You were always a clever one. I knew Madam Caro was the fool for thinking you were as stupid as you looked. Where is the money?"

"That na my problem," he said. "Your concern na the video."

"That is where you are wrong, young man," Dele said. "I can have you arrested right now if I want. I've got some men outside. I can get them beat you senseless until you tell me where you kept the other one. Or I can hand you over to your boss."

"I no get boss," he said angrily.

"Whatever. I need some of that money. I need the other drive too."

Robert sighed. He knew it might come to that. It was time for plan B. He regretted the fact that men just had to be greedy and force the hand of other men. When the news broke someone would accuse the perpetrator of being evil, like there was much of a choice.

"Okay," he said. "If I give you the drive and some money you go leave me alone?"

"Sure," Dele said. "I'm not a greedy man. I give you my word."

"How much?"

"Twenty million," he said.

Robert knew there was no point negotiating with him. He stood.

"Make we go," he said.

"Where?" Dele asked.

"To my friend house. That na where the money dey. But we go alone. I no want make you harass my friend later."

Dele looked a bit unsure but stood anyway.

"Don't try any silly games with me," he threatened. "I am not as stupid as your boss."

"Wey your car?"

"In the parking lot. Let's go."

The two men walked out of the restaurant. He had not paid for his coke and did not forget. No one stopped them. The car park was full. He almost gasped as he saw all sorts of exotic and expensive cars parked there. As a kid, he had often wondered why the rich never seemed to be satisfied. He was beginning to understand. There was too much competition amongst them. Again, he could not blame them. Even the poor had the same competition. The only difference was that while the wealthy compared houses and cars, the poor compared shoes and watches.

"That's my ride there," Dele said proudly. "You can see I need an upgrade."

Robert said nothing as they got in. He had come alone as he suspected. He started the engine as he gave a brief history of the car and some of its special features. He was not interested. The toys of the rich represented to him the very reason the country was one of the most corrupt in the world.

"You are not talking much," Dele said. "Don't worry. You will still have a lot left. Don't be greedy now. By the way, let me have the drive before we go."

He reached into his pocket and produced the drive. Dele took it from him, kissed it and put it in his pocket.

"That woman had me by the balls because of this," he said. "I'm going to take her down soon. I'm sure you are happy to hear that."

"That na your problem," he said nonchalantly.

Dele was in high spirits as they drove away. He could not stop talking about what he would do with the money. Robert directed him as he drove. Eventually they got to a neighborhood known for its high crime rate. Even Dele was not comfortable. Few police ventured there to respond to an emergency. He pointed at a house with no lights on and asked him to pull over in front of it.

"I'm not getting out," Dele said. "You go get me the stuff. I will wait right here."

"What if I bail?"

He laughed. "Feel free. Your mother will spend the rest of her life in prison. Besides, I will have customs looking out for you in every international airport. If you are smart you will go in there like a good boy, get me my money and the other drive and then we can all pretend we never knew each other."

"For real?"

"Sure."

He opened the door as if to come out. Dele was saying something when the shots rang out. He slumped in his chair, his temple looking like he had been in a bad MMA fight. Robert moved quickly. With his heart pounding he walked to the other side of the car, opened the door and dragged the dying man out. He left him on the ground after retrieving his cellphone, the drive and his wallet. He knew it would be interpreted as a hijack which was rampant in the area.

He drove off with the car. His plan was to ditch it someplace where it would never be discovered till he was hopefully out of the country and beyond reach. He reached into his pocket for one of his two cell phones. It was only then he realised it was not in his pocket. He searched around frantically for it. He knew it could be incriminating evidence. He believed he must have dropped it in his rush and drove back to where the body lay. There was no phone. Confused, he drove away, hoping he had left it in the restaurant.

He felt like he had when he killed Esu years back; scared and angry. He was angry because he had just done something he would prefer he had not. People would be people. The man was being greedy and he was certain he would have wanted more. It was either he killed him or he would never realise the dream he had worked so hard for. He kept shaking his head as he drove. He regretted the fact that it had to come to murder. He had a good job, a loving wife and what many in his shoes or in the ghetto would consider more than enough. He just had to be greedy.

Suddenly he began to feel nauseated. He fought the urge but it became so overwhelming that he had to find a convenient spot to pull over. He opened the door and threw up. When he was through he felt drained. Slowly he closed the door and continued driving, determined that nothing would stop him from actualising the dream he had dreamt of so much with the woman he loved. He would rather die.

He stopped by a service station and bought a gas lighter, a flashlight and a small can of fuel, all the while being careful to stay as far away from the security camera as possible just in case it worked. He got back into the car and drove on. He finally got to his destination, an isolated bush on the outskirts of town. He stopped close to a bridge. He chose it because he knew the area. There was a local hunter known for his good quality bush meat from whom Caro insisted he get all the bush meat from. He lived in the village across the bridge.

With the fear of snakes at the back of his mind he used the flashlight to scan the ground before he set his feet down. He did a quick search of the vehicle in case his cell phone was somewhere on the floor, removed every document he could find and then set the car alight. He watched the fire as it licked its way through the interior. It looked surreal. It was an expensive car. Satisfied the fire was not going to fizzle out he left the scene and began walking towards the bridge.

The hunter was in front of his house chatting to his wife when he arrived. He was in his late fifties. His wife was in her twenties. He was surprised to see him. Usually he came early in the morning when he had just come back from checking his traps.

"How you dey?" he asked. They had an oil lamp that emitted thick black smoke into the atmosphere. The area had no electricity even though it was just ten miles from the city.

"I dey," he said. "Abeg give me water make I drink."

The wife left to get him some water.

"No tell me say you walk," he said.

"Musa get the car," he said convincingly. "He go the next village go get palm wine."

"If he knows anything about palm wine he for know say the thing dey sour for night," he said. "You wan some bush meat?"

Robert nodded. "We get plenty guests. Dem no fit get enough of the meat. We need at least fifteen kilos of good meat."

"I get one big deer that I refuse to sell dis morning. My wife don cut am up and e dey smoke for her kitchen as I dey talk. Dem go like am no be small. We been wan use am for my elder daughter marriage next weekend but if money dey I go sell am. God help I go catch another one tomorrow."

"How much?"

"Twenty thousand," he said.

Robert did not argue as usual. In the past, he would have bargained so he could keep the saved change. He took out the money from his pocket and handed it to him. He saw a blood spot on his hand and quickly put it in his pocket. While they spoke one of his sons from his late first wife arrived in a motorcycle.

"Be like say bush fire dey rage yonder," he said after exchanging greetings with them.

"Hope e no go reach here," his father said. "You see any fire brigade?"

"No way," he said. "Dem no fit come quench house fire na bush dem wan quench. Na for the other village sha. I no think say e go cross the river."

Suddenly it hit Robert that he may be responsible for the fire. He stayed away from the conversation. His water came. He gulped it down. The hunter asked him to excuse him while he bagged the meat which he warned might still be hot. Robert sat and chatted with his son. The man was a bit drunk. He too was a hunter but not as successful as his father. Minutes later he returned carrying a bag of smoked meat with the help of his wife.

"When you think say Musa wan arrive?" he asked.

"I no sure," he said. "I need to get the meat back quick. You go fit lend me your motorcycle?"

"Make my son drop you," he said. "Just make sure say fuel dey inside when he return."

Robert thanked him. He pretended to make a call to tell Musa he did not need to wait for him. The two men put the heavy bag into the back of the truck. Robert thanked them before getting into the passenger seat. They drove slowly. The truck was rickety and the young man boasted about how he would inherit it one day. When they got to the highway he could see the fire. It was huge and menacing. He could make out the outline of people as they tried to contain it. It was as if the whole village had come out there to tackle it. He was sure they would find the car.

"Maybe one drunk fool drop him cigarette inside the bush," the hunter's son said.

"Maybe," he said.

He did not say much as they drove, directing him now and then when he needed to make a turn. They finally arrived at a hotel almost ten blocks from the motel he was staying in.

"Stop me here," he said.

They got the bag of meat out. He offered to help him carry it inside but he declined. He gave him some money to buy fuel and they shook hands. As soon as he was gone he hailed a taxi. The bag was loaded into the boot. He told him his destination. The man knew where it was. As they went he asked if he liked bush meat and that he could have the whole bag. He lied that it was a gift from an uncle and that it was too much for him. The man was so happy he asked him not to pay for the fare. When they got to the motel he could tell there were more cars than usual. He wondered if he should get back inside the taxi and move on. He had forgotten to pass by the chemist. The driver gave him a piece of paper with his phone number scribbled on it.

"If you get more bush meat just call me," he said as he shifted gears and prepared to drive away. "My sister get restaurant inside town. I'm sure she go need am."

He took the piece of paper and promised he would. As he walked up to the entrance he could see his room. There was no light to be seen from the window. He wondered if she was asleep. He hoped she had not overdosed. He had added more than recommended hoping it would keep her asleep till he returned. He hurried, panic gripping him.

18

CHAPTER 18

Jeff was having dinner with his wife when his phone rang. It was an unrecognisable number so he ignored it. Mason had advised him a long time ago on various ways he could make his life safer. One of those ways was to ignore calls from unknown numbers. He found others like removing the battery from his cell phone when having important conversations as well as avoiding smart TVs a bit too far–fetched.

"Who is that?" Nneka asked.

"Have no idea," he said. "Let's eat. Private number."

"It might be important," she said.

"If it's important then whoever it is should send a message," he said.

The phone stopped ringing after a while. A few minutes later it started ringing again.

"Just answer," she pleaded.

He picked it up.

"Hello?" he said.

"Jeff?"

He jumped with a start. She spoke in low tones and sounded weak but he recognised her voice immediately.

"Ehi. Where are you?"

"In a room," she said. "I think it is a hotel or some kind of apartment."

"Can you see any signs?" he asked. "Look around if you can go outside or look through the window."

There was a pause. He could hear her walk. After a few moments, she returned.

"Starlite Motel," she said.

"I know where it is. I'm coming to get you right away," he said excitedly. He was relieved she had not been back at the resort all that time.

"He may come back anytime," she said.

"Who?" he asked as he grabbed his keys, raising one finger to excuse himself. Nneka nodded quickly in agreement. She knew exactly what was going on.

"Robert," she said.

He tried to make sense of what she just said as he hurried to his car.

"Leave the room and go to a public place nearby," he said. "As soon as I get there I will call you. Look for a restaurant or a bar."

"Okay," she said.

He drove like a lunatic. Hundred thoughts crossed his mind as he drove. He could not figure out what Robert's plan was or if he was acting under Madam Caro's instructions. It was possible. Why a motel? Occasionally he called her to make sure she was fine. Eventually he arrived at the street. He drove slowly. He saw her standing beside a street vendor. She hugged him as soon as he got out of the car. He could see she had lost a lot of weight and looked drowsy.

"What on earth was he doing with you?" he asked angry and relieved at the same time.

"Let's just leave before Caro's people find me," she said.

"Which room were you in," he asked.

"Room 212," she said. "It's on the first floor. We can't go back there."

"Did he say where he was going?"

She shook her head.

"Did he tell you why he brought you there?"

"He said Caro was looking everywhere for me," she said. "He said we needed to hide until his visa was approved."

"Visa?" he asked puzzled.

"We were going to leave the country. He has all these documents there and all these bags of money. I think he was drugging me. Each time I ate I would get drowsy and black out."

Jeff thought over what she just said.

"Wait for me here," he said. "Is the room locked?"

"No. I did not think to lock it. What if he's back?" she asked.

"Just wait for me," he said. "I'll be quick."

He hurried back to his car and drove to the motel which was within sight. He hurried up the stairs and looked for room 212. He knocked. There was no answer. He opened the door and went in. Quickly he grabbed the bags and all the documents he could find, turned off the light and left. An apprehensive Ehi was relieved when he returned. She got into the car and they drove away.

"You took his bags?" she asked when she saw the bags on the back seat.

He nodded.

"Let's hope we have some bargaining chips in there," he said.

"Bargaining chips?" she asked.

"Like his travel documents, possibly his passport. I know there is money but I also know he may be more interested in leaving than being rich," he said. "What happened at the hospital?"

"I don't know," she said. "I took the pill as directed. The next thing I remember was being in the motel room. He told me Caro got wind of the whole plot and was furiously looking for me. How could she have known?"

"Maybe the doctor got scared and told her," he said. "Or maybe he is just lying."

"He wanted me to come with him," she said. "He wanted us to leave the country together. I went with him to get my passport photograph taken. He gave me a different name. He even told them I was his sister."

Jeff sighed. He knew Robert was love sick and infatuated with her. That was no justification for the abduction. Looking at her lean frame was painful. He wondered if he should take her to a hospital.

"We will go to my place," he said changing the topic. "My wife knows about you. She will take good care of you. Unfortunately, we all must find somewhere to lay low. There is no telling what Caro knows. I have something to tell you. I'm not sure if this is the right time to tell you this."

"What is it?" she asked.

"I found your mum," he said.

He did not know how she would react. She stayed quiet and remained quiet for the rest of the drive. He tried to start some conversation but she would not talk. Eventually he let her be.

Nneka was in the sitting room when they arrived. She stood and looked at Ehi.

"Is she...?" she began.

He nodded.

She held her in a warm embrace for a while, as if to absorb all the pain, neglect and suffering she had heard about. When she burst into tears he was not surprised. Ehi started to sob as well. He excused himself and left them to themselves. He went to the bedroom with the bags and began looking through them. The money did not mean much. He was curious to see what all the memory sticks contained. Robert did not strike him as the sort of fellow who would need memory sticks. But then he was a man full of surprises.

He inserted one into his laptop. He was not prepared for what he saw. He quickly went through the rest, pausing and forwarding from time to time. It was clear they all contained the same sort of information. He was aware of his trembling hands as he returned the sticks. He was in possession of information that could get him killed. He understood then that Madam Caro must have been blackmailing a lot of politicians into whatever favours she needed. He also wondered who else was in on it with her. She did not strike him as being that sophisticated and he had come to learn that whenever such a setup existed there was some criminal figure behind the scene.

He carried the bags to the passage and with the help of a chair hid them in the ceiling. He kept the memory sticks in his small bag. He had saved copies of each in his laptop. He returned to the living room where the two ladies were in the kitchen preparing dinner and chatting away as if they had known each other for years.

"I told her to rest but she insisted on helping," Nneka said.

"It's not like I need any rest," Ehi said smiling. "All I've been doing is sleep and eat."

Jeff smiled as he saw her dice onions. His biggest fear was that she would have a hard time integrating into normal life. She seemed to be doing just fine. He asked for permission to have a one on one with his wife. He gave her some money and asked her to leave the house and head to a nearby hotel. His instinct told him it was not safe to be there. She protested but he insisted. He explained that he had to attend to some important business before leaving in the car.

While he drove, he decided to pass by the post office. He put the sticks in an envelope and placed it in his post office box. He proceeded to dial the inspector's number. After receiving no response, he decided to try again in the morning. On his way back to the car, his phone began to ring. It was an unrecognisable number that was not in his contact list. He answered it.

"Where she dey?" Robert asked. He sounded like a maniac.

"Who?" he asked feigning ignorance.

"No play games with me," he raged. "The receptionist see you. She describedyou and your car with detail."

"She is mistaken then," Jeff said. He realised he was not too worried about the money and other stuff he took. He knew then that he loved her genuinely.

"I know say na you," he said. "Tell am say make she come back. I need to see her now."

"See her for what?" he asked. "You kidnapped her and lied to her that Madam Caro was looking for her. I can report you and get you arrested for kidnap."

"You no fit kidnap person wey don die already," he said. "I no shake for that one."

He knew he had a point. It was safer for all involved that Caro still thought she was dead.

"I go let you take half the money," he said.

"It's not your money to give," Jeff said. "It's Caro's and I dare say Ehi deserves a large chunk of it."

"I slave for that woman many years!" he yelled. "I suffer like dog. Na my money too!"

"I'm sorry but I can't let you see her," he said firmly. "You realise she is underage? She has not lived. Let her grow up."

"Tell her say if I no see her tonight I go kill myself," he went on. "I go shoot myself. But I go shoot that witch first."

Jeff began to get worried. The way he sounded he was sure he was losing his mind and was capable of anything.

"Alright," he said trying to reason with him. "What is your plan? You see her, then what?"

"Then we leave this country together," he said. "We go start another life far from all this nonsense."

Jeff knew he had to be careful with his words.

"What if she says no?"

There was a disturbing silence from the other end. When he spoke again he sounded subdued and he strained to hear his words.

"She suppose remember all the things wey I do for her when Caro and her thugs wan deal with her," he said. "I put my life on the line."

"I'm sure she appreciates all that," Jeff said. "But if you really love her you must be willing to respect her wishes. She is a young girl who has seen the worst this life has to offer. She needs an education. She needs to grow up. She may decide she loves you when she is ready. She may meet someone else. You may meet someone else. That's how love works.

It is not a one-man show. There is no force, coercion or manipulation when love is concerned."

"Maybe you want take her from me?" he asked.

"What?!" Jeff asked in shock. "I hope you know I am married."

"Those old men wey dey come Caro place dem marry too," he said. "I see the way she talks about you. Na you she love. She no love Robert the ape with screw face. She love handsome Jeff."

"Listen," Jeff said. "I won't listen to you insult me or suggest things you know are not real. I am telling you that it has nothing to do with the way you look. I know you have a good heart. She told me how you were there for her. I'm just saying she is not in a position to decide on things like this now."

"Who you be to say?!" he cried. "You no be her papa or mama."

"I happen to have traced her mother," he said. "She wants nothing to do with her so I can speak on her behalf as her custodian. I plan to apply to adopt her as my daughter. She will go to school. She will live like other girls her age who are fortunate to have parents to look out for them. When she is of age she will decide who she wants to spend the rest of her life with. If it happens to be you then that is good. As a matter of fact, I will wish for someone like you. You are far better in character than a lot of men I know. She just needs to heal. You need to heal too. Let's not forget you are a victim in all this too. You must see my point of view."

He could hear his breathing on the other end of the line. He hoped he was finally thinking his words over. He was disappointed when he spoke again.

"I go drive to madam Caro's," he said. "I go shoot her and any other person wey I find there. Then I go find those thugs wey dey look for me all these years. I go shoot them too. When I don shoot them all then I go shoot myself. This life no worth am. Na only suffer man like me wey no get anything dey suffer. Na God give me this face. If I go fit carry my gun enter heaven I go shoot God too."

"Wait a minute," an alarmed Jeff started saying but the line went dead. Worried and afraid that he had meant every word he tried to think of what to do. He thought of dialling 911 but remembered how appalling the emergency response was. Suddenly he remembered Dele. If anyone had any reason to protect Caro it was him. If she dies his secrets would be exposed. He was glad there was an answer this time.

"There is a man called Robert. He works for Caro and I fear he is about to go there and start killing people!" he said frantically.

"They deserve to die," Robert's voice said.

He was shocked and confused to hear his voice. There was spite and mockery in his tone.

"How come you have the inspector's phone?" he asked.

"I kill am," he said calmly. "I shoot the evil bastard. Wey police when man dey suffer? Na now you want call them? Mind your own business."

He hung up. Jeff stared at the phone in his hand in utter disbelief and shock. The only way he could have been with Dele's phone was if he had really killed him. He knew there was little he could do without endangering his own life. He returned to his car and drove away. He hoped his wife had listened to his advice and that they were already at the hotel. Just to make sure he called her. She confirmed that they were already there.

"Stay indoors," he said. "I'll be with you shortly."

He drove slowly. He wanted to believe there was something he could do to stop Robert. He dialled his number several times but he refused to answer. It dawned on him that if an investigation was carried out his number would be found in his and Dele's phones. He would be questioned and some overzealous prosecutor might want to link him to the crimes. He did not like the situation but there was little else he could do.

19

CHAPTER 19

Madam Caro and her Asian partners sat around a table celebrating the final approval of their Dubai resort. There had been hiccups along the way. Greedy officials wanted bribes every step of the approval process. She entertained them by telling them how her most trusted member of staff had disappeared with her money. She left out the part about the memory sticks. It was her key to unlocking the harsh economic environment and no one needed to know that any future threats she made would be empty. She was yet to tell her true boss about it. He was an unpredictable character with bipolar who lived in the shadows. Few had seen him face to face. Those who knew him had no idea just who he really was. He was the one who made use of the contents of the discs to push through contracts and trade deals worth billions of dollars. She only used his tactic occasionally to facilitate small favours. There was no telling what he would do. No one needed to know.

"Sex sells more than drugs and oil combined," one of the men said. He was half drunk and would be the manager of the new resort. His name was Dajal, originally from India but based in Dubai. "We have girls coming in from all over the world. Most would be from Cambodia, Nepal, and Thailand."

"What is so special about them?" Caro asked.

"High maternal mortality. Lots of orphans. Zero social support from their governments. You need to go there and see for yourself. They sell their nieces for less than fifty dollars. Those are the main sex tourism destinations in the world. There is no such thing as paedophilia in those countries. You are mature when your aunt tells you so."

"You men are sick," Caro said grimacing. "You never cease to amaze me. Why can't you stick to mature females?"

"People can be queer," he said. "We don't judge people. We are pure businessmen. To be successful in business you cannot have a conscience. I grew up in the slums of India. Do you know that some deliberately mutilate their children just so they can make it better in the business of begging? Some actually go as far as blinding their own children."

"You don't say," Abdullahi said in disgust. He was from Dubai and was there to claim his 'thank you' package from the team for approving the deal. All expenses he would incur was paid.

"Something like that happens in the northern part of the country," Caro said. "It's easy to pull a face at stories like this when you have never known poverty. The mindset of the desperately poor is very different."

"It is all about survival," Dajal agreed. "The rich would rather build bombs that are used to manipulate the economic climate to their favour than houses. They only care about their own interests. Only their own children matter in their eyes or else how can you explain Syria and Iraq?"

Abdullahi shrugged. "I'm here to enjoy my life," he said. "Can we change the topic before I grow a conscience and revoke the deal?"

Caro laughed. "Please don't. You need more wine? Drugs perhaps?"

"All," he said. "Once I return it is back to my stressful life. Let me enjoy for a little while."

"It can't be that stressful if you are making all that money," Dajal said. "We paid a fortune just to get you to sign a simple document."

He shrugged and had a sip of his wine which cost a thousand dollars a bottle. He did not see anything special about it. Dajal had explained that it was vintage wine. Vintage or not he felt it tasted like piss mixed with lemonade but did not want to offend his hosts. They had spent a lot to make him happy.

"Did you hear that?" Caro asked frowning.

"What?" Dajal asked, his eyes looking sleepy.

"It sounded like gun shots," she said looking worried.

"Fire crackers maybe," he said.

She shook her head. "Not possible. We don't do such silly stuff here and there's no one around us."

Suddenly a shot rang out and someone screamed. More shots rang out. People abandoned their tables and ran for dear life. Caro and her guests stood, looking around in confusion.

"Looks like it is your boy Robert," Dajal said pointing.

Before they could do anything, Robert was standing facing them with his gun pointed at her. Around them people were scrambling to get as far away from him as possible. The entrance suddenly seemed like a key hole.

"Have you lost your mind!?" she yelled. "You took my money and now this? How stupid can you be?"

"I don't think it is a good idea to be talking to him like that," a now profusely sweating Dajal said. He had his hands up.

"Nonsense," she said. "I gave this boy hope when he was nothing. Ugly fool! What are you going to do, shoot me? Drop that gun before I count to ten!"

A single shot rang out. She clutched her chest, her mouth and eyes wide open as if genuinely surprised that he had shot her. Musa ran out of the kitchen to see what the mayhem was all about. He saw his boss on the floor and Robert still pointing at the men with his gun, tried to run back and was shot in the back.

"Listen Robert," Dajal said looking frightened. "Is it money you want? I will give you any amount..."

A single shot stopped him and he slumped to the ground. He turned the gun to Abdullahi who was by this time wishing he never set foot on the continent and shot him too. He turned and looked around. The place was almost empty and littered with broken glasses and uneaten food. He stormed out, a look of determination in his eyes. Outside people were still scrambling into their cars and driving off at high speed, horns blaring in desperate attempts to clear the way ahead of drivers who were not fast enough. He got into the hijacked car he had come in and sped off.

The stolen car could not go fast enough for his liking. Seething with years of suppressed rage his destination was a notorious night club where he knew the thugs who had put a hit on his head years back liked to hang out. He had avoided it like a plague. Sometimes when Madam Caro sent him on errands close to the place his heart would race. The mere thought of being captured alive and tortured for hours used to make the hair on his back stand on end. He knew firsthand what they were capable of. This time he had no fear. He was not running anymore. He was going to them.

Growing up, they, the neighbourhood kids, had been fed with tales of horrific abuses by members of this gang. He remembered the sense of fear they used to have whenever they encountered any of them. They were the gods of the ghetto and used their reputation to intimidate girls into becoming their girlfriends and boys into becoming members. They also had money. In a place so poor, that meant even more power. Lots of lives were ruined by them. He never wanted to become a member because his mother who was deeply religious drove into his soul the difference between light and darkness.

Some of his mates joined. Some wanted the power. Some wanted girls. Some wanted an escape from what appeared to be a hopeless future. Darkness reigned in the ghetto. Darkness was ironically also the ghetto man's ray of hope. People like him with poor but principled mothers were rare and disadvantaged.

His was bullied relentlessly for years. Those without any gang affiliation were often the targets of rival gangs who always looked to increase their numbers. He was adamant in his refusal to join any even though it would have ended the bullying. They picked on the very sore spot in his life; his looks. He was teased in school and at home. Esu had taken it a shade further than every other person.

The gang evolved over the years. As they became more powerful and rich they began to expand into other neighbourhoods. They began to invest in things like nightclubs, drug labs, and even restaurants. They never forgot him and he always had to be careful where he went. He knew he had no chance of a normal life so long as the key members of the gang were alive. There were times when he wished he had a bomb to blow up the club which belonged to one of their older members and served as their headquarters and meeting point.

The club had two guards at the entrance and two at the back which served as an emergency escape route to the members. There had not been an attack in years. He planned to take them by surprise. The main man he sought was just an ordinary member of the gang when he was a teen. He had risen in ranks and was now a key member of their silly board. He it was who made sure his name was never forgotten. Esu had been his close friend. His nickname was Killa. He was a huge man who liked to boast about how many men he would like to kill before he passed. Rumour had it that he had murdered over twenty already.

The two guards were at the back chatting when he approached. He drove straight into them without hesitation. The car only stopped when it hit the side wall of the club. He pushed aside the deployed airbags, got out of the car and walked into the club. The place was packed with people of all ages. The stench of marijuana hung in the air and he wondered how they could even breath. He made his way upstairs where he knew Killa liked to hang out with the other members and oftentimes women.

Killa was sitting on a leather sofa with a girl on each side. He looked sleepy. They all looked sleepy. It was obvious they had been doing drugs. He shot the four men in the room before they had any chance to react. The women began to scream and some of them ran out. The others just cowered and kept screaming until he yelled at them to stop or die.

Killa peered at him for a while until he finally recognised who he was.

"My, oh my," he said. "If it ain't Ugly Face. How you take get inside?"

"Make that one no bother you," he said, his gun pointed at him. "Shebi you want me dead? Here I am."

Killa laughed. He did not appear to be bothered by the gun.

"Lots of people want you dead," he said. "You could have had a better life if you had not been so stubborn and pig headed. Look at me. I am the epitome of success. I told you with a face like yours the criminal world was the place for you. Man, was I right. That gun looks good on you. If you behave I can still help you change your life. By the way, where have you been hiding? Been living like a rat in the caves like Bin Laden?"

"I go advise you to watch your mouth," he said.

"Or what?" Killa asked smiling confidently. "You think say na you be the first person to point a gun at my head, you ugly faced cursed demon? Do you think I got to where I am by being a coward? Guess which of us is going to die tonight? You."

Robert felt like just shooting him but something kept holding him back. He was curious to know why he sounded so confident.

"Get up and raise your hands!" he said.

Killa laughed but remained sitting.

"You killed my men," he said. "Not one of them answered to you. You think the fact that you have that gun gives you any power? You think power comes from holding a gun and commanding people around? Power comes from being influential. These men were willing to die for me and have killed for me. They have been able to provide food on their tables because of me. They were loving fathers and husbands. You, Ugly Face, have created many orphans tonight."

"That na your problem," he said even though the thought of what he just said troubled him a little. The adrenaline rush was subsiding and his anger was beginning to fade. "I no go ask you again. Stand up now."

He did not know where the gun came from. When he stood, he had a gun pointing right back at him. He smiled.

"Now that there are two gods in this small room," Killa said. "Who is going to leave here still a god tonight and who is going to meet the real God?"

Robert stared at him. Without warning he squeezed the trigger. Killa fell to the ground but not before managing to shoot once. Robert screamed in pain and clutched his left shoulder. It felt as if a hot rod had pierced it. He turned and left, his face contorted in pain. Downstairs the loud music was still playing and it seemed no one was even aware of what had transpired above. He stumbled out, found an unlocked car in the parking lot and got in. He managed to call his mother. Blood was trickling down his arm. He struggled to breathe but managed to get the words out.

"Rob?" his mother asked. "What is going on?"

"I'm dying mama," he said.

"Where are you?" she asked, her voice trembling with fear.

"Sorry say I no become the engineer wey you want make I be," he said. "Fear dey catch me mama. I fear say I dey go hell."

She said a short desperate prayer.

"Plead the blood of Jesus," she said. "No cross that line without surrendering to him! Remember the thief on the cross."

"Too late mama," he said shaking his head. "Too late. I know say na hell I dey go. I don kill too many people today."

"Where you dey, my son!" she asked. "Make I call ambulance."

"Make I die mama," he said. "I don suffer too much for this life. If I die...if I see God...I go ask am why. Why you give Ugly Face this ugly face?"

She started to cry. He ended the call and proceeded to dial Jeff's number. While he dialled, he remembered the story of the thief on the cross. His mother always told it to him as a child. The threat of an early death was always real growing up where they did. Her greatest fear was always that he may die without being born again and end up in hell where, in her words, there was no hope of escape or respite from suffering. He prayed as he waited for Jeff to pick up.

"Dear Jesus, remember me in your kingdom...no let Ugly Face go hell. Make my spirit get better face this time around."

"Robert?" Jeff asked. He was back in the hotel room with his wife and Ehi.

"I am dying, sir," he said weakly. "Just wan talk to her one last time."

"Is this some gimmick or what?" he asked.

"Sir," he said. "I am dying, I no dey joke. Make I talk to her one last time."

Jeff looked at Ehi. She was sitting on a couch watching television beside his wife.

"Is it him?" she asked mouthing the words.

He nodded. "He said he is dying. He wants to speak to you. Not sure if that is a desperate attempt to elicit sympathy or not. Do you want to speak to him?"

She nodded and came to take the phone.

"Hello?" she asked.

"Angel," he said weakly. "I hope the angels over there go be like you."

"Robert what's wrong?" she asked in apprehension.

"I am dying," he said. "Killa shoot me. Pray for me, my angel. I wish you good life. Pray for me. Remember that time wey you almost die? Now I know how e be. I love you angel."

She did not know how to respond. Jeff and his wife watched her.

"I don kill madam Caro. I don kill Musa. All the people wey trouble you, I don kill dem. Now I dey go meet my maker wey give me ugly face. I go ask am why. Thank Jeff for me, my angel. You dey good hands. Jeff na good man. Go school. Make sure you no follow all these mad women of today, women of immorality. Wickedness dey for this life. Marry better man. Remember me, ugly face Robert. Ugly Face loved you no be small. Hope I see you again one day on the other side."

"You are beautiful inside," she whimpered. She meant it. "You are the only nice person I met in that place. If I did not meet you I would have been dead by now. Where are you? Please don't die. Go to the hospital. We can come and get you."

"Live for what?" he asked. "I don tire. Tell Jeff to give my mama some money. My sister must finish school. Call 0-4-0-7-6-5-4-5-3-1. This life, no peace. Only you...only you...."

"Rob!?" she cried.

She could tell the phone had dropped from his hands. She could hear him struggling to breath. Panic gripped her and she started sobbing. Jeff rushed forward and grabbed the phone from her. He heard him as he fought to stay alive. He could hear the terror and the determination to live as the heavy breathing became more frantic. Finally, he let out what sounded like a long sigh and it became quiet.

"Where is he?" he asked.

She shook her head.

"I don't know," she said. "Is he dead?"

"I have no idea," he lied. He knew he was dead. He put his arms around her and held her while she sobbed. He signalled to Nneka. She put her hands over her mouth in shock. No one spoke. She sobbed for hours while he held her, not knowing what to do or say. His wife sat on the bed, her hand over her mouth. For a while the only sound in the room was that of Ehi sobbing. After what seemed like hours she stopped. He held her still, not knowing what to say or do.

"I should have stayed with him," she said weakly. "None of this would have happened."

"Don't," Jeff said, himself overwhelmed with the turn of events. He wished he could wake up and discover it was all a dream. He wondered at what point he would prefer to wake. Every waking moment since he came across her had been a nightmare. Yet, he would still prefer to have met her than to live on in blissful ignorance unaware of the travails many like her faced.

She disengaged herself and started walking towards the bathroom.

"Where are you going?" he asked.

She turned. They were looking at her with concern in their eyes.

"I'm going to take a bath," she said. "Don't worry, I'm not about to kill myself. I'm beyond that now. I want to live to fight evil on this planet. I really do. I just feel...overwhelmed."

She went into the bathroom and shut the door. Jeff sat beside his wife. She put her arms around him. None could find the words to say. They could hear the water running into the bath and Ehi humming a song neither of them knew.

"I think she would be a great person," he said.

"I do too," she said. "She has known and seen a lot. Out of great suffering comes the greatest of minds and the gentlest of souls."

"If they see their suffering the right way," he said. "Many become bitter and angry. They become monsters. It's all about letting go. I am happy she has turned out this way."

"We become what we choose for ourselves," she said. "Love or hate, resentment or forgiveness...it's all about choice. One can make an angel out of you. The other will turn you into a living demon."

"And we all suffer the consequence," he said thoughtfully. "We all suffer the consequence."

They listened as she sang to herself. Jeff had a smile on his lips and a frown on his brow. Eventually he went to the bags. He had hidden them behind a tall boy hoping to find a better place later.

"What are in those bags anyway?" she asked.

"Money. Lots of it. Robert stole it from Caro."

"You should take it to the cops," she said.

"And tell them what?" he asked. "I wish I could but the situation I find myself in is complicated. If I hand in this money I will be charged with murder."

"He committed suicide," she said. "You were here. We were all here. You have alibi."

"Not Robert," he said. "Inspector Dele."

He explained everything while she listened, shaking her head from time to time. Even she could see how easily he could be implicated.

"What do you plan to do then?" she asked when he was done talking.

"Invest in her future. Invest in the future of others like her," he said. "Not a dime would be spent on even a haircut for myself."

"How much is in there?" she asked.

"A lot. Millions."

He opened one of the bags and did a rough estimate. He was sure there was over twenty million in it. Next, he opened the side pocket. He whistled.

"What is it?"

"This is a lot of money," he said. The real reason he had whistled was that he had touched what he knew to be another memory stick. He had a good idea what was in it. He took it and pushed the bag under the bed.

They watched television together afterwards. Ehi eventually stopped singing. Nneka eventually slept off. He listened for any sound from the bathroom. It was eerily silent. He was relieved when he heard her coming out of the bath. She spent some time drying her hair with the blow dryer. When she re-emerged, he asked if she was hungry. She was not. He advised her to sleep with his wife on the bed. He would sleep on the couch. He had no intention of sleeping.

He waited till they were deeply asleep before taking out his laptop. He used his ear phones to minimise the noise. He sat on the table, inserted the disc into the laptop and waited. It contained lots of videos and images just as he had suspected. He was not prepared for the number of familiar faces in it. There were powerful men in cabinets past and present. He whistled softly as he scrolled down. It was obvious to him that Caro had been blackmailing some of them for various favours. He also suspected that some international interests were using her to obtain lucrative contracts. From experience, he knew the type of gadget needed to obtain such high definition images would have been imported.

After hours of analysing the contents of the USB he sat back and heaved a huge sigh. What he had could lead to his death if anyone knew he had it. It was every journalists' dream to come across what he had. He knew corporations both home and abroad that would pay millions to obtain the information in his possession. Gbenga would gladly have him back just so that he would have control over them.

He created an email account using false names and sent many of the videos as an attachment. Next, he opened a second YouTube account and uploaded the videos. He set it to publish in a few weeks. If anything happened to him the videos would be uploaded to the entire world. If he stayed alive he had the option of stopping it. It was his only way of ensuring his safety. He knew sooner or later someone would figure out that he now had the memory sticks.

He checked the second bag. There was a similar stick in the side pocket. He plugged it into his laptop. It contained similar videos, only this time they were mainly businessmen. Some he knew. Most he did not. Suddenly a familiar face came into view. He felt as if the very air was sucked out of his lungs when he saw it. He sat and stared at the face for what seemed like hours, all the while trying to figure out what connection he could have with someone like Caro.

Just before five in the morning he packed up his laptop and stretched out on the couch. His mind was busy. Eventually he dozed off. When he awoke, it was almost eight. Nneka was fully dressed. Ehi was still asleep.

"Still have to work," she said.

"Not today," he advised. "Let's just lay low for a couple of days and understand what is happening."

He wondered if he should tell her about the videos. He decided it was the sort of information he would prefer not to share with her for her safety. If anyone knew she had any idea about it she would be on the same hit list as he knew he would.

"Don't be paranoid," she said and stooped to plant a kiss on his forehead. "Breakfast is in the microwave. Make yourself a cup of tea or coffee."

"What's for breakfast?" he asked.

"Bread," she said as she walked out the door.

He sat up after she was gone. He still had no idea where to hide the money. The banks would be immediately suspicious if he walked in with such an amount in cash. He decided the safest thing to do was to take it to the Hausa men who operated semi-illegal exchange bureaus. They would change any amount of money without asking questions. He reckoned if he changed it to dollars and euros the quantity would be much less and the value more preservable. The naira was nosediving in value everyday due to the diving crude price.

He took a quick shower, dressed up, put the discs in his pocket and left with the bags. He decided to leave Ehi sleeping.

The Hausa money changers were all over his car when he pulled up. When he told one of them who introduced himself as Dogo how much he wanted to change he told the rest to calm down, there was enough to go around. He was invited into his office. They chatted about the weather and politics for a while. When he asked what the delay was all about he was told the others were rallying around to raise the foreign currency he needed.

"Relax" he said. "You are in good hands. It is not every day we change such a huge amount. For safety reasons, we do not leave more than a certain amount in the office."

"Do you know any place where I can deposit some money without drawing any attention?" he asked.

"You mean a bank account or safe deposit box?" Dogo asked.

"Any. I need to travel soon and I can't be carrying such an amount with me."

"Easy. I will ask one of the men here to take you to Alhaji. He is the manager of one of the banks in town."

He made the call. In less than two minutes the deal was set.

"He said you can come," he said grinning. "Do you want us to give you the money at the bank? It's safer. We all use the same bank."

He thought over it. He trusted Hausa men.

"Why not."

"Let's go then."

He stood. They left the office. Dogo spoke to the men outside. They hurried into three SUVs parked under a mango tree.

"They will follow us. Security," he explained.

"Are they armed?" he asked.

"If they are not armed then they are as good as nothing," he said. "Let's go in my jeep. It is bullet proof. If you need one like mine I can get it custom made for you. These are no times to be gambling with life. Hiding in a cheap car does not always work. Kola?"

"No thanks," Jeff said.

Two men relieved him of the bags before he got into the car. They drove in a convoy. Dogo never stopped talking while Jeff listened, asking questions now and then. A bullet proof car would cost over two hundred thousand dollars. He said he would think about it and was advised to do so quickly. The price keeps going up.

The bank had security personnel all over it. Only a crazy thief would dare rob it. It was obvious some important personalities had their money in it or they would not have been allocated military personnel to guard it. They were ushered straight to Alhaji's office. He was a small man with a stern look. The picture of the president graced the wall behind him next to one in which he is seen shaking hands with him. Point made. Jeff relaxed when he saw the pictures.

He was a man of few words. His commission was a reasonable two percent. He would not even have to leave his office. He agreed. In less than ten minutes he was given some documents to sign. Afterwards he was given a thick envelope that was supposed to contain his ATM card, deposit and withdrawal booklets as well as a booklet advertising other services they could render. He thanked Alhaji and was driven back to the bureau where he was once again advised to get a bullet proof car. This time he offered a huge discount on the price.

His first destination was an ATM machine. He withdrew some cash just to be sure. With the money, he went to the shop and purchased some food and clothes. Eventually he returned to the hotel. Ehi was awake. She was in high spirits which surprised even him. It was as if Robert and Caro were erased from her mind. She was reading a book he believed Nneka had given her.

"I want to start school as soon as possible," she said.

"That's good," he said. "You know you have to start from primary school."

"I don't care," she said. "I just want to start."

"Still want to be a lawyer?" he asked.

"Yes," she replied.

"Good. I will make the necessary enquiries later today. My wife is a good teacher. She will make sure you catch up quickly. You may even start before the end of the week."

"Great!" she said.

He gave her the clothes he had bought. She was ecstatic. He did not want to bother her about how mean kids could be. He knew there were some who would tease her about her age. He hoped she would be able to deal with all the bullying and mockery that was part and parcel of life. With a face like hers, he knew it was only a matter of time before all sorts of men start hovering around her like vultures. He would leave that to his wife. She must be taught that dreams were easy to dream. To stay focused in the face of distractions and the human pressures was the hard part. He knew she was resilient and would succeed. Life had prepared her well. She was one girl far above her peers in wisdom.

He turned on the television in time for the afternoon news. Robert's rampage was reported as an act of terror. Inspector Dele's murder was also announced. No link was made between the two. The man who replaced him was a no-nonsense man who threatened fire and brimstone on all terrorists who dared try to make his state their home. He could not remember seeing him in any of the videos. To him that was a good sign. The rest of the news was about the various man-made disasters all over the world. He was not interested.

He watched as she held the dress in front of her, sizing them up in front of the mirror one after the other, a faint smile on his lips. He began to think of something The Ethiopian had once told him about the will. She had desired to be free more than the others. She had resisted slavery with everything within her. Her cry for help had been heard and he had no doubt that his going there with Mike that night had been divinely arranged.

CHAPTER 20

Osun sat staring at the wall in front of him. He had been sitting there for hours. He blamed himself for delaying too much. Robert's actions were not one he or any other person involved could have anticipated. If he did not find the money and the memory sticks, then all the money and time spent had been a waste. He should have been forthright with her from the start. He should have asked her about the money from day one. It was, after all, his money. He blamed Spiro for his soft approach. If it was up to him he would have cut to the chase from day one.

He heaved a heavy sigh as he sat on the sofa to plan his next move. Word reaching him was that she had survived the gunshot wound but would be in hospital for a while. She may wake up a vegetable. She may make a complete recovery. No one was sure of anything. The police were investigating her too. Her crimes were not his business, shocking as they were. He wanted his money and his life.

His mind went back in time as he stared. He began to believe that karma might be real when he arrived the United States. His money had gone quickly, too quickly. The conversion ratio was outrageous. Bags of money suddenly fit into a briefcase after being converted to dollars and euros. It was like a magic trick except it was a real trick with his money, a trick he blamed on the elite who used the financial system to keep third world countries disadvantaged. To make things worse, the cost of houses was, in his opinion, criminal. Rent was even worse.

He had arrived confident. The money he had in his account was enough to set him up for good, or so he had thought. Weeks later he realised he needed to start making money or he would be back to where he started; broke. Getting a job was not easy. Not that he tried too hard. He was never the type to work under anyone. He found people too crafty and selfish which was ironic considering what he did to his friends.

He had rented an apartment in downtown Chicago. His neighbours were mostly white folks who worked in factories. The real estate agent he had contacted warned him about crime in black neighbourhoods. She had made him watch hours of World Star Hip Hop videos on violence in black neighbourhoods. He was convinced after five minutes of watching but since he was stuck in the waiting room he had to watch the whole thing while she got together his documents in some inner office. He used to be sympathetic to them when he watched how the police treated them. The more he saw of the lack of control especially amongst black teens, the less he felt sorry for how they were treated. It was not the criminality that bothered him. It was the fact that they had no discipline whatsoever. There was a complete breakdown of the traditional system of law and order which relied on the family structure which in turn imbibed the respect of the elderly in youths from an early age. No society could survive that kind of indiscipline and no society should tolerate it.

Caro had a cousin who had travelled to Europe via Libya years before they met. He had made his way to Canada and eventually the United States and had settled in Chicago. She had begged him to try to look for him when he arrived which was one of the reasons he had decided to settle there. He had his picture, last known address and phone number. He had tried his best to contact him. Whenever he could he would show someone his picture and ask if he knew him. To his surprise, none of the people he asked did. It was a big city though. Even when he was settled enough to go to the last known address he still could not see a single soul with any meaningful information which he found odd. He should have stopped searching. That would have spared him all the trouble he was later to face. He should have known that the people he asked knew but would not say. He should have known that something was amiss.

Life was good initially. He hooked up with a dude who went under the alias Tiko. Tiko was from Mexico and lived illegally in the States. His biggest fear was deportation. They had met at a car wash. He had a nice car too and they quickly bonded. He opened his eyes to the night life in Chicago which was sicker than anything he had ever known. They went to places he would never have known existed if not for Tiko. Innocent looking pizza shops suddenly turned out to be underground casinos. Dark alleys suddenly became the back entrance to illegal fight clubs where men and women placed bets that were worth hundreds of thousands of dollars. It quickly became apparent to him why many black youths were so messed up. It was the clubs and illegal joints set up by the adults that was messing them up. There was never a dull moment and he spent recklessly. He knew his money was suffering a huge hit. He hoped on the big win that never happened.

When his money and his pride finally ran out, he got a job in a construction company owned by a black man who wanted cheap labour. He was trained on the job and was used to do just about anything from tiling to roofing, whatever needed an extra hand. The money was decent and reliable. He even began to wonder why he always hated honest jobs. He would have appreciated money more if he had ever had a day job. He blamed the erroneous thinking on his friends back home. They considered themselves gangsters who did whatever they wanted and considered work as slavery. The real slavery, he had come to believe, was being broke all the time and always running from the law.

He inevitably began to think of settling down. When a woman called Maria from Venezuela told him she was pregnant with his child he decided to settle down with her. Her father owned a fast food restaurant in town and most of her siblings were involved in the business. Most did not approve of her marrying a black man. It simply was not done in their culture. To him, that was just the same racism they complained about.

They visited now and then. He could tell they were eager to find evidence of abuse so they could find an excuse to end the marriage. It was stressful but he put up with it for the sake of peace. They always came in twos as if they expected a fight to break out or something. Her siblings were a nuisance but he reminded himself it was to her, not them, that he was married. He could see why their marriages never lasted long. They were too prying and protective of each other. Even when they were in the wrong they would find a way of blaming the spouse in question.

They had kids. Three to be exact. He sometimes thought about Caro but decided it was not worth the effort. Home represented danger. His money was still with her and he preferred to let it stay there. His call became less frequent. He ignored her calls most of the time. She liked to ask when he planned to come back or invite her over. He would lie that he still needed to get his green card. He was happy with Maria. He stopped calling altogether after a while and changed his number. He had grown tired of lying.

One day he was in his lounge room watching a movie when his front door was kicked open to reveal four men who looked like demons. He knew they had been watching him because they came barely a minute after Maria had left with the kids for a play group and some gossip. As soon as he saw them he knew he was in trouble. He tried to figure out who they were. As far as he was concerned he was not in anyone's black book, at least not in Chicago. He had been living life crime free and even wondered why it had been so hard for him to do so back home.

"You the guy from Africa looking for Ikenna?" the biggest of the men asked in a thickset voice that came from fat laden vocal cords.

"Yes?" he answered reluctantly. It had been months since he asked about him.

The big man walked towards him. For his size, he was surprisingly fast. The last thing he saw was a fist so huge it amazed him coming towards his face. He did not have any time to duck. When he came to, he was in a room with thick curtains that blocked out any external light and tied to a chair. A small dimly lit bulb provided some light. He was gagged too. He had no idea how long he had been there for. He could tell there were others in the house. He could hear cars approach and leave. People were always talking and laughing from somewhere in the house. It was a busy place. The man he assumed to be the owner was called Spiro and appeared to be some sort of leader or authority figure. The men and sometimes women who came there revered him.

Just when he had begun to wonder if they had forgotten about him Spiro came to pay him a visit. He was a surprisingly small man with a voice that belonged to someone bigger. His eyes were like those of a hawk; small, sharp and darting all over the place. He reminded him of pictures he had seen of a Saudi prince who liked to take photos surrounded by the expensive toys his wealth could buy. He always looked like the expensive toys belonged to his master and not him. Two of the men who had come to his apartment were with him.

He apologised for leaving him tied up that long but made no attempt to untie him. They removed his gag and spoon fed him some porridge to help his memory and speech, as Spiro put it. He did not like lies, he was told. He sat on a similar chair that had been placed in front of him and watched as he was fed. Despite his ego, he ate. He was starving. They wiped his mouth with a wet cloth and then gave him water to drink. Despite the audience, he enjoyed the meal.

"How is Africa?" Spiro who had been watching curiously asked as if he was talking to a friend.

"Alright" he replied trying to stay calm.

"All we hear from the news about Africa is bad stuff. Is it really that bad or is it the media?" he asked.

Osun shook his head. "Don't trust the media. It's not all war and hunger," he said. "We've got disease and genocide also. I've seen more homeless people here than I did over there. We just face the same struggles as every other person. I for one have never been kidnapped in Africa."

"That's good to know," he said ignoring his last statement. "These mainstream media make it seem like it's all war and famine over there. Makes you want to thank the slave owners for bringing our ancestors over here. I've seen how you guys talk over there. You guys are freer than we are. If it's not that bad, why do you risk death just to come over here and Europe to eat the same shit we have been eating for centuries? Why not stay home where you at least have no racist nonsense to worry about?"

"It's the same," he replied. "It's never about race. Always about the haves and the have nots. Skin colour has nothing to do with it. We all trying to be one of the haves so our children don't have to go through the same. It's the sacrifice we make for our kids."

"Then the same kids of previously have not parents who now have treat the have not kids of their time the same way you were treated and the cycle continues," he said. "It's actually the same. Now, I understand you are looking for Ikenna. He died some years back. He was a stubborn idiot. He sat on a chair quite like the one you are sitting on in this very room. Had to repaint the room after what we did to him. Are you listening?"

He nodded. He tried to explain to him that he had no ties with the man. He was just trying to reunite him with his cousin. Spiro would have none of it. Ikenna had been involved with Spiro's business partner in some sort of shady deal that he would not divulge the nature of. It had involved a lot of money, dirty money. He had kept the money to himself thinking he could easily disappear and start a new life in Miami. He was caught and brought back to Chicago where he was tortured for days. He refused to say what he had done with the money or where he hid it. Someone took the beating too far and he died. He had gone home just before he went to Miami. They believed that someone in the dark continent had it, someone close to him.

"You are going to help us find my money," Spiro had said. "You are going to return home and start asking questions. We want the money found or your family may go missing.

He had pleaded with them to let him go. He could not go back home. He might as well have been pleading with an owl. Sometimes they would leave him for days with no food, water, or opportunity to use the toilet. During those days, he would think of what he had done to his friends and wonder if it was bad karma paying him back. He did not see Spiro for a long time after the first day. His instruction was that they should bring him to him only when he had agreed to their request. He was left in the chair and tortured periodically until he agreed to do whatever they wanted him to do.

Spiro asked the men to leave the room. It was then he divulged the real reason he wanted him back home. It was not all about stolen money. His friend had been a victim of blackmail. He was a politician who had ambitions to one day become a senator. The problem was that he had gone to Africa as part of a delegate and had partied too hard in a resort that belonged to Ikenna's cousin. He had suggested the place to them as the go-to place for fun. Most people let down their guards when in third world countries. Someone had made a video of him that would hurt his chances of running for any office. Ikenna had somehow known about this or was involved and was using it to milk the poor man.

The blackmail was not the issue, bad as it was. The issue was that his friend could not move on politically with such a video in existence. His opponents would no doubt find it. To make matters worse, they feared others in the African delegate who had acted stupidly were being blackmailed too even though they did not tell anyone. He wanted him to find whoever had the video and destroy it and every copy of it or his family would disappear. He promised to pimp out his wife and kids if he failed. This made him angry but he was in no position to show it. He had to be patient and bide his time.

He returned home looking like he had been kidnapped by ISIS. An apprehensive Maria wanted to know what had happened. She had filed a missing person's report. She wanted to involve the police when she learnt what had happened. He warned her against it. He had a better plan. Involving the police would only get them killed. He had no idea where Spiro lived. He had been blindfolded on his way out of there. All he knew was that it was in a ranch because while there he had smelled cow or horse dung.

He eventually left for Africa. He knew they were watching Maria and his kids. He also knew he had enemies back home. The money, minus the one he had left behind, was gone. He did not feel sorry for them.

He just wished he had spent it better. Spiro had not divulged who this politician was but the man was so relieved something was being done about the issue that he had offered to pay for his air fare and hotel accommodation. He had to deliver.

Caro was easy to convince. Convincing women that he loved them had never been his problem. Making money had always been his real problem. So far, he had had zero luck when it came to money. Spiro's plan was simple: get back into her life, get his money, find where she was keeping the videos and steal it. Left to him he would have been more direct. He would have told her exactly what he was there for and asked her to give it to him. They wanted to be more cautious. A politician was involved. Politics and scandals were never good together. The rest was history.

He stood and walked to the bar where he poured himself some scotch. He knew if he thought hard enough he would come up with a solution. The videos were somewhere. Suddenly the phone began to ring. He answered it.

"Hello?" he said, phone in one hand and scotch in the other.

"Who the hell are you and what are you doing in my mama's house?"

"If this is your mama's house then I must be your daddy," he said.

"My father's an idiot and he's in the States so shut your mouth. I heard she was shot. Is she dead?"

He chuckled as he realised he was just like his dad.

"No," he said. "She's in an induced coma."

"Well tell her to die quickly. I need that house."

The line went dead. He was stunned. For a few seconds, he stood there motionless. It suddenly dawned on him that he had inadvertently created a monster. He thought of his kids back home and how protective he was of them. No one had been there for his son. He dialled back. An impatient Akpu answered.

"Who's this?" he asked.

"Hello son," he said a bit more gently. "I am really your dad."

"Sure. Don't keep saying that 'cos I've made a vow to shoot my dad in the head if I ever see him," he said. "You must be the dude that we are after. You shot my men. Bad move."

"They came after me," he said. "I had to defend myself."

"Well you better run back to wherever you came from 'cos we never gonna stop till we get you," he said. "I heard about what you did to your friends. What sort of man does that?"

"That was a long time ago," he said.

"So?" Akpu asked. "Have you returned the money yet? You belong to the ground and I'll personally make sure I put you there. The devil can take it from there 'cos you deserve no rest in the afterlife."

"Son..."

"Don't ever call me that," Akpu said angrily. "I don't know you and I don't wanna know you. The only thing I need from you is your death. And even if you are my dad, what difference do you think that would make now? I'm not one of those Dr Phil folks looking for some runaway idiot. I stopped searching years back. You think I don't know why you came back? You came for my mum's money and them videos. Word goes around quickly. Guess what? Robert is dead. He took them. Now the journalist has them. Go home to your wife before they get pimped out."

Osun felt a cold chill run down his spine. He wondered how he came to have known so much about his mission. In the criminal world, there really were no secrets.

"What journalist?" he asked.

"So now you want my help," Akpu said mockingly. "Why don't you do me a favour and go jump in front of a moving truck. This world would be better off without you."

"If you know as much as I know you do, you will know my family is not safe," he said. "Please, tell me where to find this journalist."

"Tell your people to send ten million dollars for information on who has them," he said laughing like it was a huge joke. "And don't tell anyone you are my dad. People can decide to kill me instead. Let me know what your sponsors say. Got your genes, don't I? You should be proud of me."

The line went dead again. Osun went to sit on the couch. It began to dawn on him that whoever was behind the blackmail scheme was well known to his son. One good thing that had come out of their conversation was that he now had a lead. A journalist likely had the videos. It should not be too hard to find any journalist linked to Robert or Caro. He knew exactly the person to ask. He dialled a number and sipped his scotch as he waited for him to answer.

21

CHAPTER 21

Jeff sat on a tree trunk as he waited for The Ethiopian to arrive. He had decided that the best thing to do was to send Ehi to a school far away from the eye of the storm. He had an aunty whom he trusted. She had agreed to accept her into their household. She was a woman who still believed in everything modern people no longer believed in. She believed in Christianity, that the man was the head of the home, that children had to be taught to speak and act respectfully, and that a healthy home gave rise to a healthy society.

She was a member of the Deeper Life Church founded by a no-nonsense preacher who discouraged members from owning television sets. Women in the church were not allowed to wear trousers. Sex before marriage was completely prohibited, not even those who are engaged were exempt. Jeff believed that was simply Christian teachings and not his own personal laws. He used to think his views about television was quite extreme but was beginning to change his mind. It was only getting worse. It should be considered child abuse to let children feed their minds on such degrading material.

Then came the era of cell phones and other hand held devices connected to the web. Anyone could upload the contents of his polluted mind to be made accessible to the whole world. Not many had the discipline or spiritual understanding to avoid certain degrading material. The whole world was indeed drinking from the cup of fornication in the hands of the whore of Babylon written of in the book of Revelation.

He could think of no other person better equipped to nurture her. His wife would have been the perfect foster mother but he felt she was safer away from the mayhem. Once he was through tidying things up he would relocate to join them. He could afford to.

It was a decision he had not taken lightly. There was the need to integrate versus the need to avoid modern society's depravity. He knew raising her the way of the church would place her at some advantage when it came to dealing with the so called real world which, in his view, could also be known as the devil's world. Little about the real world had any place for God or the godly. Sex, drugs, alcohol, wild parties, and complete disregard for existing laws was the order of the day. He could not be bothered.

He had swum in the darkness and knew how it worked. It was only fair that she at least be allowed to develop some spine before being thrust into the wildness where she would have to make up her mind how she wanted to live. He was not the type who would even judge people for choosing Satan and his ways. If God himself allows humanity to choose, who was he to judge how they chose? He only wished people knew that the choice has always been between God and Satan. Those deluded into thinking it was between God and freedom or independence had no clue. They would wake up one day.

He had his concerns. The flesh was the fall of man. From the lusts of the flesh stems all manner of evil deeds. He still had his urges despite years of knowing the truth. He found it amazing how much was available to humans through the internet at the click of the button. To the lost, it was utopia. The flesh had never had it so good. Whatsoever pleasure the mind could imagine, there was somewhere it could be realised. He knew it was slavery. To keep mankind trapped in the flesh and its lusts was to cut them off from their divine maker and aspirations.

The day of reckoning was approaching. God is spirit. Those who desired to know and encounter him must spit out that which they were being force fed, deny the flesh that is the devil's handle upon their lives, and live in the spirit. The spirit and the flesh would always be contrary to each other. Their desires were contrary. This he had observed to be true.

He often wondered why this was so, since God created both. Why should the creator ask the created to deny one and embrace the other? Even in his dark days he had contemplated this irony. He had always known deep down that there was something hopelessly wrong and evil with humans. The days of the crusades and the escapades of the colonial days were full of horrific tales better forgotten than remembered.

He could understand it when men kill during war. He could even excuse the man who kills to survive. What he found sickening and frightening was the man who, having overcome, would keep his victims or captors for mere sport or depraved acts of torture. Set them free or else kill them! That part of man that derived any pleasure or satisfaction from seeing a helpless victim in torment for no apparent reason was the part he feared the most.

He had studied animals. They killed for a reason. He could not even compare the immoral actions of humans to the behaviour of animals. To describe human misbehaviour as animalistic was a misnomer. Animals were not depraved. There was always a certain order or reason for their behaviour. Humans acted like beings off their hinges. Something had gone horribly wrong. They were off on a tangent and were moving further away from the centre, wherever or whenever that was.

He used to wake up at night to ponder his ways. He would wonder at his conscience. Mike had told him that the best way to silence the conscience was to bastardise it. He believed the more you ere the quieter the conscience became. He did try to ere a lot. His conscience did get quieter but never truly died. He would lay awake early in the morning and make promises never to repeat his deeds of the previous day. Hardly would the sun rise before he was back in the old ways of sin. It was a battle he hopelessly waged with his very self. If it was his very self who desired to sin, who or what then was that part of him that desired to stop? He was always aware of this contrasting nature he called himself. Mike had even argued that God had given man flesh to enjoy and a conscience to battle. God was a sadist. This reasoning made no sense to him since God's ways generally led to a better life for all. No part of the ten commandments would cause a human to hurt another. The reverse was the case.

When he met Nneka it was more than her beauty or even her character that attracted him to her. He saw someone who seemed to have no dichotomy between her body and her conscience. She seemed to be at peace with herself. When he learnt firsthand just how devoted to her faith and God she was, he began to formulate his own theory.

Mike and his likes believe that true freedom could not be achieved until a complete break from God and conscience was achieved. He had tried that and failed. Mike's ways of so called freedom only created more disorder and grief in the world. Women were discarded for getting pregnant. Bastard children became bitter and angry when they grow up uncared for. Adultery wrecked homes and made a mess of once beautiful relationships. He could tell easily that what he called freedom brought much disorder to society.

He would never dream of getting married to a woman whom he knew would cheat on him. Even Mike was known to throw tantrums whenever he heard of any of his multiple girlfriends having an affair. Was freedom good for him then and not for them as well? Should not the same freedom as defined by him be the right of everyone? That was a selfish way of thinking.

Nneka was a woman who had followed the teachings of her parents. Many men desired her, including those making a mess of other women. Many wanted to make her their wives. The wild ones were good for pleasuring but not for the home. Even Mike joked about this. He was beginning to learn that some women were promiscuous because they had bipolar. Humanity would always take from the vulnerable. Few stopped to protect the vulnerable. Even those who thought they were innocent because they were not as promiscuous were guilty in his eyes. They were guilty of the sin of omission. Inactivity when action is demanded is a sort of evil. People are supposed to act on behalf of the helpless, especially orphans and widows.

There was also the issue of drugs and alcohol. If men were free to indulge in these, why then do they struggle to break free when the addiction sets in? Should not freedom involve knowledge? The responsibility to know is an aspect of true freedom many feel they can overlook. Contemplation before activity is now regarded as an aspect of slavery. Men and women are urged to be spontaneous. Why call that which would ruin you in time to come freedom? Only a fool would jump out of a plane without a parachute and claim to be free because he finds himself flying without any harness or impediment. Is not the violent landing what all who are rational should fear? Is not the fall the reason many avoid the leap? For freedom to be freedom, there must be no eventual enslavement or negative consequence. It must not lead to bondage or pain. The very definition of freedom to many was therefore flawed.

He had studied Nneka for weeks. At the time, she represented to him an impossibility. How could she remain so calm and yet live without the necessary evils he had been told no human could do without unless they were liars. He had confirmed that she had no secret lovers, did not sneak out to engage in any untoward behaviour and never used any foul language that was the order of the day. How did she do it? Some began to rumour that she was gay. He knew this was not true. He did not find any secret lovers, male or female. Others began to say she was depressed and had an unhealthy mind. Again, he found this to be unjustifiable. She was as motivated as everyone else and always had a smile on her face.

When he started going to her church the truth hit him. Before then he had used the many allegations of paedophilia against certain churches as evidence that trying to live life devoid of sin was akin to mental illness. Week after week he would sit in her church and listen to the young pastor preach. He realised that there were others like her. He saw murderers who became the gentlest of souls. He saw adulterers who became faithful to their spouse. He saw prostitutes who became chaste. Each new week saw a new testament of another soul rescued from the clutches of darkness by the salvation of The Christ. His mother had been a Christian and he had thought of her as a silly woman who allowed an undeserving man to ruin her life in the name of marriage. In a way, he had believed that faith would make a fool out of him and he had stayed as far away from any converting influence as he could.

He began to study the phenomenon known as The Christ. He read the entire bible. He even read texts that were not included in the bible such as The Book of Enoch. The fall of man as stated in the book of Genesis was an intriguing mystery. Nneka became his spiritual teacher of sorts. He would ask her a hundred and one questions about things he had read. She was very patient with him and would explain things to him in a way even a kid would understand. Sometimes she would invite her pastor to explain the things that she could not.

Gradually he began to realise that Jesus, the Christ, was the most important phenomenon that had ever occurred in the history of humans. To him, it came down to some simple questions: Was he the son of God or not? Did he die and rise from the dead or not? Was it a hoax or was it real? If it was a hoax, why then were the disciples willing to defend that hoax to the point of death? Only John, the author of the last book of the bible, was spared a violent death. Why did they not just come out and renounce their claim that Jesus rose from the dead? Were they themselves deceived? If so, how could one explain the miracles they themselves did in his name that caused multiple others to believe? What did Paul, a vicious persecutor of the church, see on his way to Damascus where he was going to persecute Christians that made him turn around and start believing in Jesus?

His rational mind told him there was truth in the gospels and that truth was evident in Nneka and others like her. They were truly free. Their freedom had no consequence save that which came from the persecution of the world, a persecution that Christ warned would be the price of following him in a world devoted to the evil one knowingly or unknowingly.

He had delved into the topic of salvation and spirituality like a maniac. He researched anything and everything that had to do with the soul. He even studied psychology and the works of men like Freud. The theme of the serpent kept creeping up. He realised that this mystical creature was at the core of every ancient religion and culture. Even the renowned Satanist Crowley referred to 'the serpent that giveth light', the same serpent that encouraged its followers to do every despicable act known to man. It was obvious to him that the serpent had one goal, the same goal he had in the garden of Eden: to deceive man by offering him mystical knowledge that he believes would make him a god while in fact enslaving him. That a small percentage of humanity were privy to knowledge which the rest of humanity were not privy to was obvious. Someone or something was responsible for this knowledge.

What do the beings who give secret knowledge to vain humans demand in return? The answer he got after years of research was as shocking as it was revealing. In ancient times, they demanded human sacrifice. This was evident in documented texts of the practices of those who worshipped Baal or Molech and what he now knew to be fallen angels aka demons under various guises. The same mystical being or beings kept popping up in ancient Maya, Egypt, India, Africa, Greece, and even Europa.

He had interviewed countless victims of modern human trafficking and ritualistic abuse. Human sacrifice was a recurring theme. One would have thought that humans had become wise enough to know that there was no link between the murder of a man, woman, or child and wealth or power. Or was there? What if that which they sacrificed to was real? What if they did indeed reward them with power and riches as claimed by their victims and even escapees of these dark cults? Why would the elite gather year after year at the Bohemian grove to practice what looked like ancient rituals?

He, like many others, always assumed the American Statue of Liberty to be an innocent symbol of freedom. Little did he know that it was a monument orchestrated by Freemasons, the same organisation believed to be behind the pyramid symbol on the one dollar bill. The designer, Frederic Bartholdi, was a Freemason. Few knew that Egypt was his first choice to have the statue displayed. Few also knew that it depicted an ancient god. Something was going on that had its origins in ancient times and was concluding in his time.

Lucifer always wanted to be at the centre of human power. He wanted to be worshipped. He would do so by force or, when this was not possible, by craftiness. Many events in history made sense when looked upon with this view in mind. Almost every past ruler had a link to the occult. The priests of their day and the demons they served were the true forces behind thrones. Once a powerful ruler was taken over, his next goal was always world domination. Humanity was heading towards an era of Satan worship believing they were heading towards an era of illumination; an age of freedom and enlightenment devoid of all religion. This was why most world events were littered with the symbolism of the all-seeing eye. To the uninitiated, it was just art. To those who understood the ancient mysteries, it was a declaration that the new order was almost upon humanity.

His view about a lot of things had changed. Ancient myths no longer seemed mythical anymore. The serpent was a real creature depicted in many cultures and ancient religions. That serpent still lives. He also realised that God did not leave mankind helpless in a world full of dark entities seeking to destroy it. The name Jesus was given to humanity as a shield to ward off evil, the same name that many made mockery of. It was a name and a being whom the darkest of entities knew and recognised. Even Enoch in his book referred to him.

He used to laugh at how they made a big deal of the name. Now he knew better. It was not just a name to be chanted like some magic word by whosoever. It involved a deep belief and understanding of who he truly was. When the name is uttered from a believing heart, it triggered a response in the kingdom of light! It was akin to a victim's cry for help. It was like a woman dialling the police when an intruder was in her home. It was a lifeline giving to believers. The name was backed by real authority that is recognised in the spirit realm.

Why was it so hard for humanity to accept that they are not alone? Why, despite the evidence, did many still think there is no God? He used to laugh at those who thought the earth was stationary. One day he decided to listen to the argument for a motionless earth. In the end, he was left to ashamedly agree that they did have some points. He only believed that which he had been taught without questioning how they got their facts.

He had laughed at religion while committing the same error with so called science. Even Einstein acknowledged that there was no evidence for a rotating and revolving earth. He did not say that it did not rotate or revolve, just that there was no scientific test that had proven it did during his time. If simple issues as these were still debatable, why were some still too sure that the concept of God was nonsense?

The concept of an indefinite universe proves that the human mind was limited in its ability to grasp certain realities. What stood at the edge of the universe? Was there endless space? That made no sense. The human mind had much it did not understand and those who claim to represent science arrogantly lay claim to the fact that one day, that which is unknown would be known. If humans cannot presently figure out infinity, how can they figure God out? What happens if one day humanity finally realises that there had always been a creator? He still remembered a statement he read from the bible. At a time when concepts such as atoms and the string theory were unheard of, someone had made a startling claim.

Through faith we understand that the worlds were framed by the word of God, so that things which are seen were not made of things which do appear.

Hebrews 11 verse 3, King James version of the Holy Bible.

The man was talking quantum physics at a time when subatomic or even atomic particles were not even comprehensible! He knew there are some who would interpret the words to mean something ridiculous. There are some who are willing to put forward any possibility concerning the origin of the universe except that of creation by God. This to him was completely unscientific. No possibility should be off the table.

"What a beautiful day," The Ethiopian said.

He turned around, a bit startled by the intrusion. He had been so lost in his thoughts that he had been completely oblivious to his approach.

"Beautiful day indeed," he said. "A clear blue sky, birds chirping away noisily...a lagoon as clear as spring water, it is astonishing."

"Let us praise God who made these things and gave us the senses to appreciate them."

He nodded. The Ethiopian came to sit beside him.

"Have you decided?"

He nodded.

"It's not going to be easy," he said. "This is a sacrifice. You are called to be a fisher of men. You have the good news which will liberate many if they will believe. You will be hated. Many will try to kill you. False accusations will be levelled against you. The world is under the influence of Satan and he will use men and women who have not laid down their lives for God to attack you in ways unimaginable. I have been there.

Christ has been there. Never lose heart. Focus on what you are doing. We have but one life to live here. What better way to live it than to be vessels of the Spirit of the almighty; allowing him to use us to do his will in this wicked and adulterous generation?"

Jeff nodded.

"I know what I am getting myself into."

"How is the girl?"

"She left today. I keep worrying about her. I pray she makes the right decisions."

The Ethiopian smiled.

"She will decide what she will decide. You have done your part. Pray for her and give directions when needed. In the end, she, like every other human, must decide if they want to be a part of this darkness or embrace the light that is Jesus Christ. It is a decision that no man can make for another man. She is a girl today, tomorrow she will be an adult. Quit worrying. I know she is like a daughter to you. When you have your own children, even they will make that decision."

Jeff nodded.

"God never lets go of anyone easily," he continued when he realised he was still troubled. "Whatever love we have for our fellow beings, he has even more. Even those who have chosen darkness are not abandoned by God. Amidst the darkness, he still calls and pleads, calling men out of bondage even though they see it as freedom. Were we not born into the darkness? Only true love perseveres like that. This is the hour of grace. It is grace that calls you and many like you to this ministry. I was called by grace. We are called to deliver the good news of salvation to those who hate our very guts and the very notion of life under God. How fun is that?"

Jeff managed a laugh. He had seen videos on the internet of how Christian ministers were being treated around the world. Some were burnt alive. Some were beaten to coma. Some had been beheaded. It was no different to what it had been at the beginning when all but one of the disciples were murdered.

"I have laid down my life," he said. "Even to the death, I shall never look back. I have seen the darkness. It is not a good place to be. Men and women need to know that they need not stay in it. Light came over two thousand years ago."

The Ethiopian patted him on the back.

"I leave for Cambodia tonight," he said. "Then from there I depart for The States.

Jeff was surprised.

"Why Cambodia?" he asked.

He shrugged.

"Wherever the Spirit leads, there I will go. I will find out when I get there. The baton is now in your hands. The same Spirit who watches over me watches over you. You are a good man. I need not say more. God told me he will send a man my way. The day I saw you I knew it was you."

"Why me, if I may ask?" he asked. "There are a lot of pastors and preachers. I am just a journalist."

"To be a true shepherd, you must lay down your life for your sheep. Motive. You have a genuine heart. You have come to an end of yourself. It is hard to use a man who has not come to an end of himself. Those who have not only see it as a means to self-enrichment."

"What does that mean, to come to an end of yourself?"

"It means to die to self," The Ethiopian said. "It means you have come to realise that nothing good comes out of the flesh. To see your depravity and corruption is not easy. Many still think they are a bit better than the thief or the murderer. We are all the same. Before salvation, every man is wanting and falls short. Unless a grain of wheat falls to the ground and dies, it cannot bear fruit. You have died. Now Christ can live through you.

"This battle is yours now. It is a spiritual battle. The evil on this earth is witchcraft. This is behind the entertainment industry. This is behind the drugs, the night clubs, strip joints, pornography, and family destruction. They are casting spells on people while they dance in their ignorance. You are being called to tell a stubborn people to leave the fun they are used to. They will hate you for it. Some will listen. Most will think you are a lunatic. You thought I was. Now you know better. You may never see me again. Go strong. God is with you. Jesus is your banner and strength."

He stood. Jeff stood too. As he looked at the man in front of him he recalled the day he had come into the camp thinking he was there to record a story. A lot had happened since. The two men embraced. He had tears in his eyes when they separated. The Ethiopian's assistant arrived to escort him out. Without a word, they left.

He sat on the trunk and began to think of the days ahead. He had no idea what to expect. Nneka had been puzzled but, in the end, she declared that she could never argue with the will of the almighty. If the early disciples had not made similar sacrifices, salvation would never have come to their generation. If the early missionaries had not made similar sacrifices, Africa and India would still be under the complete control of dark spirits and practices. Now they had a choice.

His phone began to ring. It was Mason. Puzzled, he answered it. "Where are you?" he asked.

"In the middle of nowhere," he said. "Did they let you go?"

"We will talk about that later. I need to know where you are staying," he said. "I need to come over. We need to talk. This is very important."

He hesitated. There was something in his tone that was odd. Suddenly a lot of things began to make sense. He began to realise the reason he was the go to person when it came to solving kidnap cases. He was the ring leader. He was the one behind Caro. He was the mastermind behind the blackmails. He wanted his address because he wanted the memory sticks. He was never kidnapped.

"I will send you a text," he said and ended the call. Next, he called his wife and advised her to call a cab and move to the apartment he had rented for Ehi. After the call, he removed his phone battery. He also removed his sim card, broke it in half, and threw it into the bush. He dismantled the phone and did the same with it. He stood and walked to the hut. The Ethiopian had no phone. He would not need one.

Six people were waiting by the hut when he got there. They greeted him with reverence. They had been told. He went into the hut and waited. He listened to the first person, a woman whose video had gone viral. She had a mental illness. During a manic episode, she had done stuff that she would never have imagined doing and those around had taken videos while they cheered her on. The uploaded videos had been shared hundreds of thousands of times. She suddenly started crying.

"Not one person could even cover me up with a piece of cloth or something," she said when she found enough of her voice to continue. "Those were my so-called friends and family. They were laughing even though they knew my medical condition."

Jeff shook his head sadly. The story of the woman caught in adultery came to his mind. He did not know at first how to respond.

"I watched the Ejigbo market assault video where some women were tortured for hours just because one of their children stole pepper worth less than fifty cents," he began. "Those men showed no mercy. It is a video that haunts me and many who saw it to this day. Mankind have a funny way of excusing their own crimes. We judge and even punish others for the same things we have done. You know Christ?"

She nodded.

"I know him but I have not yet committed," she said. "To be honest, I really do not like Christians. All they do is judge. My own cousin was abused by a priest. He wanted to be a priest and used to hold them in high esteem. Now he is a drunkard and suicidal. The abuse wrecked his life."

Jeff sighed.

"Listen to me," he said. "Every and any genuine man or woman who has encountered Christ was once a sinner. You cannot encounter Christ without being aware of your sinful nature. Everything we receive from him is by grace, an act of mercy. 'It is by grace,' said the apostle Paul, 'Lest any man should boast.' There is only one being who is the accuser and his name is Satan. Satan means the adversary. Heaven rejoices when one sinner repents.

"What basis do I have to judge another? Do I not have favour before God simply because Jesus cleansed me of my sins? Without his mercy, my sins remain. The same Jesus cleanses us when we repent and forsake our evil ways. What happened has happened. Forgive them who shared the videos. Be like your father in heaven, forgiving and kind. Make that commitment. You know him who died and yet lives. Give your life to him. What holds you back? It is not the abuse of your cousin. It is not other so called Christians who are in fact hypocrites. This is between you and Christ. Do you believe in him or not? When will you commit? Come into the light. Embrace life and flee the darkness and bondage."

She nodded repeatedly.

"I have a boyfriend," she said. "I live in sin. I love him so much. I don't want to be one of those hypocrites who have one leg in church and another in sin. When I am ready to commit, I will. He is a nice guy."

"The devil will always put something or someone between you and Christ. You will always have to choose between him and the world and the lusts therein. This is an issue of life and death. Where will he be when you stand before the judgment seat? You hinder him the same way he hinders you. If God is good, then serve him today, not tomorrow. Who knows the number of his days?"

She listened in silence, her head bowed. He understood how hard it was to give up those things and those people the flesh had become accustomed to. He also understood that unless they are given up the better life of holiness would never be seen or known. Abraham gave up Isaac and got a nation. There was always something far better on the other side of the decision to give up the world for God. Sadly, many held unto what they were used to, what they knew and had in their hands. They would never know that that which they refuse to let go of is the very thing that keeps them from untold blessings. God in his wisdom had made it so that without faith, it would be impossible to please him. To get the new, the old must be surrendered.

They talked for what seemed like hours. She was laughing again by the time they said their goodbyes.

The next person had even more complex problems. He was a member of a cult he had joined in his teenage years. He had been promised unspeakable wealth which he had been enjoying ever since. The only problem was that he was told from the onset that he would die just after his thirty-fifth birthday. It was a few weeks away and he was beginning to hear voices telling him his time was near. The man was scared. He had never seen such fear in anyone's eyes.

"Why now?" he asked. "Why wait till you are at the brink of death?"

The man smiled sheepishly despite everything.

"Time flies when you are having fun," he said. "To be honest I never took them seriously. Deep down I never really believed I would die young."

Jeff looked at him for a while.

"What is it you really want?" he asked him.

"I don't want to die," he said. "I want to break off from the agreement. I want you to pray for me."

Jeff could tell he was a man used to bargaining his way out of difficult situations. It was all about getting a good bargain that would take him out of a bad one. He had no interest in knowing God or changing his ways.

"Let me tell you something," he said sternly. "God is not mocked. I have seen many men and women who decided to play around and disregard every moral law until a day before marriage. They think they can play games with God. I have seen that, in the end, we are the ones who lose. We will face the same circumstancewe faced when we rejected God. That thing we held on to will represent itself. The choice will always be there. He knows when we put him off because we prefer the pleasures of this world. The choice will not get easier."

"What are you really saying?" the man asked a bit arrogantly. "Where has the other fellow gone? I was told he is a good guy who understands."

"The spirit is the same. I am saying that you will face the same circumstance you faced when you made the deal with Satan. You will lose everything. Your blessing will come one day, but first you must learn to trust in God, to work hard, and to value material things less."

The man sat still for a few minutes. Suddenly he stood and left. Jeff shook his head sadly.

By the time he was through with the sixth person it was night. He went outside thinking he was done. He was shocked to see scores of people waiting to see him. He went back into the hut and sat down. It was going to be a long night.

He took a deep breath as he waited for the seventh person. Too many had serious issues to deal with. Someone paid a terrible price to set them free. The least he could do was be his mouth piece.